moon dance

To Dyani:
Blessings,
Susan K. Earl

moon dance

 a novel

SUSAN K. EARL

TATE PUBLISHING & *Enterprises*

Published by Tate Publishing & Enterprises, LLC
127 E. Trade Center Terrace | Mustang, Oklahoma 73064 USA
1.888.361.9473 | www.tatepublishing.com

Tate Publishing is committed to excellence in the publishing industry. The company reflects the philosophy established by the founders, based on Psalm 68:11,
"The Lord gave the word and great was the company of those who published it."

Book design copyright © 2009 by Tate Publishing, LLC. All rights reserved.
Cover design by Kellie Southerland
Interior design by Jeff Fisher

Published in the United States of America

ISBN: 978-1-61566-412-2
1. Fiction, Christian, Romance
2. Fiction, Historical
10.01.21

dedication

In memory of my own Maggie, Margaret Hendricks, who persevered through many heartaches of her own, even as she inspired others with her strength of character, her faith in God, and heaps of love for all who knew her.

chapter 1

I was such a simple child before that dreadful day, and the suffering wrought that sorrowful afternoon nearly broke my heart in two. Seems a day don't pass that my feet don't wind down this solitary little path through the woods where I seek to find some comfort, some peace to quiet my aching spirit. Even today, as I wander unhurriedly through the dense trees, the simple cry of a mockingbird pierces the silence, and I tremble mightily as I sweep the shrubs aside and rush deeper into the woods. The warmth of the sun on my face and the stillness of the woods surrounding me seem to cradle me in their embrace, and while I should be filled with peace, my heart aches with pain and shame.

As daylight dwindles, soft breezes caress the evening, and I slide silently to the ground and stare into the darkening waters of Johnson Creek. I struggle to keep my thoughts away from all the ugliness that haunts me, but even the beauty of this day can't chase away the chill that fills my soul. Time seems to stand still as I breathe in the musky night air, and my thoughts once again wander back to a time and a place that once was and never since has been, a time of innocence, long ago lost.

⌒⋎⌒

It began like any other; just another carefree, lazy May afternoon, happily singing songs with my younger brothers and sisters as we ambled carelessly down the dusty road, our laughter echoing merrily through the trees as we heedlessly headed toward home. Then, without warning, as we rounded the corner my heart commenced beating rapidly, and just like that, I knew—I just knew something terrible had come to pass even before my forlorn little house came into view.

My hands shot out to stop my sisters from going any farther toward home. "Hey!" they shouted at me. "What's the matter with you, Maggie?" I shook my head but couldn't voice what I was feeling. Then I whispered to my brother Will to take the kids on over to the neighbors' house.

I slowly rounded the bend in the road, fearfulness filling my very soul. My breath caught in my throat when I caught sight of our yard jam packed with dozens of dusty cars and my Papa's baby, his 1926 Ford Model T, just left completely forsaken in the midst of the others with the doors flung wide open—he would never do that to his precious car! My heart racing, my breathing difficult, I panicked. "Oh God! What's wrong? Has something happened to Mama?" I frantically raced the rest of the way home.

Men were walking around the yard, quietly smoking and shaking their heads, their faces closed and hard. I tried to get an answer from one of them, but he just turned away, tears shining in his eyes. "God, what is happening?" I screamed to myself. My feet seemed to leave the ground as I floated into the deathly still house. As I set foot in the room, I caught my breath and let out a deep moan. "Oh, oh, there's Mama; she's all right. Papa's here too." I frantically prayed, "Thank you, God … thank you they're all right."

Papa was bending over Aunt Rachel, who was crying hysterically. I glanced around for Papa's brother, my uncle William. He wasn't in sight, but I spotted several of my papa's friends lumbering around with their hands in their pockets, eyes red, looking lost and out of place.

I froze for a moment, unsure of what to do or say. Then I felt Mama's eyes on me, so I hurried to her and fearfully laid my head in her lap. She gently stroked my hair as my frightened eyes spoke to her, asking her all the questions I couldn't voice. As she rubbed my icy hands in hers, her anxious eyes searched mine. Finally, she choked back a sob and mournfully explained, "It's your uncle William, Maggie ... we've ... we've lost him." Her tear-filled eyes peeked over at Papa. His red-rimmed eyes met hers in sadness.

I didn't understand. "Mama ..." My voice faltered. Finally, after several fearful moments, I was able to go on, so I squeezed her hand hard and asked, "How, Mama? What happened?" I was almost afraid to hear her answer.

"Oh, Maggie," Mama cried softly. "Your uncle William was fatally injured in a terrible car accident early this afternoon." She struggled to wipe away the uncontrollable tears slipping silently down her sorrowful face.

Tears pooled in my eyes and silently spilled over. "No!" I cried. "What happened? How?" I was repeating myself, but my mind couldn't yet comprehend what Mama was telling me.

Papa staggered over to us and balanced himself on the arm of Mama's chair. He draped his arm around her and gently rubbed her back. "Maggie, it's just hard to talk about, but ya have a right to know, girl." He rubbed his hand over his face and heaved a heavy sigh. "William was drivin' the dump truck, and we was takin' a load over to the new construction goin' on across town, when all at once, out of nowhere another truck comes tearin' out in front of us."

He took a deep breath then rubbed away a tear that threatened to spill from his eyes. "That driver ... he lost control and spun around in his old truck. Then his truck hit us full on ... on William's side ... it just hit him." Papa couldn't go on, so he simply laid his head on the back of Mama's chair and wept like a baby.

Mama tenderly drew his head to her shoulder and began whispering softly in his ear. I turned away, afraid to ask more. After a little bit, Papa sat up and cleared his throat. "Jo, you tell her the rest. I just can't." He restlessly wandered around the gloomy room and then at length trudged despondently outside to the front porch.

Mama stroked my hair. "Maggie, baby, you're sixteen now, my oldest child. In my heart I still think of you as my little girl that I have to protect from the ugliness of the world." She hung her head and heaved a long sigh. "But sweetie, I know...I believe...you're grown up enough to help us get through this heartrending time. And right now your papa 'specially will need all our love and support." Her eyes searched mine for understanding. "Your papa was ridin' in that dump truck too, but...oh...thank God he wasn't injured." Mama broke off, crying.

I didn't—I couldn't say anything. It felt as though all the breath in my body had left me, and I couldn't breathe. Mama reached out and hugged me so tightly then exhaled a heart-felt cry and continued. "The dump truck spun round on impact, and William fell out of the cab. He was knocked out, but Papa thought he'd be okay 'cause he was clear of the truck when he fell. Then ..."—Mama paused then finished quietly as more hot tears coursed down her already tearstained face—"in less than a fraction of a second, the dump truck teetered and turned over...and all the dirt in the dump bed spilled...it spilled all over him...and buried him."

My throat froze, and I felt as though I couldn't draw a breath. Then I finally choked out, "Mama, no! No...why...how? Oh God, Mama, couldn't anybody help him?"

"They tried, Maggie, they did. Your poor papa and some men who were nearby tried to dig him out straight away, but all they had use of was their hands." She closed her eyes and whispered, "Your papa was frantically trying to save William. He just kept diggin' and diggin' and diggin', but there was so much dirt ...In due course they reached him, but it ... was just ... too late." She cried and hugged me to her. "Oh, Maggie, when I think of what your papa must be goin' through, it about breaks my heart."

I sat there in stunned silence, not knowing what to say or do to comfort my family, so I just hid my head in Mama's lap and cried softly.

At long last, Mama took a deep, shaky breath. "It must have been so awful." She blew her nose and wiped at her eyes with her handkerchief. "Your papa said when they finally got him over to the hospital in Ft. Worth, there was nothin' anyone could do. Our William was lost to us." She took my cold hands and held them tightly as a shrill wail once more escaped Aunt Rachel's trembling lips.

That day, that dreadful day began it all, yet there was nothing else to do except what my mama did, because in her eyes she had no other choice. My aunt Rachel had two small children and no job, nor any hope of one for that matter, what with the Depression going on. What else could we have done? I have asked myself this question a thousand times since that day Aunt Rachel and her girls moved in with us, but every action has a reaction, so they say.

At first after Aunt Rachel moved in, we all crept around silently like ghosts because no one wanted to upset her with sounds of laughter or idle talking. Our school even closed for the week after my uncle William was killed, seeing as most of us at the school were related to him in one way or another. I would have just as soon gone to school instead of staying quietly at home, watching my mama, papa, and Aunt Rachel cry. Mama floated around the house taking care of Aunt Rachel's every need, and Papa finally went back to work later in the week. After a while, things seemed to fall into a pattern and began to settle down, or so I thought.

The sun hung low on the horizon as I slowly began to make my way back through the darkening woods. The lush, unrestrained spring foliage hindered me as I slipped silently back down the dusky path; nevertheless, as my bare feet met the soft earth, I felt at home.

As I emerged from the woods, my thoughts drifted back to those left behind me, and in my mind again, I saw Papa standing out on the back porch, his rough hands cupped gently around Aunt Rachel's face; her, red faced and crying, looking all soft and needy, him looking at her like he wanted to eat her up.

Papa looked at me like a mad dog when I stomped up onto the porch that day. His edgy eyes followed me, and I heard him nervously call out as I passed, "Maggie, you go on in the house now and help your mama. Your aunt Rachel's havin' a real hard day, and right now she just needs me to help her get through it."

You can't fool me with your wicked lies, I thought as I furiously stormed into the house that blustery October day. I knew my papa was up to no good with Aunt Rachel, but what could I do to stop him. I could only try to show him my disapproval with a cold, icy stare and stomping feet. What I really wanted to do, I just won't say!

A sudden gust of wind roused me once more from my daydreams and drew me back to the reality awaiting me at home. My feet quickened as I approached our tired, worn-out house, and I heaved a troubled sigh as I caught sight of Mama staring sadly out the kitchen window. I rushed rapidly into the house and embraced her gently, hoping to ease a little of the pain I knew she endured. She hugged me tightly and sent me off to bed. I sighed sadly as her weary voice followed me down the long, dark hallway.

Night sounds filled the house, and the unrelenting feeling that a storm was not far off churned through my being as

I slipped quietly down the hall. I slid unobtrusively into my sagging, rickety bed, careful not to wake my little sisters, who shared the bed with me. The feel and smell of my freshly washed sheets, which only a short time ago were hung out to dry in the warm spring air, comforted me with a feeling of belonging, of home. I snuggled deeper under the covers as the lonely sound of the wind rustled the trees outside my window, and as shadows crept across the darkened bedroom, the chirping insects grew louder, their sounds comforting and familiar to me. My eyes started to close just as the first rumble of thunder sounded in the distance, and I wondered once again if this shameful time would soon be over. After all, it had been almost a year since Uncle William died.

His eyes followed her as she traipsed silently down the dark, lonely road, her sadness evident even from a distance. He yearned to race up and talk to her, comfort her, but he felt too unsure of her reaction. His heart beat quickly at the thought of what she might do or say if he ever got up the nerve to ask her out.

He caught a glimpse of her almost every day as she walked unhurriedly home from school, and occasionally they waved or called out a greeting to each other. He'd known her all her life, spent time with her in church, and sometimes they'd even crossed paths at social gatherings, but lately his feelings for her had changed. She'd developed a certain grace and courage over the past months that inexplicably drew him to her.

Today she hadn't come by the corral after school as she did most every day, and that had bothered him. He'd thought he might just head out to her house after work and ask her if she'd like to go out for a stroll with him, just to make sure everything was all right. After a few minutes of tortured imaginings about what could have happened, he'd decided to go on and leave work a little early. As he'd come up over the hill, he'd spotted her walking home with her brothers and sisters. His heart felt relieved that she was safe and sound.

He quickened his pace to try to catch up with them, but before he could, she'd turned away from her siblings and detoured into the woods. He stopped and gazed off after her, afraid to follow her because he didn't want to frighten her. After all, she was only seventeen. He was twenty-one, but he knew deep within his very soul that she was meant to be his.

He sat down on an outcropping of rock, trying to will himself to go home, but he couldn't. He just wanted to be close by her, possibly find an opening to convey how much he'd come to care about her.

After a bit she emerged from the darkening woods, her face a study of sadness. He stood up and stretched then kicked a small rock across the road, hoping she'd turn at the sound and catch sight of him, but she seemed too deeply lost in thought to take notice. He watched compassionately as she turned into her yard and ran into her house. He watched as she hugged her mother, and he dreamed that one day she would be his. As the clouds rolled in and the starlight faded away, he sighed deeply, turned, and trudged slowly toward home.

"Joe! Hey, Joe!"

He paused as he heard his name called and then squinted in the shadowy moonlight. "Who's that?" he called back.

"Geez, Joe, don't ya even recognize your own brother!"

"That you, Rueben? My mind's a million miles away," he said, brushing his hair back with his hand as if trying to clear his mind with the gesture.

Rueben ran up and slapped him hard on the back. "Snap out of it, Joe. That Maggie's got ya all hot and bothered, and ya can't think straight. Pop wanted ya home an hour ago to help him bring in the cows, so he sent me out to round ya up. I knew for certain I'd find ya moonin' over here by Maggie's house."

"Look, Rueben, Pop's gotta understand, I work all day now for Johnson. I'm a man now, not just Pop's son."

Rueben laughed and slapped his leg. "Yeah, yeah, Pop'll never take that kind of talk, not till you've moved out and married that girl, Maggie. Maybe not even then!"

He turned away and sighed deeply. "Yeah, I know you're right, even if ya are just a scrawny kid."

Rueben pulled on his sleeve. "Did ya hear what happened down to the Walkers' place this mornin'?"

"Nope, I've been tied up all day workin' Johnson's horses. What come about?"

Rueben whooped loudly. "Strangest thing I ever heard. When Mizz Walker went out to her barn early this mornin' to milk her cow, someone'd already beat her to it."

"What do ya mean, 'beat her to it'?"

"Someone had stoled the cow's milk, Joe! They waltzed right in and milked the cow themselves then up and took the milk!"

He stopped and stared at Rueben. "What come to pass? Did they catch 'em?"

"Naw, but Mizz Walker was fit to be tied! Everybody said ya could hear her yellin' a mile away, and she was hotter than heck, runnin' round, screamin' 'bout thieves stealin' her children's milk. I never heard anything so dang foolish in my life!"

Joe shook his head sadly. "Foolish, yeah, this Depression can drive a man to do a lot of foolish things, but ya never know what you'd do till you walk in the other man's shoes, Rueben. Times are hard for ever'one, and that man or woman was probably pretty dang hard up to steal another family's milk."

Rueben stopped and looked back at him. "Mizz Walker said whoever stoled her family's milk should eat hay for a week. You could have lit a fire with the sparks flyin' out of her eyes … or so I heard."

Joe dejectedly kicked at a loose rock, and dust flew into his eyes. He brushed away the tears he said were caused by the dust, but Rueben knew better. "Come on, Joe; I'll race ya home."

chapter 2

The ringing of the alarm clock jarred me out of my dreams. I reached over and slapped the alarm button, sending the clock flying off the table. My little sisters stared accusingly at me in the early morning light, so I smiled sweetly and threw my pillow across the bed at them. Screams erupted as I hurried out of our tiny bedroom. Here I was, the oldest of eight, and I shared my room with five little sisters. I wondered if I would ever have a room of my own, much less a bed of my own. Money was so tight, almost nonexistent in my family. The Depression had hit everyone hard, but it seemed as though it had more or less destroyed my family.

Light shone through the open kitchen door, and the tattered curtains were pulled back to capture every bit of light the morning offered. Darkness had filled our hearts and home for so many months now that even the brightness of this beautiful March morning couldn't ease the throbbing pain I carried inside. My heart ached so for Mama, and anger at my papa burned inside me like fire.

This morning my thoughts once again turned to the turmoil that roiled inside me. My papa was gone. Not just to work, but really gone. He'd gone off with that other woman. How he could do that to my mama was a mystery to me. She said it was the Depression. Everything was blamed on the Depression. My thoughts darkened as I remembered the day he told us he was in love with Aunt Rachel. I felt sick to my stomach just at the thought of my hairy old papa and Aunt Rachel together, and it gives me chills even now.

It was a cold and rainy Sunday afternoon in late December. I was sitting behind Mama's big chair, trying to let the heat from the fireplace warm me up, when I heard Papa come in from outside. He grunted something at Mama, and she asked him, "What?" I peeked around the back of the chair.

Papa's face was as red as a beet as he sputtered out, "Rachel's pregnant, Jo." I thought I was going to throw up. Nevertheless, I curled up quietly and tried to make myself as small as I could so Papa wouldn't notice me.

Mama looked angrily at Papa. "William's been gone almost eight months, so there's no way the baby is his! What have you done, John?"

Papa reached over and shook Mama hard. "You listen to me, woman. If ya hadn't been so tired and washed out all the time, if you'd given me even five minutes o' your time—"

Mama angrily jumped up and slapped Papa hard. "Don't you even try to blame your lust on me, old man. You and I were just fine till Rachel came and tried to soften you with her needy little ways."

"I can't talk to you when you're like this, Jo. I have a responsibility to this girl, and she loves me like you never did."

"Oh, without doubt," Mama muttered icily. "I had eight children with you 'cause I couldn't bear the sight of you. What about your responsibility to me, to our kids?"

"I don't want to discuss it; my mind's made up, Jo. I need to be with Rachel and our kids." He turned and stormed out of the room, and the whole house shook like an earthquake when he finally slammed the front door.

Mama fell back in the chair and started to cry softly, but I was in such a state of shock I couldn't even move to comfort her. So that day Papa left us, left us high and dry. No remorse, no money, no support, just up and left us. Luckily, my mama wasn't conniving like Aunt Rachel. She seized the only job she could find and commenced working at the button factory. It didn't pay much at all, but it didn't take someone else's papa away from their family either. Mama said it was honorable work, but she had to leave every day before daylight, so it was up to me to figure out how to feed my younger brothers and sisters breakfast.

I skipped supper last night because I knew there just wasn't enough for all of us, so now my stomach growled noisily to remind me I needed to eat too. I looked out the back window at the poor little garden we'd planted last week, and I yearned for the taste of juicy red, ripe tomatoes and Mama's pinto beans. Maybe soon we would have a few fresh vegetables on the table, but for now I'd have to do the best I could with what little we had. I opened the cabinet and took out an almost empty box of oatmeal, poured the oats into a pan, and added twice the amount of water called for on the box. I gazed sadly at the meager offering, but I knew it would have to do; it would just have to be enough.

My thoughts wandered back to last spring, just one short year ago. The smell of freshly cut hay lingered in my mind, the sounds of my papa coming home at night, and he and Mama laughing softly in the twilight about something one of us kids had done—everyday, normal things. I hated that my safe world had suddenly changed. Times had always been hard, even when Papa was here, but never like this. My papa had made just enough to keep his head above water and us out of the poor house, but somehow I didn't notice being poor so much back then because that was just the way it was.

Then that horrible day happened and she came. My uncle's widow came to stay. She didn't even seem to care that my uncle William was dead. She just wanted everyone to take care of her.

My mama had welcomed her, comforted her, and sheltered her. And what did she do in return? She stole my mama's husband, took my papa away from his children, and sent my mama to work in the button factory. Anger bubbled over in my heart just thinking about her.

Impossible, he thought as he tried to catch the unbridled wild mustang he was being paid to tame. The horse reared back and charged to the other side of the pen just when he thought he had it. He took his hat off and slapped the dust off his pants. As he wiped his brow with his dirty bandana, he saw her coming down the road with all of her brothers and sisters in tow. She was so beautiful, and he wanted so badly to take away the pain he knew she was in.

He'd heard the rumors that were flying around town all last summer and into the fall. Then at last, when the rumors were proven true, he could hardly bear to see her shame. How could a man up and leave his family to starve while he went off and started another family with his brother's widow. It was unthinkable. He coughed loudly as the horse charged by, kicking dust into his nose and mouth.

She turned and looked over at him. Her face crinkled up in a sweet smile as she waved and playfully called out, "Good mornin', Joe. I see that horse is tryin' to tame you today."

He laughed and waved back at her, but his tongue suddenly felt as though it was glued to the roof of his mouth. His face reddened, and he thought it was high time he started to act like a man and not like some fumbling little boy. Today he would go to her and ask her out. There was a barn raising and dance at the Fredricks' place on Saturday, and that would be the perfect opportunity to let her know how much he cared about her.

He turned back to the job at hand and circled up next to the uncontrollable horse. The stallion snorted and threw its head back as he approached, so he cautiously held out his hand and gently stroked the horse's mane. It jerked away but didn't run. Then he began to lightly rub its neck and back, trying to calm it down. After a while, he was able to quickly slide the bit into the horse's mouth and gently pull the bridle over the jumpy animal's head.

He continued to stand very still and stroke the horse softly, and in due course he carefully placed a worn saddle blanket on the anxious horse's back. The unruly stallion tossed its head and snorted some more but stayed where it was. He reached out and held on to the horse's head as he slowly slipped the saddle over the blanket. He felt the ripple of agitation and fear run through the horse when the heavy saddle settled into place on its back. He waited several minutes, continuing to try to keep the nervous horse calm; then he cautiously reached underneath the great beast and drew the girth to the buckle. He cinched it tightly and then unhurriedly stroked the horse's neck and shoulders. The stallion stood its ground, snorting and shaking but becoming a little more docile. He decided to let the horse rest before trying to ride it. He would let it wear the saddle for a few hours and get used to the weight on its back; afterward it would be time to truly break it. This was always an exhilarating feeling for him, even though it seemed ironic that in taking away the freedom of the horse, he felt freer himself.

⁓ჟ⌒

Laughter filled the air, and I experienced lightness in my heart this morning that I hadn't felt in many months. I grabbed Hannah's hand as we left the classroom at lunchtime. "Come on, Hannah, and let's find a place to talk." We raced to our favorite spot under the live oak tree and collapsed breathlessly onto the grass. I hauled out my bag and took out the few meager scraps I'd put together this morning for my lunch.

Hannah shook her head as I emptied my bag. "Maggie, when are you goin' to start takin' better care of yourself? I swear you're goin' to blow away in the wind if you don't start eatin' proper."

"I'm fine, Hannah. Look, I want to tell you 'bout this mornin'."

"Here, take half of my sandwich. I won't eat it all anyway. Mama always makes way too much for me."

"All right, Hannah, but I really, really want to talk to you about—"

"About what, Maggie?"

"I feel silly now, and it's probably just my wild imagination takin' off. I always seem to make more of things than they really are, but—"

"Okay, out with it. You can't not tell me now! Does it have somethin' to do with your papa and mama?"

My heart seemed to weep a little, but I pushed those thoughts aside. "No, no! I took the kids on a roundabout way to school this mornin'—"

"Oh…you seem to be followin' this roundabout way a lot lately, Maggie!"

"Well…anyway, I saw him."

"Did you talk to him?"

"Sort of…I was watchin' him workin' with Mr. Johnson's horses, and he kind of looked over at me and a horse ran in front of him and kicked up dust all over him. I laughed and made a little joke. He didn't answer me, though, so I don't know if he really noticed me or not."

"Oh, I think he did. I think he's been noticin' you for a while."

"How can you tell? He never really comes over and talks to

me, so he probably just thinks of me as a foolish child. He's all grown up, and I'm just seventeen."

"My mama was married at sixteen, and she had my brother by the time she was seventeen. Just 'cause you're seventeen don't mean he can't think about you as his future wife."

"Hannah! I never said I was goin' to be his wife! I just think he's cute and nice."

"Sure, Maggie."

All at once, it felt as if all the breath in my body had been squeezed right out of me. I heard my name called, but I couldn't move. The half-eaten sandwich fell from my hand unnoticed as I squeezed my eyes shut and prayed that this unbearable moment would pass quickly.

My youngest sister, Lilly, came running up, pulling on my hand, crying out to me, "Maggie, come on, it's Papa. He wants ya! Come on, come on!" I shook her hand away and angrily turned my back on the road. I could hear the kids acting all excited, shouting out and crying to Papa. I wouldn't—I couldn't turn to look at him. I heard him call my name again, but his voice just sliced into my heart like a knife.

Hannah reached over and took my hand. She whispered something to me, but my mind was buzzing with fury, and I couldn't understand a word she said. I felt hot tears slide down my cheeks, their salty taste caressing my lips and tongue. Papa's booming voice as he played with the children made me cringe, and when I heard Rachel's voice, it only added to the anguish I was in.

My feet found the well-worn path into woods, unguided by any conscious thought. As I reached the creek, I slid down onto the warm earth as softly and quietly as a leaf dropping from a tree. The day had seemed endless, and I simply couldn't keep my mind on what I was supposed to be studying in school. Arithmetic just wasn't important to me today.

Seeing Papa and Rachel walk by the school at lunchtime took me to a deep, dark, ugly place I didn't want to be. *How can he act like I should just run to him like I used to? How can he think I've forgiven him for tearing apart our family? The little girls still love him.* They screamed his name. "Papa! Papa! We miss you so much!" They ran and jumped on him. "Papa, when are you and Aunt Rachel comin' home? We have so much to show you!" Even the boys couldn't wait to rush out in the street and share all their news with him, and Rachel's girls ran out too. They even called him *Papa!* I wanted to scream at Papa, rant at him, make him understand how much he hurt me, but I didn't. I sat there, and my blood boiled. Papa called out to me. He wanted me to come and see him. I used to be his "favorite girl," which was something I never, ever desired to be again. I turned my back on them and pretended to be deep in conversation with Hannah Rogers. Hannah's frightened face was as white as a ghost, and I think the anger I felt—and tried to keep inside—exploded like fireworks out of my eyes. I suppose that scared her more than just a little.

Hot tears fell uninvited onto the warm, sandy banks of the creek. I frantically wiped at my face, willing myself not to cry. Papa didn't deserve my tears, so why should I waste them on him. My heart ached so badly for Mama and for all of her children.

I don't know how I got through the rest of the afternoon at school. I barely made it home with the kids before my feet automatically tracked their way to my secret place. Will seemed to know I needed to be alone, so he quietly took the kids the rest of the way home. I think he knew how upset I was, but he just didn't understand how I could hate Papa. After all, he is Papa!

I sensed movement in the nearby brush, so I silently glanced about, trying to discern who or what was approaching near me, when suddenly a soft, wet nose pushed its way into my weepy face. As a drooling tongue licked at my tears, I desperately reached out and hugged the warmth of my big, overgrown puppy to me. My tears could no longer be restrained, so I sat and cried the tears of shame, the tears of pain, the tears of the unknown, into the coat of my faithful friend. He didn't judge me or condemn me or tell me I was being silly. He just sat and tried to lick away my mournful tears, and unknowingly, he brought great comfort to my lonely, lost, broken heart.

❧

I must have fallen asleep there in the woods because my recollection of where I lay was slow in coming as hazy, unsettled images crept unwittingly into my mind. I rubbed my face, stretched out, and discovered Jack's warm, furry coat beneath my hand. I felt so weary and confused that I couldn't even budge, so I closed my eyes for a few more minutes and let the calming trickle of the creek soothe me gently back to life.

My face felt rough and swollen, my eyes burned, but my aching heart felt a little less raw. Somehow this unbearable day had started a healing inside me, and I reckoned I had cried all the tears I could ever cry; or at least it felt that way right now.

I sat up slowly and hugged Jack. The sun was very low on the horizon, and I knew Mama would be getting worried; so I quickly bent over the sandy creek bank and scooped up some of the cool water. I splashed my hot, puffy face and felt somewhat better. It had been almost a year, a whole year, and for that reason, if not others, I needed to start forgiving people, even if I wasn't doing it for them but for my own peace of mind.

I scooped up a bit more of the cold water and rubbed it vigorously over my puffy face then ran my damp hands through my hair. I took a deep, cleansing breath of the cool night air, called Jack to come, and quickly wound my way back through the darkening woods to the dusty road home.

As I emerged from the woods I saw a tall, lanky figure walking ahead of me on the road. At first, I felt frightened, and then I realized it was Joe. What was he doing way out here at this time of day? I wasn't sure if I should call out to him or just keep pace behind him. I felt really awkward whenever I was around him, so maybe Hannah was right—maybe I did care a little too much about him.

Suddenly, Jack let out a sharp bark and took off running down the road toward Joe. Tail wagging, body quivering like jelly, Jack almost knocked him down in the excitement of finding him near our house. Joe stooped down and rubbed Jack's ears and talked to him.

"Hey, Jack. What ya doin' out here on your own? You best get back home straight away. Come on now, boy; let's go."

"Joe, Jack's out here with me. He's not just runnin' wild," I called as loudly as my voice would allow, but it appeared I'd lost the power of speech because my voice was no more than a loud whisper.

Jack turned back and gave a sharp bark, as if to say "Hurry up!" Joe paused and turned around. He saw me and waved, so I hurried up to where he waited.

"I was just on my way to see ya, Maggie," he declared.

"Me...you wanted to see me?" I was stunned.

"I wanted to ask you if you'd like to go with me to the Fredricks' on Saturday. Their barn burned down a few weeks back, so there's a group of us from the church goin' over to help rebuild it. Then there's goin' to be a dance in the evenin' in the new barn. Ya know, to kinda celebrate gettin' it built."

I felt really stupid as I stammered, "Me...you want me to go with you?"

I watched his slow smile form and move up into his dark eyes. "Well, as long as you don't find me too offensive, I'd like to take ya, Maggie."

My stomach quivered, and I had to clear my throat before I could speak again. "Of course, that would be very nice, Joe.

I'd really like to go with you. Thank you for asking me." I felt my face flush, and I was really glad it was getting dark outside. Awkwardness overcame me, and I longed to simply run away as fast as I could, even as I desired to remain near him.

"Good," Joe answered. "I'll probably head on over there 'bout eight Saturday mornin', and I can either stop by for you round seven thirty, or you can meet me over there whenever you get ready." He smiled sweetly at me. "I know Sarah Fredrick would appreciate help settin' up food for the men since her baby's almost due, so if you want, you can come early and help her some."

"I'll be ready at seven thirty Saturday morning. Thank you for asking me, Joe," I stuttered. "I guess I better get on home so Mama won't be worried."

Joe looked at me, and I felt a little scared. No one had ever looked at me that way before. Then he raised his hand in a quick wave, turned back toward town, and called, "See ya Saturday, Maggie." My heart throbbed in my throat, powerfully pulsing and pounding and making it hard for me to breathe. I stood there immobile watching Joe's form fade into the gathering darkness.

Without warning, Jack awakened me from my stupor by jumping up and pushing my backside really hard, as if to say, "Stop wastin' time; supper's waitin' for us at home!" I laughed and called out, "Come on, Jack. Let's go eat!" My heart felt less burdensome as I raced joyfully toward home. It had been a roller-coaster day for me, but I was glad it had ended on a happier track.

chapter 3

My eyes felt glued together as I stretched and yawned sleepily. I tried to will them to open, but it felt like a losing battle. I wasn't sure I'd gotten any sleep at all last night. First of all, I was so excited about going to the barn-raising dance with Joe that I couldn't fall asleep. Then when I did start to drift off, Lilly began her nightly wiggling and kicking. I swear that child couldn't stay in one place more than a second. I would turn on my side, and she'd sling herself over me. I lay on my back, and she crawled up on me. Every time I tried to gently move her off me, she clung to me even more. Her nightmares were silent and forgettable to her, but to the rest of us who shared the bed with her, they were never ending.

At length she settled down, but it felt as if I had just closed my eyes when I heard our ornery old rooster start to crow. I glanced at the hands of the clock and realized I could have had ten more minutes to sleep. I didn't know how rooster stew would taste, but at that moment I seriously contemplated making it!

I truly knew it was time to get up and get ready for the day with Joe, and I really, really wanted to jump out of bed and fly through my morning routine, but the bed just felt so good. I lay there a few more minutes, willing my mind and my eyes to work, and then Lilly rolled over and wrapped her arms around me. Her tousled curls tickled my neck as I bent to kiss the top of her head. She snuggled closer and whispered, "Do I have to get up now, Maggie?"

"No, love, just go on back to sleep." She didn't need any persuading, so I quietly rolled off the bed and headed down the hall to the bathroom.

I'd just finished eating a hurried breakfast when I heard Joe stride up on the porch. He was whistling a familiar tune, but I couldn't quite place it. I started humming it too as I grabbed my bonnet and landed a quick kiss on Mama's cheek.

I calmly opened the kitchen door and caught sight of Joe leaning against the porch rail, his strong hands lightly resting on it, and he looked beautiful as the glowing sun rose behind him in the eastern sky. A slight breeze ruffled his thick, dark hair, causing a stray curl to fall softly over his brow as he turned to me with a smile.

"Hey, Joe," I said quietly.

"Hey, yourself," he replied, looking me over and making me blush. "You ready to go?"

I nodded, feeling myself turn red as his eyes met mine. We headed out down the long, dusty road, past my favorite secret place, past the muddy creek bed, and over the rolling green hills out of town. It wasn't a long walk, just a couple miles, but it seemed as though the silence between us could've been cut with a knife. I wasn't usually so shy and tongue-tied, but I felt really awkward walking along beside him. Then out of the blue he started whistling that same tune again as he kicked at a rock in the road.

"That's a pretty tune, Joe. I know it, but I just can't think what it is," I stammered.

He started singing, "All of me, why not take all of me ..." He stopped and grinned at me; his chocolate eyes sparkled. "It's the new Louis Armstrong tune. I really like it." He reached out and took my hand, and as he softly hummed the song he twirled me around like we were dancing.

I laughed out loud, realizing that was the happiest I had felt in months. After a bit, he dropped my hand, and we ambled on toward the Fredricks' place. Our conversation was still scarce, but I didn't feel so self-conscious anymore. It just felt kind of natural to be walking alongside him.

He paused right before we reached the Fredricks' gate. "I hope you don't mind, Maggie, but Rueben and Dorrie wanted to come along today too, so I told 'em it'd be all right. Rueben can help me with the barn raisin', but Dorrie's too little, so I told her to stay with you. I hope that's okay. They'll be coming along round lunchtime."

"I would love to have Dorrie stay with me. She's a little sweetheart, Joe." I went and blushed again as I said this.

Joe trekked out to where the men were gathering around the old burned-out barn. He turned and waved to me then disappeared into the crowd. I headed on up to the house and hoped Sarah Fredrick wouldn't mind that I'd come. I didn't know her very well since she was already into her late twenties with two young boys and another on the way, but I always saw her at church, and each time she was right nice to me. I don't know why I kept feeling so flustered about everything; I wasn't usually so unsure of myself, but it felt as if I'd stepped into a whole new world, away from childhood and into some sort of scary unknown.

I rapped on the door, and Sarah opened it. Her face was wet and bright red from the heat in the kitchen, her swollen belly covered in yards and yards of bright green fabric, but it couldn't conceal the baby beneath. Sarah smiled at me and waved me inside the kitchen.

"I'm just gettin' the bread ready to knead if you'd like to help me." She didn't wait for an answer, just nodded toward the back of the house. "The boys are still sleepin', so it's peaceful for a bit. But once they wake up, we'll be in for a trial."

My nerves got the best of me, so I stammered, "I'll be happy to help you any way you need me, Sarah."

She smiled. "I saw you come up with Joe this mornin'. Is there somethin' new I should know about?"

"He just asked me for today. I don't know if that's somethin' to know about, but I was happy to come and help him...and you," I stuttered. "I think he's a really, really nice boy...I mean man." I could feel the telltale blush coming up on my face once more.

Sarah grinned knowingly. "I think this'll be an important day, but maybe you just don't know it yet. I can see it in the way the two of you look at each other. Not just today, mind you, but at church and in town. I can see things that are goin' to happen clearly sometimes, and my feelin'." She paused as she rubbed her belly. "He's an active little fella; can't stop kickin' his mama."

I tried to change the subject as I pounded on the soft bread dough. "How do you want these loaves shaped, Sarah?"

He watched her as she slowly made her way to the kitchen door, and he could feel her nervousness as if it were his own. He sighed and wished there was a way he could just take her away from all the ugliness filling her life. He felt so fortunate that his family had always been so close and loving. His mom and pop had endured plenty of heartaches along the way, but their love for each other had held their family together. He was their only child that survived until Rueben came along when he was barely four. Then, more than ten years later, little Dorrie, his mom's only little girl, was born. He was fifteen, almost old enough to be her pop, when she came into their lives. He smiled as he thought how blessed he was to be a part of his family. He wanted Maggie to feel the love he had for her too. He wanted to shelter her from all the pain her papa had caused her. He wanted her—he knew his reflections had best stop right there for now. He cleared his throat and shook his head to clear his mind, and then he sprinted up the hill toward the men and the tremendous task of rebuilding the burned-out barn.

Dozens of men, young and old, were scattered around the piles of lumber. He heard his name called and turned around to see his buddy Fred hurrying up the hill toward him. "Hey, Joe, we saw you come up with Maggie." He laughed loudly. "So you finally got up the nerve to ask her out. You been hankerin' over her for months, so I'm mighty glad you're finally doin' somethin' about it!"

"She's a good girl, Fred, nearly a woman. I can't help but care 'bout her, and I want to make her smile more'n anything else in the world."

"Oh, brother, you got it bad! Just wait till you're married, though; then ya won't feel that need quite so much. Mary Jane and I been married goin' on two years now, and I used to feel that way about her too."

He swore, "I'll never stop feelin' that way about Maggie."

"Time will tell, my friend, time will tell."

He strode away in frustration as he heard the men calling to them to come help lift the first wall, so he rushed up and grabbed on to the frame.

"Heave up!" Tom Fredrick shouted. Then in unison, the men began lifting the wall up into place. Hammers pounded and nails flew, and almost before they turned around, most of the framing structure was up.

Wearily, the tired men settled on a break, and he was surprised to learn it was almost noon already. He wiped the sweat from his brow as he spotted his brother, Rueben, and his little sister, Dorrie, heading up toward the house. He shouted and waved then went to join the men by the well for a cool drink of water.

⌒⑦⌒

"**M**aggie, hey, Maggie, ya in there?"

I heard Rueben shouting out to me, so I quickly wiped my hands on my apron and scooted out the door. "Hey, Rueben." Rueben was the same age as me, so it felt a little awkward that I'd come here with his big brother, but to me, Rueben was just a kid. I didn't know how that was logical, but it's how I felt. I gazed off past Rueben and queried, "Where's Dorrie?"

"She's over to the flower garden. Ya know how she is with gardens 'cause she and Mama spend all their time there. I just don't know what they'll do when she starts school in the fall, seein' as how she's Mama's little shadow. Aw, anyway, you'll find her over by the flowers."

I grinned and nodded. "Well then, I'll track her down and try to coax her to come inside with me."

Rueben waved then jogged off toward the men clustered on the hill. I hopped down the steps two at a time and set off toward Sarah's charming little flower garden. Dorrie sat nestled prettily among the bright yellow daffodils, her blonde curls shining like a halo in the glow of the morning sun. She was talking to the flowers as if they could hear her, telling them how beautiful they were and how wonderful they smelled. I smiled as I watched her, her innocence a delight to behold.

"Hey, Dorrie, what ya doin'?" I called softly.

She looked up and smiled at me with a smile as bright as the sun itself. "I'm just talkin' to my friends the flowers. Do you wanna come talk to 'em too?"

I lightly touched her soft silken hair. "Not right now, baby. Will you come inside and help me get lunch ready for your brothers? Then after lunch we can come back out and talk to the flowers some more."

"Okay," she complied. I took her little hand in mine as she happily chattered away, and we strolled leisurely back to Sarah's kitchen. Just as we arrived at the kitchen door, I heard a loud motor roaring up the road, and then I caught a glimpse of the Model T turning into the driveway. I thought my eyes had to be deceiving me when Papa proudly stepped out of the clattering car, walked around it, then opened the door and lovingly helped Rachel out. After that he opened the back door, and Rachel's two girls came bounding out, shouting and laughing. I thought I would die right there.

Dorrie pulled gently on my hand. "It's all right, Maggie. Let's go sit with the flowers." Unbidden tears filled my eyes, but I angrily brushed them away with the back of my hand. "No, sweetie, I promised Sarah I would help her get lunch ready for the men, so let's get that done; then we'll head back to the garden." I hurried Dorrie inside the safety of the kitchen.

We had just started putting slices of ham on plates when Rachel promenaded in. "Sarah," she called out. "Where are ya, cousin? I'm famished and dyin' o' thirst. That man don't want to stop for anything. Rushin' me here and there. If I didn't love him so much—" She paused quietly as she noticed me and stretched out her hand to me. "Oh my goodness, now I didn't know you were comin' today, Maggie."

Her self-indulgent smile seemed more like a smirk; her words felt as if she were taunting me, begging me to blow up at her, but I wouldn't give her the satisfaction. I just looked at her hard then quietly asked, "Rachel, how are ya?"

Sarah rushed into the room, intent on preventing a fight. She came up short, stopped, and smiled nervously at both of us. "Rachel, you look good. How're ya feelin'? You come on into the sittin' room and visit with me for a while. We'll just let these girls finish up with the lunch. Come on; let's go visit. It feels like I haven't had a chance to talk to you in ages." Sarah took Rachel's hand and quickly pulled her into the other room. The other women in the kitchen looked blankly at me, their stares asking more than words could, and I fervently wished I could just disappear.

Warily, little Dorrie tugged on my skirt. "Maggie, let's make a picnic for Joey and Rueben. Then we can eat near the flowers."

I thought that was a splendid idea.

The older women turned away from me and started discussing their vegetable gardens. It was as good a time as any for them to brag about why their garden was the best and about the right way to get canning done. The younger wives began swapping recipes and discussing the best way to get rid of diaper rash. I felt totally flustered, but I appreciated their kindness. In a place as small as our town, there wasn't much room for secrets.

$\sim\!\mathscr{K}\!\sim$

Dorrie smiled as I lifted the bulky basket of food off the table. "Joey and Rueben are really gonna like this lunch! We don't usually eat all this kinds of food at home."

"It's kinda nice when everyone brings a little bit of their own dishes to share, isn't it, Dorrie. Then we get to sample a little of everything." My stomach growled loudly, reminding me that I'd only had a small hunk of bread with last year's blackberry preserves on it for breakfast. The smell of the freshly baked bread, smoked ham, and the pickled vegetables was almost too much for me to bear, so I hastily hurried Dorrie out the door, and we set off in search of Joe and Rueben.

We discovered them out in back of the half-finished barn, tossing dried cow chips past a stick they'd haphazardly planted in the ground several yards away. My heart raced as I watched Joe, his stance strong and tall as he brought his arm back to lob the cow chip at the stick. Then as that cute little curl tumbled lazily across his brow, I experienced a sudden, strong yearning to reach out and stroke his hair, but after I considered it, I resisted.

"I wanna play, Joey!" Dorrie cried out happily.

He spun around and picked her up, lifting her high into the

air and spinning her around and around. She giggled joyfully as he plopped her back on the ground. "Let's go wash up and eat first." He winked at me and then teasingly tickled Dorrie. "I'm so hungry I could eat all the flowers in the garden…in one big bite!"

"Not my flowers, Joey!" she cried, stomping her foot down hard.

"Nope, not even one," he replied as he kissed her chubby little cheek. After that, he and Rueben headed over to the well and began pumping water out to clean their hands.

"Stop it!" Dorrie screamed merrily as Rueben turned and splashed water on her. He laughed and scooped up another handful of the cold well water. "You'd better run fast, or you'll be the old wet hen." His eyes sparkled with mischief as he hurled the water at her. She laughingly screamed and then merrily raced off down the hill. He grinned mischievously, hastily grabbed the basket of food, and darted after her. Their laughter was contagious, and Joe and I caught it as we dashed down the hill after them.

All of a sudden, my shoe caught in a hole and I began to pitch forward, but Joe smoothly caught my arm and pulled me up to him. We were so close I could feel his breath in my hair. My heart thumped loudly, and I felt afraid to speak and break into the amazing moment. He drew back from me and gazed longingly into my expectant eyes. Everything else around me dimmed, and I was aware of only him. He appeared to want to say something, but instead he stepped back and lightly touched my hand. Then he heaved a sigh and said softly, "Let's go catch up. I'm a starving man after all that work this morning, and that ham smells mighty good!" He winked and smiled at me with a sparkle in his dark eyes that just about melted my heart right then and there.

Dorrie and Rueben had found a perfect spot under a huge old oak tree. By the time Joe and I arrived, they'd already sprawled out comfortably on the grass, and Rueben seemed quite content with his plate of ham.

Joe plopped down, leaned up against the tree, stretched out his legs, and sighed contentedly. "I could lay here all day, what with the breeze and the good food and"—he looked straight at me—"the mighty fine company. Life just don't get better'n this."

I think I blushed again for about the millionth time that day. I handed Joe a heaping plate of food and turned away to fix something for myself. I'd gotten to that tongue-tied place again and was really beginning not to like it, so I filled up my plate and boldly looked back at Joe with a bighearted smile. His grin inspired me to blush again. Fortunately, Dorrie broke the awkward moment when she crawled up into Joe's lap and asked him to tell her a story.

I was just thinking how adorable Joe looked as he made each character in his story come to life, when suddenly a cold shiver crept up my spine. I shook myself to get rid of the feeling and then glanced up as I felt his eyes on me. The concern I detected deeply touched me. I laughed and started to say I was all right when I heard Papa's voice behind me, and I knew then what that creepy sensation foretold.

"Maggie, hiya, girl. I been missin' you and your brothers and sisters. What say we go have us a talk for a minute." Papa's voice was soft and smooth, a voice I used to love to hear, a voice that used to make me feel so safe, a voice that now revolted me.

I stood up awkwardly and caught on to the tree for support. I looked needles at Papa and hoped he felt every one. Then I stormed determinedly away from my friends and stopped by the well house. Papa followed me, his eyes full of hope.

"Maggie, I just can't stand that ya won't see me or talk to me, girl. I'm still your papa; I'm still the same papa you've always had. You're just gonna have to forgive your aunt Rachel and me and let us be a family again. You need us, Maggie, and we need you. You're my firstborn." Papa stopped rambling, but his impassioned eyes continued to plead silently at me.

My heart was torn because I'd loved my papa so much. As I stared sullenly into his despairing eyes, my suffering soul fluttered with sweet remembrances of happier times. I twisted away from him as hot tears burned my eyes, and I tried to block out the haunting memories piercing my heart.

I squeezed my eyes shut to try to stop my tears from falling, except then tender images of my papa filled my mind. I pictured him as he arrived home from work when I was only a little girl and how special I'd felt when he'd pick me up and put me high up on his shoulders and then ask how his favorite girl was. And sometimes on summer nights he'd take us kids up to the top of the hill, and we'd sit and gaze at millions of stars while he'd tell us wonderful stories about them and help us pick out all the constellations. I remembered how my papa taught me to recognize all the different birds by their calls and to love the beauty of the earth that God created.

I cringed as all of these visions cluttered my mind, and half of me yearned so badly to just throw myself into his arms and say, "I miss you too, Papa," except the injured part of me was too strong. The pain he'd inflicted on Mama and all of us the past months was just too much to bear. I desperately wanted to grab something, throw it, and shatter it into a million pieces, like my life had been shattered, but I couldn't. So I did the only thing that I could—I calmly told him how much I hated him.

The luminous moon shimmered above the horizon, the stars glittered in the night sky, and my heart soared as I waltzed into the newly made barn with Joe by my side. It was my first time ever to actually be present at a barn dance. The closest I'd come before had been playing with the other kids outside of the barn while the grownups danced merrily inside.

As far back as I could recollect, folks around here had celebrated the planting and harvesting seasons by means of barn dances. Mainly because it didn't take much to get ready for one, and, most importantly, the cost was trifling. And everybody got a chance to just relax and partake of a little enjoyment after all the week's work. All it takes is a hay wagon backed way into the back of the barn and turned crossways for a stage; then the fiddlers take their places, and a caller jumps up on an old box or bucket and starts his calls. Then the magic happens…and tonight I was a part of the magic.

I remembered in happier times when Papa and Mama danced, how delighted Mama felt when the musicians tuned up their fiddles and the dancing began. My heart swelled with comparable joy, and it was just about the most exhilarating feeling I'd ever had when I finally heard the caller shout out, "Pair off!"

The new barn sparkled like diamonds from the light cast by dozens of kerosene lanterns. The smell of the fresh wood, the laughter, and the feel of Joe's hand in mine as we began to dance all made me feel blissfully dizzy.

Too soon the dance was over and done with, but it had been just about perfect. My head was still dizzily spinning from my last wonderful dance with Joe as we strolled out of the crowded yard, and I sighed unconsciously in sweet satisfaction. I simply couldn't believe he was interested in me! He seemed so grown up, and I felt like such a child, but tonight had been pure magic. My heart soared once again as I looked up at the glistening stars and the full, pure white moon, and I deemed I could never be more contented.

Joe reached out and squeezed my hand. "Penny for your thoughts."

I beamed at him and nodded. "Thank you for takin' me today, Joe. I had a grand time. It was right pleasurable helpin' the Fredricks raise their barn. And the dance…oh, it felt just like a fairy tale."

Mary Jane giggled behind me. I had almost forgotten that she and Freddy were walking home with us. I sighed. "The only dark spot to the day was when Papa and Rachel showed up. I don't know how she could come, what with her belly all swelled out and her knowin' how everyone feels about her."

Mary Jane cried out, "But Maggie, you know Sarah Fredrick is Rachel's cousin. It would've looked awful funny if they hadn't come." She stumbled, and Freddy reached out to steady her.

"Whoa there, girl. Time we get you home. We'll turn off here, Joe. See you two at church in the mornin'." Freddy and Mary Jane slipped away into the moonlight and soon disappeared down their shadowy dirt road toward home.

All of a sudden Joe stopped and gently grasped my trembling hands. I felt overjoyed and scared to death at the same time, and it was as if lightning raced rapidly through my veins. He gazed searchingly at me and then quietly cleared his throat. "Maggie, I know you've been through a lot this past year, and I can't begin to understand how ya feel." He hesitated a moment then caringly continued. "I noticed how you reacted when your papa tried to talk to you this afternoon. Your fear when he spoke was like a cloud of darkness surroundin' you." His dark eyes spoke kindly to my fluttering heart. "I don't want you to have to be afraid or be in this anguish anymore, Maggie. And if I could magically make ever'thing right for you, I gladly would."

I blushed and stammered. "Oh, Joe, I'm so sorry. I hope I didn't embarrass you today, what with losin' my temper and all with Papa...I—"

He lightly squeezed my hands. "Wait, Maggie, please. It's difficult because we don't know each other very well yet, but I'd like to change that. And if you'd allow it, I want to be here for you whenever you need me to."

"Joe..." I began, but his fervent expression stopped me. His passionate eyes lingered on my face for a long moment, and heat seared through my body.

He declared tenderly, "I aimed to ask your papa's permission to court you, but now I know that's the wrong thing to do, so I'll just ask you, Maggie, if you'd be at all interested in me."

My heart stopped, or at least that's how I felt. Didn't he know I'd been watching him for a long time, never thinking he'd have any thought of me? I took a deep breath of the night air and exclaimed, "I would! I really would, Joe!" I gazed happily into his warm, dark eyes. "I'll be eighteen in June, ya know, so I'm not really all that young."

He smiled sweetly and draped his strong arm around me, and I lightly situated my shaky hand on his back as we moseyed along down the dusty road toward home. As we rambled down the road, my mind mulled over the what-ifs, and I was sorely afraid he might try to kiss me when we rolled up to my house. I didn't know what I'd do since I'd never even kissed a boy before, much less a grown man. I so hoped my nervousness didn't show because I absolutely, positively didn't want him to think I was a baby.

I sighed softly, and his arm tightened around me. I gazed thankfully up into the shimmering black velvet sky, its darkness broken only by the glimmering moonlight and countless brightly shining stars that really did look like sparkling diamonds, and I felt so content just to be right there beside him.

As we rounded the bend in the road, the lights of my tired little house blazed harshly into the darkness. Stark reality assaulted me, and I came back from the fairyland I'd existed in for such a short time. My stomach tightened, and I felt a mixture of anger and fear settle on me. The delight I had experienced so sweetly merely minutes ago was suddenly replaced by a heavy weight of dread.

I lightly grasped Joe's hand and whispered fearfully, "I best get inside, Joe. Something feels wrong."

Concern filled his voice. "Do you want me to go in with you, Maggie?"

"No…no, it's all right. I'll see ya tomorrow, Joe." I fixed my eyes on his sweet face for one last, lingering moment. "Thank you for a wonderful time."

chapter 4

My instincts had been right. Mama should have been in bed hours ago. She had promised to leave the kitchen light on for me, but not every light in the house. I crossed the darkened yard and raced into the kitchen. Mama was there, sitting all alone at the table. Her head was bowed, and I could hear her crying.

"Mama!" I cried out.

"Hush, Maggie, you'll wake your brothers and sisters." She looked up at me, and I saw the bruising on her face. Her right eye was swollen and puffy, and her poor lip was still bleeding a little bit. She tried to smile at me and winced at the pain.

"Mama, what happened? Who did this to you?" I watched as she tried to stand up and walk over to the stove. She limped slowly back to the table with a rag she'd soaked in hot water. I kneeled down in front of her and gently took her hands. "Mama, your foot! Is it broken? My God, what happened here! Did someone break in? Please tell me, Mama. I'm old enough to know!"

Mama bent her head in despair. "Maggie…it was your papa, honey. He stormed over here this evenin' after the kids were asleep, and he was fit to be tied. I don't know how much he drank after he left the Fredricks', but he's a mean man when he drinks."

"Papa…Papa did this?"

Mama nodded sadly. "He didn't like the way everyone treated him today. He said he felt like a leper, and he kept screamin' that I'd even turned his own daughter against him. I told him he'd done all the turnin' himself. That's when he lost all control and just started hittin' me. I tried to fight him off, but when he's been drinkin', he's too strong." She rested her head on the table in shame and misery.

"Mama! No!" I cried in anguish.

She trembled as she remembered her terror. "I didn't mean to, but I screamed really loud when he stomped down on my foot. That's when Will ran in. Papa snarled when Will told him to just go and leave us alone, but then, thankfully, he left."

"Oh, Mama, I'm so sorry. I'm so, so sorry! It's all my fault!" I was grieved.

"No, no, Maggie." She reached out and stroked my hair. "I've just been sittin' up and waitin' 'cause I'm so afraid he's goin' to come back." She paused again and then said quietly, "I'm even fearful of what he might do to your aunt Rachel."

"Mama, how can you take up for her after what she did? I hope Papa hurts her and that baby!"

"Maggie, I never want to hear you talk like that! God knows our hearts, he knows what everyone does, and he'll take care of any retribution needs takin' care of. You go on to bed, now. I'm goin' to wait the night out here in the kitchen. I've got your papa's old shotgun right here beside me, so I think I can scare off anyone who tries to bother us."

"No, Mama, you're half dead and hurtin' right now, and your foot might even be broken. You go lay down with the girls, and I'm goin' to stay up and wait out the night."

Mama looked as if she was about to protest, but then she wearily nodded her head and thanked me softly. I helped her up and walked her down the hall to my bed. I pulled the covers up gently as I lightly kissed an unbruised spot on her face. Mama sighed deeply and fell into a troubled sleep.

Menacing shadows formed around me as I slipped quietly back down the hallway, turning off lights as I went. I knew in my heart it was only the trees swaying in the blustery wind that seemed like ghostly arms reaching out to grab me, but even so, I rushed to lock up the front door and the kitchen door, something we very rarely did. Then I sat resolutely in my mama's big rocking chair in the living room, Papa's shotgun resting on my lap, infinite fear raging in my heart. My eyes burned with tears I couldn't shed, my body trembled uncontrollably, and I felt hot and cold at the same time. I wasn't sure if I was afraid my papa would come home and I'd have to shoot him, or if I was afraid he would never come home again. Truthfully, I didn't know which would be the worse fate.

"Oh, God," I moaned, "I can't even pray." That perfect day, that perfect night that happened only moments ago had faded away and was replaced by a living hell. The fiendish wind kicked up suddenly and tossed the shuddering tree branches against the windows and walls. I stared at the looming shadows and listened intently for footsteps on the porch, and as the endless night crept by, the tempestuous wind strengthened, and my angry tears began to fall.

He watched as Maggie ran quickly toward the lighted house. He just didn't feel right leaving her and going home. Moreover, he knew something was definitely wrong. He didn't know what it was, but he knew he couldn't leave her alone and unprotected for the night. He quietly crossed the yard and sat down under an old live oak tree that gave him a direct view of the house. He was surprised when Jack slunk in beside him and gave a happy yelp. "Shh, quiet, Jack." Jack responded in his usual way—several large licks to his face, a little happy panting—and then he stretched out and lay down. He scratched the dog's back gently as he watched the shadows for movement. He saw the lights start to go out one by one in the house. Then he saw Maggie creeping through the living room toward the front door. He saw her check the lock, and as she turned toward the window, he saw her strained face. Whatever had happened that night wouldn't happen again. Not while he was on watch.

⁂

The wild wind whistled and whipped through the trees, and it looked as if it was going to be a long, cold night. After the warmth of that beautiful March day, the cold felt even colder, but at least it wasn't raining. That was a blessing in itself. He leaned his head back and thought back over the day. Maggie was beginning to mean even more to him than he'd ever imagined. His heart beat faster as he thought about her. She was so beautiful; her light brown curls bouncing around her sunny smile and her brown eyes glowing like amber. He was utterly captivated by the way she moved him. He closed his eyes and felt warmer just thinking about her.

Jack let out a low growl but was quieted when Joe put his hand on the dog's back. His eyes searched the darkened yard. Jack softly growled again, and he knew someone was nearby. He stood up slowly and walked out toward the road. The eerie moonlight cast shadows all around, which helped to hide the intruder that he knew was there.

Suddenly he felt breath on his neck. He turned and stood face-to-face with Maggie's drunken papa.

A low voice snarled in his ear, "Who're ya and what're ya doin' on my property?"

He stepped back and looked into the intruder's eyes. "It's Joe Gilley, Mr. Bowen. I'm just here to make sure no one disturbs

Maggie or her mama anymore tonight. Do ya understand what I'm saying?"

Maggie's papa leaned into him. His breath smelled like a brewery, and his eyes looked wild and lost. "I come home to my family, and whadda I find, some wannabe boy tryin' to act like a man and keep me off my own place. Step aside, boy; don't make me hurt ya."

He placed his hand on Mr. Bowen's chest to prevent him from getting any closer to the house. "I don't think that's a good idea, Mr. Bowen. I think you'd best get back home now and think about what you're doin'. Maggie's never gonna forgive you if you go carryin' on like this."

"Whadda ya think ya know about my family, boy?" Bowen vehemently spit out.

"I don't know what happened in that house tonight, but I know it wasn't good. I saw Maggie's face. Only somethin' brutal could make her look like she did."

Bowen roughly shoved him and tried to run toward the house.

He caught hold of Bowen's arm and spun him around. "Come on now, Mr. Bowen. Let me walk ya home. Your ..." He faltered, at a loss for words because he knew Rachel wasn't Bowen's wife yet. He knew there'd been no divorce. He cleared his throat. "You need to get on home and get some sleep. Things'll look different in the mornin'."

Bowen hissed, "Move aside, boy. I have a right to act and do anything I please on my own place."

He did the only thing he could think of—he pulled back his arm and let it fly, making firm contact with Bowen's nose. The crunch he heard didn't sound good, but he couldn't worry about that now. He hoped the sound of the wind had blocked the skirmish in the front yard from the ones inside the house, and he knew he had to get Maggie's papa off the property, and fast. So he firmly grabbed hold of Bowen's limp arms and roughly dragged the drunken man down the dark, gloomy road toward town.

chapter 5

I awoke slowly, unsure of where I was. My eyes felt as if they were weighted down with lead. As I moved in the chair, the shotgun slid off my lap, and I remembered the terror of the night before. I rubbed my weary eyes and sighed sadly.

The sun was just beginning to turn the sky pink when I heard Mama rattling around in the kitchen. Did I want to go talk to her? My feelings were so jumbled. I wanted to be there and protect her, but I also felt so resentful that my evening with Joe had ended in such a horrific way. I picked up Papa's shotgun and headed down the hall.

Will stuck his shaggy head out of the boys' bedroom, rubbing his eyes and yawning. "Mornin', Maggie. Where ya goin' with Papa's gun?"

"No place, Will. I was just fixin' to put it up on the closet shelf in Mama's room. I don't want any of the little ones to find it and play with it."

Will grunted, "Mmmhmm. Mama all right?"

"Don't know yet. I heard her in the kitchen, but I didn't go in. She was pretty done in last night." I turned around and fixed my eyes firmly on him. "I'm glad you were home, Will. Who knows what Papa would have done if you weren't."

"I didn't even recognize him, Maggie. He was ragin' mad. He looked like the devil had ahold of him, and I was really scared."

Tears burned behind my eyes. "He was mad at me, Will, and he took it out on Mama." I shuddered as I thought about what Papa'd done. "I shouldn't have created that scene yesterday, but... I just can't stand the sight of him! And Rachel, how can she pretend she hasn't done anything to us. Miss sugar and spice and nothin' very nice. She kept gigglin' and talkin' to Sarah, talkin' 'bout how much she wants her baby to be a boy for Papa. Papa has sons already. She just makes me sick!"

"It's hard not to hate her. I feel that way too. I just wish things could go back to how they was before. It'd be good to have Papa home the way he used to be."

"I don't want him home ever!" I said, storming down the hall a ways.

Suddenly a loud wail came from the back room. "Mama!" I turned away from Will and hurried into my bedroom. Lilly was sitting up in bed, thumb in her mouth, holding her blanket up under her chin.

"What's the matter, baby?" I crooned. "Did you have a bad dream?"

Lilly snuggled into my arms and sighed. "Maggie, I wet my bed again." Her little face puckered up, and a silent tear slid down her cheek. "Papa's gonna be so mad at me."

I hugged her tightly and gazed into her large brown eyes. "Papa won't be mad, baby. Come on; I'll help you get cleaned up; then we'll get ready for church together."

I blamed Papa for this too. Lilly never had accidents in bed before Papa and Rachel took off together. Lilly was only six, hardly old enough to know what was going on, but unconsciously she was reacting to the tension in the house. *Poor baby*, I thought. *How else are you going to damage us, Papa?*

꒰ᴍ꒱

His eyes opened slowly when he felt warm, wet breath on his face. He saw Maggie's dog, Jack, leaning over him, tail wagging, tongue hanging out, ready to play. He gently pushed Jack away, stood up, and stretched. It had been a really long night, and he felt almost too tired to move, but he wanted to get home before Maggie knew he'd camped out in her yard all night. He stretched again as he looked up at the house.

Suddenly, he saw the front door open and Maggie's mama come down the porch steps. He thought about jumping behind the tree, but he knew she'd already spotted him. He ducked his head and then looked up shyly. He tried hard not to react to the bruising and swelling on her face as he uttered softly, "Didn't mean to disturb you, Mrs. Bowen. I just felt a little uneasy when I dropped Maggie off last night."

"No reason to feel guilty, Joe. I'm glad you were concerned enough to stay around. Things haven't been too good lately." She tried to smile, but the split in her lip made it lopsided, and she cringed as the cut opened up again.

"I really don't want Maggie to know I was here, Mrs. Bowen. She might just think I'm intrudin' upon her family matters, so I'd appreciate it if this could be just between us."

"Maggie would feel honored you care enough about her to stay all night, Joe, but I won't mention it, though, if you don't want me to. Did you have any problems with—"

"No, ma'am. Jack kept me company for the night." He glanced over at the timeworn house and heaved a tired sigh. "I'll walk out with you if you don't mind."

She limped a little as they headed off together down the dusty road.

⌒ℳ⌒

"Mama?" I called as I entered the darkened kitchen. The sun was just beginning to rise, and shadows still filled the house. "Mama, where are you?"

"I think she's already gone to town, Maggie," Will called from the living room. "She said yesterday that she wanted to get to church early and talk with the pastor, so I guess that's what she's done." His troubled face appeared at the kitchen door. "I'll go rouse the kids so they can get ready for church."

I leaned heavily on the sink and stared sullenly out the kitchen window. I blinked twice when I thought I saw Mama walking off down the road with Joe, but it couldn't have been. My mind and my eyes were so tired; I knew I had to be imagining things.

I groaned then started putting together a few things for breakfast, and I felt so relieved that Will had bartered for a few laying hens last week. I walked out back, and the freshness of the air revived me a little. My step quickened as I headed over to the hen house, reached under the hens, and gathered an egg or two out of each nest. They would make a nice breakfast when I put them together with the eggs we got yesterday.

It didn't take long for all the food to disappear once the kids landed at the table, and just as soon as they finished eating, they vanished just as quickly. It took me longer to cook breakfast than they spent eating it, and I groaned loudly when I took in all the mess still waiting for me to clean up. I threw down my dishcloth and sat heavily in a chair, shaking my head in disgust. After a few minutes of silent self-pity, I rubbed my tired eyes and reluctantly pulled myself up out of the chair.

I stuck my head in the living room and found most of my sisters and brothers sprawled on the floor or lazing in a chair. "Mary, Frank, Kate, Janie, y'all come on now and hurry up, or we're goin' to be late for church," I called. "Where'd Lilly and Jessie run off to, Will?"

"Don't know; I think they headed out back after they ate." Will had his head buried in a book, and it didn't appear he planned on helping me find the girls.

I stumbled out the back door again, calling for my two youngest, most mischievous sisters. "Lilly, Jessie, time to go to church! Mama's already there, so you girls better get a move on it now!"

I saw two pairs of eyes peeking out at me from the hayloft. "You girls know you're not supposed to be up there! That floor's not strong enough to hold anymore. Get down here, the both of you." I used my sternest motherly voice and hoped they'd mind me.

Suddenly, I felt their little hands grabbing mine, and I pulled the two girls in close to me and hugged them tight. Unexpectedly, I broke into tears, and I couldn't stop sobbing. I squeezed the girls tighter to me until they began to scream and cry too.

Jessie cried out, "Stop it, Maggie! You're hurtin' me! Will! Help me! Maggie's gone plum crazy!"

The other kids came running out of the house, and Will roughly seized me by the shoulders. "Maggie, stop it, stop it now! You best get in the house and rest. I don't think church'll do you any good today." He took Lilly and Jessie by the hands, and they all started off down the road to town.

I sat there on the ground, rubbing my face, trying to clear my jumbled mind. Too much had happened in the last twenty-four hours, and I just felt so afraid and unsure of what might happen next. *God, why do I have to be the oldest? Why does it feel like I have to be the one to save everyone else?* I crawled over to the barn door and slowly pulled myself up. I just needed to make it to my bed, and then everything would be all right.

Bit by bit I managed to get myself into the house, my refuge. My mind was a clutter of erratic thoughts, and even the dirty breakfast dishes scattered on the table accused me as I crept by.

All of a sudden, fear overwhelmed me, and I was seized by an irresistible urge to simply conceal myself from the world. As a result I rushed down the hallway to my bedroom, my sanctuary, and held on tightly to the doorposts, breathing heavily as I gazed longingly at my bed. The only thought running through my weary head was that it would be so nice to have the bed all to myself for once.

I quickly pulled my soiled cotton dress over my head, threw it carelessly to the floor, and climbed despairingly into bed. From nowhere I heard a stark cry of desperation. It took me a moment to realize the wail had been mine, but finally the dampness of the sheets penetrated my consciousness. I jumped up as if I'd been burned then abruptly sank down into a heap on the floor. "No no no!" I sobbed.

I lay on the floor weeping for the longest time, wallowing in self-pity. What was happening to me? What other misery lay in store for me? These were questions I couldn't answer, at least not right now. Resentfully, I gathered myself up and stubbornly started stripping the sheets off the mattress. I wouldn't let Papa destroy me!

I carried the sheets out to the washtub and threw them in none too gently. Then I marched back inside and dragged the old soggy mattress out onto the porch to let it dry in the warm spring air. Lastly, I gathered up the soap and clothespins and set off angrily to wash the sheets.

Laughter filtered in through the open bedroom window. I languidly stretched and plucked a pillow into my arms. I lazily rolled over and buried my face in its downy softness, willing myself back to sleep. In my dreams I had been dancing with Joe. His arms were around me, his hand lightly touching my back. I sighed softly and opened my eyes. For a moment I was taken by surprise when I realized I was in Mama's bed. Then I remembered Lilly's accident. It felt so good to just lay there in the bed, all alone except for my dreams. It felt even better to realize that this dream had actually happened, and it had happened only last night.

I felt so different today, as if I had shed a little more of my childhood. Part of the grownup world called me to hurry up, but another part of me wasn't yet ready to give up my childhood. I still wanted to walk barefoot in the creek in the dead of winter. I wanted to whirl around and pretend I was a movie star. I wanted to play as freely as my little brothers and sisters were now as they ran joyfully back and forth through the clean sheets hanging on the line. They could pretend and imagine themselves flying when the sheets slid over them and they escaped them on the other side, and it seemed like only yesterday that had been me.

I leaned out the window and playfully called out, "Now you kids don't go messin' up all of my clean laundry, you hear me!"

"Oh, Maggie." They giggled.

There was a quiet knock at the door, and then it slowly opened. "Are you okay, Maggie?" Mama's sympathetic tone brought fresh tears to my eyes.

"Ummhmm." I hung my head. "I'm so sorry, Mama."

Mama sat down beside me and took me in her arms. "Whatever for, baby?"

"I should've talked to you this mornin', Mama. I should've told you what I did!" I blubbered.

"Maggie, honey, I don't understand what you're talkin' about."

"I said horrible things to Papa. Horrible things! And I told him I hated him. And then he came ... he came ... and hurt you!" I pulled away from her in shame.

"Maggie, baby, this isn't your fault. Your papa is a grown

man, and he's responsible for his own actions, not you, child."
She stroked my hair gently.

"He wouldn't have turned up here if I hadn't angered him,
Mama!"

"Don't, Maggie, don't ever think that. You know this isn't
the first time your papa has brought violence on me. He's not in
his right mind when he drinks. Although that's not an excuse."

"Mama, what if Will hadn't been home!"

"But he was, honey. God protects us from evil, Maggie. I
truly believe that. And last night, he protected us in the form
of Will and—"

"And what, Mama?" I hiccupped a sob.

She smiled sweetly. "And you, my darlin' girl, and you."

"Mama, I thought I'd go crazy this mornin' when I didn't get
to talk to you before church, and then I let all of my emotions
take over, and it really scared me."

"But sleeping helped, now didn't it?" Mama asked gently.

"You help me, Mama." I laid my head on her shoulder and
sighed, half ashamed that Mama was comforting me when she
was the one who had suffered most.

chapter 6

After two weeks the early April rains finally stopped, and the saturated earth could hold no more. Johnson Creek had overflowed its banks, and everywhere we looked there were huge puddles. He caught sight of Maggie and her flock just as they rounded the corner on their way to school, so he dusted off his hands on the seat of his pants, pushed back his hat, and sauntered over to the fence rail. Maggie ran up to the fence, as she had every day for the past few weeks. Her warmhearted smile greeted him and made his heart swell.

"Hey, Joe. Looks like we're gonna have a beautiful day today," she exclaimed breathlessly.

"Looks like it," he replied with a grin. "What say we go ridin' tomorrow, seeing it's Saturday?"

"Yeah! We're going ridin'!" the boys shouted.

"Not you," Maggie whispered. "Just me!"

"Dang it." Will grimaced. "I ain't been ridin' in forever."

"Maybe next time, Will," he began. "I think it'd be nice this time if only Maggie and I go."

Will kicked at the dirt, but his sixteen-year-old mind understood where Joe was going. "That's fair enough. Anyway, I told Frank I'd take him fishin' down to the creek tomorrow."

"We better get goin', or we'll be late for school," Maggie reminded the kids, but she hung back for a minute with Joe. He reached out and tenderly brushed a stray hair off her face, his fingers lingering, caressing her face. "You all right, Maggie?"

"You always make me feel like I'm all right, Joe." She paused, closing her eyes in satisfaction as his fingers brushed lightly against her skin. Then she looked up at him with an affectionate smile. "I can't wait till tomorrow. It will be so wonderful to spend the whole day with you."

He frowned a bit, his fingers remaining near her lips as he whispered, "I hope I can always make you feel this way." He drank in her loveliness for another moment then suggested, "You better go catch up, and I'd best get back to work. See you tomorrow, Maggie."

The gentle warmth of the morning sun on my face caused a feeling of serenity to settle upon me as I sat contentedly on the front porch waiting for Joe to arrive. The last few weeks had been calm and uneventful, and Mama was doing so much better, for which I was extremely grateful. Her bruises were only faded shadows now, and fortunately her foot wasn't broken, just sprained. The doctor told her it would take a few weeks to heal properly, and our dear papa hadn't been seen or heard from by any of us since that horrid night.

Will and Frank came out on the porch and sat down next to me. Frank was thirteen and thought he was old enough to be thought of as a man. What a notion! Seems like just yesterday he was toddling around, putting on Papa's old boots that came up to the top of his legs and trying to walk like Papa. Mama threw an old cowboy hat on him, and he looked too cute for words. Right now, though, his face looked as if it were dragging on the ground.

I reached over and hugged him. "What's wrong, Frank?"

"Mama says we can't go fishin' till the creek goes down. I really wanted to go today! Why's she have to be so mean?"

"Could be she loves her little man and don't want anything to happen to him...like maybe fallin' in the flooded creek," I teased.

"Ah, Maggie." Frank shook his head. "Do ya think we can go ridin' with you and Joe? That would make me feel a whole lot better. Can we, Maggie, can we?" he pleaded.

"Not this time, boys. Why don't y'all play 'Cowboys and Indians' out back? You've got your six-shooters and hats. That's always fun. Or maybe you could set up a camp and pretend you're on a safari," I offered.

"That's old borin' stuff. I wanna do somethin' fun," Frank grumpily complained.

I tried a different tactic. "You know there's a circus comin' to town in late July. Maybe y'all could put on a pretend circus for the girls."

Will smiled and tried to play along. "Yeah, we could make Jack be our lion."

Jack barked happily when he heard his name. Then he spun around and started barking out toward the road where Joe had just come into sight, riding up on his horse and leading another behind him. The boys and I waved happily and started walking out to meet him.

"Wow, those are some mighty big horses, Joe," Frank exclaimed as he admired the rusty brown quarter horses. "I wish I was ridin' with you."

I could see Joe thinking. He pursed up his lips and slightly closed one eye, and then he suggested a plan that made both boys start whooping and hollering. "How 'bout you and Will climb up on Princess and we'll take a short ride 'fore Maggie and I head off?"

Sunlight danced with shadows as we quietly walked our horses down the narrow path through the woods. Joe rode ahead of me, and I watched him affectionately as we meandered along the beaten trail. I wasn't exactly sure where we were headed, but he'd said it was one of his most favorite places in the whole world.

All at once I heard movement in the nearby brush and turned quickly to see what might be approaching. A beautiful little red fox slipped by, intent only on treading as far away from us as possible.

Joe gently reined in his obedient horse and glanced back at me. "We're 'bout to cross a little creek up ahead, and there's a lot of low branches; so be careful Princess don't try to rub you off on one. She's bad that way. Just keep her head tight, and it'll be fine."

I laughed. "Oh, so that's why you brought Princess for me to ride."

His face reddened as he grinned. "No, course not. She's gentle, just stubborn sometimes, and when she gets ready to head home, she'd like to take over the lead from you. Just don't let her."

The gurgling creek was more than just a little trickle after all the rain we'd had in the last couple of weeks, but Joe calmly urged his horse, Redwing, to jump over the creek, and it did with no problem. Princess, on the other hand, decided she didn't want to have anything to do with it, so Joe tethered Redwing on a nearby tree and crossed back through the water to me.

"She don't cotton to jumpin', so we'll just walk her through the creek. It's not too wide or deep at this spot, and the water's not runnin' too fast either." He took the reins from me and guided Princess through the waist-high water. The willful horse hesitated a bit but then passively followed him.

"You're gettin' soaked, Joe. I guess we should have turned around and ridden somewhere else today."

"No reason to. I've done this lots of times." He cocked an eyebrow at me and continued. "Sometimes I even decide to go skinny dippin' if the water's warm enough." He grinned broadly. "Hmmm ... too bad it's not warm enough today!"

"Joe!" I giggled to cover my embarrassment.

"We're almost there." His mischievous smile beamed like sunshine.

⌒⁄ℓ⌒

The concealed clearing had always been a special place for him. His gramps had taken him there often from the time he was a small boy. He wasn't sure if it was the mystical feeling he had whenever he visited, or that it always felt like an extraordinary place because of the wondrous times he'd shared with his gramps. Whatever it was, he had always kept it a secret until today. He couldn't wait to share the mysterious spot with Maggie and see if she experienced the same enchanted feeling he did every time he visited.

"We're almost there, Maggie. We'll need to tether the horses then hike just a little ways 'cause the path is too narrow and brushy. I just haven't kept it cleared like it used to be when I came here with Gramps 'cause I didn't want anyone else to find it."

"What is it we're goin' to, Joe?"

He glanced back with an enigmatic smile. "You'll see." He dismounted, quickly tied Redwing's reins to a low branch, and helped her down off Princess. As she slipped softly into his waiting arms, his strong hands lingered at her waist, and his expressive eyes held hers for the longest moment.

"Joe?"

He moved to kiss her, but she quickly ducked her head, and his eager kiss landed instead in her soft curly hair. He breathed in her sweet perfume as he gently hugged her, and although he felt disappointed, he recognized she just wasn't ready to move into a deeper relationship yet. He smiled as he brushed her hair back out of her embarrassed face, took her hand, and murmured, "Come on, Maggie; it's right through here."

He led the way down an almost nonexistent trail, tugging the tangled vines aside as he plowed through the dense brush. Finally, they drew near the clearing, so he casually stepped behind her, giving her an unhindered view of the area. He gazed longingly at her lovely face as she took in the perfectly formed circle before her. It measured about fifteen to twenty feet in circumference, and mysteriously, nothing at all grew in the fine white sand. The tall, lofty trees and bushy shrubs surrounding the clearing angled away from its center, leaving an unobstructed view of the azure blue sky above.

He tentatively watched Maggie to try to gauge her reaction, and he felt gratified when he noticed the wonder dancing in her mesmerized eyes.

"How strange! Who keeps this place so cleared out?" she asked in awe.

"No one; it's just always been this way, and no matter how many years I keep comin' here, it's always the same. My gramps said he found it as a boy." He lifted his eyes to the clear blue sky in silent praise. "This place has always had a spiritual feelin' to it for me. I'm not the least bit sure why it does, but Gramps alleges that folks round here believe it's sacred Indian ground."

He stretched out his muscular arms to take in the whole of the clearing. "It has an air of spirituality to it, so I like to imagine that native priests might have come here to pray for their people and for all this fertile land and the creatures livin' round here."

He took a deep breath of fresh air and looked around. Nothing grew in the sandy white circle, yet beauty surrounded it, and the magnificence of the sky above filled him with admiration. He'd camped out here many times and felt an unexplainable closeness to God. He loved the peaceful solitude, gazing at the stars shining brilliantly in the dark night sky and the total mystery of the place itself.

He gently grasped Maggie's hand and led her over to a sizeable sycamore tree. He swept his hand in the air and pointed at a spot where the tree's roots had grown in such a way that they formed a perfect chair. He offered, "Let's sit a spell and just relax. Then in a bit we'll head back to the creek for lunch."

⁓

The native Texas prairie grasses were dotted with colorful wildflowers; pink and yellow buttercups, bright orange paintbrushes, and dazzling yellow sunflowers danced wildly in the swift breeze. I marveled in the beauty around me as our spirited horses galloped swiftly over the open prairie.

We'd decided to head back a little earlier than planned because ominous storm clouds were gathering in the northeastern sky. The tall grasses were almost lying down in the sudden wind gusts, and little drops of rain begin pelting us. The clearing was about eight miles out from home, which meant about an hour's ride at a trotting pace, but with the sudden storm coming in, we were trying to make it back quicker.

Our strong quarter horses' strides increased as thunder rumbled loudly in the blackening sky. Joe rode ahead of me, scoping out our route, and at one point when the sky looked ready to burst, he turned back and yelled, "We should make it in plenty a time. We're only 'bout fifteen minutes from your house now."

I just nodded my head and held on tightly to the reins. The intense lightning streaking nearby might not spook Princess, but I hated it; so in view of that, I tried to take my mind off the approaching storm by reflecting back over the day. For the most part, it had been exquisite, but I felt like such a fool when I considered what Joe must have thought of me when I'd nervously evaded his kiss, but I was just too scared. I'd really, really wanted to, but...at least he didn't appear upset with me.

We'd sat close together on the sycamore roots, holding hands and watching the birds flutter about. We even tried to name all the ones we saw, but my useless mind was just too distracted what with being so close to him. Then when he twirled me around, scooted up close behind me, and lightly wrapped his arm around my waist, my heart about jumped into my throat. Turned out he just wanted me to notice a family of rabbits that had come up to nibble on the grass at the edge of the clearing, although we did keep sitting close like that even after the rabbits had left.

After a while, Joe had lightly brushed my neck with his fingers and asked me if I was hungry. It sent a tingle all through my body, and I had a hard time answering. Then he stood, helped me up, and draped his arm around my waist. I followed suit as we unhurriedly wandered back across the clearing, down the narrow path, and back to the place where we'd tethered our horses. My jittery heart fluttered with emotion to be so close to him, and too soon we reached our destination.

We quietly led our horses back to the little creek and tied them nearby so they could easily get to the cool water. Then Joe unpacked one of the saddlebags and spread an old quilt on the ground. He offered me his hand, and as he held mine, he tenderly kissed it. Warmth flooded me, and I sighed contentedly. He winked at me and then kindly saved me from embarrassment by reaching back into the saddlebag for our lunch.

His mom had helped him put together a really nice picnic for us. He'd brought some cold chicken, carrots fresh from their garden, and a couple of ripe red apples. We shared the apples with the horses, and they seemed quite delighted.

My beautiful daydream was broken when a sudden sharp

shaft of lightning streaked right out in front of us. I jumped halfway off my horse, and Princess sensed my nervousness and acted skittish for a bit. Joe yelled back that we needed to pick up the pace, so I followed his lead and gave Princess a quick kick to get her into full gallop. An exhilarating sensation surged through me as we charged over the stormy prairie toward home. We made it just as the sky opened up and poured buckets, and I wondered for the hundredth time if the April rains would ever end.

chapter 7

He knew It would be a hard day for her because it was exactly one year ago that her uncle William had been killed. That in itself was a terrible tragedy, but the aftermath that unfolded had proved far harder for her. He wanted to do something out of the ordinary to help her get through the day, and since it was a Saturday, he didn't have to work at Johnson's.

"Joe!" He heard his mom calling him just as he was about to set out for the barn. He turned back and headed over to her.

"Joe, I need you to run a quick errand for me in town this mornin'. Your sister and I are goin' to plant some more tomatoes and a few black-eyed peas in the back garden, and I need a few things. I don't want to have to stop now and get ready to go, so I thought if you have time you could just pick up what I need."

"Sure, I have a couple of stops to make on the way. Then I'll bring back whatever you need. I thought I'd ride over to Maggie's and maybe bring her over here for a while."

She handed him a quickly scribbled list. "That'd be real nice, Joe. I like that Maggie so much." She planted a quick kiss on his cheek and headed back into the house.

May twentieth, just a short year ago, Maggie's future had

looked so different, and he wanted more than ever to prove to her that she'd have a good future with him. Her birthday was coming up in about a month, and she'd be eighteen. He already had a pretty good idea about what he'd like to get her.

He sprinted up to the barn, called out to Redwing, and his trusty ride trotted over to the gate expectantly. He held out his hand, offering the horse a bright orange carrot, which Redwing immediately crunched down on and continued to enjoy while he carried out the horse's tack from the barn. He thoughtfully rubbed Redwing's velvety black nose then gently pulled the bridle over the trusting horse's head.

As he slowly rode out over the overgrown pastureland, his thoughts drifted back to his passion, his Maggie.

I'd been up since before daylight trying to help Mama round up our newly acquired little pink pig that Will had brought home last week. Lately, he'd started bargaining and bartering for all kinds of things, just doing whatever farmwork folks needed, and then he'd trade his labor for something we had need of. Only thing is, I think the girls became a little too attached to their new pet pig. Will hadn't bartered for a pet, though; he'd bartered for the bacon, yet the girls had already named the little pig Missy. Nevertheless, whether it was bacon or a pet, we found ourselves outside for the longest time, chasing the ornery little pig around and around the yard, just trying to get it back in its pen.

The cantankerous pig squealed loudly as I grabbed at its leg. Then all of a sudden my feet began slipping and sliding on the rain-soaked sod, but fortunately I found my footing. In due course I managed to once again grasp the stubborn pig's back leg. I held on tight and tried to maintain my balance, but little Missy had other ideas and forcibly jerked away from me, literally pulling me facedown in the mud. I let out a frustrated scream and irritably stood up, covered in gooey mud from my chin to my toes. Mama about fell over laughing at me, and at first I just stared daggers at her. Then I wordlessly glanced down at my mud-covered self, and likewise, I couldn't help laughing because I knew I must have looked a sight.

Will stuck his head out the back door, wondering what all the noise and fuss was about. Then he commenced to laughing too. He nimbly swung himself off the back porch and in about three strides caught up to the stubborn little pig. He skillfully swooped her up and nonchalantly deposited her back into her home sweet pen. Then he fixed his laughing eyes on us and sauntered arrogantly back into the house.

Mama put her hands on her hips, still laughing. "That boy is gettin' to be quite a man…if ya know what I mean."

All the kids were up by the time Mama and I wandered back to the house, and they let up a righteous howl when they spotted me. I openly ignored the giggling little creatures and strutted by with hardly a glance. Then Mama told them to come on and help her get breakfast fixed.

I finally managed to shove my way into the bathroom and clean myself up, but by that time the oozy black mud had dried on my skin and clothes. It might take a month of Sundays to get all the mud out of my disastrous dress, but I fervently hoped it'd wash off my skin without too much trouble. I heard more silly giggling as at length I finished scrubbing up in the shivery cold water, and I felt extremely thankful that at least it was Saturday morning and not a school morning so I wouldn't have to hear them tattling all about my great pig chase to the other kids at school.

I'd just dropped my favorite blue sundress over my head when I heard the thundering of hooves pounding down the road. I quickly peeked out my bedroom window and glimpsed Joe riding up on Redwing. My hair was still all wet, and I felt a mess, but I was really excited to see him. I quickly pulled my unruly hair back in a ponytail, tied in a matching blue ribbon, and proceeded outside to the front porch.

He slid off his horse and strode casually over to the porch. "Thought we might take a walk this mornin', Maggie."

I smiled in reply as Joe extended his hand to me, and I happily placed mine in his. Then I hollered to Mama that I'd be back in a bit. We strolled hand in hand down the tree-shaded road till we came across my favorite path into the woods. The lofty trees were fully leafed now, the fluttering birds had built their nests, and the whole forest was alive with the lively sounds of nature as we trailed contentedly down the narrow path to the creek.

We slid down the creek bank, and I heedlessly dangled my bare feet in the cool water as Joe picked up a small twig and unconsciously started scratching lines on the ground. He peered up at me compassionately as that stray silky curl of hair fell softly over his concerned eyes. "I kinda thought this might be a difficult day for you, Maggie, and I just wanted to be here in case you needed to talk or somethin'."

I reached out and brushed the wayward curl back off his face, and it was such a natural gesture I didn't even pause to think about it. He caught my hand and kissed my wrist. I quickly drew in my breath as his lips touched my skin, and I closed my eyes to try and compose myself before I mumbled, "I did have a hard time sleepin' last night just thinkin' about it all. And you know, I really do miss my uncle William; he was such a fine man."

I waited a bit as I tried to control the tears that threatened to spill out at any moment. Finally, I sniffled and softly affirmed, "I remember when I was younger … this was before he married Rachel, and he lived with us. He could get you laughin' just lookin' at his face. Sometimes when Papa'd be gettin' on to one of us kids, Uncle William would stand behind him makin' faces and pretendin' to be Papa. It liked to killed me not to laugh right out loud, but I always had to wait till Papa walked off. I don't think he meant to be disrespectful to Papa; he just didn't like us kids to get in trouble."

"He was a good man," Joe replied sadly.

"Papa and Uncle William could get into a mess of trouble on their own too, ya know. I probably shouldn't be talkin' 'bout this, but it reminds me of the kind of free spirit Uncle William always had."

"What come about?" Joe smiled as I hesitated. "From your lips to my ears is as far as this'll go."

I ducked my head, feeling shy for the moment. "Well," I began, "at one time Papa and Uncle William were runnin' moonshine, and they had a still way back in the woods that nobody was supposed to know about."

"No, you're pullin' my leg!" Joe grinned broadly.

"They did; how else do you think Papa could have afforded that car of his?" I laughed a little, thinking back to how the two of them conspired to keep it a secret from Mama. "One day they both came tearin' out of the woods like a bear was chasin' 'em."

"It wasn't a bear, now was it?" Joe hooted.

I laughed, thinking back to the picture they made. "No, it was Mama. She had her broom after 'em, and as far as I know, there's no more still."

"I would have liked to have seen that," Joe exclaimed.

I frowned a bit, thinking of how much I'd lost when Uncle William died. "I think when he died it took a little spirit out of me too."

He reached out, took my hand, and held it gently, waiting patiently for me to go on.

"Seems I not only lost my favorite uncle, but I also lost my papa that day, though we didn't know it at the time." Tears began to well up in my eyes again, and I blinked hard to control them. "I sorely miss how my mama used to be home with us all the time and how she used to take time to laugh and play with us kids even though she had a lot of chores to do." I brushed at my tears sadly. "Now she's so busy tryin' to make ends meet, workin' all the time, it feels like I've lost her too."

"Your mama probably feels the same way, but she's tryin' her best. And I know how much she's come to depend on you, baby," he offered kindly as he gently brushed away a lone tear trailing down my face.

"Sometimes I just don't know how to feel." I idly picked up the stick he'd been fiddling with and scratched at the ground for a bit. I shuddered and then looked up at Joe as I nervously whispered, "Mama talked to me 'bout filing for a divorce from Papa." I watched Joe for his reaction before I went on; his eyes showed me only concern. "She said she'd discussed it with the pastor, and considering all that's gone on, he supports her."

"I realize how much this hurts you, baby, but you have to know that none of what's gone on is your fault."

I paused for a moment. Then my tears fell once more like big, slow raindrops. "I do know that, Joe, but I just wish Uncle William hadn't been killed and our lives hadn't changed so drastically."

"Sometimes we just don't understand why such things come to pass, but I don't think God plans on bad things happenin' to us. I believe he helps us through our troubles and helps us realize that even in hard times there's been some good things happen this past year."

I fixed my eyes on him and whispered softly, "You're my good thing, Joe." I lowered my eyes. "I feel so very blessed that God put you in my life."

His fingers trailed lightly down my cheek, and he lifted my face to his as he softly whispered my name, "Maggie."

This time I didn't duck my head when he kissed me, and it was about the sweetest, most wonderful moment in my life.

⌒∦⌒

"Mama," I called as I skipped up the steps and onto the front porch. "Mama, Joe wants me to go over to his place for a while this afternoon." I continued talking to her, even though I hadn't yet found her. "Mama, did you hear me?"

Joe followed me through the house as I searched in vain. "Maybe she's out back, Maggie."

We headed out the back door and heard voices coming from behind the barn. "Mama, Will, Frank, anybody…where are y'all?"

"We're here," several voices chimed at once.

Lilly ran out and grabbed both of our hands. "Hurry, come on! I thought…somethin'…was wrong with my kitty, but guess what," she continued breathlessly. "She's a mama…she's havin' baby kitties." Her sweet face was flushed with excitement as she pulled us behind the dilapidated barn.

Kitty lay contentedly on a blanket, surrounded by all of her "nurses." Beside her were three tiny mouse-sized kittens, mewing softly with their eyes closed tightly. Lilly was beside herself with joy. "Aren't they beautiful, Maggie?"

I couldn't do anything but agree with her.

Mama pulled herself up from the ground, a smile playing around her mouth. "Well, little ones, I think that's all I can do to help Mama Kitty. It's up to her now to take care of her babies."

"Can't we stay here and watch 'em, Mama?" the eager girls cried.

"Of course, sweeties, but I've got chores to do in the house." She paused and turned to Joe and me. "There's a home-demonstration agent making her rounds today and tomorrow in Johnson Station, and if she gets out here with some food supplies, I'm goin' to need a block of ice for the ice box. I'm hoping someone will have a surplus of milk that she can bring us. It'll be all right for a while without keeping it cold, but I'll feel better if I can put it in the ice box."

Joe nodded his head thoughtfully. "We'll be happy to pick it up for you, Mrs. Bowen, and if there's anything else you need, we can get that too."

Mama meekly turned her face away as tears filled her eyes. She wiped her eyes with the back of her hand and sighed. "It's this darn Depression! I never thought I'd have to depend on the charity of others to feed my babies. The pastor mentioned to me he'd put us on the list at the county courthouse as a deservin' family needin' help, albeit I'm just so ashamed to take charity, but it's a blessin' from God all the same."

I quickly leaned over and hugged her tight. "Mama, you've given so much of yourself to this community over the years; no one minds helpin' you now. It's fittin' for you to take surplus goods from these farmers. They're our neighbors, and you know they don't want to see good food go to waste any more than you do."

She smiled sadly. "I know, honey, but I just want better for you, Maggie…for all my children." She sighed heavily. "You two go on now and have a fine day. If you're able to bring me an ice block later on, I'd surely appreciate it."

After we stopped in town to pick up the supplies Joe's mom needed, we decided to take the longer route back out to his parents' farm. He heaved himself up onto Redwing and then pulled me up behind him. I wrapped my arms around his waist and felt very satisfied with life.

We meandered down wooded trails, trotted beside little streams, and gloried in God's world around us. Joy filled my soul every time I thought about that moment by the creek when he'd kissed me, and the way he kept glancing back at me made me think he was just as content as I was to be together.

The sun was at high noon when we finally reached our journey's end. I deemed it had already been an especially nice day, and I looked forward to spending some time with Joe's family.

His mom and Dorrie came around the house just as we rode up. Mrs. Gilley delicately tried to wipe the sweat off her brow but only succeeded in streaking her face with dirt, and little Dorrie was dancing all around, chattering to everyone about her favorite little flowers that were finally starting to bloom.

I glanced over at their charming little farmhouse and yard, which looked well cared for and loved, and thought sadly that my house looked tired and shabby in comparison.

Joe gently held my arm as I slid off Redwing's back. Then he rode off toward the barn. "Be right back," he called.

Dorrie ran over and grasped my hand, dragging me with her as she ran. "Come see, Maggie! Come see what Mom and I planted today."

I laughed happily, and as we ran off, Joe's mom warned me not to let Dorrie wear me out. We raced around the house and over to the flourishing kitchen garden, where globes of round ripe tomatoes hung from vines, and green beans, okra pods, and various peppers were all ready to be picked and enjoyed.

"Mom and I planted some more tomatoes this mornin', so we'll have some late in the summer. We planted black-eyed peas and some pumpkins for pies too. My mom makes the best, best, best pumpkin pies in the whole world," she exclaimed.

"I bet she does, sweetie," I agreed.

Dorrie twirled joyfully around the yard, spinning so much she made herself dizzy. She plopped down on the ground next to the flower garden and motioned me to come over. "Do ya want to see somethin' really pretty, Maggie?" she asked shyly, her blue eyes as round as buttons.

"I'd love to, honey. Show me."

She led me to the farthest corner of the garden and pointed

at a patch of bright pink, yellow, and red flowers floating on long wispy stems. "These are my most special flowers," she chortled. "I planted these hollyhocks last year, and this year they've finally bloomed."

"They're very beautiful, Dorrie. You'll have to teach me your secret to growin' such pretty flowers and healthy vegetables."

She crossed her little arms and broodingly thought about this for a minute. "Well, I guess if you marry my brother, I will."

Joe walked up just at that moment, and I found myself blushing again when he winked playfully at me.

"What's that, half-pint?" He laughed as he swung Dorrie up into his arms and then dangled her upside down.

"Joey!" she screamed. "Put me down right now." She giggled, twisted around, and tried to tickle his stomach. "I just meant that we have to keep Mom's special secrets in the family!" She squirmed some more and then sassily added, "You better look out! Pop and Rueben are coming up from the field, and they'll get you."

He laid her on the ground and tickled her. "No, they won't. I'm bigger'n both of 'em." He winked mischievously at me. "Anyway, Maggie'll protect me, won't you?"

"Don't get me involved in this!" I held my hands up in laughing protest.

〜

He had one more surprise in store for her this afternoon, and he hoped she'd enjoy it enough to keep her mind off the anniversary of her uncle's death. As they finished up lunch, he turned to her. "Johnson has a couple of his quarter horses runnin' over at Arlington Downs this afternoon, so I thought it might be good fun to go watch a couple of races if you'd like."

Rueben jumped right in and excitedly exclaimed, "That'd be

somethin', Joe. I've always wanted to go to the races ever since they opened up that track. What say we all go?"

"Joe, I don't want you boys down at that racetrack, especially not with Maggie. That's no place for church-going families like us." Joe's mom spoke softly but firmly.

He groaned in exasperation. "Mom, there's nothin' wrong with that racetrack. Johnson runs his horses there ever' chance he gets, and we won't be doin' any bettin', just watchin'. If you don't want Rueben to go, that's fine, but I'm a grown man now, and I can make my own decisions."

His pop's face grew red as he blurted, "Joe Edward, don't you be back talkin' your mom now."

"No, no. He's right, Pop," his mom affirmed. Then her face puckered up in thought, and she turned to Pop. "What do you think about lettin' Rueben go with Maggie and Joe?"

Pop turned sideways in his chair, stretched out his long legs, and exhaled slowly. "Well, long as he stays with 'em, I don't see no harm in it."

Joe looked at Maggie and winked. This was about as much of an argument as ever went on at his house, but he didn't want to upset her even a little, especially on this day. "Looks like it's settled then," he stated. "Maggie, would you like to go to the races this afternoon?"

"I believe that'd be right pleasurable, Joe. And it'd be great if Rueben comes along too."

⌒⋎⌒

My curiosity grew as we rode closer to Arlington. "I've never been over to Arlington Downs before, Joe. I've heard some about it, but not a lot."

"It's huge, Maggie," Rueben said excitedly. "I've never seen anything so big as that grandstand! Pop, Joe, and me rode by a few weeks ago, and you could hardly pass on Randall Mill Road it was so thick with people, horses, and cars."

Joe nodded. "That's the truth." He glanced back at me. "Well now, I've picked up quite a bit of talk when I've been over there with Mr. Johnson. That grandstand everbody's so impressed with can hold about six thousand people, and if I remember rightly it was built back in '29 or '30. I've heard tell it's outdated already, though, 'cause there's been as many as twenty-five thousand people out there on big race weekends."

"That's more than six times the population of Arlington!" I exclaimed.

Joe continued. "Yep, it's a huge draw for folks all over the country, and a big moneymaker too. Mr. Johnson has two of his finest quarter horses racin' there today, Desperado and Amigo."

He slowed the horse a bit and glanced back at me then proudly exclaimed, "I helped train both horses for racin' last summer, and Johnson's picked up a couple of first-place purses from his wins. I'm not rightly sure which races we'll witness today, but I'm hopin' we'll see the ones our horses run in."

I wrapped my arms a little tighter around him as the muscular horses broke into a gallop. The wild wind whipped around us, and I was really glad I'd changed out of my sundress and into slacks before we left my house. It would have been really hard to keep my dress under control, what with the wind and traveling at such a rate of speed.

At length we found ourselves barely a stone's throw away from the tiny town of Arlington, which was about seven miles from Joe's family farm out near Sublett. As the horses slowed down to a trot, I carried on with our chat. "I seem to remember hearing that Mr. Waggoner spent almost three million dollars building his racetrack. I can't even imagine that much money, so it seems simply incredible to me."

"To cut a long story short, he was already a millionaire, but I hear tell he's makin' 'bout a hundred thousand a day on the races; so it didn't hurt him none to build it. He had the mile-

and-a-quarter racetrack built out on his stock farm, along with the grandstand and stables, and it's become a pretty remarkable place altogether."

The horses slowed to a walk as we rode into the little community of Arlington, although it appeared big to me compared to Johnson Station. The main street was a bustle of activity. People, cars, wagons, and horses—it looked as if everyone from miles around had come to town today. I tightened my arms around Joe, feeling a little nervous to be in such a crowd. He reached back and patted my leg reassuringly. "No need to worry, baby. This place is crowded most ever Saturday. Arlington draws folks from all over the country, what with the racetrack and their mineral well."

I gazed around in wonder at all the hustle and bustle. Then I noticed a little stand out in the middle of the road painted red, white, and blue and decked out with flowerpots filled with some pretty red geraniums on each of its four corners. I leaned closer to Joe and asked, "What are they sellin' out in the middle of the road?"

He grinned. "That's the famous mineral well. You haven't ever tried it?"

"No, I've heard tell of it, but usually when Papa came to Arlington he'd only bring Will or Mama with him. This is probably the farthest I've ever traveled from home, at least that I remember."

There was an older man standing nearby the well, waiting on water customers. Joe called out a greeting, "Afternoon, Mr. Shelton. Looks plenty busy here today." The man smiled and nodded in agreement.

Rueben looked askance at Joe then jumped off his horse, Sugar, and tied it to a nearby hitching post. Then he sauntered over and helped me off Redwing.

Joe dismounted and tied Redwing next to Rueben's horse. He walked up to me and draped his arm around my shoulder. I sighed happily and moved a little closer to him. He held me close for a minute, dropped a kiss on my forehead, and then we walked hand in hand to the well. I smiled at Mr. Shelton as he handed me a little cup of water straight from the well. I started to drink it then pulled the cup away in surprise.

Mr. Shelton chuckled. "Water's warm now, it'n it? People round here know and are used to it, but folks never tried it are always surprised." He stopped and grinned at me. "Wanna hear my spiel?"

I nodded, and he continued. "Well, let's see now, it was way back in 1891 when Mr. Hammack got the idee to drill a water well for the folks in Arlington, but ever'body was sorely disappointed 'cause the water was so hot that ya couldn't even drink it, and the taste was sumpin' awful. For a long while nobody dared use the water. They just run it down the gutter. Then a bit later on someone had darin' enough to taste it and discovered this here water has medicinal value. Sooner than not, peddlers was toutin' it for curing ever' sickness under the sun, and folks from near and far started demandin' our water here for all their complaints. This went on for a good twenty years or so, and folks was afraid the well'd done gone and dried up, but 'tweren't so. Arlington folks come up with a system to force the water up and out. Then 'bout nineteen and twenty-seven, that stopped workin' and folks drilled this here well, and believe it er not, the water in this here new well is even better and twice as strong as what that old well gave us."

I peered at the water in my cup and decided to give it another try. It had cooled off somewhat, so I took a tiny sip then wrinkled my nose up at the taste. Joe wrapped his arm cozily around me and grinned at my appalled expression.

"Maggie!" I heard my name called and turned to find my dearest friend, Hannah, hurriedly scampering across the road toward me. "What a nice surprise to see you on a Saturday, Maggie," she called breathlessly. "Papa needed a few things from the hardware store, and Mama wanted us to bring her back a few jugs of mineral water." She paused to catch her breath. "We were just fixin' to head back home when I caught sight of your curly head."

I gave her a quick hug. "Hannah, you know Rueben and Joe from church."

She nodded her head as she looked wide-eyed at Joe.

I laughed and continued. "We're goin' to Arlington Downs this afternoon to watch a couple of races 'cause Joe has two horses runnin' today."

Joe cleared his throat. "Now, they're not my horses; they belong to the man I work for." He smiled sweetly at me as he playfully ruffled my curls. "I did help train 'em, though."

"Hannah, why don't you come with us? It would be so much fun if you could!" I cried excitedly.

"I don't know, Maggie. Papa and I came in our truck, so I don't have any way to get there or back home later."

Rueben blushed a bit and stammered, "You could ride on my horse with me."

"Yes," I exclaimed. "That's a fine idea."

"Papa will say I'm not old enough to go out there," Hannah protested.

"Hannah!" I exclaimed in annoyance. "We're almost finished with high school! One more week! Just ask him. Tell him Joe works for one of the owners, so we'll be protected. We can tour the stables and watch a few races. Then we can be home by suppertime. Please ask him, Hannah. We haven't had much time together lately at all."

Hannah beamed and glanced casually at Joe. "I wonder why, Maggie…" She gazed over at her papa, who was deep in conversation with another farmer. "Well then, I reckon I'll make an effort to convince him, but I'm certain he'll say no."

"Don't claim that, Hannah. He'll allow it; I know."

She shrugged her shoulders and rushed off toward her papa's truck. We could see her begging and pointing back at us. After a short spell, she turned and excitedly nodded yes. She kissed her papa on the cheek and hurried back over to us. "I just can't believe he said yes! Let's go quick before he changes his mind."

⌒✄⌒

He skillfully steered Redwing down the tight path through the crowded stables and finally spotted one of Johnson's jockeys down at the far end of the row. "Willie!" he yelled out loudly.

Willie turned around when he heard his name called. "Hey, Joe! Glad y'all could make it down today."

He pulled up near Willie and beckoned him over. "Appears it's goin' to be a fine afternoon for racin'," he commented. "What's the schedule look like this afternoon?"

"Danny's ridin' Amigo in the next race, which'll start in about twenty-five minutes or so. I'm ridin' two races after his."

"Sounds good. We were hopin' to get to see both horses run today, and it appears we will." He grinned happily. "What are the odds on Desperado?"

Willie scratched his head and thought for a moment. "Last I heard he was at twenty to one, but I think he's gonna do real good today 'cause he's itchin' to get goin'."

"We best let you get ready, Willie, so we'll move on and take our horses over to Johnson's stable boy." He nodded at Willie as he maneuvered Redwing back into the flow of traffic. "We'll see ya at the track."

He guided Redwing out toward the back of the stables while Rueben and Hannah followed close behind on Sugar. After talking with the stable boy for a few minutes, he turned back to the group. "Wanna go meet a few of the horses?"

Maggie seemed enchanted as she walked from one stall to the next, talking to each horse and stroking those that would let her gently on their noses. She turned to him in excitement. "Oh, Joe, they're so beautiful and strong!"

He thought, *Just like you, my love,* but he didn't voice it there. He just draped his arm around her and agreed with an affectionate, "Mmmhmm."

Rueben and Hannah rambled on ahead of them, unaware

that they had lingered behind, and as the two vanished around the corner, he found an unexpected moment alone with Maggie.

He watched her with affection as she had a one-sided dialogue with one of the young horses and suddenly realized just how much he was genuinely captivated by her charm. His arms encircled her waist and drew her to him. "Did I tell you yet today just how beautiful you are, baby?"

She wrapped her arms around him and laid her head on his shoulder with a happy sigh. He took the opportunity to lovingly kiss her neck. As a consequence she lifted her face to his, and once again he savored her sweet lips.

From a distance he heard Rueben calling his name and unwillingly awoke from the spell she'd put him under. "Hold your horses, Rueben. We're comin'."

Anticipation filled the crowded grandstand because at today's races horses from all over the country had come to compete. People from nearby and faraway wandered confidently around the racetrack, knowing that the races would be magnificent, given that when Colonel Waggoner and his sons undertook something, it was bound to be extraordinary.

The huge crowd surged forward in excitement as some of the best horses in the country lined up to compete for one of the large purses, which had generously been put up by the Waggoners.

My interest increased when I heard the announcer call out, "Number twenty-two, Amigo, ridden by Daniel Jones, owner, Mr. Robert L. Johnson." I grabbed Joe's hand and practically squealed in delight. He was as intense as I was when "Taps" sounded and the eager horses swiftly charged through their gates. The enthusiastic crowd roared out their favorite horse's name with fervor. Their chants increased and soon grew to be one uproarious reverberation along with the pounding pulse of the horses' hooves on the hard track.

Hannah jumped up and down, daringly screaming for Amigo, and she surprised Rueben when in her excitement, she grabbed him and hugged him as Amigo swiftly passed the leader at the last turn in the race. The crowning glory of the race—and of the day—was the look on Hannah's face when she realized what she'd done, but Rueben didn't seem to mind in the least.

The sun exploded in myriad colors; gold, red, and orange splashed their brilliance through the evening sky, enveloping me in their warmth. Joe had just left, after first depositing Mama's ice block into the icebox for her.

I hugged myself as I sat contentedly on the front porch, offering thanks to God for the excruciatingly beautiful sunset as well as the wonderful day I'd just shared with my friends. I felt so happy that Hannah had come with us, and it had been so good to laugh with her again. When we dropped her off at her house, she was practically bursting as she joyfully conveyed everything about the day to her parents. Afterward, Rueben looked a little lovesick as he rode off ahead of Joe and me, but we were kind and didn't tease him.

Then we rode on over to Joe's for a bit and sat out on the porch with his mom and pop. Right before we left, Joe's mom suggested Mama and all of us kids come over for some of her homemade ice cream and blackberry cobbler next Saturday. Although she did warn me that we'd all have to help pick black-berries first, I assured her it would be our pleasure.

It's strange sometimes how things come about. Just a short year ago my life had been so different, and I'd been so very different too. I'd meant what I said to Joe about Uncle William; I would give anything if he were still here with us. Moreover, I knew deep within my very heart and soul that even if all the turmoil that had come into my life as a result of Uncle William's death hadn't happened, Joe and I would've still found each other.

His delightful kisses as he said goodnight still lingered on my lips, so I closed my eyes and experienced his lips yet again. I realized right then, beyond a shadow of a doubt, that Joe was my true soul mate.

As the sun dropped down under the horizon, leaving only shimmering remnants of the glorious sunset behind, I laid aside my musings and hauled myself up off the steps. I leaned on the porch railing, gazed contentedly off into the distance, and then wandered into the house with my head still lost in the clouds.

chapter 8

Early Saturday morning, chaos broke out in the Bowen house. At least that's how I saw it. Kids were running everywhere, no one was able to find what they needed, and Jack was running back and forth among us, barking his head off. Then, just as suddenly as it began, it stopped.

Mama solemnly marched out on the front porch and called us to order. She proceeded from one of us to the next, carefully inspecting our freshly washed clothes, as well as Frank's ears and feet, trying to make sure we were presentable enough to go visit the Gilleys. It appeared we all passed her rigorous inspection because Mama whirled around and out of the blue began skipping merrily down the steps. The little girls cried out in delight and happily skipped after her. Will and I just stared blankly at each other for a moment. It had been a long time since Mama had played with us kids in this way. Suddenly, Frank gave a loud whoop and swiftly charged off down the road, Jack close on his heels. Will grinned broadly and grabbed my hand, and we joyously scampered down the steps after them.

We arrived at the Gilleys' in record time with Mama laughingly leading the way. I spotted Joe up by the house and waved happily at him just as Dorrie and Rueben came charging out of their house, buckets in hand, all ready for the day.

"Mornin', Mrs. Bowen," Joe called. "Mom's in the kitchen, and she said to tell you to go right on in."

"Thank you, Joe," Mama exclaimed, gathering herself back into a semblance of order. She winked at me as she hopped happily up the porch steps.

"We have a bit of a walk down to the berry bushes, but it's not too hot yet," Joe explained. "What say we head out there now, and then we can come back and relax in the shade while the cobbler bakes."

I wrapped my arms around his and gave him a little hug. He laughed and enfolded me in his arms. "Okay, gang, follow me," he commanded.

It seemed as if miles and miles of blackberry bushes grew along the back pasture fence, all heavy with ripe, juicy blackberries just waiting to be picked.

Frank pushed back his hat and exclaimed, "You sure got a lot of berries, Joe!"

Joe scratched his head as he gazed with satisfaction down the fence line. "Well, my pop always says, 'Plant one to rot, one to grow, one for the farmer, and one for the crow.' You always gotta expect some of the bushes to die 'fore they ever' bring forth fruit, but I do believe these bushes have gotten a little carried away."

We picked berries till our fingers were stained purple, and the bushes still looked full of fruit. I stopped and stretched, lifting my arms to the sky. Then I focused on what was happening around me. Frank was sprawled out near a haystack, gobbling up berries as fast as he could. Will and Rueben were leisurely walking back up to the house, each carrying two buckets of berries and deep in conversation. The girls appeared to be enjoying themselves, given that I heard lots of giggling and playing going on in the midst of picking berries. Lilly must have felt my eyes on her because just at that moment she whirled around and gaped at me with a big purple grin, and even her teeth looked as if they'd turned purple.

Laughter bubbled out of me as I felt Joe's strong arms encircle my waist. "I do believe we got sufficient blackberries to make enough cobblers for a church picnic."

I contentedly leaned back against him. "I do believe you're right, sir." I laughed playfully.

"What say we call the kids and set off to home?" His voice was like a gentle caress to my soul.

I started to holler out that it was time to go, but Joe beat me to it by whistling loudly and motioning for them all to follow us. I took hold of his hand, and we all paraded down the cow path to the house.

Mama and Mrs. Gilley sat out on the back porch talking. They waved cheerfully when they spotted us, and Mrs. Gilley loudly declared, "We got the cobblers started with the berries Rueben and Will brought up, Joe. They're bakin' now."

Joe nodded. "You need me to crank the ice-cream churn yet?"

Mrs. Gilley shook her head. "Nope, Pop and the boys are already at it, so why don't you just go get your guitar and entertain us with some of your pickin'."

The girls jumped around in joy, and Frank pulled an old harmonica out of his pocket. "I can play along with ya, Joe."

"Well then, looks like we'll have us a concert, Frank. Hang on, and I'll go grab my guitar," he replied as he shot off into the house.

A gentle breeze ruffled the trees, and I looked to the heavens in praise for such a glorious afternoon. Joe quickly returned and plopped down on the ground beside me. He strummed a little and worked at the keys to tune up his guitar then began with "Bill Bailey," an old favorite that we all joined in singing. Then Mama and Mrs. Gilley called out their favorites, "Red River Valley," "Let Me Call You Sweetheart," and several other much-loved songs that everyone knew. Mr. Gilley, Rueben, and

Will came around the house toting the ice-cream bucket, and they blended their voices in song with ours.

After a bit, Joe's mom wandered off into the house to check on the cobblers. The girls surrounded Joe and Frank, dancing and singing happily, but almost too soon it seemed Mrs. Gilley returned and called out that the cobbler was all ready to be served. Joe abruptly stopped in midsong, smiled sweetly, and winked at me. "One more song first. It's a particular one I've been workin' on 'specially for Maggie."

He began picking out a tune I was more than familiar with. Then he gazed intently at me and began singing. "All of me, why not take all of me. Can't you see, I'm no good without you, Take my lips; I want to lose them. Take my arms; I'll never use them."

My heart quickened, and I so wished we were alone.

Stars sparkled like jewels displayed in the black velvet sky. Our afternoon of delight had lasted until well after dark, and then Joe had driven us back home. The girls and Frank all piled into the backseat, and Mama settled in up front with Joe and me. Will had ridden off earlier with Rueben and his pop to help with the evening roundup, so we'd left him to fend for himself since the little girls' sleepy yawns called for bed.

Joe helped carry Lilly and Jessie inside for Mama, and then we wandered out in the yard with Mary and Frank to sit a spell and visit. Joe leaned up comfortably against a tree, so I settled down in front of him and cuddled cozily back against his shoulder. He wrapped his arms around me, and contentment overflowed my very soul. Frank sprawled out in the grass, staring up at the sky, and Mary plopped down next to us. She gazed thoughtfully over at Joe. "Do you like bein' a cowboy?"

He laughed. "Well now, guess I never thought much about

it. Growin' up on a cattle ranch, it's kinda just a natural conclusion. But yeah, I guess I do pretty much like it."

Frank flipped over, chewing on a blade of grass. "I'd like to work the horses the way you do. That'd be my dream job."

"Maybe someday you will, Frank. I started workin' for Mr. Johnson back when things first started gettin' rough and Pop needed help keepin' things runnin'."

Mary nodded. "Do you like the horses better?"

"It's hard work one way or another, but I really take pleasure in trainin' the horses. They respond well once ya get 'em to trust you, and each one has its own unique personality, so it's challengin' from time to time."

I softly caressed his arm and felt his lips gently brush against the back of my head. "I love to watch you workin' with the horses, honey. You're very skilled in knowin' just what to do."

Frank laughed. "I believe you just like watchin' Joe no matter what he's doin'."

Joe covered my hands with his. "Nothin' wrong in that. It's an honor to me that your sister cares enough about me to even notice me."

Frank groaned and sat up. "I sure wish I was old enough to work with you."

"I'm blessed to have a job I love and make a little money to help my family when they need it most."

Mama strolled out on the porch. "Frank, Mary, y'all come on in. It's gettin' late, and we have church in the mornin'."

Mary jumped up and headed toward the house while Frank collapsed back on the ground, complaining.

Joe stretched out his long leg and nudged Frank with his toe. "Hurry up, Frank. Show some respect to your mama."

Frank responded quickly. "I'm comin', Mama." Then he turned back. "Night, Joe."

I laughed softly. "Frank's quite enamored by you too, honey. Don't think I ever witnessed him mind Mama any quicker than tonight."

He ran his hands up my arms then tenderly massaged my shoulders. "He misses his papa, baby. I'm just a poor substitute."

I turned around and gazed intently into his eyes, and whatever it was I'd planned to say flitted completely out of my mind. His hands enveloped my face and drew me to him. My lips lovingly met his, and I melted sweetly into his kiss.

chapter 9

May days fell into June, and school let out for the summer. The days were busier than ever as I rushed around and tried to take care of everyone and everything. I hardly ever got enough time to spend with Joe. Mama had started working longer hours at the button factory, which left me in charge of the house and kids. Will had hired on with the railroad. He brought in a much-needed four dollars a week, but he had to leave for work almost as early as Mama, and sometimes he was gone several days out of a week because he had to go where the track was being repaired.

"Maggie!" I heard Frank calling me, and I tried to ignore him. I just needed five minutes to myself. I thought longingly of my secret place in the woods, sitting quietly by the calming creek, no one around to annoy me.

"Maggie, hurry up. Someone's comin'." He frantically gestured to me to hurry. "It's Papa's car, but I think it's Aunt Rachel drivin'. Then again, I can't tell for sure."

My stomach did a double turn. I'd tried hard to avoid seeing Papa since that day at the Fredricks'. Lately, though, he'd been coming around and taking the little kids off to do things, but Will and I wouldn't see him. I couldn't imagine why Rachel would dare to come to Mama's house.

"Maggie!"

"I heard ya, Frank. I'm comin' as fast as I can." I walked out on the front porch and saw Rachel clumsily climb out of the driver's seat. She put a hand to her lower back as she walked awkwardly toward us. Lilly came up behind me and hid her face in my skirt.

"Maggie." Rachel breathed heavily. "Maggie, you gotta come now."

I looked hard at her. "What do you need me for, Rachel? You have Papa. Let him take care of you. The doctor's in town, or the midwife if you need her."

Rachel's breathing was labored, and her face was so red that I was afraid she'd have the baby right there on our front porch. She stammered, "No, no, Maggie, it's not me. It's your mama. She's been hurt. They called your papa from the hospital in Ft. Worth, and he sent me to get you. You need to come now!"

"What happened? How did Mama get hurt?" I asked anxiously. Lilly started crying, and the other girls ran out and started pulling on me too. I tried to hush them and tell them it was all right, but they wouldn't stop. I stared heatedly at Rachel as she grasped the railing on the porch to help keep herself standing and demanded, "Rachel! What happened to Mama?"

She shouted back, "I don't know! All I know is your papa called me screamin' and hollerin' and tellin' me to come get you. Luckily, he left the car home today, or I wouldn't have been able to make it here."

"I can't take all these kids with me," I started to say, but Frank quickly interrupted me.

"I'm old enough to stay with 'em, Maggie. I'm almost fourteen."

"I guess you'll have to for a while, Frank. At least till I know all of what's happened. You girls stay in the house and mind Frank. I'll be back shortly."

The little girls screamed, "No, Maggie! We want Mama! We wanna go see Mama too!"

I peeled them off me and started walking toward the road. Rachel turned and followed me. "Maggie, get in the car. You can't walk to Ft. Worth! Get in the car, and I'll drive you there."

Rage and worry fought within me. I'd sworn I'd never have anything to do with Rachel, but Mama was hurt and Rachel had the means to get me to her. "If you'll just take me by the Johnsons' place, I'll see if Joe can come out and stay with the kids after he gets off work. Then we can go on to the hospital."

Joe wanted to come with me to the hospital, but I felt better having him stay with the kids because I didn't know what I'd find there or how long we'd be gone.

As John Peter Smith Hospital came into view, my anxiety grew and heaps of unanswered questions of how and when Mama got hurt kept running through my mind. Rachel didn't look good at all, but she and her baby weren't my concern, so I urgently begged her to hurry. She needlessly turned her sweating, red face to me and nodded her head.

I shivered uncontrollably as we raced up to the emergency entrance. I quickly bounded out of the car, hurried to the nurses' station, and edgily asked for Mama. The nurse looked carefully at the patient information and impatiently told me to have a seat in the waiting room. By this point I was on the verge of screaming, but I did as I was told.

I tried to sit still, but my agitation was too great. So I aimlessly wandered around the bleak room. Finally, after about five really long minutes, I caught sight of Papa quietly tramping through the double doors near the nurses' station. He spotted me, calmly walked over, and sat down. He wearily patted the seat next to him. I sat.

"Maggie, girl." He sighed softly. "Maggie, your mama's not doing too well just now."

I reached out and grabbed his hand. "What happened, Papa?" I anxiously pleaded.

He held on to my hand so tightly it hurt. Then he cleared his throat a couple of times. "Well, it appears someone left a hole open on the road down near your mama's job. They'd opened it to work on a water pipe, but somebody didn't finish the job and left the hole uncovered."

"How does that matter? I don't understand what that has to do with my mama," I cried.

Papa cleared his throat again and began to speak sadly. "It was still dark when your mama was headin' to work, so she didn't see the open hole. She dropped right in, and when she fell, she cut her head pretty bad. The doctor said it was lucky someone found her when they did, or it could have been a lot worse."

"How could it be worse than this?" I sobbed softly.

"Now, Maggie, you listen, girl. Your mama's gonna need you to be strong for her right now. We'll head back to see her in just a minute, but you need to know before you go in that she looks real bad. She was conscious when I left her, but she don't make much sense when she's talkin'. I believe the doctor said it was the concussion makin' her all confused." His eyes were actually tearing up, and for a moment I felt sorry for him.

"Can I go back and see her now, Papa?" I begged tearfully.

"Let's go back together. She'll want to know you're here."

At this same moment, Rachel breathlessly wobbled in. "I finally found a spot to park the car, Johnny. What do you need me to do now?" Her face was ashen, and she looked about ready to faint.

"Sit down here, Rachel, and I'll come back out in a bit." He guided her to a chair and stroked her head gently before turning back to me. "Let's go, Maggie." I flinched when he touched my arm.

Mama's room was at the far end of the hall, and my stomach

turned cartwheels all the way down it. I tried to put a reassuring smile on my face before we walked in because I didn't want Mama to see how scared I was. When I finally got a look at her, I felt really frightened. Her poor head was covered in thick white bandages, and her whole face was swollen black and blue. She had some sort of tube running down into her arm, and that scared me even more.

A nurse was adjusting her bed covers, and she turned and spoke to us as we entered. "Mrs. Bowen is restin' comfortably now. We gave her some pain medicine and something to help her sleep, but now she just needs to get some rest to help her recover quicker."

I sobbed softly as I walked toward the bed. "Can I just sit here next to her till she wakes up?"

She patted my shoulder. "That's fine, but just one of you at a time. Your papa may want to stay now, but y'all can decide. The doctor will be here in about an hour or so to talk to you both."

I looked askance at Papa. He nodded his head. "You stay with your mama, Maggie. She needs you right now." Then he turned and walked off down the hall, and I was left feeling very small and alone.

As I waited for the doctor, I held Mama's hand and continuously prayed that she wouldn't die. Her breathing was so shallow, and her skin felt cold and clammy. I trembled violently as I carefully laid my head down on her tender shoulder and told her how much I loved her.

"Maggie." A soft whisper reached my ear. I nervously raised my head and gazed into Mama's deeply shadowed eyes. "I'm okay, honey." She managed this much before she slipped back into unconsciousness.

I was still holding her hand and fervently praying when the doctor finally arrived. Papa quietly followed him into the room. "Mr. Bowen, Maggie," he began. "Mrs. Bowen has been through a serious trauma, and she's going to need weeks, maybe even months to fully recover from her injuries."

"What all's wrong with her, Doc?" Papa asked.

"Well, to begin with, she has a deep, jagged wound on the back of her head, which caused her to lose a lot of blood. We've already given her a transfusion, and her vital signs are all stable now, which is a good sign. She's also sustained multiple contusions to her ribcage, back, face, basically all over her body."

He paused and looked straight at me. "Her body was subjected to considerable shock in that fall. It appears she fell about ten feet, and as she fell, her body was bashed about against the sides of the hole, so she will need complete bed rest for at least the first few weeks of her recovery."

I drew in my breath and squeezed Mama's hand tightly. I tried not to cry out in front of the doctor because I wanted him to think I was brave.

He looked at us both and continued. "The head wound is what really worries me the most because of the danger of infection. Right now we're also monitoring her closely because she's shown signs of a slight concussion. Even so, we did make the decision to go ahead and give her pain medication because she was in such physical distress."

Papa kept shaking his head as though he understood everything. "How long will she be in the hospital, Doctor?"

"We can't keep her here too long, I'm afraid. We're already overcrowded with only eighty beds, so most of her care's going to depend on you."

I couldn't contain myself any longer, so I burst out with questions I really needed the answers to. "Doctor, what can I do to help Mama? Is she goin' to be okay? Can I stay the night with her? How—"

The doctor interrupted me with a tight smile. "Maggie, your

mama will be fine. It's just going to take her a little while to recover from all her injuries, which are mighty painful right now. Of course she'll be sore for quite a while, but none of her injuries are life threatening at the moment."

He sat down in the chair next to Mama and began to take her pulse. After a moment he looked up and addressed me. "I know you're worried because your mama's sleeping a lot now, but this is caused from all the medication she's taking. I understand from your papa that you'll be her primary caregiver, so I do want you to watch over her carefully for the next few weeks. The nurse will give you instructions on how to treat her wounds and, just in case, how to tell if a wound has become septic. As I said before, that's my main worry right now."

Papa patted my shoulder. "We need to let Mama rest for now, Maggie. I'll drive ya home. Then tomorrow we'll come back and see her."

"We'll monitor her tonight," the doctor said, "and if her vital signs continue as they are, I plan on releasing her tomorrow afternoon."

Dusk was settling in when he heard a car approaching. It turned in slowly, its headlights flashing across the yard like a watchful beacon on a lighthouse. As the roar of the engine died, he watched Maggie slowly climb out of the backseat. Mr. Bowen stepped out and walked over to her. She nodded her head in agreement to whatever he was saying. Then she stumbled up to the porch, where he sat waiting. Solemnly, she sat down next to him and then wordlessly laid her head in her lap. He reached over and took hold of her hand to try to comfort her. Right now, it seemed, was not the time for words.

He glanced up and watched the kids running about in the far pasture, chasing fireflies in the twilight. They hadn't noticed

Maggie yet, but he knew when they saw her they would all descend upon her like flies at a picnic.

Mr. Bowen and Rachel were still sitting in their car, the darkness growing thick around them, when he glimpsed a shadowy figure running toward the car. He finally made out that it was Frank, and the little girls weren't far behind him. They swarmed around the car until their papa got out and started hugging each one.

Maggie stirred beside him, looking up and off into the distance. He scooted a little closer to her and draped his arm around her shoulder.

She spoke softly. "Thank you for being here, Joe. You don't know how much it means to me."

He kissed her tenderly. "I'm glad I could be here to help you, Maggie. I wouldn't want to be anywhere else today."

She nodded and looked up toward the heavens as her tears began to fall. He leaned over and kissed away a tear or two, wishing all the while that he could kiss away all of her pain.

Tears clung to her lashes. "Mama's goin' to be okay, honey. She has a lot of bad cuts and bruises … and when I saw her, it just scared me all to pieces, but the doctor said she's goin' to be okay."

"How long'll she be in the hospital?"

She sighed tiredly. "They're goin' to send her home tomorrow afternoon. That's what Papa was talkin' to me about at the car. He's going to come by for me round noon. Then we'll go get Mama and bring her home."

I awoke to the sound of Jack's enthusiastic barking. I stretched out and realized I was alone in bed and all the girls were already up and gone. The sun shone brightly through my open window, letting me know I'd slept way past my usual time to get up. Nevertheless, I lay abed, thoughtfully reminiscing about the past months and wondering what tomorrow would bring me. I remembered what Joe had said to me only a few weeks before, that even in the midst of tragedy, God continues to bless us with his goodness. This time it had come in the form of a man who heard Mama cry out as she fell into that terrifying hole. If he hadn't been nearby, Mama might have bled to death all alone. A shiver ran through me at the thought, and I knew it was something I couldn't dwell on. I tried to pull myself together and remember that today Mama would be coming home. I knew I really should get myself up and moving so I'd be ready when Papa came, but the bed felt too good.

Nonetheless, my lazy contemplations continued even after I'd unhurriedly dragged myself from my cozy bed. I wandered restlessly through the lonely house, thinking about Papa. Yesterday he'd seemed like the papa I had always loved. He was so concerned about Mama at the hospital, and even on the way back home. I almost forgot Rachel was there … almost.

It's as though I have to make a heartrending decision every time I see Papa. If I don't or won't see him, I feel more at peace. But then he comes back into my life, and the torment of loving him comes streaming back again.

My distraught meditation was suddenly broken by footsteps pounding up the porch steps and Jack barking as though there was no tomorrow.

"Will's come home, Maggie!" Jessie screamed. "He's comin' into the yard right now. Hurry up, Maggie! Let's go tell him 'bout Mama."

"I'm hurryin' as fast as I can, Jess," I told her patiently.

Dust was flying everywhere from all the fast, furious feet running out to meet Will as he hurriedly approached the house. Jessie and I watched from the front porch as five little bodies collided with Will in joyous greeting. Jessie jumped off the porch, not even bothering with the steps, and ran enthusiastically to him. Jack couldn't be left out, so he added four furry paws and his wiggly tail to the mix.

I had to laugh at the sight of Will dragging the kids with him as he headed up to the house. "Hey, Will," I called. "We didn't think you'd be home for another couple of days."

"I heard 'bout Mama last night from some of the men who'd been in town yesterday," he explained.

"I'm really, really glad you're home, Will. Mama's goin' to need all of us today."

"She over to the hospital in Ft. Worth?" he asked.

I nodded thoughtfully. "The doctor said he'd release her this afternoon."

"They're gonna let her come home already?" Will asked in surprise.

"Mmhmm, the doctor thought she could recover just as well at home as at the hospital. He said the hospital don't have room to keep her there unless she's in a life-threatenin' condition."

"I wanna go with you to the hospital today and see for myself how she's doin'. I'm just not sure I trust those doctors sendin' her home so soon," Will exclaimed.

I groaned and shook my head. "Papa was there too, Will. He did a lot of talkin' to the doctors and nurses, and he signed the papers sayin' he'd be responsible for her release."

"Papa!" Will shouted. "What right does Papa have to say he's responsible for Mama now?"

"Will, be careful, the girls are right here," I warned.

"Maggie, they should know a thing or two by now, and if they don't, then let's educate them!"

"Papa is still legally Mama's husband and her guardian. He's the only one who can have a say in it," I answered angrily.

Papa arrived right at noon. Will had calmed down a little, but when the car turned into the yard, I could see his anger returning. So I placed my hand on his shoulder and pleaded softly, "Not now, Will. Let's be kind for Mama's sake."

Will heaved a sigh of frustration but shook his head in agreement. "For Mama. But I tell you, Maggie, that Rachel better not be in the car with Papa. I just don't think I could take lookin' at her right now."

I peered out the kitchen window at the car. "I don't see Rachel, but Papa has another man in the car with him. They're gettin' out now and comin' in!" I panicked. "Why would Papa be bringin' someone here now?" I didn't wait for Will's reply. I just took off out the door to make sure Mama was all right.

Papa caught sight of my frantic face as I rushed down the porch steps. "Whoa there, girl! Your mama's all right. This here's Mr. Milton; he's a lawyer over in Ft. Worth."

Will jumped down the steps and stood bristling beside me. "What'd we need a lawyer for, Papa?"

Mr. Milton cleared his throat. "I'm going to be representing your mama and papa in a lawsuit against the town. They're liable for the cost your mama has incurred from her accident."

I covered my face with my hands. *What is Papa up to now?* I wondered silently.

Papa looked a little embarrassed as he said, "Your mama can't take care of things herself right now. Consequently, I'm just makin' sure she has what she needs to get by for the next few months."

I wasn't sure I believed that Papa had hired this lawyer for Mama's benefit. He hadn't been very trustworthy in the past year. Therefore, I wasn't sure I could trust him now.

"Mr. Milton is goin' to ride along with us to the hospital, so it's probably best if just Will comes with us right now, Maggie. Your mama'll probably need to stretch out in the back, and Will's strong enough to help me get her comfortably into the car."

I burned with emotion as I gazed angrily at Papa. "No, Papa, I told Mama that I'd come this afternoon."

"Now, Maggie," Papa began.

I stood my ground. "I'm goin' one way or another, even if I have to walk there!"

Mr. Milton looked uncomfortable. "Mr. Bowen, you won't need to drop me back by my office after we leave the hospital. I can easily have my secretary pick me up. There should be plenty of room in your car for the four of you."

"That settles it, then," I yelled as I marched determinedly toward the car. I slid into the backseat and forcefully slammed the door.

I looked back at the group by the porch and saw Will grinning from ear to ear. He was probably remembering that just a few minutes ago I had told him to be kind for Mama's sake. Looks like I was the one who couldn't control her fiery temper.

chapter 10

A cooling breeze whispered almost imperceptibly through the trees, offering me a mere breath of fresh air. The sweltering sun still sat stubbornly on the horizon, and I continually fanned myself as I sat out on the front porch waiting for Joe. The temperature had climbed close to ninety-five today, and staying inside the house had not been an option, so the kids spent most of the day off playing in the creek and I'd stayed back taking care of Mama.

Today she appeared a little better than that first day, two weeks ago, when Papa had driven us home from the hospital. Even so, she had still slept through more of the day than she had been awake. Fortunately, so far there'd been no sign of infection from her injuries, and she'd had a little bit of an appetite again.

I'd opened up all the windows and doors and turned on the attic fan to try to pull a little touch of coolness into her room, but it still felt too sticky and hot. For that reason I'd draped a few wet rags around the bed and prayed the breeze created by the fan would draw the coolness over Mama.

The kids had come home and had their supper and now lay sprawled lazily around the yard, still trying to keep cool. After a while Mary ambled over and plopped down beside me. "Wish that breeze would bring us a shower. I just feel all clammy, like I can't even dry off."

I grinned at her. "The summer solstice hasn't even come about, and so it looks like we're in for a blisterin' summer."

She groaned and lay back on the porch. "Think I'll sleep out here tonight."

I started to answer her then heard hoofbeats pounding on the road. "I think that's probably Joe."

"Well, I'm not movin'. You two wanna be alone, you'll just have to find someplace else."

I laughed. "Is that a challenge, Mary?"

"Nope, just a fact."

I playfully tossed my fan at her and hopped down the steps, intent on meeting up with Joe down by the road. I turned back and called out to Mary, "Listen for Mama for a bit, Mary. I'm goin' to take a short walk down the road."

I met Joe as he rode into the yard. He slid easily off his horse and draped his arm comfortably around me. I stretched up and kissed him. "Looks like you've had a long day, sweetie."

"Mmhmm, it gets long what with helpin' Pop ever evenin' after I leave Johnson's, but it's only right I help him." He kissed my cheek sweetly as Frank appeared out of nowhere.

"Think I can ride Redwing a bit, Joe? I won't go far." His eyes pleaded, but his crooked smile was the victor.

"Take care, Frank, and don't get him runnin' too fast 'cause he's already had a good workout this evenin'," he advised as he handed over the reins.

We watched amiably as Frank rode happily off down the road, and then we strolled down the other way, wrapped in each other's arms. We stopped at the outcropping of rocks down past my path into the woods. Joe graciously offered me his hand and helped me climb up.

Red and gold splashed the sky as the brutal sun finally dropped below the horizon, leaving us in that twilight zone just between daylight and darkness. We settled back comfortably, and Joe lazily snaked his arm around my shoulders then unconsciously started rubbing that spot just behind my ear that just about melts me, and I sighed contentedly.

He affectionately laid his head against mine. "Did you remember 'bout tomorrow?"

"No, I can't recollect anything, but with so much goin' on with Mama—"

"Mmhmm, I know, baby. I probably would've forgotten, but Pop and Rueben are all whipped up about it, and the boys out at Johnson's ain't been talkin' 'bout much else."

I sat up and stared intently at him. "What'd I forget, Joe?"

He kissed me and grinned. "Tomorrow's the Friday Roosevelt's passin' through Arlington."

"No! Oh gee, I really wanted to go with you and see our president and Mrs. Roosevelt. I admire her so much!"

"Well, I may have a solution for you, Maggie. Pop wants to get over to the Masons' home by ten thirty or eleven in the mornin' to get a good spot to stand, so we'll stop by and pick you up round ten or so—"

I interrupted him. "But honey, I have to be home with Mama. I can't just leave her with the kids."

"Just wait a minute now; I'm gettin' there." He gently brushed my frizzy curls back and then softly caressed my face. "Gramps is goin' with us, but Grammy thinks the heat'll be too much for her, so she suggested comin' over and stayin' with your mama for the day. That way you can get away for a bit with me. And I think you deserve a little time off, sweetie, 'cause you been nursin' your mama twenty-four hours a day now for two weeks."

"It would be nice, but will y'all have enough room in the car?"

He playfully nuzzled my neck. "In any case, baby, if need be, you can just sit up on my lap, and I won't mind one bit."

᷉

I thought my eyes had to be deceiving me, for if truth be told, I don't believe I'd ever laid eyes on so many people all in one place at one time. We drove through the town of Arlington around ten thirty, and everywhere I looked people, cars, horses, even a few carriages crowded the streets. Joe's pop headed down Division Street, intent on reaching the Home for Aged Masons. The director, Mr. Woodward, had promised to save a smidgen of space for us because both Joe's gramps and pop were Masons.

When we finally arrived, I was flat flabbergasted when I spotted all the elderly men lounging on benches and chairs that had been placed out by the highway near the entrance to the Masons' home. One and all carried little American flags, and some even carried the Texas flag; and everybody looked right proud to be there, just as I was.

Joe's gramps meandered through the crowd and captured Dr. Woodward's attention. They talked happily for a bit. Then Dr. Woodward handed him both flags and took a snapshot of him smiling proudly as he held up the flags. It touched my heart so to see all those proud folks waiting to honor one of our finest presidents.

Joe and I wandered casually through the excited group of ancient men, listening to their stories and laughing at their jokes. One age-ripened man hesitantly caught on to my hand as we drifted by, anxious to share his wealth of tales with us. His squinty eyes peered up at us under bushy brows as his voice quavered. "I hear tell you young'uns is waitin' to see our new president. I could tell ya 'bout a president er two, maybe even entertain ya with one of my war stories if you've a mind to listen."

Joe squatted down and pulled me onto his knee. We were now eye-to-eye with our newfound friend. I nodded politely. "Why, we'd be delighted to learn anything ya care to share. This here's Joe, and I'm Maggie." Joe stuck out his hand, and the elderly Mason vigorously shook his hand.

"Now let's see, must be seventy years er more since I served under my first president, that'd be back to the Civil War, but I tell ya now there weren't nothin' civil about it. I's no more'n sixteen myself when I run off from home, anxious to handle a gun and join up in the man's army. Run off to Houston I did. Told 'em I was older, and they handed me a gun and set me to guardin' prisoners. Two, three days at a time, long hours at it. Not wholly what I planned on 'fore joinin' up."

Joe smoothly shifted me to his other knee as our storyteller continued to weave his tale.

"Must have been six, maybe seven months of this when without no warning atall we heard all variety of commotion down near Galveston way. I's so charged up thinkin' now I'd get to use my gun and do battle ... 'tweren't so."

We both sighed heavily in disappointment for him. Joe shook his head and remarked, "Seems to me you'd not known much of war 'fore joinin' up, what with thinkin' it such a thrill to do battle."

"Now, son, ya just hit the nail on the head, so to speak. I's from down in the far parts of East Texas, growed up a farm boy. Not much goin' on round me but crops growin' and animals needin' tendin'. Most times we didn't see another soul 'cept family more'n once a month er so." He scratched his head and groaned. "But I did so want to rush off to Galveston and win myself a war."

I laid my hand on his arm. "What happened?"

"We all fell around, tryin' to ready ourselves and rushed right on over to Galveston. Once we made it there, we scattered around, waitin', rifles drawn. Then we heard a train a comin'; saw it loaded with soldiers. I aimed to get me my own prisoners that day, but come to find out, it was our own boys. They was comin' home 'cause the war done ended."

He shook his head sadly. "All them soldiers come down on Houston lootin' stores and takin' whatever they wanted. I'm sorrowed to say I joined right in. Took me some cloth for my mom and sisters; took some guns and ammunition for my brothers and myself. I didn't know no better at the time, but now I'm right shamed when I think back on it."

His eyes took on a glazed look, and he sank deeper into his chair. I leaned over and dropped a quick kiss on his cheek, and he smiled up vaguely at me, already forgetting our shared chat.

I popped up off Joe's knee and obligingly tugged him up. He lazily stretched and rubbed his legs then affectionately took my hand as we headed back to find his family. As we strolled back through the dense crowd, I was right surprised when we came upon an elderly woman sitting up proudly in the midst of the men. I curiously stooped down next to her to say hello, and she warily leaned toward me. "Speak a little louder, child. I'm not gettin' any younger. I'm near 'bouts ninety-two years old, so speak up now." She looked so cute in her stylish dress as she delicately twirled a white silk parasol with the six flags of Texas printed on it. Moreover, it surprised and delighted me when she coyly flirted with Joe as if she were only seventeen instead of ninety-two. After chatting with her for a bit, we discovered from Mr. Woodward that she was the proud widow of another Civil War veteran.

Finally, round about two thirty in the afternoon, we heard the screaming sound of sirens ever increasing in volume as they drew nearer to us. My hopeful heart thumped loudly in my chest in anticipation of what we were about to behold. I clung tightly to Joe's arm and leaned out toward the road to try to catch a first glimpse of the procession.

The very first thing we laid eyes on was twenty-four motor police proudly preceding the car that held our president. My impatient heart did a double flip as at long last I sighted the motorcar of our very own president, driven by his son Elliott, proceed right in front of us. Both President and Mrs. Roosevelt smiled graciously and bowed, and I about jumped for joy when the president even cheerfully waved his hat at us. A little ways down the road, right in front of the gate, the presidential car came to a sudden stop and President Roosevelt called out to the assembled men, "I am glad to see you." Everyone cheered noisily and cried out, "Thank you, Mr. President."

I stood in awe for the longest minute then happily hugged Joe's poor arm again. He must have thought I was trying to break it off as hard as I'd been squeezing it for the last half hour, but he just wrapped me in his arms and kissed me sweetly right in front of everyone.

⁓

We all piled haphazardly back into Pop's car, still enthralled with the history we'd just witnessed. Everyone eagerly chattered at once as we struck off toward home, one and all incapable of holding back excitement over being so close to our very own president.

As the car bumped along the rutted roads, Joe's gramps rattled on about what a great turnout there'd been at the Masons' home, and his pop commented on the fact that our president's own son had a huge home right over in Ft. Worth. I simply sat contentedly in Joe's lap and listened quietly, still awestruck from the incredible experience.

All at once the car roughly bounced in a pothole, and I felt Joe's strong arms tighten around me as he laid his head gently against my back and just about groaned. I started to say something, but I caught sight of Rueben's laughing face and decided I'd best not.

As we drew closer to the town center, his pop remarked that he'd like to stop off at Carter's Hardware and look over a new contraption he'd heard tell of. We slowly made our way through the throng of traffic and eventually found a place to park the car. Joe's mom, pop, gramps, and Dorrie all hiked off through the heat to the hardware store.

Joe held me back as Rueben stuck his head back into the hot car and teased, "You two best hurry and catch up. Y'all wouldn't want to miss seein' Carter's new contraption." Then he raced off laughing.

I turned sideways on Joe's lap and laughed. "I just don't know 'bout that brother of yours sometimes." His fervent expression stopped me.

He softly stroked my face then drew me close. "It's right difficult bein' so close to ya, baby. I believe I just need a minute or so 'fore we head off after the others."

I laid my head on his shoulder and gazed up at his sweet face. Soon I found myself trailing my fingers lightly through his soft hair as I lovingly kissed his sweet lips. He cuddled me closer as our passion sparked, and feelings I'd never experienced before flowed pleasurably over me. I felt so vulnerable as his soft lips lightly caressed my face, and I sighed longingly as he whispered my name so sweetly.

Without warning, the car door was wrenched open and his pop let out an exasperated sigh. "Joe Edward, seeing that your mom is out waitin' on you two in this heat, you'd best just walk it off right now, son."

My face flamed as Joe's pop strode doggedly back down the road. I glanced at Joe, and his deep dark eyes drew me tenderly back to him. I felt his heartbeat so close to mine as we kissed once more. Then we reluctantly climbed out of the car and traipsed off down the road.

We noticed the long line of people impatiently waiting outside the store, and I had no notion why so many folks could possibly have need of a hardware store. The noisy, crowded streets repelled me. Consequently, I clung nervously to Joe's hand and just followed along.

We sighted his family about halfway through the line and ran to join them. Dorrie immediately jumped up on Joe, begging him to hold her. He easily swung her up into his arms, and she laid her tired little head contentedly on his shoulder. Then he reached over and wrapped his arm around me, drawing me close beside him.

After what seemed an eternity, we advanced inside the store, every one of us drenched in sweat from the sweltering sun. I playfully joked to Joe and Rueben that what with this heat and all, I might even consider trying another cup of the mineral water, and they readily agreed.

We slowly trudged through the store, following the trail of people in front of us. Once we finally reached the back of the store, a cold breeze hit us, and the temperature dropped at least a good ten degrees.

Joe let Dorrie down on the floor and placed his hands on my shoulders, standing so close behind me that I could feel his breath in my hair. I leaned comfortably back against him as the store's owner, Mr. Carter, hopped up on his stool. We peered at the large hole cut out in the back wall of his store, which had a large fan carefully mounted in it. The air blowing in from it was surprisingly cold, and this aroused my curiosity. Everyone surged forward until Mr. Carter held up his hand. At that juncture he explained how on a recent road trip to California he'd started noticing signs along the highway advertising cooled air. He decided to stop in at one of these places and discovered a newfangled cooling system that he thought just might work in his store.

He'd sketched out what he'd need to assemble his own water-cooled system, and he began building it almost as soon as he arrived back home. Seemed all he needed was a bale of hay, some boards, a small amount of nails, chicken wire, a fan, and water. He built up a large frame, filled it with the bale of excelsior, and strapped that down with the chicken wire. Next, he cut a large hole in the back wall of his hardware store, fitted in an old fan he had lying around, secured the frame onto the outside of the store behind the hole he'd cut, then added a water line that slowly dripped water into the hay. He alleged that as the water dripped through the hay and evaporated, it'd come out nearly as cold as ice when it was pulled into the store through the fan. We could truly attest to this, seeing as it felt at least ten degrees cooler in the back of the store than it did in the front of the store.

We trailed out of the store and stared at all the people still waiting to go in. It appeared as if the line was twice as long as when we'd first joined it. I picked up my pace and tugged Joe along, anxious to get out of the crowds and back to the car. He grinned at me and shook his head, knowing how much I disliked being in crowded places.

We reached the car a good five minutes ahead of his family, so we just strolled off down a nearby trail to bide our time until they arrived. It wasn't long before we heard Joe's pop blow the car's horn, so we hurriedly made our way back. I blushed when I noticed measures had been taken to make certain Joe and I wouldn't be sitting so close together on the ride home.

Today had been well worth the discomfort I felt, what with actually witnessing the parade of President and Mrs. Roosevelt and afterward sharing such an extremely exhilarating experience with my own adorable Joe. As we neared home, I sighed blissfully and knew beyond a shadow of a doubt that this glorious day would forever be etched in my memory.

chapter 11

Late nights and early mornings had left me feeling drained. It'd been almost three weeks since Mama came home, but she was finally able to get up on her own for the first time yesterday, so she spent the morning contentedly sitting out on the front porch watching the kids play.

This morning her face was pale and still heavily shadowed with fading bruises, but a smile played around her mouth as she sat outside in her rocking chair and watched Jessie, Lilly, and Frank run races from the porch steps to the road. Jack barked happily as he raced with them, continually putting himself in harm's way as he darted in and out between the three. Janie and Kate sat contentedly over in the side yard, stirring up mud pies, intent on making Mama a masterpiece, and our little caregiver, Mary, was draped in a chair next to Mama, fussing around and aiming to stay by her side and take good care of her.

Will had gone back to work a couple of days after Mama'd gotten home. His anger toward Papa hadn't abated a bit, so it was really for the best that he'd left since Papa came around most every day now to "help" Mama. I didn't trust Papa, but I tried to be civil when he was around. Yesterday, Papa said

Mr. Milton was working on a settlement with the town that he thought was pretty good, and Mama just told him to do whatever he thought was best. I had to hold my breath to stop from screaming because sometimes Mama could be so naïve.

That day I turned eighteen, but it seemed no one remembered because so far it had been like every other day. Although my heart swelled with joy as I peered out the window and set eyes on Mama. She sat contentedly out on the front porch and watched the kids playing peacefully together, which was enough of a present for me. I shuddered still when I thought we could have lost her.

A soft sigh escaped me as I finished washing up the breakfast dishes. My mind was a jumble of thoughts—my hopes, my dreams. I leaned my elbows on the edge of the sink and gazed longingly out the window. My blissful daydream was suddenly broken when Frank yelled out, "Hey, Maggie, Joe's comin' up the road."

I quickly wiped my hands on a dishtowel and ran my fingers through my hair. I wasn't expecting Joe to come by this morning since today was a workday. He turned into the yard just as I walked out onto the front porch. "Joe! What a nice surprise!"

"Well now, I couldn't miss spendin' your eighteenth birthday with you, Maggie," he said with a wide smile.

"Oh, Maggie, how terrible of me!" cried Mama. "I can't believe I've let this day slip by me!"

"It's okay, Mama. You've been through a lot in the past few weeks," I soothed her.

"That's no excuse for forgetting the birthday of my firstborn child!" Mama moaned.

Frank scampered up the porch steps two at a time. "I remembered, Maggie. I got ya a present right in the house." He tore into the house like greased lightning, loudly banging the door in his haste.

Joe laughed out loud at Frank's enthusiasm, and then we all

burst into laughter, which helped to ease the awkward moment for Mama.

Mary, Janie, Kate, Jessie, and Lilly all crowded around me in excitement. "We wanted to surprise you, Maggie!" they shouted.

"We wanted it to be a real good surprise, Maggie. Papa even said he'd bring all the things we need to celebrate your special day," Janie exclaimed.

Lilly and Jessie both hollered and danced around me. "A cake for Maggie! A big ol' cake for our Maggie!"

I looked at Joe and grimaced. I didn't want a cake from Papa, but I couldn't say it because I didn't want to disappoint the kids or dampen their spirits.

Joe picked Lilly up and sat her on the porch rail. "Well, peanut, y'all might have to wait on that cake till this evenin'. I've got a special day all planned out for Maggie, and she's already agreed to come with me." He winked at me as he said this.

Lilly looked at me sadly as I replied, "I'm sorry, Lilly, but I can't disappoint Joe, now can I?"

"I guess not." She sighed. "Papa's comin' after lunch, and he said he had a good, good surprise for ya too."

"I'll see it later, Lil. We can have cake and everything this evenin' when I get back," I appeased.

She hopped down and grabbed Jessie's hand. "Okay. Come on, Jessie; let's go play with Jack."

The two ran off, leaving Mary, Janie, and Kate staring daggers at me. "Papa's bringin' cake, Maggie. We haven't had cake in a long time! Please, please stay so we can have cake!" Kate pleaded.

"You can cut the cake without me, girls. You can even make a wish for me, as long as it's a really good wish," I teased.

"But Maggie—" they began, but they were interrupted by Frank as he dashed back out onto the porch.

"Frank Bowen, slow yourself down right now," Mama admonished him. "There's a lot you could break racing around like that, including yourself!"

"Sorry, Mama." Frank looked remorseful for about a half second. Then he bounced back, holding out an object wrapped up in the dishtowel I'd recently used to dry my hands. "I hope ya like it, Maggie," he offered shyly.

I sat down on the top step, took the package from him, and gently opened the dishtowel. Inside lay a beautiful little wooden carving of a horse. "Oh, Frank, this is wonderful! Did you make it?"

"Mmhmm. I saw how much you liked Joe's horses, Maggie, so I made you one of your own," he stated proudly.

I pulled him down next to me. "Frank, this is about the best present I've ever received. Thank you, sweetie!"

He turned red when I planted a kiss on his cheek. "It's nothin', just foolin' around with wood." He scrambled up and started down the steps. "Happy Birthday, Maggie," he called over his shoulder as he ran off in pursuit of the girls.

Mama sniffled then smiled at me as I caught her wiping away a tear. "All my children are growin' up so fine."

∽⁂∾

Joe caught my hand as we strolled slowly down the secluded road toward his family's farm. He affectionately intertwined his fingers with mine as he said, "I thought we'd walk a bit today and have us a little more time alone."

"It's a wonderful idea, Joe." I inhaled deeply, enjoying the familiar fragrance of rich farmland air. "This is so nice, and I really needed to get away from the house for a while," I declared as I snuggled up to him. "Spending my birthday with you is exactly what I was wishin' for right before Frank shouted out you were comin'."

He nodded and dropped a little kiss on my willing lips. "I aim to please." He kicked at a small rock in the road, sending the dust flying up around us. I laughed and raced to where the rock had stopped then kicked it farther up the road. We played happily as if we were only twelve, enjoying precious moments together.

When we reached the turnoff for his house, he stopped and soberly took my hands in his. His expression was so serious I was almost afraid of what he might say. "There's somethin' I've been wantin' to say to you for a long time, Maggie." He paused briefly before saying firmly, "I think you might already know, but I need to speak it to you."

His impassioned eyes held mine for the longest moment before he softly vowed, "I love you, Maggie Bowen."

"Joe!" My heart pounded with joy, but I fell speechless as I looked into his radiant, hopeful eyes.

He tenderly caressed my face. "It's okay, baby, you don't have to say anything right now. I just really needed you to know how I feel about you." He squeezed my hands in assurance, but this precious man, my man, looked heartbreakingly sad.

I trembled with emotion as I lovingly put my hands on his shoulders and pulled myself up so I was looking him square in the eye. I gazed at him longingly with tender affection then boldly wrapped my arms around his neck and eagerly kissed his sweet lips. My heart about burst as I exclaimed adamantly, "I love you too, Joe." Then I laid my head on his strong shoulder and whispered softly, "I love you with all my heart!"

⌒*⌒

Dappled sunlight filtered through the trees as we strolled casually toward the horse barn. Contentment embraced me like a warm fire on a cold winter's day, and I could only hope my face wouldn't reveal to Joe's family all the passionate emotion that was running through me right now. I tried to hold in my desire to shout out that Joe loved me and that I loved him, but it wasn't easy to do. It seemed this sweet secret just kept bubbling up inside, relentlessly threatening to burst out, and I just wasn't sure how long I could contain it.

Joe's joyful eyes followed me as I swiftly skipped up the slope toward the barn. His wide smile was all I needed to know that he was feeling the same way as I was. I waited for him at the top of the rise, my smile beaming down at him. When he reached me, he tipped my chin and gave me a quick kiss before we headed hand in hand to the modest red barn.

Joe's pop and Rueben were in the corral with Princess when we arrived. Rueben paced anxiously back and forth, and Mr. Gilley didn't look too calm himself.

"What's wrong, Pop?" Uneasiness flickered in Joe's voice.

"Don't know if something's wrong or not," Pop replied soberly. "We've just been waiting on Princess to foal. Don't seem like she's havin' problems, but she's been showin' signs of laborin' for a couple days now."

Rueben climbed up on the fence. "Yep, but she really started actin' like she was in serious labor 'fore sunup; now it's near noon. She oughta had the foal by now." He jumped down and started his pacing again.

Joe smiled wryly. "Rueben, ya know it can take hours and hours of labor 'fore a horse foals."

"Yep, but this is the first time I've been so involved in it. Most times I've been stuck away at school."

Pop chortled, "You'd think he was the pop the way he's actin'."

"Aw, Pop!" Rueben complained.

Princess snorted then produced a long, low whinny. She began pacing around the corral nervously.

"Joe," Mr. Gilley called. "Get over here and hold her head. Rueben you stand by her side. I'm goin' to take the business end."

I climbed over the fence and stood quietly by Joe. I'd never seen a foal born before. Kittens and puppies, yes, but not a foal.

Excitement filled me as I saw the little horse's head poking out a bit at a time. Princess kept trying to turn her head toward Mr. Gilley, whinnying and snorting, so Joe grasped her head firmly to keep her still.

Rueben held steadfast to the horse's side, running his hand down her neck and back to try to keep her calm.

Finally, the whole head appeared, and after what seemed like only a moment, Princess shuddered and snorted one last time, and amazingly, the little foal slipped silently out all at once. It lay there all wet and slimy, looking around at its new-found world. Princess turned her head and gently nudged her baby, and miraculously, at least to me, the tiny foal stood up on its trembling little legs and began to walk beside its mother around the corral.

"Oh, how wonderful!" I cried in delight.

"See, nothin' to be worried about, Rueben," Mr. Gilley exclaimed with a proud smile. He picked up an old blanket and commenced rubbing down the little foal. "Looks like a fine little fellow, he does," he remarked.

Princess had been keeping a close eye on her newborn, standing nearby until Mr. Gilley finished with him. Then she nuzzled her baby gently and looked over at us as if to let us know who was in charge. Mr. Gilley chuckled softly as he slowly ambled back over to us.

"Dorrie should see this," Joe remarked. "I'll be right back," he called as he hopped over the fence and tore off down the hill.

He reappeared shortly with Dorrie in tow. Her ecstatic cries when she saw the little foal for the first time thrilled me all over again. "Pop, can he be my own little pony? Please, Pop, please!" she begged.

Mr. Gilley heaved her over the fence and into the corral. "Looks like I don't have any say in the matter. I believe you called first claim on him, baby." He smiled happily in response to her delight.

They walked calmly over to mother and baby, and Dorrie gently patted the newborn foal. "He's so beautiful. Look at him! He's all black, except for he looks like he's wearin' white socks. And look! He has a star on his forehead."

Joe looked amused. "What you gonna call him, Dorrie?"

She appeared lost in thought. Then she confidently declared, "I'm gonna name him Starlight."

"That's a pretty name, Dorrie, and I think it's just the right name for this little one," I agreed.

"Come 'ere, Maggie, and pet him," she implored. "He's so, so, so sweet!"

"Starlight, star bright," Maggie whispered softly in his ear. "I have the wish I wished tonight."

His heart raced as he felt her breath gently sweep across his neck. "Me too," he replied with a wink.

Pop finished checking Princess to make sure she was all right. Then he tiredly wiped the sweat from his furrowed brow, took a well-earned breather, and watched Rueben and Dorrie laughing happily as they admired the newborn foal. The little foal had taken a liking to Dorrie as well because when she walked away, it followed her every step.

"Joe, that surprise you told me bout is kickin' up quite a fuss back there. Might be good if y'all take a look at it." Pop nodded toward the barn.

In all the excitement going on, he'd almost forgotten Maggie's birthday present. Today felt more like his birthday, what with the joy he'd received.

Maggie's eyes twinkled mischievously. "What surprise, Joe?"

She held out her hand, and he clasped it firmly. "Close your eyes and come with me, baby." He led her back into the shadowy recesses of the barn, where sunlight slithered through cracks in the walls and shimmered in through tiny windows built high up in the hayloft.

They stopped at the last stall, and he took hold of her shoulders and started to spin her around to face her next birthday surprise. "Can I open my eyes now, Joe?" She laughed.

"Not yet," he began. "First…" His lips eagerly found hers, and she responded feverishly to his kiss, both glad for this unexpected opportunity in the shadowy barn, far away from the curious eyes of his family.

After a bit, she sighed deeply and laid her soft curls against his chest.

"Okay, baby," he whispered softly in her ear. "You can look now."

"I don't think I can. I think I'm meltin' right away." She sighed again as she intimately clung to him. He held her close and caressed her face. "Thank you for lovin' me, Maggie."

She snuggled up even closer to him as they swayed in the dark, their passion rising. Suddenly, something shoved him roughly from behind. He held Maggie tightly and tried to steady them so they wouldn't fall. "What the heck!" he exclaimed.

A loud snort came from the stall, and he laughed. "Um, I almost forgot what we came in for." He took her by the shoulders and turned her to face the stall. "Here, Maggie, meet your birthday present."

Her eyes lit up when she caught sight of the beautiful golden palomino shaking its head vigorously, as if annoyed at being ignored for so long.

"No! Oh, Joe, is he for me?" she stammered. "He's beautiful!" She reached out and stroked the horse's silky mane.

"Nothing can compare to your beauty, baby." Her smile lit up the barn, and he felt like the luckiest man in town. "When I saw him at the auction last week, I knew I had to get him for you."

She hesitated. "It's too much, Joe. You shouldn't spend your hard-earned money on a horse for me."

"You don't worry bout that now. I had a couple of heifers up for auction, but instead I made a trade with the man who owned this horse."

She reached out and hugged his arm to her. "Oh, he's wonderful, honey!" She gently stroked the horse's soft nose and offered, "Let's take him out in the sunshine. I think he's feeling lonely way back here in the back of the barn."

He embraced her as he teased her kindly. "I kinda like it way back here in the back of the barn, especially when I'm back here with you." He kissed her sweet lips once more, unlatched the stall door, and led the vivacious horse out into the corral.

"Boy, that took y'all long enough," Rueben chortled. He winked at Maggie and made her blush.

"You just go on now, Rueben, and leave these two kids alone," Pop commanded. "Won't be long till you're gettin' yourself lost in a barn."

Rueben about fell off the fence rail laughing.

"What's in the back of the barn, Pop?" Dorrie asked innocently.

Maggie tried to save Pop from answering. "Look, Dorrie, we found another fine-lookin' horse way back in the back o' the barn."

Dorrie came running over, but Pop quickly caught her up in his arms. "This one's not so little, half-pint. You gotta take it easy round horses that don't know you."

She dropped a kiss on his cheek. "Okay, Poppy."

Pop walked over and carefully examined the palomino. "This here's a fine thoroughbred, Joe. You made yourself a good deal last week with Mr. Turner."

"I thought so myself," he replied warmly as he lightly ran his fingers through Maggie's silky curls. "My Maggie deserves a fine thoroughbred for her eighteenth birthday."

✐

Twilight had begun to set in, and the first tiny twinkling stars appeared at about the same time Joe and I reached my house. We'd decided to leave my new "pal" at Joe's since I didn't have the means to take care of him properly. Also, I didn't want to spoil the glory Frank took from making me the little wooden horse. Altogether it had been an amazing day, a truly breathtaking, momentous, life-changing day.

Joe pulled on the reins and brought Redwing to a standstill a couple hundred yards from my front porch. "What say we just keep ridin', darlin'?" he joked.

He reached back to help me down off the horse, but I laid my head on his shoulder and embraced him once more. "Thank you for a glorious birthday. I couldn't have dreamed anything more perfect."

"It's been pretty nice, now hasn't it?" He nodded toward the house. "Appear to be a few pairs of eyes peering at us through the front windows."

"Oh gosh! I forgot about my cake! I hope they ate it without us." Joe lightly held my arm as I slid to the ground.

"I'll go take care of Redwing and then meet y'all in the house." He winked as he rode off toward the back of the house.

The front door flew open. "Maggie, where you been? We were all worried about you!" Janie put on her best angry face. "I bet y'all forgot all about us, now didn't you?" she accused.

"Not for one moment, sweet pea," I lied. "There was some excitement over at Joe's house, and it kept us tied up most of the afternoon, but we're here now."

"What excitement, Maggie?" Frank roughly pushed Janie out of the doorway.

"Stop it, Frank! You don't have to push me," Janie complained as she gave him a light shove in return.

Frank shook his head. "Girls! Why do I have to live with so many girls?"

"Someday, Frank, you won't think that's such a bad thing," Joe called out as he sauntered up to join us on the porch.

"Remember Joe's horse, Princess?" I asked.

Frank nodded. "Oh yeah, that's the big red horse Will and I rode a couple months back. Did somethin' happen to her?"

"When Joe and I got to his place, we discovered Princess was about to foal."

"What's that mean, Maggie? Is she sick?" Mary asked in a concerned voice.

"No, Mary, it means Princess was going to have a baby horse," I explained.

"Oh, I wanna go see!" cried Lilly.

"Maybe you kids can come over one weekend and see him. He's a right cute little fella." Joe looked at me, and his smile warmed me all over.

"Did y'all eat all my cake?" I teased.

"Papa didn't come, Maggie. We waited and waited, but he didn't come," Mary said morosely.

Frank tried sheepishly to cover up for Papa. "Probably he got tied up at work or somethin', but Mama has a special surprise for you in the house, Maggie." He paused thoughtfully. "She's been lyin' down for a bit, but I bet she'll want to get up now since you're home."

"No, let's not wake her. I can see it tomorrow. How 'bout we all sit out here on the porch and look at the stars comin' out. It's a really beautiful night, and since it's my birthday, my wish is to spend it out here with all of y'all."

Joe sat down beside me and entwined his fingers in mine. Frank climbed contentedly up on the porch rail, and Mary quietly sat down in Mama's rocker while Janie, Kate, and Jessie ran happily out into the front yard calling for Jack. Little Lilly just plopped herself down in Joe's lap and dejectedly stuck her thumb in her mouth.

I brushed her hair from her face. "It's all right, baby," I tried to comfort her. "Mama will be all better soon."

"I know, Maggie, but I really wanted cake."

I awoke to the sound of the front door slowly creaking open. I peered into the shadowy darkness of my bedroom and listened hard. I couldn't tell what time it was, but I knew it had to be way after midnight. I slipped quietly out of bed and crept lightly out into the hallway. I paused and listened again before I tiptoed silently past Mama's bedroom. I was glad her door was shut, but I wasn't sure she would hear anything anyway because of the pain medicine she was still taking. I fervently wished Will was home, but he wasn't due in for another couple of days. I cautiously peeked around the corner into the living room and glimpsed a ghostly figure filling the doorway. My heart was beating like a drum in my throat. Fear gripped me as I quietly stepped back into the hallway. All of a sudden, the old floor creaked loudly in the deathly stillness of the night. I froze and waited.

I about jumped out of my skin when I heard footsteps approaching. "Maggie! What's got into ya, girl?" Papa whispered harshly.

I sank down on the floor in relief. "What's got into me?" I whispered back. Fright made the anger in my voice all the more powerful. "What's got into you, sneakin' around at all hours of the night, scarin' me to death?"

"This is my house, girl. I can come and go as I please."

I stared at him long and hard. "It would please *me* if you'd leave."

He reached out and roughly grabbed my arm, pulling me up. Then he dragged me toward the door and out onto the front porch. I jerked away from him and practically spit out, "How dare you! How dare you!"

Papa backhanded me hard. My hand flew to my injured face, and I looked at him as if he'd stabbed me with a knife. I collapsed down on the porch in a heap and cried softly.

"You got a lot to answer for, girl," Papa growled.

I didn't answer him; I didn't look at him. I was afraid of what I might do or say.

He grabbed my arm again and tried to pull me up. "You hear what I said, Maggie? You answer your papa, now!"

"You're not my papa anymore!" It was the meanest thing I could think of to say to him at the moment.

"You been trampin' round town with that Gilley boy! Don't you deny it, girl. I saw you!"

"What are you talkin' about? And what business of yours is what I do anyway! You haven't seen fit to be a part of my life in over a year," I cried.

"Seems like I shoulda!" he roared.

"Be quiet!" I hissed. "Maybe you don't care, but my family is asleep inside the house."

"My house, girl!"

I heard the door creak behind me, and Mama's pale, wraith-like face appeared in the moonlight. "John, you've been drinkin' again." Sorrow spilled out as she spoke. "I want you to leave now!" she reprimanded him firmly.

"You stay out of this, Jo. I got a right to discipline my own child!" he slurred.

"She's not a child anymore, John." Mama continued to walk toward him, her hand out in front of her, ready to do battle by pushing him off the steps.

"You stop right there, woman. You don't know what this girl's been up to."

"Just what do you think she's been up to?" Mama tried to walk him down the steps.

"I saw her and that boy together today. Drove right past 'em, and Maggie looked straight at me and didn't even know I was there." He was crying now, weeping like an old woman.

"John, go back to town. You don't want to wake the little ones. You've already driven your oldest children away from you;

don't do that with the rest of them." She gave him a soft shove toward the road.

He stumbled off drunkenly and was soon consumed by the darkness.

Mama laboriously climbed the steps, wincing in pain a time or two. She stooped down on the porch beside me and gathered me up in her arms. "He don't mean it, Maggie. He lets the liquor fight his battles for him. Unfortunately, all his battles are his own doin'."

She kissed me gently on the forehead. "Joe's a fine young man, Maggie. A fine man." She sighed sadly. "Did your papa hurt you?"

I lied for the second time that day. "No, Mama, I'm just fine." Little did she realize that not only had Papa hurt me physically, but he'd scorched my soul with hatred, for which I didn't know if I'd ever forgive him.

Time seemed to stand still when he saw her face. She'd sent Frank out to tell him she was feeling poorly, but he wanted to see for himself. He wandered into the kitchen and found her sitting alone at the table. She looked at him, and her silence spoke volumes. He knew in his heart what had happened, so he turned and stormed off out the door. He heard her call after him as he angrily jumped on his horse and fiercely galloped away.

He knew right where to find Bowen at that time of day. He rode hard and fast then pulled up sharp in front of the rundown rental house. Anger seethed out of him like steam from a kettle, and he was afraid of what he might do when he found Maggie's no-good papa.

Rachel's chalky face peered out at him from behind a curtain. She turned and yelled something back into the house, but he didn't wait for anyone to answer the door. He just exploded into the room and yelled, "Bowen, get out here and be a man!"

The two little girls cowered in the corner, crying. Rachel spread her arms in front of the entrance to the kitchen. "No, Joe, don't go in there. He's feelin' bad enough as it is. Just leave him be … please."

"Move, Rachel. I don't want to hurt you." She stepped aside in fear.

Bowen sat at the table, a bottle in front of him and shame in his eyes.

"Get up!" he commanded.

Bowen looked at him then looked away sadly. "There's nothin' you can do to me to hurt me worse'n I already hurt myself."

"Let me try!" he shouted. "I said get up! Do it now, or I'll have to help you!" He shook with fury at the man who had dared to hit Maggie.

"Won't do ya no good. Maggie don't hold with violence, boy." Bowen laid his head in his arms. "Go on now; get out of here."

His head buzzed with rage. He grabbed Bowen's collar and hauled the man out of the chair. The chair fell over with a deafening crash, and Bowen let out a whimper. Somewhere in his mind he heard Rachel scream.

He looked at the poor excuse of a man and dropped the scoundrel as though something dirty had touched him. "You're not worth it."

As he headed out the back door, he turned angrily to Rachel. "Sorry to upset you, Rachel, but next time, keep him home 'cause I won't be so generous."

She held on to her belly with one hand and the doorpost with the other. She nodded an acknowledgment as hot tears streamed down her face.

He found Maggie curled up on her bed. He laid down beside her and pulled her into his arms. "Your papa won't hurt you again, baby, I promise you."

"Oh, Joe, what did you do to him!" Her eyes were round with fear.

"Nothin', nothin' at all. Just talked to him and let him know to stay away from you from now on." He gently brushed her hair out of her face and looked searchingly into her tear-filled eyes. "God help me, I wanted to kill him, Maggie. But I saw your sweet face in my mind, and I knew it wasn't worth losin' you to satisfy my anger against him." He tenderly caressed her red, swollen face. "Dear God, Maggie …"

"I'm okay, Joe. I'm strong enough to make it through this." She kissed his hand as he softly stroked her injured face.

"I don't want to leave you alone here. You don't even have a party line telephone way out here or any way to get in touch with me if you needed me."

"I'm not alone, honey. Mama's here, and the kids. Jack's here too, for all the good he did last night." She sat up on the bed and looked sadly at him. "He didn't even bark to let us know someone was around, but I guess he knows Papa."

He pushed himself up and declared, "I'm stayin' here tonight, Maggie."

She blushed. "Joe!"

"Not *here* here," he said as he patted her bed, "but in the house. I still feel uneasy 'bout your papa. He was drinkin' again when I got there, and this is twice I've seen him bring violence upon this house."

She snuggled up close to him, and he wrapped her tightly in his arms. She heaved a tired sigh as a tear trailed slowly down her face. "I just want to stay right here in your arms forever, Joe."

chapter 12

Long summer days had set in, and I had spent most of the past two weeks secluded inside our sweltering house, but today I proclaimed my freedom, my independence, along with the rest of our country.

July 4, a day I had so looked forward to, was finally here. Joe and I, along with all our brothers and sisters and Hannah, planned on spending a fine day down on the banks of Village Creek.

I quickly pulled on my coolest slacks for riding and pinned my hair up into an attractive bun. I attached a pretty matching red ribbon into my hair then glanced in the mirror and examined the bruises still evident on my face. They had pretty much faded, except for a few traces of yellow and brown blotches. For this reason I wandered into Mama's bedroom and borrowed a little of her face powder. Now I felt ready to celebrate the day.

Sounds of laughter filtered down the hallway, growing louder as I approached the kitchen. The girls were happily packing up a picnic lunch, replete with vegetables from our own little garden as well as generous donations from the county.

A smile played around my lips as I watched their happiness,

and I grinned as Mama winked at me with a twinkle in her eyes. It was so good to see her smiling again, considering she'd been so frail for so many weeks now. I strolled over to her and wrapped my arms around her. "Are you sure you'll be okay alone today, Mama?"

Her smile warmed my heart as she proclaimed her own independence. "Maggie, honey, you just stop worryin' 'bout me. I'm doin' fine. I haven't had a dizzy spell in over a week, and I'm gettin' around real well on my own now. You know I can't be out in that hot sun yet, so I'd just as soon sit right here in my chair and think about all the fun you children will be havin' today."

She pulled me into her lap as though I was a little child. "Even if you think you're all grown up, you're still my baby, ya know." Our captivated audience of five stared at us then burst into another fit of giggles.

Frank and Will scampered in hollering that Joe was riding up the road to our house right at that very moment. Excitement overflowed as they dashed in and out of the kitchen.

I hopped up off Mama's lap, gave her a quick kiss, then flew out the door myself just as Joe and Rueben cantered up to the house on their horses. Each brother led another horse beside his, and Dorrie rode comfortably in front of Joe on Redwing.

Joe waved at the throng awaiting him on the porch as he called out, "I think we can all ride on these four horses if we triple up with the little ones."

My beautiful Pal stood waiting for me next to Joe. As I drew near him, he gave a little whinny of recognition, and it appeared he was nodding his head in greeting to me. Every time I saw my wonderful birthday treasure, I felt the same excitement I'd felt when Joe first gave him to me. I wasn't quite sure if the excitement came from receiving such a grand present or from the marvelous moments Joe and I spent together way back in the back of the barn.

During the past two weeks, Joe had ridden Pal over to the house almost every day after he got off work. Then we'd taken short rides each evening in the gathering dusk so Pal and I could get to know each other. Today I knew those rides had paid off because I had no fears at all about riding Pal and taking two of my little sisters on the horse with me.

After giving Pal some good attention, I held on to the saddle horn, fixed my foot into the stirrup, pulled myself up, then swung my other leg up over the saddle, and all the while Pal stood perfectly still as I mounted. I laid my head down on his strong neck and gave my cherished horse a huge hug.

Joe jumped off Redwing and tethered him to the porch rail. Then he swung Kate up into the saddle. "You girls stay still up there till I get everyone settled," he cautioned them. Next, he lifted Lilly up into the saddle right in front of me and helped Mary to get situated right behind me.

He smiled up at me. "You girls all right?"

"This works perfectly, honey," I amiably replied.

Will sauntered over to the horse Rueben was guiding. "You want me to ride this one, Joe?"

"Yep, that's exactly what I want you to do. We'll put Janie in front of you, and Jessie and Frank can ride with Rueben till we stop off to pick up Hannah. Then we'll rearrange and maybe let Frank ride with you too."

After everyone was settled on his or her horse, we merrily rode off toward Hannah's house. As we rounded the bend in the road, I glanced back at the front porch and saw Mama still standing there waving good-bye to us, and I knew she'd stand there and wave until the last one of us was out of her sight.

⌒✱⌒

The gentle gurgling of the creek greeted them even before he could see it. He glanced back and smiled at Maggie, admiring how well she rode Pal and marveling at how beautiful she looked as the sunlight slanted down through the trees and lit her hair into a glowing halo. Their leisurely journey down the dusty country roads had been filled with laughter and love. The girls squealed in delight when they set their horses to a gallop for a few miles, and Maggie's brother Will sat up proudly on his horse, looking every bit the man he was fast becoming.

He heard Rueben laughing with Hannah and Jessie as they trailed behind the others. He thought there might be a new romance in the air blossoming between Hannah and Rueben, and he knew that would make Maggie happy, seeing as how Hannah was her best girlfriend. It would be kind of nice to have them all together in one family someday.

He slowed Redwing to a walk, turned right, and led the horses down the narrow path through the dense trees and on down to the banks of Village Creek. On the way he spotted a redheaded woodpecker busily drilling a hole in an old birch tree, so he leaned over and pointed it out to Kate and Dorrie. They gazed at it in silent admiration, craning their necks to look back at it as they passed it by.

Redwing stopped obediently when he gently pulled back on the reins. He hopped off and tied the horse to a nearby bush. Then he helped the two impatient little girls down and watched happily as they rushed to the creek, joyfully slid down the creek bank, and squealed in pleasure as they dipped their feet into the cool water of Village Creek.

Maggie pulled up beside him, her eyes dancing with delight as she spied Dorrie and Kate happily kicking their feet and splashing water on each other. Lilly eagerly called out to him, stretching out her arms so he could help her off Pal. He lifted her gently down to the ground, and she practically flew down to creek where the other two little girls were splashing in the refreshing water.

Mary shook her head as he reached up to help her down. "Kids! What are you gonna do?" Then she too ran down the winding path to the water's edge, dipping her toes carefully in the water to test it out before jumping right into its irresistible coolness.

"You're such a precious blessing to me, Joe," Maggie proclaimed as he helped her dismount. He drew her into his arms and tenderly kissed her, but the moment was broken when Will and Rueben rode up beside them on their horses.

"Give us hand, will ya, Joe?" Rueben called.

"Yeah, stop horsin' around, Maggie. We've got some serious fishin' to get to," Will complained with an impish grin.

He helped the rest of the bunch down and then gave Rueben and Will a hand tethering their horses down near Redwing. Maggie followed behind, leading Pal. He gently took the reins from her as she wandered over to him. His yearning to be with her grew stronger every day, so much so that he felt that he was only half alive when she wasn't by his side.

After all the horses were secured, he removed the saddlebags, which held their picnic lunch, took her hand, and led her over to a nearby tree. She opened one of the saddlebags and took out an old quilt, which she spread out on the sandy ground. He lazily plopped down alongside her, leaned back against the tree, and wrapped his arm comfortably around her. She contentedly laid her head on his strong shoulder and then affectionately kissed his neck as she mumbled sweetly, "I love you, honey."

He gazed longingly at her then hungrily kissed her waiting lips. "And I love you, baby, more'n you'll ever know."

He had just commenced sinking into a lazy doze when he heard Frank hollering for him. He hugged Maggie, dropped a light kiss on her cheek, and sprang up to see what all the yelling was about.

Frank motioned him over to the water. "We need your knife, Joe, to cut down some of these bamboo canes. Will brought some string and a number of hooks to set bait, but we can't break the cane without your knife 'cause it's too green."

He reached in his pocket and pulled out his knife, swiftly cutting several thin stalks of bamboo. Then he sliced a notch at the top of each cane and handed the poles to Rueben. Rueben tied a few yards of twine through each notch then handed a pole to each of the eager hands reaching out to him.

Maggie called out, "I've got some baloney you can use for bait over here if y'all want it."

Joe chuckled as the kids swarmed around her. Then he ambled back over to her. "And who said fish like baloney?" he asked with a grin.

"Why, everyone knows fish hunger for baloney," she laughingly replied. "Besides, it's what I have on hand right now."

He stretched out and laid his head in her lap. "Well now, I guess if it was you holding that baloney out for bait, I'd come rushin' up to be caught by you too."

<hr />

The sweltering sun streamed brightly in the cloudless blue sky, its rays penetrating through the trees and striking Maggie's sleeping form. She stretched lazily and gazed out toward the creek. Frank and Jessie were intent on digging a huge hole a few feet from the creek's bank, and everyone else lounged contentedly nearby, their fishing poles dangling lazily in the creek.

He heard her stir, so he strolled back over to the quilt and offered her his hand. She reached up, took his hand, and laughingly tugged him back down on the quilt with her. "Hello, sleeping beauty," he whispered. He stroked her hair, lovingly tucked a stray curl behind her ear, and kissed her.

"I think I'm ready for that picnic lunch we brought. Unless, of course, y'all already caught a good mess of fish. Then we can just cook 'em up instead," she teased playfully.

"Well, let's just go see what we got. Don't know with this bunch, though. They might have felt sorry for the fish and let 'em all go."

"I heard that!" Rueben called. "We ain't caught nothin' much but crawdaddies, but I reckon that's due to Maggie's baloney bait," he joked as he tweaked Hannah's ear and grinned at her.

Hannah's face turned bright red as she laughingly replied, "Maggie always figures out somethin' practical to fix any problem, so maybe it was meant we should catch all them crawdaddies." She leaned close to Rueben, and her bright eyes sparkled as she teased, "Too bad you tossed 'em all back in the creek."

Just at that moment, Lilly darted up, complaining loudly as she tugged Maggie and Joe down toward the creek. "Look what a mess Frank and Jessie are makin', Maggie! And they won't even let me play with 'em," she pouted playfully.

He leaned curiously over the hole. "What y'all lookin' for anyway?"

"Tryin' to find arrowheads." Frank grunted as he carefully brushed the dirt away from an object that was barely peeking through the soil.

Rueben ambled over to them. "Arrowheads? What makes y'all think there's arrowheads round here?"

Jessie eyed him ruefully. "Don't you know anything?" She pointed to the uncovered earth. "This here's Indian ground."

Maggie looked pained. "Jessie, don't be so rude!"

"I'm not tryin' to be, Maggie. I just asked him a question."

Joe grinned at Maggie then turned to Rueben. "Yeah, Rueben, don't you know anything!"

Frank glanced up at them. "Well, ya know, at school the teacher told us that all this land along the creek used to be Indian villages."

Jessie stood up and held her hands out plaintively. "See, that's why it's called *Village* Creek."

"Yep, there were Caddo, Cherokees, and Tonkawa all round here...even Comanche. The Indians mostly lived peacefully till settlers wanted this land along the creek. Then they had some rough battles, and the outcome was that the Indians lost. I wish

I'd been round back then so I could have learned more about 'em," Frank affirmed.

Will crawled up behind Frank and grabbed hold of his hair. "They'd probably have just scalped the hair right off your head."

Frank pulled away. "Naw, they finally just up and left after the Texan scouts came back and burned down most of their huts. I don't know why they couldn't have just shared the land. Seems to be plenty here."

Jessie stooped down next him and began brushing at the dirt with a pine frond. She looked up sorrowfully. "It's just like the Reeds who used to go to our school. One day they lived in their nice little house. The next day the bank people came, and the Reeds just up and moved away. It's so sad."

Maggie wrapped her arm around Joe's waist and rested her head on his shoulder. He pulled her close as he gazed thoughtfully out over the peaceful creek. After a bit he let out a heavy sigh. "Well now, y'all holler if you find anything. Meanwhile, we'll go set out the food 'cause I know all this work must be makin' you two mighty hungry."

chapter 13

An unexpected summer cloudburst surprised us all this morning. I snuggled up with a blanket in Mama's old rocking chair and gazed sightlessly out the rain-streaked window as tangled reflections of the past few weeks consumed me.

Time heals all wounds, so they tell me. So much pain, so much joy. Physically, Mama and I have both pretty much healed, but deep inside my heart still bleeds. I think Mama's does too, but she's so good at forgiving Papa, even after all the grief he's bestowed upon her.

I don't see how Mama can trust him, what with all he's put her through, but I'm afraid she still loves him even now. I can't think of another reason why she'd so willingly turn herself over to his care. For instance, just this morning Mama needed to go to her doctor over in Ft. Worth for her weekly checkup, and even though I didn't like it, she had Papa drive her there. I stayed back in my room when he came for her because I can't—won't—forgive him. I wish Mama would just see the doctor and come right back home, but they're supposed to stop off at the lawyer's afterward to sign some papers. As they left, Mama hollered out for us kids to stay close to home because she thought it might be late before she made it back.

"Mama—"

"Maggie, I just want this to end so I can get on with my life! And this way I won't have to cower to your papa anymore. He won't have any right on this place ever again, not unless I allow him over."

"Jack!" I yelled, coming out of my reverie. My faithful dog had just emerged from the creek and vigorously shook the slushy creek water all over everything, including me. I jumped up and tried to wipe the sludge off my face, clothes, arms, legs, but to no avail. I looked daggers at Jack's puppy grin and then laughed. "Come on, Jack; let's head home."

I retraced my steps back through the woods as Jack raced ahead of me, barking happily. My journey to the creek hadn't resolved a thing, but I felt a little calmer just letting my anger swell and dissipate as the surging water rushed noisily by.

A soft summer wind swirled over him as he relaxed on the front porch steps waiting for Maggie. He closed his eyes and leaned back against a post, enjoying the coolness of the breeze that had, if only for the moment, vanquished the heavy stifling heat. He listened to the laughter of the girls playing over in the side yard, glad that Dorrie had driven over with him that morning after the rain had finally stopped and pleased that she had someone near her own age to play with for a while. Lilly was just a year older, and they seemed to have forged a tight friendship. He thought it was too bad they wouldn't be going to the same school in the fall. Even though they weren't too far apart distance wise, the townships weren't the same.

He sensed movement behind him, glanced through slitted eyes toward the sound, and caught sight of Frank perched up on the porch rail, staring back at him. He grinned. "Caught me off

I pushed these thoughts aside and strayed to happier contemplations, like the Friday Joe and I celebrated the Fourth of July together. It feels like it's always been Joe and me together. I can't imagine it any other way now, but really it's only been about five months, five wonderful months, in which so much has happened.

The sound of the rain lulled me into a drowsy, sleepy state of mind, and I decided it was too hard to try to stay awake, so I wandered sleepily down the hall to my bedroom and curled up comfortably in bed. Lilly, Kate, Janie, and Jessie were playing dolls over in the corner of the room, but even their chatter couldn't keep me from drifting into dreamland.

I stretched sleepily and turned over, burying my face into the softness of my pillow and giving myself over to more joyful thoughts. I really wished it wasn't the middle of the week and that it wasn't raining, and most of all I wished I could spend the lazy afternoon with Joe.

Lilly came over to the bed and lifted up my eyelid. "What'd you say, Maggie?"

I pushed her hand away, opened one eye, and looked at her. "Nothin', why?"

The four little girls jumped up on the bed next to me. "Yes, you did, Maggie. You were talkin' to yourself," Jessie assured me.

"I don't think so, girls. I've been asleep."

They giggled as Kate stood up and spread her arms wide. Then she pretended she was me. "Oh, Joe, I love you!"

"That's what you keep sayin', Maggie," Jessie declared.

They started jumping up and down on the bed and screaming, "Maggie loves Joe, Maggie loves Joe!"

All of sudden the mattress dropped to the floor, and we all tumbled right down with it. The astonished girls just covered their mouths with their hands and giggled louder.

"Now look what you've done," I reprimanded them. "You've broken the bed. Y'all know there's only one thing I can do now!"

"No, Maggie, no!" they screamed as I began to tickle them

relentlessly. Suddenly, Frank and Mary were in the middle of the whole thing too. We all froze when we heard a creaking, grinding noise. Then all at once the whole frame gave way, and everything collapsed to the floor, including us.

"Uh-oh!" Frank exclaimed. "Looks like you girls are gonna be in big trouble when Mama gets home."

We chased him down the hall, laughing and grabbing at him, but he moved too fast and ran safely into his room, unharmed. He quickly slammed the door and barricaded himself inside.

We were still laughing when I heard someone pounding relentlessly on the front door. I cautiously opened the door, and like a bolt from the blue, I discovered Rachel's oldest daughter, Pearl, standing there. Her small frame was soaked to the bone, and she shivered violently as she stood weeping before me.

"Pearl, whatever are you doin' here?" I asked fearfully.

"Mama needs Papa right now, Maggie. Somethin's powerful wrong with Mama, and she screamed at me to go find Papa." Her little body quivered as she continued. "I heard Papa tell her he was headin' over to your place this mornin', so I ran as fast as I could."

"Pearl, honey, Papa's not here. He's in Ft. Worth with my mama," I quietly explained.

Pearl's little face puckered up, and fresh tears streamed down it. "Mama's sick, Maggie. I need Papa, please ..." She broke off, crying harder.

All the kids anxiously crowded around me. Then Mary graciously reached out and pulled Pearl into her arms. "Don't cry, Pearl; we'll help you. Won't we, Maggie?" Her tender eyes pleaded with me.

"Of course we will. First, though, let's get you dried off, Pearl."

"No, Maggie. Mama needs me home. Please come with me. I'm so scared ..." She broke off, crying harder.

Frank patted my shoulder. "Go on, Maggie. I'll be here with the girls."

My mind was arguing with me, screaming at me, accusing me of going to the enemy, but my heart won out. "All right, Pearl. Let me get us both somethin' to keep the rain off us; then we'll hurry on over to your house."

Pearl gratefully grabbed me in a wet hug. "Thank you, Maggie."

❦

As luck would have it, the minute we stepped off the front porch the rain fell harder. I grasped Pearl's hand, and we ran quickly down the road toward town. Finally, thankfully, we reached our destination. The old house looked lopsided and tired, and the porch creaked louder with every step we took, as if it was just too worn out to hold us.

Pearl slammed back the door. "Mama!" Only the sound of silence echoed back. "Mama, Lucy, where are you?"

The unexpected squeaking of a door split the silence, and I jumped. "Pearl?" The tiny whisper pierced the air.

Pearl ran toward the voice. "Lucy, where's Mama?"

"She's sleepin' now, back in her bedroom." Lucy nodded her head toward the back room.

Fear filled my soul. "Stay here, girls," I commanded.

I inched my way into the room, afraid of what I might find. Rachel was sprawled across the bed; sweat drenched her face. She didn't appear dead, but I had to be sure. I stepped toward her in trepidation and placed my hand on her head. She moaned faintly.

"Rachel, Rachel, it's Maggie." Her eyes fluttered open with alarm.

"I need John, please. Somethin's not right this time. Please, Maggie, please find him."

"Rachel, why didn't you send for the doctor or the midwife? Why?" I asked anxiously.

"Don't hate me so much, Maggie."

I cringed with shame and then quietly replied, "Rachel, I don't hate you." Her face contracted in pain, and I implored, "Please, let me get the doctor."

"I just…want…Johnny—" She let out a sharp scream that made me tremble even more.

I ran to the door. "Pearl, go next door and ask them to get the doctor here as fast as they can. Run fast, Pearl; please run fast as you can!"

She was out the door before I finished speaking. Little Lucy came and hid her face in my skirt. "I'm scared, Maggie."

I wrapped my arms around her. "It'll be all right, Lucy." I kissed her little cheek and gently led her to a chair. "Let me go back in with your mama now, Lucy. You just sit down here and wait for Pearl." Her frightened eyes implored me, so I fibbed, praying that it would turn out to be truth. "It'll be okay, baby; your mama will be just fine."

I wandered restlessly around the bedroom, unsure how to help because my very presence seemed to make Rachel more anxious. I didn't know what I'd do if the doctor didn't get here soon. I'd been around when Mama had the little ones, but she'd always had the midwife nearby, and she'd always had an easy time birthing her babies.

I got down on my knees beside the bed and prayed. I prayed like I'd never prayed before, not just for Rachel and her baby, my own little brother or sister, but also for forgiveness for all the hatred I'd carried inside me over the last year or so. I held on to Rachel's cold, damp hand and prayed for guidance to know how to help her.

Without warning the bedroom door flew open, and Pearl ran in, breathless and dripping wet. She stuttered, "Mrs. Michaels is comin', and they called the doctor on their party line."

I stumbled up from the floor and peered out the bedroom door. Mrs. Michaels, God bless her, was bustling in with an energy that surprised me. She pushed her girth through the bedroom door and then turned back to give instructions to the two little girls. "Pearl, you and Lucy go wait for the doctor at the front door. You send him back to me as soon as he arrives, you hear me now?"

I waited nervously as she examined Rachel. "This here baby's breech, Rachel. We gotta get him turned around so you can deliver him."

"I can't, Bertha. I'm just so tired ..." Her voice drifted off.

"Nonsense, girl. Now you help me, and we'll get this done 'fore that doctor has time to get here."

I breathed in deeply, and Mrs. Michaels noticed me. "Get over here, Maggie, and hold her hand. I gotta do some reachin' and turnin', and it's bound to be painful."

I took hold of Rachel's limp hand. "I'm afraid for her, Mrs. Michaels."

She looked sharply at me. "Someone should have come and got me or the doctor hours ago."

"Rachel was here alone with the girls, and she wouldn't let them go."

"Where's your papa, Maggie? He needs to be here," she stated adamantly.

Rachel groaned and tightly squeezed my hand. She cried out, "Stop, please stop! I want Johnny! Please stop ..." Her voice died away in a whisper.

Sweat dripped off Mrs. Michaels as she tried tirelessly to get the baby to turn. All at once she leaned back and said, "I think we're there, Rachel. Give it a good push now."

"I can't ... I'm too tired." Her voice was so weak that it scared me even more.

"Rachel," I begged, "Rachel, Papa's waitin' on you to have this baby for him. He wants his little one with you. Please, Rachel, push for Papa, push for Papa's baby."

"It hurts!" Her face contorted as she gave one big push, and the baby surged out. She shrieked in pain. Then her cries faded into a deathly silence, which to me was even worse.

I grabbed her hand in fear and looked over at Mrs. Michaels, but she was tending to the baby, so I was left to help Rachel. Her breathing was shallow, but at least she was breathing.

I dipped a rag in a cup of water and lightly brushed it over her face. Her eyes flickered, and she moaned softly, "My baby ..."

I tried to comfort her. "The baby's goin' to be fine, Rachel. Mrs. Michaels is takin' care of him." I glanced over at Mrs. Michaels for assurance, but her back was to me, and it didn't seem she'd heard me.

Suddenly, the door burst open and the doctor rushed in. He quickly shooed me out of the room, so I slipped down the hall and quietly gathered up the two frightened girls. We sat together in tearful silence, waiting for the doctor to come out.

My heart churned with emotion as we waited for word from the doctor. Lucy had grown tired, so she curled up on the floor next to my chair and fell fast asleep. It had been a hard day for the little one. She looked so vulnerable and young lying there, her damp hair curling up around her face and her thumb stuck comfortably in her mouth. She looked much younger than her eight years. I pulled a worn-out quilt off the rocking chair and laid it gently over her.

Pearl's eyes stayed glued to the bedroom door. She, like me, was her Mama's oldest, the ever-vigilant caretaker in her little family. I hoped she would grow up wiser than I had, and with less of a fiery temper.

The rain had finally let up, and the sun peeked out and burned off the clouds; but it couldn't dispel the chill in the room. We kept our silent vigil as shadows crept across the room and the sun began to set. It startled us all when footsteps pounded loudly across the porch, and the door crashed back against the wall, sending reverberations throughout the house. Papa had arrived.

Pearl and Lucy rushed to him, crying, but he brushed them aside without a word as he hurried into the bedroom. Lucy ran to Pearl and embraced her, and then they both looked at me with big, tear-filled eyes. I held out my arms and cuddled the two terrified girls close to me.

After what seemed to be hours, the bedroom door opened and Mrs. Michaels came traipsing down the hall, carrying the tiny infant in her arms. She smiled kindly at us as she brought the baby over to us.

"Here he is, girls, your new baby brother, William." She glanced compassionately at us. "Your mama named him after your papa, Pearl."

Pearl sniffled as she peered into the blanket at the tiny red baby. Lucy peeked over her shoulder and offered her opinion, "I thought he'd be purdier, but he's just all squished up and red."

I smiled and tried not to laugh, but Mrs. Michaels couldn't restrain her mirth. After a moment, she proclaimed, "Well now, Lucy, most babies come out lookin' like this, but they usually straighten out in a day or so."

I gazed at her in suspense. "What about Rachel, Mrs. Michaels? Is she goin' to be okay?"

"Well now, that's for the doctor to say, but judging by what I saw back there, I'd say she's gonna be fine."

"I was so afraid for her—"

"She worked really hard in there, Maggie. Now she's gotta rest up a bit; then she'll be fine and dandy. I think the doctor had to do a little repairin' where she tore, but he grunted out that it weren't much." She handed the little one to me and turned toward the door. "I best get myself home. Y'all don't need me, what with the doctor and your papa home now."

I held the tiny breath of life in my arms and marveled at the miracle of life God had blessed us with. I had a new little brother, and as I held him I felt so ashamed of the angry thoughts I'd had against him over the past months.

I watched him as he moved and stretched on my lap. "Hello, little William; you are a fine baby."

Lucy leaned into his face. "Do you think he knows me yet, Maggie?"

"I'm perfectly sure he does, Lucy," I fibbed.

She nodded happily and smiled at me. "Now we can all be one big, happy family."

Moonlight spilled into the window of the rundown rental house. Pearl and Lucy had gone to bed long ago, and the doctor had merely tipped his hat at me as he left without saying a word.

Loneliness draped itself on my shoulders, and a tiny tear of self-pity slipped down my face. Papa had come out once and gathered little William up. Then he'd disappeared back down the hall and was instantly swallowed up in the shadows as he reentered the bedroom. I wasn't sure why I stayed. I could've walked home hours ago—I guess I should have—but something held me back. A tugging on my heart perhaps, or just plain stubbornness because I always liked to know what was going on.

I leaned my head back against the unforgiving wood of the rocking chair, closed my eyes, and pulled the quilt up over me. I must have drifted off to sleep for a bit because the moon was much higher in the sky when I heard Papa coming quietly out from the bedroom.

He held out his hand to me, and I took it. His hand had always meant trust and safety to me when I was a little girl, but lately it had caused me only anger and fear. I pushed aside these thoughts as I followed him outside to the porch.

The moonlight danced around us, casting deep shadows on

Papa's face and making him unreadable to me. He yawned, buried his face in his hands, and then rubbed it roughly. After a bit he glanced over at me. "Thank you for what you done to help Rachel today, Maggie. I know it was a hard thing for you after ever'thing that's gone on with us."

I sat silently waiting, not really knowing what to do or say. Papa cleared his throat. "I know I owe you more than an apology, and you've had more'n your portion of grief to contend with lately, and most of it's my fault."

We sat in silence for a while until Papa unexpectedly cracked his knuckles, and I jumped. He gazed into the moonlight and began softly, "When William died, a part of me died too. I should have saved him." He paused for so long I was afraid he wouldn't go on. I watched silently as a lone tear trailed down his cheek. He took a deep breath then forcefully let it out. "I was right there, Maggie … and I should have saved him."

My mouth was so dry I couldn't speak. I turned my head away so he wouldn't see the tears filling my eyes.

His voice was no more than a whisper. "I didn't plan on fallin' in love with Rachel. My God, I still love your mama, Maggie, but being with Rachel, takin' care of her, I feel like I'm keepin' William alive. And she just needed me so much."

I forced myself to speak, but my voice was so soft it could barely be heard. "We needed you too, Papa."

"I know … I do know that, and I tried to make it work, but I did ever'thing wrong." He groaned softly then stood up and stared at me, but I don't think he really saw me because it seemed his eyes were looking right through me.

He shook his head in sorrow. "It felt like I was doin' the right thing. Your mama is a strong woman with a deep faith, so I knew she'd be all right. And you, Maggie, you're so like your mama."

I stood up next to him. "Papa, I need to get home. It's late, and I know Mama's probably wonderin' and worryin'." I turned away from him, afraid my voice would give away all the turmoil and emotion I was feeling. "I'm glad I could be here for Rachel today, and I'm sorry I've carried this hatred around inside me for so long. It's just been really hard to love you lately, Papa."

Tears threatened to fall as I falteringly continued. "We can't just make believe the past months didn't happen…and I don't think we'll ever get back to how we used to be."

He looked at me as if he'd never seen me before. Then he sighed deeply and nodded in silent agreement. He swiped at a tear trailing down his cheek. "Come on; I'll drive you home. Rachel and the baby are both sleepin', so they'll be fine while I'm gone."

He started off to the car then turned back to me. "I don't think we'll ever get back to what we had before either, Maggie, but maybe we could try and start over. There's a lot you need to forgive me for, and even more I need to forgive myself for."

We drove most of the way in silence, both lost deep in our thoughts.

chapter 14

Steam rose from the ground, and the heat felt oppressive. Yet another morning shower had greeted me today, bringing a burst of coolness to the air, only to be followed by stagnant, muggy heat. Jack stuck close to my side as I wound my way down the overgrown path through the woods.

I hadn't spent near the time I used to down at the creek, but today I'd felt irresistibly drawn back to its banks, spurred on by the need to be alone and sift through my jumbled feelings. Just a few weeks ago I had witnessed the miracle of birth, actually assisted in it. And Papa...I was so torn in my attitude toward him. He held out the olive branch, and I almost took it because the emotionally charged atmosphere of the day and the tiredness of the night had left me so vulnerable. I meant it when I told Papa it had been hard to love him lately, but what I hadn't said was that it had also been hard not to hate him so much.

The brush had grown thick in places, and I paused to push aside a new crop of saplings struggling to find a bit of sunlight to grow in within the dense woods. They seemed almost like a metaphor of my life at that point in time. Ahead of me lay the swiftly running creek, just waiting for me to tell it all my woes and let it carry them away with its flowing waters.

I settled in on the roots of a cottonwood tree while Jack quickly jumped into the muddy creek for a cooling swim. Pictures of the past few weeks swept through my mind. Little Pearl pounding at the door, Rachel almost completely dependent on a person she thought hated her, and Papa seeming so lost and sad. And Mama...

I didn't know what to think about Mama. That night, after leaving Papa at the road, I quietly snuck into the house, hoping not to disturb anyone, but there was Mama, sitting in the dark, waiting up for me.

As I quietly closed the front door, she awoke from a light sleep and held out her hand to me. I grasped her cold hand, dropped down on the floor beside her chair, and laid my head in her lap. She stroked my hair lightly and asked softly, "You okay, Maggie?"

I looked into her caring eyes and wearily described the events that had taken place at Papa and Rachel's house. Mama kept her eyes locked on mine, listening intently, watching me, perhaps to see if the stress of the day had been too much for me. I ended my story with a short version of what had conspired between Papa and me.

Mama shook her head sadly. "Your papa has always been one to proceed without caution. He thinks more with his heart than with his head, and his heart's intentions aren't always purely good."

"I don't know what to think about Papa. I do understand how hurt, how torn apart he was when Uncle William died in such a dreadful way...right in front of him, and Papa was horrorstruck that he wasn't quick enough or strong enough to save him."

Mama nodded. "It's hard to fathom how one o' us would react in the same situation. I can't even imagine the terror he felt." Her voice drifted into silence.

I tried to speak, but only a trace of a whisper escaped me. "But Mama,"—I waited a moment then continued softly—"Mama, even though Papa hurt bad, he shouldn't have left us. He shouldn't have hurt you or us kids so terribly."

"No, sweetheart, he shouldn't have," she conceded. "He's always been one to want things to fall his way. And when he can't control his life, he falls prey to the bottle."

I stood up and walked aimlessly over to the window and gazed out into the velvet darkness. "Papa shouldn't hurt us just to try and stop the hurtin' inside himself."

Mama walked up behind me and wrapped her arms around me. "My wise little girl. You see things clearly in a way others can't...even your papa."

"What are we goin' to do, Mama? I'm afraid I can't just turn off these hateful feelings I have toward Papa and Rachel, but I'm so tired of this hurtful conflict."

She turned me around and gazed tenderly at me. "Maggie, your feelings are your feelings, and only you can change them...in your own time." She lifted my chin and fixed her eyes on mine. "I've suffered some hard feelings against your papa too, 'specially in the past year, but even before that...times you kids knew nothin' about."

Her eyes teared up, and she turned away and spoke so softly I strained to hear her. "But for some reason, only God knows why, I still care about what happens to him, and I wish him no harm, Maggie."

My own telltale tears threatened to fall, so I turned back to the window, hoping Mama wouldn't notice. After a few moments I asked, "What did the doctor say today?"

Mama crossed the room and sank pensively into her chair. "He was very positive. He said I was healin' nicely, but he still wants me to wait another month or so before I go back to work. But..." her voice trailed off.

"But what?" My nerves were on edge as I waited for her to answer.

Her voice cracked a little. "I know what you're goin' to say, Maggie, when I tell you—"

"Mama!" I exclaimed, exasperation evident in my voice. "What else did the doctor have to say?"

"It wasn't what the doctor said; it's what I did," she whispered.

"Mama!"

"Okay, but Maggie, remember your brother and sisters are sleepin', so don't react like your papa might."

I felt my face reddening, and I felt wounded because I never wanted to be compared to my papa.

Mama looked me square in the eye. "At the lawyer's, I was offered a settlement from the town."

I started to interrupt her, but she held up her hand and stopped me. "Wait, Maggie; let me finish." She cleared her throat. "The town offered me a settlement of five thousand dollars plus a monthly stipend of twenty-five dollars for each month I have to miss work and continuin' for one full year after I go back to work."

"Oh my God, Mama! That's wonderful!" I cried.

"Wait, Maggie. The lawyer had two checks. One was for fifty dollars to cover my expenses for the past two months I've not been able to work, and I'm to receive another check for twenty-five dollars on the first of each month, beginnin' in August."

"But that's a good thing, Mama." I didn't understand the distress in her voice, but she soon made it apparent to me.

"Maggie, the other check was for five thousand dollars. It's to cover the doctor and hospital expenses and my pain and suffering." Her voice faltered.

I moved toward her in concern, but she held up her hand once again to stop me. She looked down at the floor. "Maggie, sit down and try not to get too upset with me."

I did so willingly. "Okay, Mama, why do you think I'll be upset with you?"

She seemed to sink deeper into the cushions of her chair as she stared at me with tears burning in her eyes. Then she looked away and whispered, "Because I gave that check to your papa."

She rushed the words out so quickly I was afraid I hadn't heard her properly.

"What?" I whispered in disbelief.

Her voice trembled as she whispered. "Your papa said he would take care of payin' all the medical bills with it, and he signed at the lawyer's that he'd be responsible."

Astonishment, disbelief, it was like a kick in the teeth. I just couldn't believe what I was hearing. "But Mama, the bills won't be anywhere near five thousand dollars! Why would you give it up to him?"

She sat up straighter. "Because, Maggie, your papa promised me he had a good investment all set that would help you children in the future. He said he found a good parcel of land over off Arkansas Lane that he can farm, and it'll provide for you children in years to come."

I repeated myself. "But Mama..." I stopped, at a loss for words.

"I got something out of it too, Maggie," she whispered. "Your papa is willing to give me a divorce...with no problems."

I felt my blood begin to boil. "He's willing!" I hissed out. "Papa should be begging you not to prosecute him for all he's done to you!"

"Money won't bring things back to how they used to be, Maggie. Even if I wanted it to, which I don't." She looked off into the distance, lost in her thoughts. "This house belonged to my mama and papa—this house, this land—and it's mine, mine and my children's. Your papa signed a paper saying he didn't want any part of it. I couldn't have my family's land taken away from me in a divorce." She peered over at me sadly. "The law favors the man, Maggie."

"Oh, Mama."

"I'll have my twenty-five dollars a month, which is almost twice what I made workin', and after that when I'm able to go back to work, I'll have my stipend plus my pay. I'm blessed, Maggie...we all are."

guard there, Frank. Think I might have dozed off for a minute or so."

Frank nodded. "Ya know, it's good to have another man around the house, Joe. Sometimes I get so lonesome with just girls around." He picked at a scab on his arm and looked down at the ground.

"Well, I guess you've had to do a lot of growin' up lately, Frank, what with Will off workin' most days. Makes it kinda hard on you."

"Naw, not too hard, but I do miss Papa and Will bein' here. We always did things together, ya know—fishin', workin' round the place fixin' things. Just stuff like that." He kicked at the post with his bare foot. "Mama says I'm her little man. Wish I wasn't so little. Then I could go off to work with Will."

"Will's taken on a man's job at a young age, Frank. He probably wishes he could be here fishin' and such with you too instead of workin' so hard." He pushed his hat back. "Times like these we just gotta be thankful we got work atall. Many's the folks that don't."

Frank looked off down the road. Sadness tinged his eyes and touched Joe's heart. "What say you and me go fishin' tomorrow afternoon after church? I know I'm not Will or your papa, but I'm a pretty decent fisherman all the same."

Frank's eyes lit up. "You're my brother too, Joe ... almost anyway," he added shyly.

"Not any such thing as almost, Frank. I'm right proud that you call me your brother. Us boys gotta stick together," he staunchly observed.

Out of the blue, Joe collapsed back onto the porch, covered by a sopping wet, rowdy dog happily licking his face and shaking water all over him. He laughingly tried to shove Jack off, but the dog was bound and determined to shower him with eager affection. Frank clamored off the porch rail and tried to help pull Jack up off Joe.

Maggie's laughter rang out and blended with his. She called

out, "Jack, come here right now!" Jack bounded back to her, jumping up and placing his muddy paws on her already muddied blouse.

"Good boy," she exclaimed, patting him and sending him into happy rolls on the ground.

Joe smiled at her disheveled appearance. "You're lookin' mighty pretty today, Maggie."

She laughed. "Why thank you, sir. I worked really hard this mornin' to get just the right look."

He grinned. "Dorrie and I drove over to see if y'all wanted to come to our house with us for a bit. She's really keen to show off her new little colt to the girls."

"That sounds like a right fine idea, and I'm pleased you brought your pop's car 'cause this August heat is really somethin'. I don't think the little ones could make the walk in it."

"That's what I was thinkin' too. Pop said he wouldn't need the car at all today, so we can take our time and enjoy the ride."

"What about me, Joe? Can I come?" Frank asked sheepishly.

He lightly slapped Frank on his back. "You bet, Frank. We wouldn't leave you behind. Maybe you can give Princess a little exercise later as well. She hasn't been ridden since the colt was born, so I think it's high time someone takes her out for a run."

Frank let out an ecstatic whoop and took off like greased lightning around the side of the house, hollering at the girls to hurry up and get ready. Joe winked at Maggie as she plopped down beside him on the steps. He reached over and rubbed off a little mud that still clung to her nose and then landed a kiss on it.

Her lovable smile warmed his heart. "I'd best get cleaned up and let Mama know what our plans are." She stroked his face softly. "Do you need anything before I go in, honey?"

"Only you, love." He fixed his eyes on her. "I'll take you muddied or not, baby, 'cause I'm crazy in love with you, ya know." He drew her close and kissed her eager lips.

She lovingly caressed his face, lightly running her fingers

along his chin and across his lips, whispering intimately, "I love you so much, Joe." Then she captured his lips with hers. He held her closer, and after a bit he quietly laid his forehead against hers and whispered, "If your mind's set to go clean up, you'd better do it soon, or I won't be able to let you go, baby."

She sat back and gazed earnestly into his eyes, and after a moment she nodded. "Me too." Then as laughter danced toward them from around the corner of the house, she sprang up, still burning with emotion, and scampered straight away into the house.

⁓ℳ⁓

"Long as I remember, I been on this land," Pop explained from his perch on the porch swing. "My mom and pop still live over to the old house on the back forty. That's where I was born, and my brother after me, God rest his soul."

He watched his pop's eyes take on the glazed look they got every time he talked about the old days.

"Now Joe Edward here and Rueben, they're bred to this land as well, and they know how hard it can be to scratch a livin' out of. But once the land's in you, it don't stop callin' you back, no matter how hard things is. Now you children just don't know how tough things was back when I was a boy. We didn't have the 'lectric lights or runnin' water in the house, but we did all right. We even had us a fine two-seater outhouse with a little window carved up in the door. Now you might not think that's so wonderful, but when you had to go out there in the middle of the night, havin' moonlight streamin' in sure helped."

Joe winked at Maggie. "Pop, didn't y'all have to walk about a hundred miles to school ever' day in deep snowstorms—"

"Now you just go on with yourself, Joe. These kids need to know their history, and how else they gonna learn it if not from us older folks. What you need to do is take 'em out to see your gramps and grammy."

"Maggie and I were out there last week, Pop. And they love her almost as much as I do," he offered.

Pop stroked his chin thoughtfully. "Well, Frank seems to be more'n interested in the old days, so I 'spect he'd like to hear their tales. Wasn't till this past year we was able to put some 'lectric lights in their old house. Let's see, my grandpa built that house near 'bout 1860, I believe."

Frank perked up when he heard his name mentioned. "Do you think they'd know 'bout the Indians that used to live round here? I sure would like to come across some more particulars about 'em, 'cause last year at school my teacher talked about archeologists, and I'm figurin' that's what I want to be."

Pop smiled. "Well now, you get Joe to take y'all out to his gramp's house; they just might surprise you with what they know."

Lilly pulled on Maggie's arm. "I wanna go see Starlight."

He stood up and stretched. "Well, Pop, I think we best let these little ladies go meet Starlight, and Dorrie's been dancin' around behind you, barely able to wait for you to finish your stories so she can show off her colt."

Pop laughed. "Didn't mean to hold you young'uns up." He tweaked Lilly's chin. "What say we head out to the barn right now, little bit?"

The girls set up a cheer and tore off up the hill to the barn while Frank followed after Pop, listening intently to more stories of days gone by.

He gazed out at the fertile farmland spread before them, glistening in the afternoon heat, and contentment filled his soul. He felt fused with this land, his roots buried as deep in the soil as the huge old oak tree down by the pond. His labors, his pop's, and gramps' had all played a part in taming and cultivating a once-wild land. He felt Maggie's eyes on him and turned to her with a ready smile. She stretched up and lightly brushed his lips with hers, and her innocent charm attracted him like a magnet to steel. As a result, he couldn't restrain himself from drawing her close to him and sealing the moment with an impassioned kiss full of promise and love.

He groaned and held her tighter, whispering her name softly. She stroked his neck tenderly as he confessed, "I don't think I ever want to let you go, Maggie. I just don't feel complete anymore if I'm not with you."

Her fingers in his hair, on his neck, flowing down his back, sent sweet, shimmering sensations coursing through him. He stepped back and gazed earnestly at her. "It's kinda like there's this emptiness in me that only you can fill, and when I wake up in the mornin' or the workday is done, my first thought is I can't wait to come home to you."

Her eyes glistened with tears. "You have my heart, Joe, always—"

He swore softly when he heard Frank hollering, "Maggie, Joe! Come on, hurry up!"

Emotion as strong as electrical energy surged between them. Maggie brushed at tears that threatened to fall then gave him a shaky smile. He shouted, "In a minute, Frank!" Then he turned back to her, his eyes radiating. "I reckon what I need to say to you is too important to me to put up with all these dang interruptions, so maybe we should finish this conversation a little later, sweetie. I know now isn't the best of circumstances for me to get so wrought up, but being close to you … I can't help lovin' you, Maggie."

Her eyes exposed her, like windows to her soul, revealing her deepest passions in one fervent look as she nodded compassionately. "I understand. It's hard for me to focus on anything else when I'm with you, Joe." She clasped his hands in hers. "I yearn for you every moment of every day, and I love you more with every breath I take."

He started to speak, but a shout from the hillside above broke the fragile spell he'd lingered in. "Can't even have a moment alone around here," he complained. He cupped her face gently in his calloused hands. "Heaven blessed me, Maggie, the day I laid eyes on you, and I promise you that tonight we'll have us a more private chat. But for now I guess it's best we go see what all the fuss is about up at the barn." He draped his arm affectionately around her shoulders as they trudged reluctantly up the hill.

⟨∦⟩

"Don't think I ever seen anything like it before," Pop commented. "That colt thinks he's just another kid runnin' around and playin'. Look yonder, what y'all make out that young colt's tryin' to do?"

Maggie laughed as she watched the girls running around the pasture, the little colt chasing them in hot pursuit, bumping its nose against one of the girls then quickly turning and running the other way.

"Looks to me like that colt's tryin' to play tag with the girls; seems to be enjoyin' it too," Joe remarked. "I've seen plenty of fillies and colts chasin' round with each other, but nothin' like this little fellow."

Maggie agreed. "Dorrie must have trained him just by playing with him so much, and Starlight surely seems to enjoy their game."

The lively little girls' laughter drifted through the air like a joyous melody. Jessie spotted them watching, raced over to the fence, climbed up on the rail, and shouted, "Did y'all see Starlight tag me? It sure feels strange to be playin' tag with a pony!" Her bright blue eyes glowed, and her lopsided curly brown hair bounced around her smiling face as if it had a life of its own.

He grinned at the picture she made hanging on the fence rail. Her unreserved smile was appealing even with several missing baby teeth. He thought about when Maggie told him Mary had decided to give all the little girls haircuts, except she didn't quite get it right.

He stifled a laugh as he saw what was about to take place. The little colt had noiselessly followed Jessie to the fence as if it was trying to sneak up behind and surprise her. Without warning, it pushed up against her with its soft nose, whirled around, and kicked up a great cloud of dust as it charged back across the pasture.

They all burst into unrestrained laughter, and Jessie coughed noisily as the dust cloud swept over her. "Dang it all!" she shouted impishly. "Watch out, Starlight, I'm comin' to get ya!" She jumped off the rail and flew lickety-split after the little colt.

"Well, if that don't beat all." Pop chuckled, slapping his hat against his pants leg to clear the dust off the brim.

He heard hoofbeats approaching and turned to see his pop's nearest neighbor, Jim Banks, riding up. The man's wrinkled face broke into a slight smile as he took in what was happening in the corral.

"Sorry to interrupt your Saturday, Henry, but I wanted to let you know 'bout a possible problem with a couple of cows."

"What kinda problem, Jim?" Pop inquired.

"I was out ridin' fence, checkin' things over one more time 'fore sundown, when I spotted a couple of cows scuttle off into the ravine back near where our farms meet up. Looked like they got spooked by somethin'."

"Do you need some help roundin' 'em up? Me and the boys'll be right happy to help you," Pop offered.

Jim slipped down off his horse and led it over to the corral. He parked his boot up on the rail, pushed back his hat, and wiped the sweat from his furrowed brow. "I checked the fence line and noticed it'd been cut. Then I rode down into the ravine to check on the cows. Them dang cows had scurried right into the heapin' middle of trouble."

Pop grimaced. "Let me get my horse saddled, Jim, and I'll ride out with you. Maybe we can just head 'em off and then lead 'em out with the horses. Seems to me to be the simplest plan."

Jim frowned and nodded. "Would be simple if that was all we needed, but one or more of them cows is tangled up in some brush and wire that blew into the ravine durin' one of them storms we had last week." He took off his hat again and wiped the unrelenting sweat from his sun-lined face. "Henry, the cows carry your brand, and seems like there might be more runnin' loose besides those tangled in the ravine. Looked to me like someone cut that fence on purpose."

Pop spoke sharply. "Joe, Rueben, go get saddled up. Bring me my horse, and do it fast." He shouted impatiently at the girls to come on then turned to Maggie. "Take the girls up to the house, and we'll be home directly."

Frank looked around like a lost sheep until Joe and Rueben came riding up, leading two saddled horses.

"Pop, we're ready," Joe called out. Then he nodded at Frank's eager expression. "Frank, you ride along with us 'cause we're gonna need your help." He looked around for Maggie and saw her gathering the little girls together. She turned around and glanced over at him as if she sensed he was watching her. He offered her a quick smile, uttered a command to Redwing, and rapidly galloped off after his pop.

He gazed down into the ravine and spotted two cows tangled up in the middle of a large pile of brush. The narrow ravine created a natural boundary between the two farms, but it was a danger if stock from either side of the fence slipped into it. He cautiously maneuvered Redwing sideways down the steep slope and carefully slid in behind the cows. From his elevated viewpoint it appeared the cows were ensnared in thick, thorny vines interlaced with strands of barbed wire.

"Could be a bit tricky freein' 'em up, Pop. There's not a lot a room down here to move about, much less budge one of the cows free!" he shouted up at the men.

"What say I send Frank down to help you? He's thin and wiry, so he'd probably be able to squeeze in and cut the cows free!" Pop shouted back.

"Works for me!" he hollered. The cows moved around restlessly, mooing loudly as if complaining to the men to hurry and set them free. He spotted Frank edging toward the ravine on his horse, so he called out a quick warning, "Frank, don't try to ride down. You just sit and slide right on down here to me." He backed Redwing down the ravine since the narrow opening didn't leave him much room to turn the horse. Then he dismounted and dropped the reins. Redwing stood silently, patiently awaiting his master's next command.

Frank scooted down the ravine on his backside and tried to slow his descent by pulling at roots and grasses growing along its sides. At the bottom he stood up and dusted his hands off. "This here's a lot steeper than I figured it was, Joe."

Pop stooped over and called, "We're goin' to go check on the rest of the herd. Either of you boys need me, holler." Then he was gone.

Frank looked askance at Joe, so he pulled out his pocketknife and extended the blade. "We'll try this first, Frank. It's got a razor-sharp edge, so be careful you don't cut yourself on it."

They stumbled through the ravine toward the nervous cows, taking care not to lose their footing on the uneven terrain. Frank slipped tentatively in next to the cows while Joe came up behind and tried to pull aside some of the brush.

"Frank, cut through this here first. That should free up a bit of room for you."

Frank expertly wielded the knife, making short work of the thick vines. "My wood carvin' finally paid off. Didn't know if it ever would."

"Yep, and I'm sure glad you're down here with me, Frank," Joe agreed. "This ravine's too narrow, and you being so small makes it a heap easier to get alongside these cows." He glanced up at the sky. "I sure wouldn't want to be down here durin' a cloudburst, though. This ravine floods fast. That's what's got Pop so upset. I think he's afraid the cows might be trapped in here and it could come a flood."

He grasped another unwieldy armload of vines and held them back so Frank could quickly hack them off. He tossed the cuttings high up over the cows and deeper into the ravine.

Frank swiped at the sweat running down his face. "Joe, I think we're at the barbwire, but I don't know if your knife will slice through it." He bent over to examine the sharp wire caught around one cow's leg. "Let me see if I can loosen it without havin' to cut it, Frank. It looks pliable." He reached down warily and seized hold of the cow's back leg, and then with his free hand he cautiously took hold of the wire, trying to avoid the sharp barbs.

"I'm gonna try to stretch this wire out some so we can shift it away from the cow, Frank, and when I do, I want you to grab the wire and hold it tight while I free up the cow's leg." He proceeded slowly and carefully, noting that the cow had a deep gash near its hoof where the barb had pierced it.

It turned out to be a lengthy ordeal, but finally he liberated the cow from the wire. He coughed and spit out the dirt that had crept into his lungs as he'd struggled with the wire. "I can't see no more wire around this one, so I'm goin' to try and back her up to where Redwing is."

Frank wound the sharp barbwire into a circle then hung it on a root sticking out above his head on the wall of the ravine. "Hey, Joe, looks like this other cow is just tangled in vines. I can't see no barbwire, but that don't mean it's not hidden by the brush."

Joe heard movement above and noticed his brother scrambling down the embankment. Rueben called out, "Pop and Mr.

Banks are headin' back to the barn with the herd. We rounded up a few strays, but most of 'em were still on our land; so Pop sent me back to lend a hand." He held a handmade halter in one hand as he grabbed on to anything along the way that would slow his descent into the ravine.

"Why don't you go ahead and take this one up with the halter. She's got a bad cut on her leg that needs tending," Joe requested.

"Might be easier to lead her out with your horse, Joe, so I'll mount up and take her home then ride back to help y'all with the other cow."

"That'd be helpful, Rueben." He held out his hand and assisted Rueben down the last few feet into the ravine. Then he pointed to the cow's back leg. "Look here. Tell Pop he'd best get this cut cleaned out and dressed right away. It looks bad."

Rueben agreed. "Yeah, I know, and Pop can't afford to lose any of his cattle right now. It's all he's got to keep this place runnin' till this dang Depression's done."

Dusky shadows settled over the land, and reassuring evening sounds filled the air, but my apprehension deepened the longer I waited out on the porch for Joe to come home.

Fortunately, the girls' high spirits had continued when we'd arrived back at the house. As a result, they'd played in the garden, climbed trees, and helped Mrs. Gilley bake a batch of cookies. Later, as I anxiously waited out on the porch, I heard their laughter floating out of the house as they listened to an early evening radio program.

I smiled to myself as the sound of their joyous, carefree laughter flitted through the night air. Sweet memories of growing up filled me. Mine were most often pleasurable, full of whistles and dreams and sorrows that never seemed to last too long, and for me there'd always been a story to tell, songs to sing, and friends to share time with. I felt so blessed that my sisters' experiences today had been happy ones that they could always remember.

I hung over the porch rail and stared at the ground, trying to keep my thoughts off what Joe might be encountering. Inevitably, I gazed back out across the yard, my mind a jumble as I anxiously kept watch on the hill for any activity.

It seemed like forever before I finally heard the cows approaching. Their lowing sounded loud and long as they headed eagerly toward the barn. I quickly gathered myself together, jumped down the porch steps two at a time, and rushed up the hill to meet the men as they arrived.

I scanned the crowded corral, trying to catch a glimpse of Joe's lanky form, but he wasn't with the others. Disappointment and concern filled me as I stared off into the distance, hoping he'd come riding up. My heart did a dance when I spotted Redwing trot up to the fence, but then the dance died when I realized it was just Rueben riding up leading a cow, not Joe.

Rueben led the cow over to his pop and talked to him a bit, and then he sauntered over to where I was hanging on the fence. "Joe and Frank are still tryin' to free up another cow, Maggie. They should be along soon, but I'm headin' back there now. So if you want, you can ride out with me."

I could have kissed him, seeing as I felt so relieved. "I'd really like that, Rueben. Should I go let your mom know?"

"Naw, Pop'll know. Meet me over to the other side where I left Redwing. Then we'll head on back to the ravine."

We met them halfway as they trailed slowly back, leading another injured cow behind them. Joe waved when he caught sight of us. He looked worn out, and so did Frank. We stopped and waited for them, and as they drew closer, Rueben held on to my arm as I hurriedly slid off the restless horse.

Joe turned the haltered cow over to Frank, and then we

watched as our two younger brothers rode off toward home. He held out his hand. I grabbed it, put my foot up in the stirrup, and he pulled me up behind him. I wrapped my arms tightly around his waist in a hug and laid my head against his sweat-drenched shirt. My heart swelled with joy to be with him again.

"I'm about done in." He sighed. "Don't know who decided to cut into our fence, but they sure caused a mess of trouble, and we just about lost them two cows." He rubbed his tired eyes in exasperation. "That first one Rueben brought back had some serious injuries on its leg, but this second cow, she's goin' to need more'n a little help to recover. We couldn't see it at first cause of the brush, but she had wire tangled all round her belly and legs. Poor thing was really hurtin'."

"I'm sorry, Joe. I wish it hadn't happened," I whispered as I tenderly caressed his neck and massaged his tired shoulders.

"Mmm, that feels mighty good." He closed his eyes and leaned back against me. The horse moved forward in response to Joe accidentally clipping its side with his boot, but he quickly grabbed on to the saddle horn to steady us. "Guess we best head for the house 'fore I fall asleep from all your tender care."

I hugged him tightly and dropped a kiss on the back of his neck. He sighed longingly. "That could be dangerous, ya know."

"Mmhmm ..."

A half moon greeted us as we rode sedately into the yard. I held on to Joe as I slipped silently off the horse, and his whispered "I love you" filled me with joy. I wandered thoughtfully toward the house and just about tripped over Rueben and Frank as they lazed under a big shady pecan tree.

"That you, Maggie?" Frank asked. He looked beat and didn't bother opening his eyes or waiting for my reply before he posed another question. "Joe all right?"

"Mmhmm. He's stabling Rueben's horse. Then he'll be back."

"I believe I'm too tired to budge from this spot, even with that wonderful smell comin' from Mrs. Gilley's kitchen."

Rueben sat up, rubbing his eyes. "Think I'll head on into the house and get a bite to eat 'fore I sack out for the night. Y'all come on. Mom's made chicken 'n' dumplins tonight, and it don't get better'n that." He reached out and pulled Frank up. "Come on now; you'll feel better after you eat."

They shuffled into the house like two old men, but Frank turned back at the kitchen door and searched through the darkness for me. "You comin', Maggie?"

I called back softly, "When Joe gets back, we'll be right in." I leaned back against the sturdy old tree and gazed at the rising moon. Its light softly shimmered through the shadows, illuminating bits and pieces of the yard while leaving the rest in darkness.

It had been a long day, and I felt weary to the bone, but as I gazed at the glorious moon, I prayed, thanking God for his generous goodness, for Joe, for our families, and for that very day of existence. Tears dampened my cheeks, not just from sadness or joy, but a mixture of the two. I closed my eyes and let the peacefulness of the moment sink into my soul.

All at once, I felt his heartbeat against mine, I felt his breath in my hair, and I imagined I heard his sweet voice saying, "Marry me, Maggie." Then I felt his kiss upon my lips and his arms enfold me, and I realized I wasn't dreaming.

I tilted my head back and gazed into his fiery eyes. "Joe, did you—" He kissed me before I could finish my sentence, and his passion blazed like a fire engulfing me in its flame.

His arms tightened around me, and he kissed me again and again. Then he nuzzled my neck and tenderly whispered once more the words I most wanted to hear, "Marry me, Maggie."

For a moment, the breath went right out of me, and I felt as tongue-tied as I'd been when he'd first asked me to the barn dance all those months ago. Then it was like a bubble popped, and tears streamed down my face as I wrapped myself up in him and exclaimed adamantly, "Yes! Oh yes, my sweet Joe, yes."

His fiery kiss put a stop to my tears as we sank slowly to the ground, arms and bodies entwined, our kisses intensifying as we snuggled up closer together. Finally, he came up for air, groaned softly, and gazed amorously into my eyes. He tenderly caressed my face, my neck, and then his warm hand slid slowly down my arm, igniting my skin. He lingered at my waist, lightly brushing the bare skin between my slacks and shirt, and everywhere his loving touch caressed me it felt as if flames erupted. I drew him down to me, filled with a deep, drenching desire to just melt into him as his lips burned into mine.

A shaft of light spilled out over the yard, and it took me a moment to realize Joe's mom was calling out to us. He laid his head on my shoulder, and I felt our hearts pounding together as one.

"Joe, Maggie, y'all come on in and have some supper. The girls are gettin' tired, and you'll need to drive 'em home soon."

"Be right there, Mom," he called. He stroked my hair then let his fingers linger by my lips, softly caressing them. "I love you, Maggie." I kissed his fingertips and felt desire throbbing through my body. "Oh, Joe, I do so love you—"

"Joe Edward!" his mom called again.

He propped himself up and sighed wearily. "Better mind my mom; otherwise she might just come on out here lookin' for us."

We strolled into the kitchen hand in hand and sat down sedately at the table. Joe's mom had her back to us, stirring a pot over at the stove. Rueben and Frank sat across from us at the table grinning, and I had a childish impulse to stick my tongue out at them; but I restrained myself.

Joe's hand found mine under the table, and he winked at me as Jessie came running into the kitchen. "Where y'all been, Maggie?" Then she stopped and looked searchingly at me. "Did you fall off the horse, Maggie?" She approached me and started picking things out of my hair. "You got leaves and twigs all up in your hair."

Frank and Rueben burst out laughing, which brought Joe's pop into the kitchen to see what was going on. He looked from one of us to the other then cleared his throat. "Joe Edward, we're a Christian household here—"

Joe stood up quickly, stepped behind my chair, and placed his hands on my shoulders. "Pop,"—he stopped and gently gathered my hair up off my neck. I felt his lips touch my skin, and I closed my eyes as desire for him swiftly swept over me. He knelt beside me and tilted my face to his. His voice was deep and husky when he spoke. "Mom, Pop ..." He couldn't finish before his lips hungrily found mine. I heard his pop step up behind him and felt him place his hand on Joe's shoulder.

I should've been embarrassed, but I wasn't. I just glanced casually around the room as if nothing out of place had happened. Joe's mom stood beside us with a skillet raised in her hand. His pop still had his hand resting lightly on Joe's shoulder. Rueben and Frank were laughing so hard they were about crying, and Jessie just stood there with her mouth hanging open.

Joe looked at his parents, his eyes shining brightly. "It's okay, Mom. You can put away that skillet. Maggie just agreed to be my wife!"

His pop dropped his hand. "Well now, that's just fine, son." He paused and stared hard at us. "There's a lot of 'lectricity floatin' round in here, so I think it'd be wise if you two marry real soon."

⌒⁑⌒

We drove up to my house close on ten o'clock. The girls tumbled out of the car, sleepily dragging themselves up the steps and into the house. I scooted up closer to Joe and laid my head on his strong shoulder. He brushed my hair aside and stroked the spot just behind my ear that about drove me to distraction and caused me to sink deeper against him with a contented sigh.

Finally, he declared, "I think Pop's right, Maggie. I don't want to wait to marry you. I love you and need you so much, and it's like a real physical pain when we're apart."

I kissed his cheek then turned his face to mine. "I'd marry you tonight if I could, Joe Gilley." Then I kissed him, softly and sweetly at first, and then with deep passion. After a bit he laid his head on my shoulder as his breath raged in my ear. I kissed his neck and quivered in his embrace as he lifted his face to mine, and we kissed once more. Afterward, he sat back in the seat and closed his eyes, and then he turned and picked up my hand. His dark eyes gazed longingly into mine for the longest moment. At that point he lovingly dropped little kisses the length of my arm, up my neck, and finally, desperately, his sweet lips met mine. My heart hammered within me, and I abandoned any pretense of trying to control myself. However, after only a few heated moments of passion, Joe pulled away from me, breathing hard. "Maggie, baby, I don't want our weddin' night to take place in the front seat of my pop's car, so we'd best stop now, or there won't be any stoppin'."

Out of the blue I heard another voice. "I don't want that to happen neither! 'Specially with me tryin' to sleep right here in the backseat."

"Frank!" I screamed. "What are you doing?"

"I was tryin' to sleep till you two got so amorous. Then I was just tryin' to be quiet and hide." He opened the car door and declared, "Guess I was so tuckered out from all our work today that I just fell hard asleep. I didn't even budge when we pulled up to home. Then when I did I tried to be quiet so as not to disturb your special moments." He laughed lightly as he jumped out of the car and quickly ran up to the house.

"Oh gee!" I laughed. "I guess I better get inside too." I touched his lips with mine once more and whispered, "Oh, how I love you, Joe."

He groaned softly. "It's murder to let you go now, but soon, Maggie, we won't have to part at the end of the day." His eyes held mine. "Goodnight, love. I'll see you at church in the mornin'."

I slipped silently out of the car, ran up the steps to the porch, and watched sadly as Joe drove off into the night. I wanted to call after him to come back, but I knew it wouldn't be the right thing to do.

I heaved a tired sigh and walked quietly into the house. Mama peeked out of the kitchen and smiled at me. "Well now, you're home. The girls were telling me all about dinner with the Gilleys, and it sounds like somethin' you and I should talk about right now."

She walked into the room, still drying her hands on a dish-towel. She calmly sat down on the couch and patted the seat next to her. "Come on over here and tell me all about it."

I plopped down on the floor beside her and laid my head in her lap. "Joe wants to marry me, Mama."

"And how does my Maggie feel about that?"

"I want to be his wife more than anything else in the whole world. I love him so much, and it just doesn't seem right any-more when I'm not with him."

"Maggie, you have a lot of passion in you for just about anything you do." She lifted my face so she could look into my eyes. "I've known for a long time how much you love Joe, and I think it's wonderful that you want to marry. I just don't want you to be carried away by your passion and not understand what real love is all about."

"I do, Mama. I know it's not all roses and sunshine, but I want to spend my good times and my bad times with Joe."

"Remember, Maggie, that God needs to be the center of your relationship with Joe. He drew the two of you together for his purpose, and you should honor that."

"Joe and I both want that. And I've known for a long time that God placed Joe in my life, and I'm deeply thankful for the love and passion that we share."

"I just want you to be happy in your marriage, Maggie. Your papa grew away from me and from God, and that liked to have broke my heart. Although, maybe I just saw him havin' a deeper relationship with Christ when I was a young girl because I fell so hard for him."

"Mama, we've talked about it, long and hard. I know where we stand," I finished adamantly.

"Okay, Maggie. I just want you to be sure because marriage is a lifelong commitment, not just a passing passion."

I gathered her hands in mine. "I'm not just infatuated with him, Mama. I love him deeply and completely." My eyes teared up, and I let the teardrops slide down my cheeks and fall gently onto her lap.

"I guess, then, we have a weddin' to plan," Mama affirmed. She leaned down and gently kissed me. "What kind of time frame do y'all want to set?"

I smiled shakily. "Is tomorrow too soon?"

Her soft laugh rang out sweetly. "Let's talk with the pastor after church tomorrow, and we'll see what we can do."

chapter 15

Sunrise had come early this morning, and he had been up at least an hour before that preparing to help his pop and Rueben repair the damaged fence. Fortunately, it hadn't taken them near as long as they thought it would, but it still left little time before church to catch even a bit more sleep.

His night had been restless, fraught with tossing and turning and very little sleep. He couldn't keep his mind off the sweetness of Maggie, of his longing and desire for her, his love that drew him to her and caused him many restless nights.

He leaned his head back against the hard wooden pew and let his mind drift off. He tried to sleep for just a moment before the service started, but it seemed his eyes had barely closed when he sensed her presence even before she sat down next to him. He opened his tired eyes and drank in her beauty. He felt totally enchanted by her smile as she gazed affectionately at him. He wanted to gather her up in his arms and hold her close, but he didn't think the congregation would take it very well if he made love to her right there in church.

She blushed a bit as if she'd read his thoughts, so he grinned mischievously and casually draped his arm around her. She'd just started to say something when his pop scooted into the pew and motioned for him to move over.

"Seems like there's a little too much heat in here this mornin'," Pop observed offhandedly. "Might need us a little breathin' space to cool things off."

Maggie's face flamed up, but even so, she leaned across Pop and whispered, "Good mornin', Joe. I had a right nice time yesterday."

He grinned at her and then quietly sat back, trying to keep himself out of trouble. Just as he thought it might be all right, he noticed Hannah slide in next to Maggie. They bent their heads together, sneaking sideways looks at him and smiling. Then Rueben plopped down next to Hannah, leaned over toward him, and saucily batted his lashes. "Mornin', hon."

Pop's face reddened. "Don't you embarrass me, Rueben. Straighten yourself up right now."

Rueben looked contrite while Pop was watching him. Then he winked boldly at Maggie and grinned. She rolled her eyes and leaned close to Pop. "Mama wants us to speak with the pastor after church, Mr. Gilley. I'd claim it as an honor if you and Mrs. Gilley would be there with us."

Pop nodded. "That's a right fine thing to do, Maggie. We'll be glad to go along with you and Joe."

The organ sounded, and they all stood up to sing. He slid his hand along the back of the pew behind Pop. She reached back and found his hand. Their fingers lightly touched, and it was enough.

It seemed an eternity before the final hymn was sung. He'd had a heck of a time just keeping his eyes open, much less focusing on what the preacher was teaching on. It had something to do with brotherly love, but in his present state of mind and the way Rueben had been carrying on, he wasn't too keen on brotherly love at the moment.

He felt his pop nudge him and noticed everybody standing up. He pulled his long legs in from under the pew in front of him, scooted along the pew behind his pop, and stood up next to Maggie. Her delighted smile rewarded him for his efforts. He put his arm around her waist and pulled her close to his side as he dropped a kiss atop her head. She wrapped her arm around him and moved as close as she could to him. Then they both sang out loudly along with the congregation.

His pop eyed him the way he used to when he was a boy, which at one time had scared him more than just a little, but today it didn't faze him at all. He respected his pop more than any other man, but his time as Pop's boy was done. Now he was responsible for his actions and for the choices he made in his life, and Maggie was one of the most important choices he'd ever made.

He took her hand as they made their way down the aisle and nodded politely to those around them. The pastor held out his hand as they made their way out of the church. "Joe, Maggie, I hear congratulations are in order. I spoke to Mrs. Bowen earlier this morning, and she asked if we could all sit down and meet for a bit. I'll be available in about fifteen minutes if that works for the two of you."

"That would be just fine," he said confidently.

The pastor held them up for another minute. "Let's meet over at the parsonage. Y'all can go on over there now, and I'll be along shortly."

Mrs. Bowen followed them outside and stopped them as they were about to cross the yard over to the parsonage. She stared from one to the other. Then she reached out and embraced them both. "Joe, you're a very blessed young man to have my oldest daughter fall in love with you. And you, Maggie, you have always been my joy, and you, girl, are very blessed to have such a fine young man fall in love with you." Tears glistened in her eyes, but she didn't bother to wipe them away.

"Thank you, Mrs. Bowen, and I promise you that no man could love your daughter more than I do," he stated emphatically. His gaze lingered tenderly on Maggie as she reached out and hugged her mama.

"Mom and Pop are comin' to meet with us too," he explained. "They should be out here shortly, but if you'd rather we can walk on over to the parsonage, and they can meet us there."

"I think it'd be nice if I could talk with your parents for a bit before I join y'all. Why don't you and Maggie take a few minutes alone to talk over what you both want to do; then y'all can share your plans with all of us in one fell swoop."

Maggie's eyes sparkled. "You're such a wise woman, Mama."

His mind was so tired that he wasn't sure how well he'd be able to focus on any important matters, but he knew that if he truly followed Mrs. Bowen's advice, his idea would be to elope with Maggie today and figure out all the other details later on. With that thought in his mind, he followed her over to the porch swing outside the parsonage.

He wearily sat down next to her, stretched out his legs, and laid his head on her shoulder. She brushed her fingers lightly across his face and tenderly kissed his closed eyes. He raised his head, turned slightly, and encircled her in his arms, drawing her face-to-face with him. "This is what I want, Maggie, to be close to you always, to love you and protect you, and share all of my life with you. Anything else you want, I'm in agreement on."

She snuggled up close to him. "How long do you think we'll have to wait to get a marriage license?"

"Maybe a week, maybe less; we can ask the preacher. I know we'll have to go over to Ft. Worth to get it, so I'll have to arrange to take some time off work this week."

"Joe," Maggie began.

"Mmhmm?" He looked askance at her worried frown then lovingly touched her puckered lips. "What's wrong, baby?"

"I have no idea what we need to plan on, other than gettin' on with our lives together. I haven't thought further than how much I want to be with you, love you, and spend my whole life with you."

He smiled kindly at her. "Sweetie, we're in the exact same place." He kissed her hand as she tenderly caressed his face. "I can see there's goin' to be some difficult roads ahead of us, baby, but with God on our side and our love for each other, we'll make it."

"Do you think your parents support us? I don't want to create any wedges between y'all, honey. My mind is just so jumbled right now."

He took her hands in his. "Maggie, my parents adore you almost as much as I do. I think I shocked 'em a bit with my behavior last night, but they didn't know what was goin' on. They didn't know that I'd spoken the most important words of my entire life to you only moments before." His lips caressed hers as he whispered once again, "Marry me, Maggie."

She eagerly returned his kiss, breathing in his essence, his love. "I love you so much, Joe, and I want to be your wife more than anything else in the whole world."

He rocked her gently in his arms. "That's all we need to know, then. Just tell me when and where, and I'll be ready."

He looked up when he heard his pop cough. "Hey, Pop, y'all want to join us on the porch?"

The pastor smiled at them. "I can see now how much you two care about each other, and it's right nice out here, but why don't we go on into the house, where we can sit comfortably and talk."

After they were all settled, the pastor looked at them kindly and asked, "Now, I can tell that planning your wedding is foremost on your minds, but I'd like to pose a few questions to you first, just so we can look a little further into the future."

They nodded in unison, and Joe replied, "We'd surely respect and appreciate any advice you can give us, Pastor."

The pastor looked from one to the other. "Okay, first and foremost, once you're married, where will you live? Now before you answer, let's think a bit. Maggie, you share a room with your sisters, your brothers have their room, and your mama has the third bedroom. And Joe, you and Rueben share your room, Dorrie has a room, and your mom and pop have theirs. If you plan on staying with your folks, who's going to lose their room?"

Joe nodded. "I guess I did give that some thought, Pastor. Maggie and I will just have to rent us a small place till an opportunity for somethin' better comes along. I make pretty good money workin' for Mr. Johnson, so I believe we can afford a little house someplace close to town."

"All right, now that's a good plan, but have you considered how long it might take you to find a rental house you can afford?"

"Well, we haven't taken that into consideration, but there's bound to be one nearby," he responded.

The pastor looked earnestly at them both. "Is there any reason to rush into this marriage, or would you be willing to take some time to carefully look at all marriage entails, spend a little time apart to pray and consider where God wants you to go in your lives?"

Maggie leaned forward in agitation. "Pastor, if what you're implying is what I think you are, then no, we don't have to rush into marriage. Joe and I have talked many times about our faith in God, and we want to share all of our experiences, both good and bad, together and follow where God leads us…together."

Joe gently clasped her hand, softly stroking it to try and ease her agitation. "We both feel that God has drawn us together for his purpose, and our love for each other is solid and strong." He smiled at her. "It's passionate, yes, as God designed, but we don't consider for even a moment that we're rushin' into this marriage. We feel it's just a natural progression for us, one that would come about whether we marry now or six months from now. I only know that I want and need Maggie in my life, more than just as a true friend and companion, which she is, but as my soul mate, my lover, my wife." He ran his fingers lightly through her hair and then soothingly rubbed her neck.

The pastor nodded thoughtfully. "I can truly see that. In spite of this, one thing I always recommend to young couples on the verge of marriage is that they take a little time apart, just to give each of you time to think about what marriage means and how drastically it will change your lives."

Joe could feel Maggie tensing up, so he spoke softly. "I don't believe we need to spend any time apart to know what we already know, Pastor. We've shared a lot these past months, and through thick and thin, I've known Maggie is the only woman for me." He glanced at her affectionately and then continued. "Unfortunately, it looks like we might have to be apart for a few days in the next week or so because I may well have to go up to Oklahoma on business with Mr. Johnson."

"Joe!" Maggie exclaimed.

"I know, baby. Mr. Johnson asked me 'bout goin' on Friday, and yesterday just passed by before I had a chance to talk to you regarding it." He gazed into her eyes. "This will give you a chance to plan with your mama and Hannah, and before I leave I'll try to put out some feelers about a rental house."

Maggie appeared distressed. "If we were already married, I could just go with you, honey."

He pressed her hand. "I'd like nothin' better, baby, but suppose we go tomorrow afternoon and apply for our marriage license. After that, we'll be set whenever we decide on a date."

Mrs. Bowen spoke up. "Maggie, he'll only be gone a few days, and the pastor is right that you both need to consider all the obstacles you may face after you're married." Maggie started to protest, but her Mama's look stopped her. "Maggie, take a leap of faith, not a leap of irresponsibility. Right at this moment is not the right time to rush into marriage. Give yourself a little time; plan so that when you are married you won't feel so overwhelmed."

Maggie gazed around the room then turned and whispered

to him, "I feel like I can't breathe without you, Joe. I see you every day, and I long for the even the shortest moments we have together. What'll I do without you nearby?"

He enfolded her in his arms. "Maggie, love, we'll put one foot in front of the other and know that no matter what, we'll find our way back to each other in just a short while."

Mrs. Bowen put her hand on Maggie's shoulder. "Honey, I really wish you'd think about what the pastor is sayin'. No matter how much you want a house to be available at a rent the two of you can afford, it's not just goin' to up and happen. There's a Depression goin' on, honey. You know that very well, seein' as how we've been living the past couple of years."

Maggie pulled away from her. "We'll just cross that fence when we come to it, Mama."

"Maggie, your headstrong determination won't always get you what you want, and you know I only want what's best for you. But if you're bound and determined to rush into this—"

Pop cleared his throat and nodded to Mama. "Beg pardon, Jo, I don't mean to interrupt you." Then he turned to face his son. "But let me say to both you kids, there's no reason to rush into anything. Just slow down a bit, take your time, and find a little place first, that's all we're tryin' to say—"

Joe impatiently interrupted him. "Come again, Pop? Wasn't it you who put the idea into our heads that we shouldn't wait?"

"Joe Edward, you just gotta get control of your emotions, that's all I'm sayin'. Think with your head, boy," Pop argued. "Think what you bring home in a month—how much of that you got saved back? Are you able to afford a wife and maybe even a family?"

Maggie's eyes brimmed over with tears, and she buried her head on his shoulder. He held her gently and stared hard at his pop. "Stop it, Pop. Just stop it."

"Now, son—"

He cut short his Pop's plea. "Pop, you keep treatin' me like I'm just a boy, but I've not been a boy for a long while. I've put up with it because I love you and Mom and I respect you, but I'm not you, Pop, and I'm not your boy anymore." He paused and ran his hand over his face in frustration. He looked at everyone. "I don't mean to be disrespectful, but this is our life we're talkin' about." He glared at his pop. "If I decide to go up to Oklahoma with Johnson, it'll mean an extra three dollars for ever' day I'm gone. I believe that'll cover just about anything we need to cover when I get back."

Maggie sat up in her chair, an air of defensiveness surrounding her. She looked impatiently from one face to another then asked him, "How long would you be gone, Joe?"

"Give er take eight days. We'll be headin' up to some of the auctions they got runnin', so I guess it depends on how many we get to."

Pop leaned over and faced his son. "That's real good money, son. If I was you, I wouldn't turn it down."

"I don't aim to, Pop. I'll head on over to Johnson's this afternoon and find out more about when he needs me to be ready to go, and I'll let him know to count me in."

The pastor extended his hands to both of them. "I think we've covered enough for one day. Let's all pray about your marriage plans, and then we can meet again when Joe returns from Oklahoma." He turned to Maggie. "It may feel as if this has been an attack against you, dear, but it wasn't intended as such. Your folks and I just want you to be aware of the seriousness of marriage. I feel we've covered a lot of ground today, and it's given you both some important things to think on and pray about. Now, I pray God's blessing upon both of you and ask his guidance over you each day as you strive to make some sound decisions."

chapter 16

The hot August sun blazed down on us as we walked up the steps of the courthouse hand in hand. Joe held the door for me and then asked for directions to the county clerk's office.

Once there, the clerk filled in all the information required on our license, stamped her county seal on it, smiled, and offered us good luck as she handed me the most important document I'd ever held.

I stared down at our names typed beautifully on the front, and I dreamily admired the picture and the fancy writing that claimed "Marriage License" boldly at the top. I felt my heart swell with joy as Joe slipped his arm comfortably around me and grinned. I stood up on my toes and kissed his cheek.

As we started to leave, the clerk called out after us. We walked back over, and she informed us that we'd need to give the license to our pastor or the county clerk on or before our wedding day so he could complete the application and mail it in to be made official.

We waltzed happily down the courthouse steps, and I felt lighter than air. Joe's grin hadn't disappeared either, so I knew he felt the same way as I did.

When we got to the car, he opened the driver's door, and I slid over on the seat just enough to give him room to drive. He climbed in and then turned in the seat to face me. "Happy?" I nodded and laid my head against his chest. He ran his fingers through my hair. "Mr. Johnson told me to go ahead and take the rest of the day off, so if you want we can drive up to a real pretty spot I found a while back and talk about our plans."

After only a few minutes Joe turned onto a country lane just south of Ft. Worth and drove up on a small rise in the road. He turned off the engine and pointed off into the distance. "This is it."

I gazed out over the rolling landscape spread out before me. "It's beautiful … so untouched and peaceful."

He scooted closer to me, draped his arm around my shoulder, and started rubbing that special spot just behind my ear. I sighed softly in satisfaction and laid my head on his shoulder. He spoke quietly. "I've heard tell this is about the highest point in the area, but I like it 'cause it reminds me of what this land might have looked like years ago before it was settled."

I snuggled closer to him. "I always feel so very blessed when I see the wild beauty God created for us: the trees, the sky, the moon, and stars. God's majesty simply abounds around us every day, just waitin' for us to notice it and drink it in."

He laid his head against mine. "I'm very blessed with the wild beauty God's placed in my life." His eyes darkened. "It is so sweet and easy to love you, Maggie, so right. I never imagined I'd love anyone as deeply as I love you."

I lifted my head, lovingly kissed his earlobe, and tasted desire. His lips slid down over my eyes, the curve of my cheek, and finally, wonderfully, met mine. The world around us faded away, and only we existed in this exquisite moment in time.

My heart hammered within me as I drew him closer in my arms. Our breathing labored, he drew back, touched my face, and whispered, "Let's take a walk."

We ambled off down the secluded dirt road, hand in hand.

Neither of us spoke, both lost in our own thoughts. Mine tended to flit from one place to another, first rejoicing in the beauty surrounding us and the love we shared, and then turning to darker thoughts about missing him and wondering how I'd make it through the coming days without him.

After a bit he stopped and took both my hands in his. "I almost didn't let you go back there, you know. It's so hard for me to keep myself from takin' advantage of your sweet love, Maggie." His hands slid warmly up my arms. "It's probably for the best that I go off for a bit, let myself cool down like my pop said."

I turned my face up to his, and he groaned softly. "I love to kiss your tempting lips, your adorable neck, and..." He ran his lips amorously along my neck then abruptly pulled away and sighed deeply. "When I get back, baby, we can do the proper thing that the world and our parents expect. We'll set a date to be married."

His eyes blazed into mine, and his words caused my heart to soar. He smiled. "I love you, Maggie, and whether we have a paper license or not, in my heart and soul you are already my wife."

His words touched my heart and flooded my very spirit with joy. I stood up on my toes and kissed him playfully then spun away when he tried to hold me. I stretched out my arms and whirled around and around. At length, I stopped and silently gazed at the heavens in praise.

"Maggie?" Joe's questioning voice stopped me.

I flashed him a mischievous smile and skipped a little farther away. Then I came to standstill and offered, "Friday mornin'."

He looked at me, puzzled. "Friday mornin'?"

"Mmhmm, if you get back next Tuesday or so, we can be married on Friday mornin'," I explained with a twinkle in my eye.

"Well, okay, but what about Friday night and the days after

that? I can't just marry you with nothin' in place yet. It wouldn't be fair to you, honey."

My grin spread out like a Cheshire cat's. "Remember what I told Mama, we'll cross that fence when we come to it."

"Maggie, sweetie, I don't want you to have to start out our marriage homeless. I want to provide for you, maybe even take you on a weddin' trip."

My eyes sparkled and teased him. "I have an idea for our honeymoon, and it won't cost us even a little penny." I scooted farther up the road away from his grasp. "It'll be very intimate and private and wonderful."

He tried to catch my hands, but I was too quick and scampered behind an old tree. I peeked out at his surprised face and giggled. "It's one of the very first places you ever took me where we were completely alone, except for God and a few stray animals, of course."

He looked stunned, and then his eyes lit up. "You're kiddin' me. Are you talkin' 'bout the clearing, Maggie? Do you really want to spend our weddin' night in the clearing?"

My laughter rang out joyfully. "I want to dance in the moonlight with you, Joe. I want to love you under the stars."

"And under the sun," he continued, his voice deepening with passion. "I want to make love to you in the moonlight and the starlight and under the rising sun." He reached around the tree and drew me into his arms. His lips caressed mine as he mumbled, "And maybe after that we'll just go skinny dippin' in that old creek."

I batted my eyes at him playfully. "Maybe so."

He spoke softly as he buried his face in my hair. "What say we get married today?"

I started to speak, but then we heard the sound of an engine start up. Joe glanced back down the road and noticed his pop's car being driven off. We took off running, yelling loudly at the man to stop.

Fortunately, he did. Joe ran up breathlessly to the driver's side, wrenched the door open, and shouted angrily, "What the heck do you think you're doin', man!"

The man calmly turned to face Joe. "Well, son, your car was blockin' my drive, and I needed to get out, so when I saw you two kids out there just playin', I took a mind to just move it myself."

Joe drew in a deep breath. "You should have just yelled out, and I'd have been more'n happy to move it for you."

The man grinned broadly. "Well now, son, you and your young lady certainly didn't look as if you wanted me disturbin' you."

Joe stepped back as the man climbed out of the seat. "No harm done." The man chuckled as he wandered back to where his truck was parked in a remote driveway.

I covered my mouth with both hands to keep from laughing. "Oh, honey, I'm sorry. I didn't even notice any houses or driveways or anything around here. This place just seemed so remote that I thought it was deserted."

Joe grinned. "Another bold adventure in the lives of Maggie and Joe." He held out his hand to me. "And now I believe it's high time we head for home. We still need to exercise the horses for a bit this afternoon."

~

We swiftly galloped over the lush pasture side by side. We'd given Redwing and Pal an exhilarating workout, for one reason to keep our horses healthy and strong, and for another to keep our minds off other frustrating matters.

My muddled mind turned over a thousand thoughts as we rode, but one thing I knew with absolute certainty was that Joe was right about our future together. And I knew beyond a shadow of a doubt that he was the man for me, my true husband, my lover, my very best friend. It was almost physically impossible for me not to touch him or hold him whenever I was near him because it was as if an irresistible force drew us together.

I'd known him since I was a little girl, but I think I first started noticing him as someone other than just Joe at church around about the time I turned thirteen. I know I was just a kid back then, but something drew me to him and kept me thinking about him all those years. I even found myself taking an extra fifteen or twenty minutes and walking the long way to and from school every day for the past couple of years just so I could catch even a little glimpse of him. Then with childish thoughts I'd giggle with Hannah about how cute he was and wish that someday he might like me a little and want to be my boyfriend.

It was meant to be, a relationship blessed by God, for only God truly knows our heart's desires, our needs, even before we recognize them ourselves. For that reason God set my thoughts on Joe and blessedly drew his to me.

It seemed as if I'd always loved him, and not just the six months or so we'd been courting. It simply amazed me how quickly and deeply our love grew and how magnificent it would be to be together as husband and wife.

I reluctantly tore my thoughts back to the present as I gently pulled back on the reins and slowed Pal to a trot. We were fast approaching the corral and the end of our wonderful day together. Parting was always so difficult, but even more so today, knowing Joe would be leaving for Oklahoma tomorrow in the wee hours of the morning. It would be so difficult to say goodbye, even for such a short time, even though I knew I had a lot to accomplish and keep me busy while he was away.

We brought the horses to a stop at the gate, and Joe dismounted and tied Redwing's reins around the fencepost. But I waited to get down, wanting instead to have him help me just to feel his arms around me one more time. Tears burned behind my eyes as I watched him, so I blinked hard to try to keep them at bay.

He turned back to me with a slow smile, sadness reflected in his eyes. He lifted his arms up to me, and I slid into them. I pressed myself against him and held on tightly as his lips softly brushed against my hair. I eagerly turned my face up to his, and his lips met mine. He drew back and gazed at me, his husky voice conveying the deep emotion he too was feeling. "I have to be up way before sunrise to meet Mr. Johnson over at his place by five tomorrow mornin', so it's probably best if Pop drops you off at your mama's on his way into town."

I heaved a sad sigh. "Just remember how much I love you, honey."

"I know, Maggie, I do. It's so hard to say good-bye to you, baby, so very hard, but it won't be for very long; I promise." He drew me closer and whispered, "And when I get back I'll shower you with all my love." He ran his hands down my back and let them linger at my waist as he kissed my eyes, my cheek, my lips. I desperately sought his mouth with mine, never wanting to end that last, lingering kiss.

We both jumped when we heard the car's horn. I quickly brushed at the tears threatening to fall from my burning eyes. "I love you, Joe." I sobbed, finally letting the tears fall unhindered.

He crushed me to him. "I love you, baby, with all my bein'."

Pal snorted, and Joe's pop blew the horn again. He sighed. "I'll take care of the horses, baby. You go ahead and leave with Pop before he blows that dang horn again."

I stretched out my hand to him. He winked and playfully patted my bottom. "Hurry up there, Mrs. Gilley; we got a future to plan for." I beamed at him and then ran down the slope to the yard where Joe's pop impatiently waited.

chapter 17

I hadn't slept well at all, and the next morning I was feeling melancholy. Joe's words, "Don't worry, baby, it'll all work out," kept playing over and over in my head. I sighed a tired sigh as I automatically finished cleaning up the kitchen.

The girls were all out back playing, and Will had left again at the crack of dawn for parts unknown. Mama had just started back to work a couple of days a week, and Frank was somewhere around. I leaned my elbows on the sink and stared sightlessly out the window while my thoughts drifted aimlessly.

I heard the hoofbeats before I saw the horses round the bend in the road. Rueben trotted up on his horse, Sugar, leading Pal behind him. Frank appeared from out of nowhere and ran down the road to meet Rueben. He took Pal's lead, placed his foot up into the stirrup, and threw his other leg up over the horse. He settled himself in the saddle and happily rode my horse the rest of the way up to the house. I walked down the porch steps, a smile on my face, even though my heart felt heavy.

Rueben waved. "Joe asked me to come over and go with you to look around for a rent house for y'all."

"That'd be great, Rueben," I called back.

"I done took care of all my chores for Pop, and I won't need to be back till close on sundown, so we'll have most of the day to look around."

Frank leaned over and laid his head on Pal's neck. "I could ride along and help y'all look."

I smiled at his eagerness. "Not this time, Frank. I'll need you to stay home with the girls."

"Mary's home," he complained. "She's practically old as me! Why can't she watch the little girls?"

"I don't know, Frank. I'll have to talk to Mama about it first, so maybe another day this week you can come and help us."

He looked crushed as he climbed down off the horse. Then he plodded dejectedly up to the porch and slid silently down onto the steps.

Rueben grinned at me. "Hey, Frank, when Maggie and I get back, how 'bout you come out to my place and help Pop and me round up the cows. We could sure use your help, what with Joe gone and all."

"I'll be ready whenever y'all get back!" Frank hollered happily.

Rueben pushed his hat back and asked if I was ready to head out, but I needed to change into my slacks first. I rushed into the house while he tied the horses to the porch railing. I hurried down the hall, listening to Frank's happy laughter as he and Rueben joked with each other out on the porch.

After I finished dressing, I pulled my hair up into a tight ponytail, looked out the back door, and called out to the girls that I was leaving. Mary came running up to the house all out of breath. "Where you goin', Maggie?"

"I'm goin' in to town to check on a rent house for Joe and me, but Frank'll be here if you need him."

She stuck her chin up. "Now why would I need him? He's not much help round here. I'm the one minds the kids most of the time."

"Well, I guess that's so, but anyway, I'll be back later on.

Mama should be home around three, like usual." I hesitated a bit, and Mary flashed her eyes at me.

"Maggie, go on; you don't need to worry none. We'll be just fine." She pushed me back through the door. "I'm practically thirteen!"

"All right, already, I'm goin'!" I laughed and headed back out the front door.

Rueben was ready and waiting. He handed me Pal's reins, and I mounted and turned my horse out toward the road. Pal was an easy horse to ride since Joe had been the one to train him, and it took only the lightest touch to get him trotting down the dusty road to town.

After a bit Rueben pulled up beside me. "How 'bout we turn here."

I smiled teasingly at him, knowing before he said it what he had on his mind. "But Rueben, town's down this way."

He blushed a bit. "Well, I just thought you might be more comfortable if Hannah came along with us, she bein' your friend and all."

I grinned at him. "Seems to me you and Hannah are gettin' to be good friends too. Y'all are spendin' an awful lot of time together."

His face reddened again. "Naw, usually just when she's with you and Joe, but she's a right nice girl."

I chuckled. "Yep, she's a right nice girl."

We set the horses to a gallop and rode swiftly toward Hannah's house. The wind whipped around me, driving away my melancholy mood and filling me with an exhilarating burst of energy. I really wanted to find a house right away, and then it would feel as though my life with Joe was a reality and not just a sweet dream that I might wake up from.

Hannah was sitting out on her front porch talking with her mama when we rode up, and her eyes lit up like sunshine when she realized Rueben was with me. We dismounted quickly and scrambled up the steps. I kissed Hannah's mama on the cheek, then Hannah. "We thought Hannah might be able to come help us look for a rental house today."

Her mama nodded. "I heard tell you and your young man are gettin' married. It must be soon if you're already lookin' for a house."

My eyes shone with joy. "Yes'm, Friday after next. Joe's gone out to Oklahoma on business this week, so I'm out house huntin' today."

She smiled. "Good luck, dear. I don't know of any place right offhand, but then I don't get into town much. Where 'bouts y'all lookin'?"

"I want to be someplace close to our folks because Mama will still need me to help her with things, and Joe still helps his pop out most days when he can. Another thing we're considering is that the house needs to be close to where Joe works, which is pretty near Johnson Station, so that'd be a good location for us."

"Sounds like you have it all thought out, Maggie." She stood up and hugged me. "Well, I wish you good luck, dear." Then she turned to Hannah. "If you go, you'd best change out of that dress."

Hannah winked at me. "Come on, Maggie; help me find somethin' to wear." She pulled me toward the door. I looked at Rueben's face as we left him all alone with Hannah's mama, and I felt a smidgen of sympathy, so I waited just a bit.

Mrs. Rogers asked him how his morning was, and he replied, "So far it's been a long mornin' of waitin'."

I laughed, strolled over to where he sat, and pushed his hat down on his head. "Give it a rest, brother."

He grinned up at me then looked longingly at Hannah, who seemed to be just as entranced with him.

Disappointment haunted me as we rode away from Sublett and neared Johnson Station. There hadn't been anything available in town, but someone had told us about a place nearby, so we'd ridden out to find it. It was a house, or at least it might have been at one time. The "For Rent" sign was about the only part of it that seemed stable. The front porch sagged into the ground, the steps were riddled with holes, and when we walked inside we noticed part of the roof was missing and birds were nesting in the chimney.

My face fell when I saw it. Hannah squeezed my hand and kindly offered, "Don't worry so much, Maggie; we'll find somethin' better." I just shook my head in disgust.

As we walked out, an ancient, rattling truck pulled up in front of the house. "Afternoon, folks," a wizened old man called out. "Was you young'uns wantin' to rent my place?"

I looked back at the house in horror and then stared in amazement at the man. "I don't believe so. We just wanted to look around."

He chuckled. "Thought as much. I'm tryin' to rent out the pasture more'n the house. That old house ain't been lived in near on ten years or more."

I felt relieved but frustrated at the same time. Rueben looked up at the sky, trying to judge the time. "The sun's near 'bout two o'clock, Maggie, so if we get a move on, we can still ride over to Johnson Station and see if anything's available."

We decided to stop off at the house for a bit and check on the kids. They were all sprawled out in the yellowing grass, carefully searching for something. Mary peered up and smiled sweetly. "Jessie's lost her pet lizard again, so we're tryin' to help her find it."

I chuckled in amusement. Jessie loved collecting bugs and such and, more often than not, lost them. She always claimed she found the exact same one she'd lost, and no matter if you told her it wasn't probable, she still believed she had.

Frank quickly bounded up. "That lady from the county came round a while ago. She left some bread and cheese and some other stuff, so if y'all are hungry, there's food." He cleverly fixed his eyes on Rueben. "Y'all go on in, and I'll go water the horses for you." Then he strutted over and offered Hannah his hand.

"Why, thank you, Frank. You're growin' up to be a fine gentleman," she exclaimed.

I grinned at him. "Good idea, Frank." I dismounted and handed him the reins. He climbed up on Pal then waited while Rueben alighted and handed him Sugar's lead. Rueben stepped back and lightly placed his hand on Hannah's back. She smiled up at him as I walked past them into the house, trying to give them a little time alone, or as alone as they could be with five kids playing nearby in the yard.

I sliced off a few pieces of cheese and some of the freshly baked bread and then filled three glasses with cold well water. I was feeling anxious about even stopping so long, even though I knew I had almost ten days to find us a place to live. I thought about Joe, and my heart ached to be with him.

"Maggie,"—I jumped when Hannah spoke—"you're a million miles away."

I blinked to ward off the tears burning my eyes. "I'm okay, just ready for Joe to come home to me."

Rueben looked up in surprise. "Maggie, he just left this mornin'! I been livin' with him all my life, and I'll tell ya, it ain't all that wonderful."

I threw the dishtowel at him and laughed. "Don't tease me, Rueben. You know you miss him same as me."

Rueben cleared his throat. "Not likely." Then he winked at Hannah as she passed him a plate of food. We sat down silently, each of us lost in our own thoughts.

Rueben stood up a short while later and stated he'd go bring the horses around front. After he left, I glanced at Hannah and smiled knowingly. "Well ..."

She blushed. "He's very sweet, Maggie."

"And ..." I teased her.

"Okay, so I like him more than just a little."

"And ..."

"Maggie, stop it! What if he hears us?"

"So."

"Maggie!"

We heard Rueben shout out from the front, so we hurriedly put away the food and rushed back out to where he waited. He helped Hannah up behind him and then waited until I was ready.

We rode into Johnson Station, and I tried not to get my hopes up too high. I hadn't been into town since that fateful night little William was born, and I really wanted to avoid seeing Papa while we were there.

We stopped in at the little store next to the school and asked if anyone had posted a notice about a house for rent. As fate would have it, there was only one place posted, and it was on the same street as Papa and Rachel.

As we rode down the street my heart filled with trepidation. Then I spotted Papa's house, and I slowly let out my breath when I didn't see anyone around outside. We finally pulled to a stop at the end of the road in front of a cute little brown and white bungalow.

I tied Pal's reins to the fence post and darted up to the porch. The front door was locked tight, so I impatiently peeked in through the front window. The inside of the house looked tidy and clean, and there was some furniture left inside. I really liked what I saw, but I knew I shouldn't get my hopes up yet.

We'd just started to go around back when we heard a woman's voice calling out to us. We waited until she caught up, face flushed and breathing hard. She held up a key. "Oh my ... the owner left this key with me ... and said to let anyone ... that was interested…in rentin' look around inside." She caught hold of the porch railing, sat down heavily on the top step, and fanned herself with her apron.

"Thank you," I exclaimed. "We'd love to take a walk through the house and look around."

She nodded. "Now if this house don't suit you, Mr. Marshall will have another house up for rent come the end of September." She pointed down the road to Papa's house. "Those folks are buildin' themselves a right purdy place down off Arkansas Lane. It's a bit of a ride from here, but I hear tell it's a real nice piece of property."

I hated to hear her go on and on about Papa's new house. It still tormented me that he'd taken money that was meant for Mama, but it was one of those things beyond my control. I knew it'd be best to just give my anger over to God and go on with my life. Unfortunately, that was a really hard thing for me to do, but I managed to nod politely. "Well, we'll just go look at this house for now. Then we can return the key to you at your house."

"Isn't that kind of you," she began, "but I believe I'll just sit out here on the porch, and y'all can take your time lookin'." She glanced at Rueben and Hannah, who stood back near the door, timidly holding hands. "When you folks think you'll be needin' the house?"

I smiled at them and then replied, "My husband and I are lookin' for a place to move into round the first of September."

"Why, that's next week, now isn't it." She glanced suspiciously at Rueben. "This here isn't your husband, now is it?"

I replied teasingly, "No, this is just my brother and his girlfriend." Rueben eyed me as he took the key from her hand, and I winked teasingly at him as he brushed by me to unlock the door. Hannah's mouth dropped open, and I playfully pulled her into the house behind me.

The house was small, consisting of a living area and kitchen combination, a tiny bathroom, and two little bedrooms. It wasn't much to look at, but it seemed clean, and the roof was solid. I wandered around thoughtfully, already dreaming up ways I could change it and make it my own.

I restlessly roamed through the rooms one more time before we left, noticing what furniture there was and figuring out what more we might need. I'd practically decided to tell her we'd take the house, but I knew first off I'd have to find out how much the rent was. Rueben and Hannah walked out in front of me and stopped dead in their tracks. I heard the little woman talking and was afraid someone else might have come up to see about the house. I hastily pushed my way through Hannah and Rueben and found her deep in conversation with Papa.

My stomach turned over. I so wanted to flee, but I decided to do the mature thing and conquer my queasiness. I cleared my throat. "Hello, Papa."

"Well, isn't this nice. I didn't know this young lady was your daughter, Mr. Bowen."

"Yep, this here's my Maggie," he said as he wrapped his arm around my shoulders.

I stepped back away from him and saw his face fall. I ignored his disappointment and asked the woman what the little house was renting for. Her answer about bowled me over.

"Why, let's see. You know this little house is one of the nicest rentals in town. I believe Mr. Marshall is asking fifteen dollars a month for it. He likes to have a month up front too. Now if you'd rather wait till your Papa's house is empty, that house will rent for 'bout ten dollars a month, plus the month up front."

I hadn't expected rent to be so much on such a little house. A decision involving this much money wasn't one I wanted to make without Joe. I was feeling a little lost and at a loss as to what to do.

"Why don't you think on it a while, Maggie," Rueben said kindly. "It's gettin' near time for me to head home to help Pop, so we can always come back out here again tomorrow."

I really didn't want to leave the day without a resolution to our housing problem, but I knew Rueben was right. I thanked the woman for allowing us to look in the house and then reached for Pal's reins.

Papa reached out and took my hand. "Maggie, come stop by the house for just a bit. William's near on a month old now, and I'd really like you to see him." His eyes pleaded with me. "He reminds me a lot of you when you was a baby."

I didn't want to go with him, but I was anxious to see little William again. After all, I'd played a small part in bringing my new brother into the world, and he was just an innocent little baby. I looked up at Papa's begging eyes. "Okay, but just for a bit. We've got to be headin' home shortly."

Rueben looked a little antsy, glancing up at the sun then back at us. I thought to relieve a little of his anxiety, so I told him to head on home and I'd drop Hannah off at her house on my way back.

He looked a little green at the thought of not taking Hannah home. "Naw, that's okay. I got time to take Hannah by her mama's. Then I'll go get Frank like I promised him. That way you can take a little more time at your papa's."

That was the last thing I wanted, but I agreed. "Okay, I'll ride out to your place when I leave here 'cause I need to talk some to your mom anyway."

I watched Rueben and Hannah ride away, suddenly wishing I'd said anything other than I'd go with Papa, but the deed had been set in place, and I had to live with it.

I led Pal as I walked down the street with Papa. He gazed off into the distance as if he were lost in deep thought. When he finally spoke, it surprised me. "Maggie, I hear you and that Gilley boy are gettin' married. I sure wish you'd have told me yourself instead o' me havin' to hear it from one of the other kids. I figure you got your reasons, though."

I waited, not really sure what to say to him. It was as if he'd forgotten everything we'd struggled through over the past year or so.

He went on. "I know you still harbor some ill feelin's toward me and Rachel, and I just hate that." He looked sideways at me. "You know Rachel and me are buildin' a house that should be ready in just a few weeks. We'd be right pleased and proud to have the two of you come live in it with us."

I stared hard at him with my mouth hanging open. Did he really think Joe and I would consider such a proposal?

He looked down at the road. "It's hard startin' out, and rentin' is costly, so this'd be a good, easy way to start your marriage out." He glanced casually at my face, trying to judge my reaction. I think what he saw was about what he expected. "Well now, here we are." He took Pal's reins from me and looped them around the porch railing. Then he jumped up the steps and opened the screen door for me. "I think Rachel's in the kitchen, so we'll just go on back there."

So far I hadn't spoken a word. Papa had done all the talking. We entered the little kitchen, where Rachel sat at the tiny table, holding the baby. The two little girls were over by the stove playing with some homemade paper dolls.

Rachel glanced up at me, a little fear in her eyes. I think she still felt afraid of what Joe might have done the night he came here raging after Papa.

I squeezed out a tight smile. "How you feelin', Rachel?"

She smiled tentatively. "Well, I believe I'm all recovered from little William bein' born. He had a right hard birth, and I just want you to know, Maggie, I'm grateful to you for comin' here to help us."

I peered down at William. "I'm just glad everything turned out okay and that William is here and healthy."

Rachel bent down and lovingly kissed the baby's downy head. "He is that." She looked up at me. "Why don't you sit down for a bit and hold your little brother."

I sat down across from her at the table, and she brought William to me and laid him in my arms. The baby gurgled and cooed and I swear smiled at me. I talked to him for a bit, and then Pearl and Lucy came over and hung on to my chair, gazing down at their little brother.

Lucy brushed back my hair and kissed my cheek. "I been missin' you, Maggie."

I smiled kindly at her and kissed her cheek. "I've missed you too, Lucy, and you, Pearl." I leaned back and gave Pearl a one-handed hug.

Papa looked pleased. "It's nice to have you here, Maggie."

I avoided his eyes and talked more to William.

Papa heaved a deep sigh. "Rachel, I told Maggie 'bout what you and I talked on, 'bout her and her new husband comin' out and stayin' with us in the new house."

Rachel nodded. "We'd like that, Maggie. The girls would too, wouldn't you, girls?"

They jumped around happily and begged me to come. It seemed strange to hear Papa call Joe my husband, but I really liked the sound of it. I knew I couldn't keep Papa in agony forever, so I kissed little William and hugged him to me. Then I stood up and gently handed him back to Rachel.

I spoke kindly. "Thank you, Rachel, for lettin' me come see William and the girls. It's right kind of you and Papa to offer us a room in your new house, but I think we all know that wouldn't ever work out."

Rachel nodded as Papa stood up. "Now, Maggie, we bought near 'bout two hundred acres of good farmland. Why don't you think on it a bit? There's enough land that y'all could build your own place and hardly ever see us."

"We'll see, Papa. Joe's out of town right now, so I can't very well talk to him about it." I looked Papa straight in the eye. "But Papa, I have a real good idea how he'd feel about it."

Papa's face reddened, and he hung his head in shame. "Maggie, girl, I don't know how else to say I'm sorry for what I done to you and your mama."

Rachel reached for his hand. "It's okay, John. Maggie knows all you been through and how it's hurt you too."

I'd had enough of the show. "Papa, Rachel, I'll let myself out." I headed quickly toward the door, intent on getting to Pal and riding away as fast as he'd take me. I'd just cleared the doorway and stepped out on the porch when I felt Papa's hand on my shoulder.

I spun around and looked askance at him.

"Maggie, I'd sure like to be at your weddin'. It'd mean a lot to all of us if we could just be there to share in your joy that day."

I grimaced. "Papa, that's just not a good idea. I may have been able to get past some of what's happened between us, but I know for sure Joe hasn't." I paused to try to let it sink in, but his eyes still pleaded with me. I touched his arm. "Papa, go inside and love the little family you have now. Come see Frank and the girls and be their papa, but please don't try to be a papa to Joe and me. I just can't say it any plainer than this, and I'm not tryin' to be cruel, but I don't want any ugliness, any remembrances of pain to take away even a second of my joy when I marry Joe."

Papa nodded sadly. "All right, Maggie, if that's the way you want it, I'll respect it, but someday, honey, I hope we can at least work out our feelin's enough to salvage a bit of what we had before all this mess happened."

I dabbed away my tears. "Maybe, Papa. I wish I could say I know we will, but my heart is still too raw. I've already forgiven you for what you did to me, but I'm havin' a harder time forgivin' you for what you brought on Mama."

He hung his head and scuffed his shoe on the ground. "I've been a fool in a lot of ways, Maggie, but I don't regret for even one day lovin' Rachel. Look what a blessin' I ... we got with our little William."

"It's gettin' late, Papa. I have to go." I pulled myself up into the saddle, and Papa handed me the reins.

As I reached for the reins, he caught my hand and held it tightly. "No matter what I done or said to you that night I was so drunk, I'm right proud of who you've growed up to be, Maggie. I hope you and your man are happy as I am right now with Rachel."

Even though I hated the comparison, I softly whispered, "Thank you, Papa." Then I bent down and kissed his cheek.

His leathery hand grasped mine once more as he passionately poured out his soul. "Please, Maggie…you just don't understand how hard this is for me. Maggie, girl, you're my firstborn child, and I never imagined in my whole life I'd be beggin' you to love me…and it just tears me up not to go to my own daughter's weddin'."

I gazed into his heartbroken eyes and pleaded, "Stop, Papa. Please don't make this any harder than it already is. It just wouldn't be right." My voice trailed off sadly.

Papa sobbed. "Girl, let's just let bygones be bygones, and you and your man try to forgive me for all I done to you and your mama."

I whispered, "Papa, please. I told you I've already forgiven you for what you brought on me, but Joe hasn't…and I don't—I won't—have anything spoil our weddin' day."

His eyes teared up, "Even if you'd just say you want me at your weddin', honey. Even if I couldn't really come, that's all I'd need to know. I think I could live with that, Maggie."

My heart fought within me, and it was all I could do not jump off my horse and fall into his arms like I did when I was a little girl. Instead, I sighed sadly, patted his hand, and rode dejectedly away as the sound of his deep sobs followed after me.

⌇

Tiny stars twinkled in the growing dusk, and the pale moonlight cast eerie shadows all around me. In my tired state of mind, it scared me more than just a little. I felt so alone as I rode solemnly toward the Gilleys' place. Just being with Papa was always so emotionally draining, and then hearing him cry so just about broke my heart.

I lightly kicked Pal to a gallop and covered the last mile in no time at all. As I rode into the yard, I saw a figure emerge from the shadows. For a single moment I thought it might be Joe, but it turned out to be Rueben. He and Frank strolled over to me, and Frank offered to go stable Pal. I gratefully accepted then tiredly dismounted and handed him the reins.

Rueben draped his arm around me, and I leaned against him with a sigh. "You've had a rough day, Maggie. Why don't you go on in the house and sit a bit with the folks, and then I'll drive you and Frank home a little later."

I rubbed my eyes and dropped a light kiss on his cheek. "Thank you, Rueben. It's been a disappointin' day all around, and I just don't know what I'm goin' to do if I can't find a place for Joe and me. I promised him, Rueben, and now I feel like I'm breakin' it."

"It's only the first day of lookin', Maggie. You can't expect miracles, and Joe don't expect you to perform magic if there's nothin' available." He took my hand and pulled me toward the lighted doorway.

"I'm such a mess right now, Rueben. I should probably just get you to take us home now. I don't want to cry in front of your folks."

He chuckled. "It wouldn't be the first time, now would it?" He turned me toward the door and gave me a little push. "You just come on in. I promised Joe I'd watch out for you, and I believe what's called for now is some of Mom's good home cookin'."

I reluctantly followed Rueben into the brightly lit kitchen and was surprised when I realized that not only Joe's parents, but his grandparents as well were gathered at the table.

"Evenin', everybody," I called, hoping my voice didn't betray my sadness.

Joe's pop quickly jumped up and pulled out a chair. "There you are, Maggie. We was just discussin' you and Joe."

Okay, I thought, *what could they have been discussing?* But instead I said, "Thank y'all for havin' Frank and me over tonight. It makes me feel closer to Joe when I'm here."

"Maggie, you look plum worn out. You come sit down right now and tell us all about your day," Mrs. Gilley replied.

"Mr. and Mrs. Gilley, I—"

They interrupted me before I could finish my thought, both speaking at the same time.

"Maggie, it's time you started callin' me Mom."

"I'm your Pop now, Maggie, not some stranger. You're family now."

My eyes teared up, and Rueben grinned broadly. I almost stuck my tongue out at him, but then I thought I really should grow up a bit and stop it. So instead I turned my back on him and hugged Mom tightly. "Thank you both for makin' me feel so welcome."

"And you'd best call me Grammy, and my old man here's Gramps."

I nodded and smiled. "Thank you all."

Dorrie dashed over to me and quickly climbed up in my lap. Her deep blue eyes stared intently into mine as she clutched my face in her tiny hands and proclaimed, "You can call me Dorrie."

Everyone burst into gales of laughter right as Frank strolled in the door. "What'd I miss?" he asked with a grin.

Dorrie jumped down and tugged Frank over to the table. "I was just tellin' my new sister my name." She stood up on her chair and stared at me. "Ya know, I always, always, always wanted a sister, and now Joey done brung me one."

Pop picked her up and plopped her down in the chair. "That's enough now, half-pint. You know your mom don't allow you to stand on her chairs." He dropped a kiss on her cheek and patted her head before he sat back down.

Frank sat down next to Rueben. "Somethin' sure does smell good in here. I could just about dine on the smell alone."

Rueben laughed. "Boy, are you full of it."

Frank grinned. "Just tryin' to be polite."

Mom passed a pan of potatoes to Frank. Then Pop tapped his spoon on the table. "Well now, Maggie, how'd the house huntin' go today?"

I rested my chin in my hand sadly. "Not so good, Pop. We found one little house that might have worked, but they wanted too much for the rent. I think we're goin' to try over in Webb tomorrow. I wanted somethin' close by, but we may even have to look farther away if I can't find anything soon."

Pop scratched his head. "Mom and me might have come up with an idea I think you may well like."

"Now, Henry," Grammy interjected, "your pop and I were the ones first thought up this plan."

"You're right, Mama, but anyway, let me explain it to Maggie."

Gramps leaned back in his chair, placed his hands on the table, and cleared his throat. "Hold on a minute, son." He pushed himself up and walked over to the stove. He came back with the pan of gravy and set it down in front of Frank. "Now, I'm in a givin' mood today, so I thought I'd start with Frank."

Frank beamed. "I'm right glad you did, sir. This dinner is great, Mrs. Gilley."

I stared at them, wondering where all this talk was going to lead. I didn't have to wait long, though, because Dorrie suddenly burst out, "Pop wants to build y'all a dollhouse just like mine."

Gramps sat back down. "Henry and me always planned on givin' the boys this property someday, so we decided that now would be as good a time as any to give a little parcel of it to you and Joe. It'd be a weddin' gift from all of us."

Pop nodded. "We was thinkin' on givin' the two of you that twenty acres down by the little pond. Joe Edward always loved that spot, and we'd really like y'all to have it."

I was so touched. "That would be the most wonderful gift I could imagine, and I know Joe would be right pleased as well because he loves this land with his very soul."

Mom smiled. "We wanted to surprise you with another little gift, Maggie, but our Dorrie here already let the cat out of the bag."

I looked askance at her, but Dorrie quickly answered my question. "'Member what I said? Pop wants to make you and Joey a dollhouse, just like he did for me!"

Pop laughed. "Well, not just like yours, half-pint, but we could build it to look like yours if that's what Maggie wants. Our plan is to give it to y'all for a weddin' gift. Then you won't need to worry none 'bout findin' a rent house. Y'all can just come on out here to your new home."

My mouth fell open in amazement. "How? It would cost too much to build a house, Pop. How can we afford such a thing?"

"You don't need worry none 'bout that, Maggie. We have some wood out in the barn that's good lumber, which Gramps and I was plannin' on usin' to build a new barn out on the property near where the fence got cut, but we feel this is a much more important project."

"But how? How can we get it built so soon? Joe and I are gettin' married in just a little over a week!"

Rueben laughed. "Maggie, never doubt my pop, because if he sets his mind on it, it's bound to happen."

I smiled. "Sounds like his sons take after him that way too."

Mom interjected. "We was thinkin' 'bout the barn raisin' people gather for. We thought we'd simply invite folks from the church to come out and help us build the house. Then we could have 'em all over the Friday afternoon after the weddin' to celebrate."

I thought about the plans Joe and I had made for the afternoon after our wedding, and I blushed just thinking about them.

"What do you think, Maggie?" Pop asked.

I pushed aside my wandering thoughts and replied, "I think

it's a wonderful idea, but Joe and I do have a little weddin' trip planned, and we were aimin' to leave just a little bit after the weddin'."

"Where y'all goin'?" Frank asked innocently.

"Well,"—I paused—"I think it's kinda a surprise." I blushed again. "If we can get a little place built, it would be such a blessing for Joe and me, but I think I'd like to keep the house as a surprise for Joe until we get back from our honeymoon."

"That's fine, Maggie," Pop conceded. "We can just plan a cookout the night after the house is finished, and that'll take care of thankin' the church folks."

Mom gazed tenderly at me. "We'll just have a little lunch with your family and ours after the weddin'. Then you and Joe Edward can go off on your own."

I got up and stood behind her, wrapped my arms around her, and whispered, "Thank you so much." I repeated this with each member of Joe's family, rejoicing in the wonderful family that I would soon be a part of.

Frank peered sheepishly at me as I passed his chair. "What about me, Maggie? I'm gonna help build your house too."

I ruffled his hair then hugged him tight and planted a big kiss on his cheek. "Thank you, little brother."

Grammy spoke up. "Maggie, Gramps and I have some extra furniture just sittin' round our house gatherin' dust, so I want you to come pick out what you need tomorrow."

chapter 18

Red dust hung sullenly in the air, obscuring the sun and making even the simple act of breathing near impossible. He readjusted his bandana over his face, leaving just his eyes exposed in hopes of keeping the unbearable dust out of his lungs.

He shook his head in disgust as he pushed his way out of the crowded auction barn. It just didn't seem possible amid all this chaos that he'd find anything here pleasing to his boss's liking, but he knew he had to try.

They'd run into some luck over in the southeastern part of Oklahoma. After arriving late on Wednesday, they'd had a full day to look over the stock and determine what they might want to bid on. Then on Friday the auction had gone so well, and everything they bid for they bought at a good price. Mr. Johnson had been exceptionally pleased with his choices and congratulated him on his good judgment in selecting the yearlings. Afterward, two of Johnson's other wranglers had headed back to Texas with the newly acquired horses, and he and the boss had moved on to an auction about fifty miles west of Oklahoma City.

He'd heard the news describing the dust but never imagined it would be so severe. And the sorrow evident in the tired, drawn faces of the emaciated men, women, and children who had made their journey there in a last attempt at survival just broke his heart. Their stock didn't fare much better, and he cringed as he looked over the skinny, gaunt cattle and the horses heaving and struggling to breathe, with ribs more apparent than any other feature on their bodies.

He bent his head down against the fine grains of sand blowing across the wasteland then trudged off toward the little cabin he was staying in. The auction was scheduled for Tuesday, and more folks were expected to bring in their stock to auction Sunday and Monday, but he didn't have high hopes that there'd be anything even worth bidding on come auction day.

He stumbled over what he thought was a rock sticking up out of the ground then about fell over when he realized it was a young boy huddled up, trying to stay out of the worst of the dust. He hauled the frightened boy up into his arms and sheltered him against his chest then jogged the rest of the way to the cabin. He quickly slammed the door, trying to keep out the dust, but even with the shutters and door closed tight, it seeped in. He set the boy down on his bunk then perched himself on the opposite bed. The tiny, shrunken boy appeared around four or five, and his anxious eyes were wide with fright as he stared up at Joe.

"Where're your folks, son?" he kindly asked the nervous boy.

"Mama's done been lost to the dust. Papa's someplace round here, but we got separated and I couldn't find him, so I just hunkered down to wait, hopin' he'd find me."

He gazed at the scrawny boy, puzzled that a child so young would be so well versed. "How old are you, son?"

The stoic boy stared back. "Almost 'leven, come the end of September."

He ran his hand over his face and rubbed at the tears burning behind his eyes. "What's your papa's name?"

"Jed, Jed Peters. And I'm Junior." The boy stuck out his hand.

He shook it and held the frail hand in his. "Why don't you stay here out of the dust for a bit, and I'll go look for your papa. There's a couple other men stayin' here too, but you just tell 'em you're with Joe, and they won't bother you none 'bout bein' here."

The child nodded and timidly glanced around as if only then noticing his snug surroundings. His empty eyes fixed on the table, and then he stared back at Joe with a glazed, hungry scowl.

Joe stepped over to the table and cut off a small hunk of bread and a quantity of hard cheese then shakily poured out a glass of water. He gazed sadly at the pitiful child and muttered, "You eat this real slow now. It appears you ain't had much to eat in a bit, so I don't want you to hurt yourself eatin' too much."

The impatient boy nodded hungrily and quickly wolfed down the meager offering.

⌐

He yanked his hat down lower over his eyes and bent into the whirling wind, intent only on making it back to the auction barn as quickly as possible. He held his bandana in place over his mouth and nose with one hand and then stretched out the other to help him avoid walking into anything. The swirling dust seemed worse than just a half hour before, and he hated the thought of spending three or four days fighting against it. He couldn't imagine how the fine folks had suffered and lived through the last few years of never-ending dust storms. It was enough to wear the soul right out of a man.

He finally felt the wall of the barn with his hand and followed it along to the doors. Once inside, the kerosene lanterns did little to penetrate the dust cloud that had settled permanently in the air around the men and animals crowded together in the barn.

He rambled from stall to stall inquiring after Jed Peters until he finally found someone who knew the man. The man nodded and pointed off toward the very back of the barn and told him that's where he'd find Peters.

He stopped at the last stall in the very back of the barn and observed a tiny, wrinkled old man carefully brushing his skeletal horse. He called out, "Mr. Peters?"

The aged man turned and nodded.

"I found your boy, Mr. Peters. He was hidin' from the dust and scared as all get out 'cause he couldn't find you."

The man looked around him. "Don't see him here. Hope he didn't cause you no trouble."

He shook his head. "No, no, he's back at my cabin. He was really scared that he couldn't find you, and I had no idea he was as old as he is. He looks 'bout five years old."

"That's Junior; he's a sight, now ain't he." Peters spit out dust then wiped his mouth on his sleeve. "Ain't never gonna get it out of my lungs."

"Junior's okay, Mr. Peters. He just got scared when he couldn't find you."

"That's what you said, son. Call me Jed. I know I look somethin' awful, but I'm only thirty-nine myself. It ain't been an easy life lately."

He heaved a sigh and adjusted his shielding bandana. "How long y'all been out in this dang dust?"

"Seems like forever, but tweren't two, maybe three years since the pond dried up, almost that long since the grass blew away. We tried to get out sooner, but there's just nowhere else to go."

"Ever'one here ... their story 'bout the same? I just ain't seen nothin' this bad in my life, Mr. Peters ... Jed."

"You won't again, 'less you come back. Can't keep the dust down." His sad eyes filled with tears, so he turned back to brushing his bony horse.

"Jed, your son was tellin' me he lost his mama to the dust. Did the pneumonia take her?"

"Naw, she actually disappeared into the dust. One day she and my baby girl was walkin' back home from what was left of the town when a dust storm blew up and took 'em … took 'em both. I searched for days; never found a trace of either one."

He leaned against the stall, his face registering disbelief. "What caused this? I never seen anything like it in my life!"

"I know, boy … what'd ya say your name was?"

"Sorry, I'm Joe, Joe Gilley. Came up with my boss to pick up a few horses."

"People here be willin' to trade you whatever they got just for a meal, Joe. But what they got most likely ain't what ya need. I's you, I'd pull out as fast as I could."

I woke up bright and early Saturday morning, counting my blessings and sweetly recalling that in less than a week Joe and I would be married. I lay there for a while, thinking about him and wishing he was there with me. Then without warning, a feeling of intense yearning came over me, and without thinking, I drew in my breath and moaned softly.

Lilly shot up and stared at me. "What's wrong, Maggie? Does your tummy hurt?"

I laughed. "Not at all, little one. I was just thinkin' 'bout Joe."

"Does he make your tummy hurt?" she asked innocently.

I rolled out of bed. "Nope, not in the least. I'm just missin' him and wishin' he'd come home."

Mary carefully crawled over Janie, Kate, and Jessie then sat down on the edge of the bed. "How come boys make your stomach hurt, Maggie?"

I let out a scream, waking all the girls up. They looked

accusingly at me, and Janie complained, "It's too early to get up, Maggie! Why'd you have to be so loud!"

"Don't forget, we're all goin' over to the Gilleys' in a bit to work on the new house. And Pop said he and Dorrie will take y'all up to the corral sometime this mornin' so you girls can spend some time playin' with Starlight too."

They scrambled happily out of bed and took off running down the hall. I laughed to myself as I took out a clean pair of slacks and a freshly washed white cotton blouse. I placed them carefully on the bed, my mind wandering again, and started to get dressed.

I heard Mary clear her throat. "I thought you scampered out with the other girls, Mary. Did you need me to help you with anything?"

She peered down at the floor then shyly raised her eyes to mine. "I just wanted to ask you 'bout somethin'."

"Okay, sweetie, what'd you want to ask me?"

She twisted around in her chair and glanced timidly around the room. "Well, it's kinda personal."

I squatted down next to her and whispered, "I'm not goin' to tell anyone, Mary. Whatever you need to ask me is our little secret."

Her face reddened, and she whispered back, "How'd you know you were in love with Joe?"

I gazed affectionately at her sweet face. "Well, I guess I'd had feelings for him for a really long time, almost from the time I was your age. Then when we started courtin', my feelings just kept growin' stronger, and the better I got to know him, the more I started carin' 'bout him. Then one day I just woke up and realized I loved him dearly."

She lowered her eyes and asked searchingly, "So do you think I'm too young to fall in love?"

"I didn't think I was when I was thirteen, but it was a different kind of love than what I feel now. But that don't make it any less real or less important. And blessedly, my first love was also my only love. What's more, all those years I had such a big crush on Joe. I never knew that someday he'd fall in love with me too."

She grinned. "I'm glad he did."

I kissed her cheek. "Me too!"

She walked over to the bed and sat down. "I think I have that same kind of crush on a boy at church."

"And who is this boy at church?" I teased.

"Never you mind, Maggie. If I ever decide to marry him, then you'll know."

"Well, okay then, but Mary, anytime you feel a need to talk more about such things, you know where I'll be."

"Yep, all cuddled up with Joe and not payin' any attention to anything else."

I laughed. "That doesn't sound like such a bad idea to me."

I hurried through breakfast and tried to get everyone out the door and on the road, but it took much longer than I'd supposed.

We finally arrived at Pop's about eight and found the men from the church had already arrived and moved most of the lumber and supplies down beyond the little pond. Frank and I hurried over to see what we could do to help, and they put Frank to work straight away.

Pop noticed my downcast face and strolled over. "Wait till we get the structure up, Maggie. Then you and the girls can come help us. There'll still be a lot to do, so while you're waitin', why don't you head on over to my folks' place. They really want to give you and Joe Edward some of their furniture and things."

I nodded. "I'll see if Mama wants to go with me, but later on I really, really would like to help with the house."

I trudged impatiently back up to the main house, feeling useless. Mama was right. It was such a man's world. I grumbled my way to the porch and into the kitchen. Mama and Mom took one look at me and laughed.

Mama teased, "They won't let you help, now will they, Maggie?"

I rolled my eyes and sighed. "I don't know how they expect me just to sit while they do everything! It's not like I've never used a hammer before."

Mom put her arms around me. "These men just aren't used to a woman who knows her own mind."

I sighed again. "If Joe was home...oh bother! Would you two like to go over to Grammy's with me for a bit?"

Mom shook her head. "Not right now; I've got the girls playin' out back, and I told 'em they could come help me bake up a batch or two of cookies when I finish up with this ham."

Mama begged off too, saying she was already worn out from the walk over that morning.

I settled on riding Pal instead. Thus I willfully headed off to the barn. After I'd set out, I heard Mary calling after me, so I stopped and waited for her. "Mama told me you were goin' to pick out furniture, so I thought I might go too if you want me to."

I hugged her, my mood improving, and we sprinted cheerfully up the hill to the barn.

Grammy rested serenely out on her porch, but she stirred as Pal trotted toward the house. She waved heartily and motioned to us to follow her inside. After I'd tethered Pal, we jumped up the steps and followed Grammy to the back of the house.

She opened up two of the back rooms and told us to explore at our leisure and grab hold of anything we saw fit. Both rooms were crammed full of boxes, trinkets, and furniture. It seemed to be an impossible task, but as we plowed through the boxes, we found treasures that made us both squeal in delight.

I put aside a few handmade doilies, and Mary discovered a beautifully made wedding ring quilt. She laid it to one side as she dug deeper into the box. I wandered over to a four-poster bedstead and climbed up on the mattress. It still felt firm and barely used, and the woodwork on the frame was beautiful. I admired the little tables that sat on either side of it and squealed in delight at the double dresser hidden under a pile of old clothes.

Grammy appeared again about an hour later, glancing over our piles of treasures and smiling. "I haven't seen this old thing in ages." She picked up the wedding ring quilt. "My mama made this for me when Otis and I married. It looks to be in good shape, and I'd be right pleased for you and Joe Edward to have it."

We let her see the fine goods we'd collected, and she happily reminisced about each and every one. I asked her about the bedstead, and she smiled sweetly. "That belonged to my dear brother and his wife. They moved back east to where her folks lived many, many years ago and left that set with us. I always hoped I'd get to see him again someday, but I haven't heard hide nor hair from him in goin' on twenty years."

She wandered over to the other room and pointed out a pair of matching chairs. "These chairs here belonged to my brother as well and was left behind. I just never seen fit to get rid of 'em 'cause I always hoped one day he'd come back to claim 'em." She sighed in resignation. "I think it only fittin' you and Joe Edward take this furniture. Tom would have wanted y'all to have it."

I hugged her and thanked her profusely. Then she turned to Mary. "You pick out somethin' too, child."

Mary beamed and held up a beautifully crocheted pink shawl. Grammy grinned. "You picked the very best prize of all, little one."

We dragged a few boxes out on the porch and cleared out around the furniture so we could come back with the truck later and easily cart our recently obtained possessions to the new little house. Then we mounted up and headed back to see how the framing work was progressing.

It was near noon when we crossed the pasture toward the little pond. All and sundry were sprawled out in the shade of the big oak, enjoying Mom's ham and potato salad, and the girls joyfully dashed around, handing out cookies hot from the oven.

Mary and I strolled over to where Rueben and Frank lazily dozed. Rueben opened one eye and offered, "Take the weight off your feet and sit a spell."

I scrutinized the building site and then plopped down next to Frank. "How close to finishin' are you?"

Rueben sat up and grinned. "Maggie, buildin' a house takes a lot of work and time. It ain't quite like constructin' a barn. Pop and I dug out the sod a few days back and readied the building site by settin' in some piers. This mornin' things went a lot faster, havin' so many hands to help out, but there's still a mountain of work to get done."

I grumbled. "Y'all should have let me help this mornin'. Then we'd be even farther along."

Frank let out a whoop, and I glared at him. "I can work just as good as you, Frank Bowen."

Rueben intervened. "Well, after everybody finishes up with lunch, you can come help pack the sod."

I looked questioningly at him. "Okay, what'll I need to do?"

"Well, first thing I'd do is go change out of that white shirt; otherwise it'll never be white again."

"I meant with the sod."

He grinned. "I know what you meant, but you're just fun to tease." I rolled my eyes at him, and he continued. "We have the inner frame up, and we built boxes akin to picture frames on the outside. Now we need to pack these boxes with the sod to insulate the walls. After that we'll board it up nice and tight, and it should keep the worst of the weather out."

Pop ambled over to us. "I negotiated with Albert Green over yonder, and he's set to come out in a couple weeks and put in a well out back of the house." He scratched his chin. "First off, we'll have to set some pipe and get your water lines situated. Rueben and me will work on that as we get time. Then we'll still need to find someone to set a toilet. That might take a bit of doin'."

"I guess I didn't think about all the effort it takes to put up a house. I really appreciate all y'all are doin' for Joe and me."

He grunted. "Tweren't nothin'."

I jumped up and hugged him. "Thank you, Pop."

"You and Joe will have to use our bathroom for a few weeks till we get finished down here." He squinted out toward the building site. "Into the bargain, we unearthed a few kerosene lanterns for y'all to use till we can afford to put in the 'lectricity."

Mary leaped up beside me. "Let's go find something to change into, Maggie, so we can get started on the sod."

Frank muttered crossly, "Mary's gonna help."

She stuck her tongue out at him and marched off. I laughed out loud and then merrily chased after her as I hollered, "Mary, wait up." When I caught up to her I tendered a suggestion. "Let's ask Mom if we can use a couple of Joe's old shirts."

⤜᷍

Every fiber of my being ached after two and a half long, exhausting days laboring on the house. We'd even worked on Sunday afternoon after church in order to finish up by Wednesday, just in case Joe turned up early.

Our little house was almost completed, and most of the grueling work over and done with. Today we'd finished construction on the front porch, shingled the roof, and laid another coat of whitewash on the outside of the house. It turned out to be a right cute place, and I felt proud that I had a part in raising it.

Our house was made up of one big room with a small kitchen and a tiny enclosed bathroom on one end, and Pop decided to put a nice-sized rock fireplace on the other end. For now we placed shutters over our little windows, but I determined that someday maybe we'd try to get some glass fitted in them. I so loved how the house looked after Pop and Rueben lined the inside walls with pine boards. This created a warm, cozy atmosphere and generated the sensation of living in an aromatic forest, and I deemed my little house to be just about perfect.

My heart overflowed with joy as I walked around that wonderful room. I hugged everyone there at least a dozen times until Mama took me by the hand, marched me outside, and we walked off some of my excitement.

Pop drove up with his truck overloaded with our furniture precisely at the moment Mama and I returned. Once the furniture was all moved in and I'd set up our belongings just the way I liked, our little house felt like a real home. As I gazed around our cozy nest, I felt mighty proud of our inherited chairs and bedroom furniture, plus the tiny kitchen table with two straight-back chairs that Mom had provided. I was just burstin' to show it to Joe, although I knew it was best to wait and surprise him after our honeymoon.

He wearily leaned his throbbing head back against the worn car seat and heaved a sigh. Mr. Johnson nodded. "Been a rough few days, now ain't it, Joe?"

"Mmhmm," he grunted out.

"Well, you just lean on back and rest a spell. Then 'fore long I'll switch out with you and catch a bit of rest myself."

He silently nodded an agreement as he sank deeper into the seat. His tired-out body ached for sleep, yet his tortured mind tormented him with unpleasant images from the past week.

His thoughts darkened as he remembered his encounter with Jed Peters and his son. He shifted edgily in the seat as haunting images of Junior flashed before his eyes, and unwillingly, he once again dredged up what took place after he and Jed found their way back to his cabin.

The cabin door easily blew open, but it took both men to

force it shut against the strength of the wildly blowing wind. An unrelenting cloud of dust followed them inside and settled around them as their eyes adjusted to the semi-darkness of the little cabin. At first Joe had felt frightened because he didn't see the boy. Then his heart about stopped when he noticed the frail, lifeless child tightly curled up in the far corner of his bunk.

Jed strode over to his son and softly shook him, but the boy didn't move. Joe's heart jumped up into his throat, and tears welled up in his eyes. "Jed," he began, but words abandoned him.

Jed gazed back at him and nodded. "It'll be all right, Joe. He's just plum tuckered out. He's still breathin', son." A silent tear slid down his face as he dropped down on the bunk and continued. "Don't know when the last time the two of us had a clean bed to lay upon. I just ain't had the energy or the gumption to do any cleanin' round our place. It about takes ever' bit of strength I find just to try and keep my boy and my stock alive."

Joe finally let out the breath he'd been holding. "Why don't the two of you come on down to Texas with us? It'd be a heap better'n here."

Jed's eyes filled with tears. "That's a mighty fine offer, Joe...a mighty fine offer. Truth is, I'm afraid to leave. Even though it's been a long spell since my sweet wife and little girl disappeared, I'm still prayin' and holdin' out hope that I'll find 'em someday."

"There's no one else could keep watch for you? No one who would let you know, even if you came for just a short while to get your strength built up?"

"Did you ever love someone, Joe?" He hung his head and sighed. "Without doubt, we'd be better off leavin', but I simply can't leave; it just ain't gonna happen. 'Sides, I've poured my whole life into my land. It's where we belong, and I rightly believe someday the rain will fall and the grass will come back. I just hope I'm alive to see it."

They'd stayed the night there, while Joe rolled out his pack and slept on the floor. Early the next morning they vanished, leaving only dismal images behind, which Joe knew beyond a shadow of a doubt would haunt him all of his life.

He groaned out loud and rubbed his face hard to try to stifle the heartbreaking images. He casually glanced over at his boss. "Need me to drive for you yet, Mr. Johnson."

"Naw, you just relax, son. I'll let you know when I need you."

He gazed off into the distance and thought how blessed he'd always been. Sadly, he closed his eyes and fervently prayed for Jed and Junior, prayed that somehow they would endure and their lives would greatly improve.

After that, his soul felt more at peace, and as his drowsy eyes finally closed, sweet images of his Maggie overflowed within him.

The last vestiges of sunlight faded, and twilight deepened as I paced nervously around the porch, anxious to hear from Joe. Mary sat in Mama's rocking chair, patiently keeping me company.

"You know he won't disappoint you, Maggie. He said he'd be home no later'n today, so you know he will."

"I know you're right, Mary. I'm just feelin' so impatient right now," I half sobbed.

She came up behind me and pushed me toward the chair. "You wouldn't be half so jumpy if you'd just sit down." She took hold of my shoulders and forced me down into the rocking chair. "Now you just sit here till I get back. I'm gonna go get you a sip of cold water, and maybe that'll help."

I smiled at her determination and thought she'd be a good help to Mama once Joe and I were married.

I sat quietly in the dark, trying to make out shapes in the yard, but my eyes kept spotting movement and I kept thinking it must be Joe. I closed my eyes and leaned back in the chair, and my feet unconsciously set the rocker in motion. I tried to keep myself from searching the shadows, but every time I closed my eyes I kept hearing the sound of a car driving up the road and I'd jump, even though I knew in my heart it was all just my wishful imaginings.

Tomorrow, Friday morning, Joe and I would say our vows, and I knew beyond a shadow of a doubt, as Mary reminded me, that nothing would stop Joe from making it home to me.

I squinted as shadows danced in front of my eyes. Jack stirred at my feet and stretched. I rubbed his ears, and he lifted his head in satisfaction. "You're a good dog, Jack," I whispered. His faithful eyes looked up happily at me when I said his name. I leaned back in the chair, staring blindly at the ceiling, and rocked slowly back and forth. The steady, rhythmic movement soothed me, and I'd about drifted off when suddenly Jack set up at attention.

"What's wrong, boy?" His ears went back, and his whole body started quivering in excitement. He whined and took off running down the steps.

I heard Joe's voice before I saw him step out of the shadows. Jack was jumping around him, begging for attention, but his gaze was only for me.

I met him at the bottom of the steps and fell into his arms. He whispered, "Lord, I've missed you, Maggie." Then he kissed me long and slow.

I sighed with sweet satisfaction and tenderly caressed his tired face. "You look so worn out, honey."

"I am, baby, just bone tired, but I wanted to stop by for just a bit 'fore I headed home. I didn't want you to think I'd stood you up at the altar." He wearily sat down on the steps, pulling me down beside him.

He wrapped his arm around me and kissed me. He sighed heavily. "Mr. Johnson stopped off at home for a bit, so I told him I'd walk on up to see you after I got the horses stabled. He's gonna run by here in a while and drive me on out to the house."

"Did you find what he was looking for?"

"Yep, we picked up a few yearlings and a couple of two-year-olds. They'll be good horses for him." He laid his head against mine and kissed my cheek. "I also found some of the prettiest land I ever saw up in southeastern Oklahoma. Someday maybe we'll get us a parcel of it."

I snuggled up next to him and laid my head on his shoulder. He leaned back against the post and drew me closer, and we sat there quietly holding hands, content just to be together in that precious moment in time.

Too soon headlights shone in the darkness, and Joe was gone.

chapter 19

In the early morning hours I arose quietly from bed, trying hard not to wake the girls. Lilly stirred beside me, smiled in her sleep, and then turned over without waking. I held my breath and tiptoed into the hallway, quietly pulling the door closed behind me. It had been the last night I'd share a bed with my sisters, but I didn't think they'd mind a bit because it meant there'd be more room for them to wiggle around.

I heard Mama in the kitchen, so I wandered in and sat quietly at the table. She turned from the stove and smiled at me. "Too excited to sleep, honey?"

"Mmhmm, a little anyway. I was feeling a little sad too 'cause I'll miss bein' here with all of y'all."

She walked over to me and cuddled me in her arms. "You won't be far away, baby, not at all, and you know we'll just be right here anytime you need a horde of kids around you."

"I'm glad Will could come home for the weddin' and you could get off work."

"There's nothin' that could keep me from bein' with you today, Maggie." Mama kissed me lightly and smiled. Then she sat down across from me, and her expression changed. "What did you decide to do about your papa and Rachel? I know he's been frettin' round 'bout comin' to your weddin' 'cause the little ones have told me all about it."

I stood up in frustration and walked over to the sink. I stared sightlessly out the window. "I didn't want to be mean, Mama, but I told him I wasn't ready to have him back in my life again. And I told him I didn't want any ugliness to overshadow this day for me."

"He's your papa, Maggie. You're his firstborn child, and no matter how he's hurt me, he still loves you. If you're afraid how it'd make me feel to see him and Rachel there, please don't worry. I haven't let it bother me in a long while."

I tenderly kissed her cheek. "You deserve better, Mama. Maybe someday I'll make my peace with Papa, but not today, not on my weddin' day. And you know how Joe feels about the way Papa has treated both you and me."

"I do know, and that's the last I'll say on it. I just didn't want to be the reason you kept him away." She crossed to the stove and started stirring the pot again. "I have this oatmeal all ready if you want some."

"No thank you, Mama. I don't think I can eat a thing this mornin'."

"Well, at least try a piece of toast and a glass of milk. You don't have to be at the church till eleven, and it's barely six now." She placed a plate in front of me. "Take this over to the table, and I'll bring you a glass of milk."

I played with the toast for a while and drank a little of the milk, but I was filled with so much nervous energy that I just couldn't eat.

After a bit Will and Frank stumbled into the kitchen. Will looked as though he'd grown a foot since I'd last seen him. It might have been exaggerating, but not by much.

He grinned at me. "You look as jumpy as a jackrabbit."

I shrugged my shoulders. "Can't imagine why."

He hugged me tightly. "I love you, Maggie. Joe's a lucky

man to win my sister's heart, and you just tell him he best be good to you or he'll have me to deal with."

I laughed happily. "Oh, I've missed you, Will."

He straddled the chair next to mine. "Did ya miss me enough to fetch me a bowl of that oatmeal?"

I stared at him in mock annoyance. "Not at all; you can just get up and get your own oatmeal, son." Then I tugged his ear playfully and walked to the stove. "What about you, Frank? Do you want oatmeal?"

Frank yawned sleepily and nodded as he laid his head down on the table.

Mama sat down next to him and ruffled his hair. "Looks like someone got up too early this mornin'." Then she turned to me. "What'd you decide to wear today, Maggie?"

"I'm goin' to wear my blue sundress."

"You look real pretty in that dress, honey."

I smiled sweetly, wondering if Joe would remember that it was the dress I was wearing the first time he kissed me. I really hoped he would.

A rumble of thunder came barreling through the house as Jessie, Lilly, and Kate tumbled into the kitchen. They all piled up to the table sleepily, and Mama grinned at them. "Did you girls sleep okay?"

They answered in unison, "Mmhmm."

"Are Mary and Janie up yet?" Mama asked.

"Janie's still sleepin'," Kate explained.

"And Mary's in the bathroom fixin' her hair. I think she has a boyfriend." Jessie giggled.

"Oh great!" Frank exclaimed. "Another girl takin' up all the time in the bathroom." He looked hard at me.

"Hey! I never took up any time in the bathroom; you must be thinkin' of another sister." I smiled and stuck my tongue out at him.

I wandered back into the bedroom and fetched my blue sundress from the closet. I held it up next to me and twirled around. Janie sat up in the bed and stared at me. "You look pretty, Maggie."

"I feel pretty, Janie, so I guess that's what makes me pretty."

"I hope I grow up as pretty as you." She sighed.

"You're already ten times prettier than me, Janie. Why, when I was ten years old, I was all legs and my curls were so tight I looked a fright, but you, baby, you're just a beautiful young lady."

She glowed at me as she reached up to hug me. "I'm gonna miss your cold feet, Maggie." She giggled.

"And I'm gonna miss your snorin', Janie."

"Hey, I don't snore!"

I laughed at the stunned look on her face. "Here, help me pin up my hair. I want to look like a grown-up lady today."

She jumped off the bed and stood behind me as I sat down on the edge of the bed. She lifted my hair up and let it fall. "I like it down best."

"Do you? Well, let's try it pinned up. Then if we don't like it, we'll let it go wild," I said as I shook my head wildly back and forth.

She giggled again as Mary came into the room. "What y'all doin'?" she asked.

"Maggie wants to look like a grown-up lady," Janie explained.

Mary strolled over to the bed. "Let me help. I'm good at doin' hair."

"I'd really appreciate it, Mary."

Mama called down the hall, "Girls, it's close on ten o'clock. Y'all need to start gettin' ready if we're goin' to be at the church by eleven."

"Okay, Mama," we all called in unison, and then we burst into a fit of laughter.

Mary straightened up first. "Now, Maggie, come sit in this chair and let me fix you."

Within minutes Mary had transformed my mop of curls into something wonderful. Most of my hair was caught up loosely atop my head, with just a few sweet tendrils floating around my face. I gazed in the mirror and thought I really did look beautiful.

Mary shook her finger at me. "Now don't you go messin' up all my hard work when you put on that dress."

I kissed her cheek. "I won't, darlin', I promise. Now you two scoot while I finish gettin' ready."

I'd barely finished zipping my dress when three little girls rushed rapidly into the room, carrying a woven chain of white clover. "Look what we made for you, Maggie," Kate cried. "It's for your weddin'. You know your 'sposed to have flowers for your weddin'."

My eyes teared up at all the sweetness my dear family was showering upon me. "Thank you, girls! They're lovely. Now go find Mary and tell her I need her."

The warm September sun shimmered softly in a cloudless sky as he waited outside the church for her. Fortunately, he'd fallen asleep the instant his head hit the pillow last night, and he'd slept like a log. Now he felt refreshed and ready for the most important day, the most important moment of his life so far because today Maggie would become his wife.

He heard their laughter before he saw them approaching. Maggie looked radiant in her blue dress with her hair pinned up and full of flowers. She glanced up at the church and saw him, so she ran ahead of her family and into his arms.

"Mornin', beautiful," he whispered as he dropped a kiss on her nose.

"Mornin', yourself. You look quite beautiful too."

"Men aren't supposed to be beautiful," he teased.

"Well, you are." She beamed.

Her family caught up to them, so he sauntered over and hugged her mama. "Mornin', Mrs. Bowen. Everybody's inside if y'all want to go on in. Maggie and I'll be right behind you."

She kissed his cheek. "You can call me Mama, Joe. You don't have to be so formal, you know."

He grinned at her. "I'd be right pleased to call you Mama Jo."

She laughed at his joke. "Be careful now. I'm not against disciplinin' my children."

After they were safely inside the church, he turned to Maggie. "You look so pretty, baby. Your hair and your dress…"

"Mmhmm."

He smiled. "I remember this dress, you know. I remember it so well 'cause it's the dress you were wearin' the first time you let me kiss you."

"You do remember," she cried happily.

"Yep." He paused and held her away from him then looked her up and down. "I do remember, and I remember how temptin' it was to want to kiss this little spot right here." He ran his fingers seductively under the shoulder strap of her dress, and the strap slipped down off her shoulder. He tenderly kissed her shoulder and then let his lips travel up to hers.

She sighed happily and started up the steps to the church door. He tugged on her hand, and when she twirled around to him, he looked at her sternly. "There's just one thing, honey, one little thing before we can go in and get married."

Her eyes widened. "What's wrong, Joe?"

"Well, look." He pointed down at her feet.

She looked stunned. "What?"

His smile broadened. "Maggie, you're wearin' shoes!"

"But Joe, we're gettin' married, and besides, I always wear shoes at church."

"No, you don't," he teased.

"I do, I always do!"

"Naw, you just wear 'em in the door; then you slip 'em off the minute you're in the pew." He laughed and kissed her tenderly. "I'm just teasin' you, honey. You can wear your shoes."

He took her hand. "Rueben and Hannah said you asked 'em to stand up with us today, so I told 'em to sit up front."

"Good, I meant to mention it to you last night, but my mind wasn't on it."

"You have a beautiful mind." He gazed lovingly at her and held her close. "I love you so much, Maggie." He kissed away her reply then whispered, "You ready?"

"No."

He looked puzzled until she reached down and slipped off her shoes. She carefully placed them next to the church steps then smiled up at him. "Now I'm ready. Let's go get married."

<hr>

We walked down the aisle hand in hand. It seemed strange to me for everyone to be looking back and watching us come in, but I felt so proud to be there with Joe that even my discomfort at being on display couldn't rattle me.

I noticed Mama's eyes on me as we walked by her. She put on her "Oh, Maggie" look as she caught sight of my feet, but her eyes sparkled with joy.

Hannah and Rueben waited at the front for us, watching happily as we drew near them. Hannah grabbed me in a big hug as soon as I reached her then turned to hug Joe. Rueben grinned at me and gave me a quick peck on the cheek, and then he turned and shook Joe's hand. Joe laughed and wrapped his arms around his younger brother in a big bear hug.

The pastor cleared his throat and smiled at us as we turned our attention to him. "Joe, Maggie, are you both ready to begin?"

We nodded solemnly. Joe reached over and took my hand, so I smiled up at him, and he kissed me sweetly.

The pastor grinned at us. "I think that part comes a little later on, Joe."

Everybody laughed, and I had to defy an almost irresistible urge to kiss him again. But he winked at me and lightly caressed my hand, so I tried to be good.

We gazed earnestly at the pastor as he began the ceremony. "May God's presence be felt here with us today as Joe Edward Gilley and Opal Margaret Bowen join their lives together as husband and wife in the holiness of his precious love."

An abundance of emotion flooded through me, and I struggled hard to focus as my heart did a little dance of joy. I whispered a silent prayer of thanks as the pastor spoke words that saturated my very soul with the essence of the spirit and the joy of lasting love.

"On this day, Joe and Maggie pledge their love for one another in the presence of God and all who are assembled here." He looked at Joe. "Joe, do you take Maggie to be your wife, to love her, honor her, cherish her, and protect her through times of feast and times of famine, to honor her as the woman God has placed in your life to love?"

He gazed tenderly into my eyes. "I do."

"And do you, Maggie, take Joe to be your husband, to love him, honor him, cherish him, and protect him through times of feast and times of famine, to honor him as the man God has placed in your life to love?"

My heart fluttered with delight. "I do."

The pastor joined our hands together in his. "Joe, Maggie, in as much as we here have witnessed your marriage, and by the power vested in me, I happily pronounce you husband and wife." He nodded and smiled at Joe. "Now, son, you may kiss your bride."

And he did … beautifully.

Everyone gathered around us at the altar, alternately hugging me or clapping Joe on the back. After a few minutes, I glanced around and caught Joe's eye. He smiled knowingly at me from across the aisle then pushed his way through the throng of family and friends to my side. He squeezed between his mom and Mama, who were happily talking to me, even though I couldn't comprehend a word of what they'd said. Joe's mom grabbed hold of him and hugged him tightly. He kissed her forehead, muttered thanks, and held out his arms to me. I squeezed past Hannah and her sister, Grace, avoided Mary's grasp, and hid myself in his arms. It felt so good, so right, just to be close to him.

Then all of a sudden, I felt myself being lifted off the floor as Joe scooped me up and pushed his way across the church, saying "Excuse me, beg your pardon," and, "Thank you," as he aggressively made his way out the door.

We'd made it to the bottom step before Joe's pop called after us. "The car's round back, Son. If y'all are ready to go, I'll go get Mom and Dorrie and we can head for the house."

Joe responded quickly, "Thanks, Pop, but I've got my horse all ready, so we'll see y'all over at the house in a bit."

"Rueben can take the horse home for you, Joe. You don't want Maggie to have to ride all dressed up now."

I called out, "We're goin' by Mama's, so I can get my bag and change, Pop. It won't take too long." I smiled sweetly at him, so he just shook his head, laughed, and moved back into the church.

Joe grinned at me. "Looks like you win." Then he lifted me up into the saddle, climbed up in back of the saddle, stuck his long legs out, and adjusted his feet into the stirrups. I wiggled my toes in on top of his boots, and he laughed happily. He wrapped one arm around me and with the other guided Redwing out of the churchyard.

I leaned back and kissed his cheek. "You're so clever, sweetie."

"It pays to have a well-trained horse. Anyway, I'd about had enough huggin' and kissin' from others. I just need huggin' with you, baby."

"Me too." I sighed. "The families will all be at your house soon, so at least we'll have a few minutes alone before we get there."

"Mmhmm, I thought about that, so we'll just mosey along and take our time gettin' there." His arm tightened around me, and I felt his lips softly brush against my neck.

We rode up to Mama's empty house, and Joe slid off the back end of the horse. I threw my leg over Redwing's back and started to dismount. He caught me by the waist and lifted me down, kissed me, and then led the horse out toward the back of the house. "I'll go water him then be back shortly."

"Okay, honey," I called. "I'll go change and put a few things in my bag. Then I'll be right out."

I wandered into the house, feeling sentimental and a little sad that I'd not be with Mama and the kids anymore, although those musings were overshadowed by the joy I felt each time I thought of my life, my future with Joe.

I stepped into my bedroom, pulled out Mama's traveling bag, and sorted through my meager collection of clothes. I folded a few things and placed them in the bag then laid out a pair of slacks and my favorite blouse.

I glanced around the room, thinking back over all the memories I'd lived in the house. I smiled when I noticed the bed was still unmade, a testament to the rush this morning with all us girls trying to get ready at the same time, so I smoothed out the quilt and plumped up the pillows. Then I reached around to unzip the back of my dress.

At that moment I felt Joe's hands on my shoulders and his lips softly kissing the nape of my neck. He whispered amorously, "Let me help you with that."

I caught his hand and clutched it under my chin in a quick

hug. He pulled me closer, kissing my neck and shoulders and whispering, "I love you, Maggie," tenderly in my ear. I moaned and spun into his arms. His hands flowed down my back, slowly unzipping my dress. An overwhelming yearning engulfed me as I wrapped my arms around his neck and hungrily kissed him.

He began walking me backward toward the bed, and I uttered a feeble protest, "We're in my mama's house, Joe."

His dark eyes burned into mine. "We're in my wife's bedroom, in her bed…" His lips captured mine as my hands found their way to his shirt, and almost unconsciously I started unbuttoning it. I ran my hands over his bare chest and wound my arms around him, kissing his neck, whispering, "Everyone's goin' to be waitin' for us at your parents' house."

He pulled me down onto the bed beside him. "That's good, baby. That means they're not here with us." Then our impatient lips collided, and nothing else mattered.

As they rode quietly into the front yard, Frank came running up faster than a streak of lightning. "Where y'all been? Everybody's already here."

Maggie grinned at him. "We had to go by the house and get my things. Then I had to change clothes and everything."

He kissed her cheek before he slid off his horse. "'Sides, Frank, y'all came in cars and we had to ride. That takes a bit longer, you know."

Frank gazed at Redwing as Maggie dismounted. "Want me to go stable him, Joe?"

"Yep, that's exactly what I want," he affirmed, knowing how happy Frank was anytime he got to be near the horses.

Laughter greeted them as they strolled around to the back of the house where everyone waited. Maggie smiled as she spotted Will wholeheartedly exaggerating about life on the railroad. She laid her head on Joe's shoulder as they stood quietly by the house, listening with pleasure.

Mary noticed them first, crying out, "Maggie, you've done gone and messed up your hair!"

Maggie reached up self-consciously and touched her hair. "I'm sorry, Mary. I guess it came down during our ride out here."

He rubbed her back gently then drew her close and was rewarded with her brilliant smile. Jessie ran over to them, looking Maggie over carefully. "Well, at least this time there's not any leaves or twigs stuck up in your hair."

Maggie rolled her eyes and blushed. "Jessie!"

"It's truth, Maggie!" Jessie argued.

He wrapped her in his arms and held her tightly, his joy in the day, in loving her, practically exploding within him. He whispered in her ear, "Maybe later we'll find us some of those leaves and twigs to decorate your hair, sweetie."

She laughed softly and kissed him. "Is that a promise?"

They were interrupted when Mama called them over to her. Maggie quickly crossed the yard, hugged her tightly, and took a seat beside her. Hannah was deep in conversation with Rueben, but when she caught sight of Maggie, she patted Rueben's arm and pointed in the direction of where they sat. He nodded, and she rushed over and parked herself next to them.

His mom wandered over to him and hugged him. "I'm so proud of you, Joe. It just makes my heart swell to think of my firstborn all married and happy."

He looked at her tenderly. "Thanks, Mom, I'm feelin' pretty dang proud myself today."

She wrapped her arm around his. "I've got lunch just about ready for y'all, but I'd really like to hear you play a little for me today. Why don't you go get your guitar and pick some for us; it touches my heart so."

"I reckon I could do that," he agreed kindly.

He noticed Maggie's eyes following him as he headed into

the house with his mom, so he winked at her and then joyfully jumped up the worn steps to go fetch his guitar.

As he hastened back outside, he caught sight of Maggie all huddled up with Hannah. He smiled at the sight they made, just like two schoolgirls telling secrets. He brushed his hand tenderly over Maggie's cheek, and she covered his hand with hers and brought it to her lips. He leaned over and kissed her, trailing away with her "I love you, honey" warming his heart.

He sat on the garden bench with his head bowed and started softly strumming chords. His heart wasn't really into playing the usual songs at the moment. He was in a much tenderer mood and wished all the while the family time would soon be done and he could slip silently away with Maggie.

His musings were interrupted when Janie came up and started pulling on his shirtsleeve. He glanced up at her and muttered, "Mmhmm?"

She bent over and looked up into his face quizzically. "I was wonderin' how come you wanted to marry my sister?"

A slow smile touched his lips, and his eyes lit up. "That's easy, Janie." He gazed over at Maggie, her gentle laugh floating over to him, her soft brown curls shining in the radiant sun, and her quick flash of a smile as she felt his eyes upon her. He picked a few more chords on the guitar and sighed happily.

"Well …" Janie demanded.

He grinned. "Sorry, I got lost in my thoughts."

Janie grinned back. "Are you gonna tell me?"

"Tell you what, pumpkin?"

"Geez! Why'd you marry my sister?" she insisted, her strident voice rising and carrying all through the yard.

His head still bent over the guitar, his hands softly picking out the notes, he tenderly expressed his heartfelt feelings. "For plenty of reasons, Janie. Your sister's brave and strong, she's got a fiery spirit that just sparks my soul, and she's the most tender-hearted woman I've ever known." He glanced over at Maggie, and his eyes locked with hers. "Besides which, Janie, I love her way down deep in my very soul. It's like..." He pondered for a moment and then asked, "Have you ever been really, really thirsty?"

Janie nodded, and he continued. "It's kinda like that, only the one thing that can quench my thirst is havin' Maggie close to me, knowin' she's nearby."

He saw her rise, and Hannah stretched out her hand to her, crying out, "Oh, Maggie," but she didn't stop. She came to him, cuddled up in his lap, and laid her soft curls on his shoulder. She tenderly kissed his neck and whispered a soft prayer. "Oh dear God, I love this man so much."

He leaned his guitar next to the bench and held her close. "Here now, look at you, honey, you're cryin' again." He kissed the tears from her eyes. "Maggie, darlin', it's okay. I love you so much, baby." He kissed her trembling lips tenderly then with deep passion, almost forgetting they weren't alone, but he was sharply reminded when Dorrie called out, "Joey!"

He laid his head on Maggie's shoulder and breathed deeply to try to bring himself back to the present. He gazed into Maggie's liquid brown eyes and replied, "Mmhmm."

Dorrie persisted, "Joey!" She pulled on his ear.

He gently pushed her little hand aside, shifted positions, sighed again, and patiently asked, "What?"

"Play the dreamy song for us."

"The dreamy song?"

"Yeah, you know, the dream a dream song," she pleaded.

He looked at Maggie and smiled because he knew she wasn't about to move. He picked up his guitar and balanced the body on one leg then reached around her and grasped the neck of the guitar. "Don't think I ever tried playin' this way, but it could be fun."

He grinned at everyone, "Guess I'll give it a try." He started picking out the chords then stopped and looked up at the heavens as Maggie laid her head on his shoulder and started lovingly kissing the back of his neck.

He readjusted his leg, looked down at his guitar, and offered, "I'm gonna give it a try, but I might just be a little distracted."

Everybody laughed, and then he began playing softly and sang, "*Stars shinin' up above you. Night breezes seem to whisper I love you—*"

Jessie hollered out, "I know that song! It's my most favorite song on the radio".

He smiled sweetly at her. "Well then, come sing it with me." He started again. "*Stars shinin' up above you. Night breezes seem to whisper I love you. Birds singin' in the sycamore tree. Dream a little dream of me.*"

Suddenly he stopped singing, but he continued playing, listening to Jessie's pure, sweet voice.

She finished proudly, and everyone clapped for her. He tweaked her under the chin. "Hey, peanut, that was right nice singin'. You keep on singin' like that, and one day we'll be listenin' to you on the radio."

Jessie beamed at him. "Play it again, Joe!"

He shook his head. "Not right now, Jess." Then he called out to his brother, saying, "Hey, Rueben, you come play for a bit." He handed the guitar to his brother and wrapped his arms around Maggie. "I think my arms are needed elsewhere."

She cuddled up closer to him and sang sweetly in his ear, "Dream a little dream of me."

He kissed her and whispered back, "Every day, love, every day."

He looked over at Rueben sitting close to Hannah and playing the guitar. "What do you think?"

Her eyes twinkled. "I don't know, but I hope so."

He nuzzled her neck. "What were the two a you all huddled up about over there?"

Maggie laughed softly. "Hannah asked me if I was feelin' nervous."

"About?"

"Our weddin' night ... you know ..."

"Mmhmm, and what'd you tell her?"

She grinned at him. "Terrified."

His grin broadened. "No, you didn't! You didn't seem so terrified earlier today."

She held his face in her hands and whispered, "Terrified of wakin' up and findin' this is only a dream."

He gazed affectionately into her eyes and stroked her hair. "Not even a bit of a dream, sweetie." He kissed her neck and uttered softly, "You are my wife in every sense of the word, and even though I feel my words just can't fully express how I feel, I hope you realize just how very much I love you."

His mom walked out on the porch and hollered, "We've got lunch all set out in here, so y'all come on in, grab a plate, and fix yourself somethin'." Then she disappeared back into the house.

He took a deep breath to try to help himself refocus on the world around them. "Let's go get a plate, baby. The sooner we eat, the sooner we can be off."

A few minutes later they found a spot under an old oak tree and sat down with their plates of food. Hannah and Rueben joined them, and they all began talking at once, which caused an outbreak of laughter that helped ease them all back into a semblance of normality.

Rueben spoke first. "How long you plan on takin' off work, Joe?"

"Well now, Mr. Johnson told me to take as much as a week, but I think I need to get back to earnin' a livin', seein' as how I have a wife to support now." He winked at her. "So I'll most likely go back Tuesday."

Hannah slid closer to Maggie. "Where y'all goin' on your honeymoon, Maggie?"

"Joe's plannin' on surprisin' me," she fibbed.

"It's a place Maggie and I both think of as really special, and we plan on headin' out soon as we finish up with lunch."

"Maggie, Hannah, and I spent some time lookin' for a rent house for y'all. We found a couple, but Maggie wanted to wait on you to make a decision," Rueben alleged with a quick wink at Maggie.

She coughed. "Yep, one of 'em was just perfect, except for the rent. I really didn't want to decide on something that cost that much without talkin' to you first, honey."

"Whatever you want, baby, we'll try and work it out. I made us an extra thirty dollars goin' up to Oklahoma, so we should be able to handle any extra expenses this month anyway."

"I know there'll be somethin' for us, so we'll see what we can find Monday when we get back."

"Pop and Mom said we can stay in Dorrie's room for a bit till we get a place of our own, and they'll just make her a little pallet in their room for the time being."

Rueben grinned, looking from one to the other. "I can't believe you two are married! Seems only yesterday I was catchin' Joe moonin' round Maggie's place, tryin' to get up the nerve to go ask her out."

"And Maggie was moonin' round school, wonderin' if he'd ever notice her," Hannah chimed in.

He draped his arm around Maggie. "And here you two are moonin' round each other in just about the same way." He looked at Maggie. "I think it's high time Rueben asked Hannah out. What do ya think, baby?"

Hannah blushed. "Joe Gilley!"

Rueben looked a little embarrassed but offered, "I been meanin' to do just that, but what with all the to-do with you two, I just haven't found the chance."

"What's wrong with right now, son?" He laughed.

Rueben eyed his brother and heaved a sigh. "Just too many people round here if ya ask me."

Hannah jumped up. "Excuse me just a minute. I think I left somethin' in the kitchen." She ran off rapidly toward the house.

Maggie leaped up to follow her. "Now just look what you two have done!"

"Wait, Maggie," Rueben called. "Let me go. It's my mess, and I'd like to try and fix it."

"Men!" Maggie sighed as she sat back down.

"Includin' me?" he asked.

"Yep, includin' you, even if I do love you and think you're adorable." She dropped a quick kiss on his nose.

He pulled her closer to him, and she lay back against his shoulder. He groaned. "Do you think Hannah will be okay?"

She sighed. "Yeah, she's just mortified right now, but hopefully Rueben can calm her down."

"Mortified. That sounds pretty bad to me."

"Embarrassed, silly."

"I know, I just thought it was a really heavy word to choose."

She flipped over and fixed her eyes on him. "Like I said, men!"

He tickled her under her chin. "Don't ya love it?"

"Hmmm ... I love you."

"Think we ought to go find 'em and try to smooth things over?"

She sat up. "No, I think it's best if Rueben takes care of all the smoothin' over." She stretched, raising her arms up above her head, and gazed at the sky. "Joe, look!"

"What you see, baby?"

"Look, the moon's rising!" she exclaimed excitedly.

He stood up and extended his hand to her. "I think this is my dance, love."

⌒✌⌒

I laid my head contentedly on his shoulder as we danced under the full rising moon. My heart swelled with happiness, and I felt lost in the magical moment, a moment when only the two of us existed. I felt his lips brush lovingly against my neck, so I gazed up adoringly into his dark, beautiful eyes. His lips met mine as we moved in rhythm to music only we could hear.

From somewhere faraway, voices penetrated my consciousness. I tried to ignore them, but Joe seemed bothered by them as well because he groaned and came to a standstill. I glanced around the yard and saw the girls hopping around excitedly, loudly exclaiming about something they obviously thought was very funny.

Pop strolled out of the house, wiping his hands on his napkin. "What's all the ruckus out here?"

Mary pointed at Joe and me. "Well, the little kids think it's funny that Maggie and Joe are dancin' without any music playin'."

Pop rolled his eyes. "Why don't you young'uns go play out front and leave those two alone for a bit."

Joe called out teasingly, "That's okay, Pop. I'm headed up to get the horses ready right now, so those little nosy spoilers can just stay and play to their hearts' content."

I followed Pop into the house, intent on putting together a few scraps of food to take with us for our wedding trip. Mama had settled in at the table and seemed deep in discussion with Grammy and Mom. I sauntered by, giving each one a hug and kiss, then asked Mom, "Do you mind if I take a bit of food for the weekend?"

Mom hopped up. "Not at all, Maggie. I already put back some of the ham, and we've got some apples, cheese, or whatever else y'all might have need of." She pulled out a basket from under the cabinet. "This here ought to hold just about whatever y'all need."

I took the basket from her. "You go sit back down, Mom. I can take care of fixin' up a few things to take."

"You'd best eat that ham tonight, Maggie. It's the only thing might spoil if it's left any longer."

Mama sat, chin in hand, gazing thoughtfully at me. "Maggie, you never did say where y'all are goin'. I'd kinda like to have an idea so if we needed to find y'all for any reason."

"Mama! You won't need to find us. We'll only be gone a few days," I complained.

Grammy spoke up. "Joe needs to let us know since it's suppose to be a surprise for you 'cause you never know when someone might just drop over dead, and then where'd we be? So it's right important for folks to know."

I kept my back to them, fussing over the stove and trying not to laugh. I could just imagine what they'd say if they knew where we were actually going. I finished packing a few essentials into the basket: a few slices of ham, a block of cheese, a loaf of freshly baked bread, and a small jar of blackberry jam. I looked around to make sure I hadn't forgotten anything and spotted the apples over by the cutting board. "Do you mind if I take about half a dozen of these apples, Mom? Joe likes to share them with the horses." I finished with a grin.

"You take as many as you need, honey. Our trees are still loaded down with 'em."

I scooped up a few extra and threw them in with the rest, and then I covered the basket with a clean dishtowel. "Well, I think I've got everything now, so I'll tell y'all bye then run on out to meet Joe."

"Maggie," Mama began.

"Okay, Mama, I'll tell Joe to let one of y'all know how to find us." I swooped down and kissed her on her cheek. "You just worry too much, you know."

"It's what mothers do. Just wait till your babies start comin'. Then you'll act the same way as me." She pulled me down and hugged me tightly. "My firstborn baby all grown up and goin' away with her new husband."

I laughed. "I like the sound of that an awful lot!" I kissed another round of kisses and hugged everyone one last time then grabbed the basket and scampered out the back door.

I glanced up toward the barn and waved as Joe rode down

the hill. He led Pal, who was acting as our packhorse and was heavily loaded down with saddlebags and a large, awkward bundle balanced on his back.

Pop strolled up behind me and wrapped his arm around my waist. "I had a good talk with that boy, Maggie. I told him to treat you kindly, and he knows what I mean."

"Thank you, Pop," I babbled, not quite ready to discuss such things with him.

"He's a good boy, and he'll make you a fine husband once he settles down. He's got a lot of tamin' to do, but I think you'll be right good for him."

"I hope I will, Pop, because I want to please him more than anything else in the world."

He looked at me curiously. "That's not quite what I was aimin' to mean, Maggie—"

I blushed from the top of my head to the end of my toes. "Oh, Pop, that's not what I was aimin' to mean either."

Joe rode up and dismounted. "What's goin' on?"

I shook my head and smiled. Pop nodded. "I's just tellin' Maggie how happy I know she's goin' to make you and how she needs to tame you just a bit; then you'll be a right good husband for her."

He raised his eyebrows questioningly at me, but I just kept smiling. He nodded. "Okay, well then, I guess we'll leave it at that then, Pop."

I caught Joe's hand, and we walked a few feet away. "Honey, Mama insists we tell someone where we're goin', so I told her I'd ask you to let one of them know."

"I'll talk to Rueben, and I'll let Gramps know. He'll get a kick out of it, I know." He noticed the basket I'd left sitting by the house. "You want that to go?"

"Mmhmm, I think I packed enough food for all three days, but I guess it depends how hungry we are."

He winked playfully, and I blushed again. He grinned

broadly. "Let's put the food in this empty saddlebag. Then I'll go find Rueben and talk to him a bit. After that, we'll head on out."

I helped him transfer the food to the saddlebag and then offered, "I noticed Rueben and Hannah sittin' on the front porch a little while ago. Looked like to me they'd made up."

He caught hold of my hand, and we leisurely wandered around the house to the front yard. He called out to Rueben, and they strolled over toward us. I quickly took hold of Hannah's hand, hauled her back over to the porch, and then firmly held both her hands in mine. "You mad at me?" I quietly asked her.

"No, I was just…"

"Mortified?" I asked with a grin.

"Embarrassed, yes, but…"

"But what?"

"Well, I think it actually kinda helped things."

"How?" I asked in surprise.

"Well,"—she peeked around my shoulder and ducked her head.

"Well…"

"He kissed me."

"And you let him! Hannah!"

"Maggie, stop it! You know how much I like him."

"Mmhmm!" I kissed her cheek. "I think he's probably goin' to make you a fine husband someday. He's a lot like his big brother, so he'll be a fine man."

She gazed over at Rueben. "He is, Maggie."

I smiled at her, and she fixed her eyes on me with a frown. "Maggie, you gonna be all right?"

"Hannah, sweetie, I'm already all right. I love Joe with every fiber of my bein', and I desire to love him always. It is exquisite to love someone the way I love him, the way I always, always want to love him."

"Maggie, I know you love him, but…"

I raised my eyebrows and looked knowingly at her then

spoke openly. "Hannah, I'm a married woman now. And it's wonderful—"

She blushed. "But you've only been married half a day."

"It's been a most magnificent half a day." I gazed over at Joe, who was deep in conversation with Rueben. "Someday I hope you feel what I do, Hannah. I pray you do."

Joe smiled at us, so I hurriedly kissed Hannah's cheek. "I love you, Hannah, and I'll see you one day next week." Then I darted over and wrapped my arms around him. "You ready, sweetie?"

"More'n ready." He clapped Rueben on the back. "Take care, little brother, and don't forget to let Gramps know what we talked on."

"No problem, Joe." He reached out for Hannah, who had followed me over. He draped his arm around her, and she scooted up close to him.

We rode off just as the sun dropped below the tops of the highest trees. "We'd best get a move on if we want to be settled before dark," Joe observed.

I rested my head on his back as we trotted over the high prairie grasses, now brown and drying in the grueling summer heat. It seemed as if the day had finally caught up with me, and I suddenly felt exhausted. Between the steady pace of the horses mingled with the heat of the day, I began to fall asleep. I felt myself slipping, but then Joe's strong hand was under my arm, pulling me up. He stopped the horses and carefully helped me down then scrambled down himself. "Okay, sweetie, let's fix you up." I climbed up contentedly into the saddle, and he jumped up behind me and lifted me up onto his lap. "Now you just lay your head on my shoulder, baby, and rest. I promise I won't let you fall." His lips softly caressed mine, and I sighed contentedly, already drifting back to sleep.

$\mathcal{M}$

He loved watching her sleep. He'd tried to keep the horses at a fast walk most of the way to the clearing, but the fading sun was setting faster than he'd anticipated. So he tightened his arm around her and set the sturdy horses to a lively gallop. She stirred sleepily in his arms and charmingly whispered his name. He softly replied, "I'm here, baby," and a sweet smile touched her lips.

They drew closer to the weather-beaten trail into the woods, so he slowed the horses back to a fast trot as he carefully shifted his weight and switched arms. After that, he let out the lead rope a little more so Pal could trail behind instead of beside them down the narrow path through the dense woods.

As they neared the gently flowing creek, he expertly reined in the dutiful horses, bent forward, and affectionately dropped a kiss on her cheek. She sighed happily, stretched sleepily, and captured his willing lips with her own. He drew her close. "We're goin' to need to walk the horses through the creek, sweetie, so I'm goin' to get down and lead 'em through. I just wanted to make sure you're awake enough to sit up on Redwing by your-self 'cause I sure don't want to lose you."

"I'm fine, honey. You shouldn't have let me sleep for so long. We could have made it here a lot faster if I hadn't fallen asleep."

"Don't you worry none. We'll be fine, and you needed to sleep. I'm right glad I could provide you with my shoulder to rest on." He smiled tenderly. "It was kinda nice just watchin' you sleep. You're a right pretty girl awake or asleep, you know." He kissed her once again and then reluctantly slid off the horse.

He grimaced when he noticed the water level in the creek had risen by at least a foot since their last visit. They'd had a lot of rain out of season, causing all the creeks to rise rapidly, and it'd even caused some flooding problems back at home. He heaved a sigh and decided to try to jump the creek with the horses, but he knew beforehand how much extra work that'd create for him. It seemed like there was really no other choice, though.

He wandered restlessly along the edge the creek, hoping to find a suitable place where the creek bed narrowed. As a consequence, he discovered a nearly inaccessible spot where fallen brush had created a little dam, keeping the creek a bit more shallow on the one side and deep and treacherous on the other. He carefully hiked back to Maggie, feeling elated that he wouldn't have to completely unpack the horses and jump the flooded creek.

He spied her happily talking to the horses as he made his way back to the trail, and he noticed how delighted the horses were to receive the delicious apples Maggie held out on her palms. She grinned at him as he loped up. "Did you find what you were lookin' for, honey?"

He embraced her. "Mmhmm, plus I found a place we can walk the horses across the creek, but I'll need to clear the path a bit first." He dug into one of the saddlebags and heaved out his machete. "Shouldn't be too long, baby."

By the time they'd crossed the creek and arrived at the tiny trail leading to the clearing, he judged they had give or take about an hour of sunlight left in the day, so he knew they had to get a move on. He helped Maggie off the horse then once again pulled out his machete. "Stay back a ways while I cut down the brush that's grown up along the trail, honey. I really meant to come out here 'fore now and get a few things taken care of, but seein' as I didn't get in till late last night, I just didn't have time."

He swung the machete back and forth through the brush, cutting out a wider pathway than usual. He was dead tired and drenched in sweat by the time they finally reached the clearing. He waited for Maggie to catch up to him then explained, "We're goin' to need to build a fire 'fore it gets dark, so if you want, you can go ahead and start gatherin' some twigs and such and I'll go back and get the horses."

She looked askance at him, and he answered before she spoke. "I don't want to leave the horses out by themselves at night. The timber wolves and red wolves have been bad this year, so I don't want to take any chances."

Her eyes widened. "Wolves! I didn't think about wolves!"

He laughed. "Not to worry, baby. They won't come near our campsite, but they might try to bother the horses if they're too far away from us." He started back down the trail but stopped when he heard her softly call his name. "Mmhmm?"

"I love you, honey." She smiled sweetly. "I just want to say I love you every time you come in or go out our door."

He grinned. "I love you, too, sweetie, but have you noticed...we don't have a door."

Her soft, melodious laughter floated in the air. "You know what I mean."

"I do, and I'll be back shortly, love." He jogged down the trail and soon arrived back where they'd tethered the horses. As he started to untie the leads, the soothing sound of the flowing creek called out to him, so he decided to take a couple of minutes and cool off in its swirling waters.

He plunged in, clothes and all, and let the water surge over him. The cool water refreshed him and helped his tired muscles relax. He heaved a sigh, sank under the water once more, and then quickly scrambled up the creek bank.

He spotted Maggie as he neared the clearing. She'd dragged two fairly nice-sized logs into the middle of the clearing and started placing some small branches and twigs in a teepee structure around the logs. He smiled as he watched her. "Looks like somebody knows what she's doin'."

She beamed at him. "I've built a fire or two in my day."

"Well, you're doin' it beautifully, baby." He walked the horses over to the far side of the clearing and tethered them to a low-hanging branch. He unloaded the bundles off Pal and then removed the saddlebags and saddles from both horses. "I'll finish up the fire and get our tent set up if you want to start brushin' the horses."

She looked over at him. "Joe! Look at you! You're soakin' wet!"

"Feels right good too. 'Sides, I won't be needin' these clothes much longer anyway."

She blushed as she stood up. "Promises, promises."

He hugged her to him. "Not empty either." Then he drew her closer, kissed her passionately, and sighed resignedly. "We'd best get set up, or we'll run out of daylight here."

He turned back to the work at hand and started digging out a small trench around the campfire. Next, he unrolled one of the packs and pulled out a handful of hay. He sprinkled the hay over the logs, lit a match, and blew softly on the fire as the flames began to lick the straw. Soon the wood had caught, and he turned his attention to the tent.

Maggie finished with the horses, so she walked over and squatted down beside him. "What can I do to help you, honey?"

"I've 'bout got the tent secured, so if you'll just pull that pack over here, I'll lay down some of the hay for us to sleep on. It'll make a nice soft bed, and we can cover it with an old quilt I brought."

She dragged the heavy pack near to the tent and started pulling out handfuls of hay. He tipped her chin up and kissed her. "I love you, Maggie."

She smiled. "I'm not distractin' you, now am I?"

"Mmhmm, but it's mighty easy to get distracted when you're so close to me."

She laughed and danced over to the horses. "I'd better give the horses some of this hay then get us somethin' out for supper. Your mom said we'd best eat the ham tonight or it'll spoil, so I thought we'd just have that with some of the bread."

"Sounds good to me, baby. I'll have this all set in about five minutes, so I'll meet you at the sycamore tree in six."

The sun had long disappeared, the full moon glimmered,

and stars twinkled brightly in the sky. He leaned back contentedly against the tree and drew her closer. His lips lightly brushed her neck, and she sighed happily. He whispered softly in her ear, "I wish I may, I wish I might have this moon dance with you tonight."

She rose and offered him her hand. He embraced it tenderly and then held her intimately in his arms as they slowly danced undisturbed in the shimmering moonlight.

chapter 20

I awoke with Joe's arm thrown comfortably over me, and an amazing joy overflowed within me. I carefully rolled over just a bit, trying hard not to wake him, and lovingly watched him sleep.

I just couldn't believe it was already Monday and almost time to head back to the real world. It had been such an idyllic weekend, and one I hated to see end, although, knowing that Joe and I would go home together to our own tiny house made leaving a little easier.

I unconsciously reached out to caress his face but quickly stopped myself before I woke him. He'd been up several times each night checking on the fire and the horses...and me. It's a wonder he'd slept at all.

I smiled to myself as I remembered the joy of the past few days. We'd spent our days exploring the woods, going beyond the usual trails we'd traveled before. On Saturday we'd saddled the horses and followed the creek as it wound its way deeper into the woods. At times we felt as if we were traveling through a darkened cavern because here and there we stumbled upon places even the sun had a difficult time penetrating. The dense, vine-entangled trees and shrubs had made traveling through the unexplored territory difficult, but Joe had gallantly forged ahead with his machete in hand and cleared away the brush enough for the horses to pass.

At one point we came upon a small waterfall that tumbled majestically over the rocks below, creating rainbows in the water as it danced with the sun. We shared our lunch, our laughter, and our love as we enjoyed the beauty of the waltzing waterfall and the peaceful woods surrounding us. We were ecstatic when we discovered that the creek deepened near the waterfall, and at that point it widened and created a breathtaking little pool of crystal-clear water just perfect for our afternoon swim.

Joe stirred in his sleep, and his arm tightened around me as he readjusted himself and sank back into dreamland. I smiled as I watched him, loving the way he looked just lying there next to me, and I fought hard with myself to keep from touching him or kissing his sweet lips.

I laid my head gently on his shoulder as my thoughts wandered back to yesterday. We stayed closer to the clearing, desiring instead to explore our deepest dreams and make plans for our future together. It surprised me that Joe so clearly remembered a single flash of a moment we'd shared right after Mama arrived home from the hospital way back in early June.

He always stopped by every evening after work to see me, and that day had been no exception. I'd had quite a time helping the girls settle down after they saw Mama arrive home all bandaged and bruised, and even Frank had looked a little green around the gills and needed some extra attention. It had really frightened me that Mama appeared so weak, and it seemed she could barely remain conscious long enough to even take her medicine. By the time Joe arrived, the kids had all gone to bed, Mama was resting quietly, and I sorely needed a shoulder to lean on. We sat quietly out on the porch steps holding hands, hardly talking. Then he'd kissed me and told me Mama was a lucky woman to have such a beautiful nurse looking out for her. I'd peeked up at the dazzling night sky and whispered that I'd often wished I could do something as important as nursing. He'd kissed me again and told me I was more than capable of doing whatever I dreamed.

I'd almost forgotten that night, but yesterday he'd tenderly reminded me of it. It touched my heart that he cared so deeply about all of my dreams and desires. We'd talked about the possibility of me going to nursing school in the spring. It'd be a hardship for us, but it would be wonderfully fulfilling for me to do something that would help so many people.

A bit later Joe happily described his notion of our future. "Someday, baby, we're goin' to have us our own ranch. It'll be huge, bigger than anything you'd ever imagine!" He stretched his arms wide open and grinned.

As he beamed at me, that cute little curl of his dropped down into his sweet face, so I just propped my chin in my hand and smiled adoringly at him.

He kissed me and then exclaimed, "It'll be somethin' similar to what Gramps and Pop have, but even better."

I swept my fingers through his thick dark hair and replied, "I know it will, sweetie, 'cause you'll be in charge of it."

His sweet smile touched my heart deeply. "Both of us, Maggie. I can't do it without you, ya know." He kissed my neck playfully before he continued. "I want our ranch to have a nice-sized herd of cattle, and we'll have lots of horses too, like Mr. Johnson has."

The more he talked, the more I fell in love with him all over again. I cuddled up to him as he proclaimed, "I love working with the horses, baby, training them for racing and for the rodeo. I don't think I could give it up, not just to ride herd on our cattle." He scooted around and enveloped my face in his hands. "We can make us some good money if I can keep on trainin' cuttin' horses for other cattle ranchers. I make an okay livin' now, but if it was our spread, we'd do right nice."

I snuggled closer to him and enticed him with a kiss. He grinned playfully, scooped me up, and headed off toward our tent, still talking. "We're goin' to build us a cute little white house where we can start a family of our own. We'll have horses, cattle…maybe we'll even get us a few sheep and some layin' hens."

He plopped me gently down on the quilt, rolled over next to me, and sighed in satisfaction. "I also set eyes on a new sort of bird up in Oklahoma when one of the farmers at an auction had these peacocks and peahens up for sale. I'd really like to get us a few of them 'cause they're just so beautiful, in spite of the fact that they're not useful for much."

I answered him the same as he'd answered me, that he was more than capable of doing whatever he dreamed and I would gladly, proudly, joyously work with him to see that all our dreams and plans came true. Then I kissed him zealously, and we eagerly explored more of our dreams we'd so longed to share together.

"Mornin', beautiful; that's a mighty wide grin you've got growin' on your pretty face this mornin'." He gently caressed my face, and I caught his hand and kissed it tenderly.

"I was just daydreamin' 'bout you, honey—how much I love you and adore you and how beautiful you look just layin' there sleepin'." I snuggled up close to him and kissed him as I'd imagined while he'd lain sleeping.

After a spell, I crawled out of the tent and stretched happily up toward the heavens. Our time together the past few days had been a glorious interlude that I never wanted to end.

Joe followed me out, drew me close, and sighed in satisfaction. He kissed the nape of my neck as he gently massaged my shoulders and asked, "Ready to head home, baby?"

I sighed. "I can only bear it 'cause you're goin' home with me."

"We'll find us a little place real soon, Maggie, so don't you fret about stayin' with Pop and Mom. I promise you it won't be for long." He trailed a kiss across my shoulders, up my neck, and to my lips.

I affectionately cuddled up to him. "We won't get home anytime soon if you keep that up, ya know."

Tired sunflowers drooped in the dying meadows, their petals turned down away from the blazing heat of the sun as we slowly rambled toward home. We rode partway and walked the horses when we chose, longing to lengthen our precious moments in our make-believe world we'd so happily created.

At one point we stopped to let the horses rest by a quiet little stream. Joe spread out our quilt and sprawled back to rest while I wandered along the stream gathering sunflowers. After a bit I skipped back to Joe, dropped down cozily beside him, and began braiding the flowers into a long chain. He watched me for a bit then closed his eyes and dozed, which might've been a mistake, seeing as how when he woke up I'd braided flowers into the horses' manes and tails as well as adorned myself with them. For some strange reason he didn't seem a bit surprised and just kissed me till my toes soared right up off the ground.

Each step drew us closer to home, and I began to feel excited at the prospect of showing Joe our new little house. As we neared the turnoff to his parents' house, he stopped the horses. "Let's rest here for just a bit, Maggie."

We dismounted and tethered the horses nearby. Joe took my hands and led me over to the side of the road. He gazed tenderly at me for the longest moment, his adoring look melting my heart. Then he spoke softly. "Ever' time I pass by this spot, I remember the day I confessed my love for you, and you brought me such joy expressin' your love for me. And I just wanted to tell you again, right in this very same place, that I love you, baby, more'n my words could ever tell. I love you."

This time I didn't hesitate or feel the least bit shy, but with tenderness and feeling I kissed his hands then drew his arms around me, wrapped my arms around his neck, and whispered, "Oh, my sweetness, I love you so deeply." Then I kissed him till his toes soared right up off the ground.

C~*H*~

He affectionately helped her up into the saddle, not that she needed his help. Then he settled in behind the saddle and wrapped his strong arms lovingly around her. It wasn't a long ride to the house, and his horse knew the way right well, so he was able to concentrate on more important things, like the sweetness of her neck and the softness of her lips. Additionally, he desperately wished they were headed anywhere at the moment but to his folks' for the night.

As they came into the yard, he gently tugged the reins and Redwing halted. Almost immediately, Pal stopped right beside him. He started to get down when Dorrie came tearing out of the house, charging toward them, shouting, "Maggie! Joey! I'm so glad you're home!"

Mom dashed out right behind her, intent on stopping her before she got too close to the horses. He quickly jumped down, dashed over, and scooped her up. "Hey there, half-pint. You'd best remember you can't just run up on a horse like that, no matter how well it's trained."

She kissed him. "Okay, Joey! But I missed y'all so much!"

Maggie walked over to them and dropped a kiss on her cheek then teased her, saying, "We missed you more."

He laughed as they began to play. Then he headed happily up to the barn with the horses. It took him about a half hour to properly care for them and get their tack all cleaned and put away. At that juncture he hoofed it back to the house and found everyone relaxing out in the backyard.

Dorrie sprang up when she caught sight of him, ran over, and began tugging him toward the pasture. "Joey, come on; let's go see the new dollhouse Pop made."

He grinned at Maggie when he took in the sunflowers now adorning Dorrie's hair. He strolled over to her. "Ya know, I had a heck of a time gettin' all those flowers combed out of the horses' manes and tails."

She smiled playfully. "Mmm, but they looked mighty pretty, now didn't they."

"Only one mighty pretty lady round here for me, and well worth the trouble she causes me," he teased.

Dorrie hollered from the far side of the yard, "Joey! Maggie! Y'all hurry up."

Pop smiled at her impatience. "Now, Dorrie, you let Joe and Maggie rest for a spell. Then they'll come look at the dollhouse." Her face puckered up, but she danced back over and climbed up in Pop's lap.

He glanced around at everyone contentedly—Mom shelling peas, Rueben strumming on his guitar, Dorrie playing and laughing with Pop, and Maggie curled up on the bench, resting her sweet head on his shoulder. He draped his arm around her and hugged her. She peered up at him as she felt his eyes on her and brushed his cheek with her lips. "Honey, let's go see the dollhouse."

He focused on her. "Why don't you go on, baby, and I'll come out and see it in a bit. I just want to sit and rest peacefully here for a bit."

"Joe..."

"Is it really important for me to go back there with you?"

"Mmhmm, please."

He sighed tiredly and then rose. "Okay, Dorrie, come show Maggie and me your dollhouse."

She ran over and grabbed both their hands. "Come on, then, hurry up! Poppy, Mommy, Rueben, everybody, let's go."

He followed her to the edge of the yard, turned, and started off down the path that led behind the gardens. Dorrie grabbed his hand and tugged hard as she pointed out toward the old live oak down by the pond. He laughed. "Dorrie, that's just pastureland. Why'd you want to go out there?"

"Just come, Joey," she pleaded.

He looked around at all their faces trying to hide big smiles. "Okay then, what say we go look at this dollhouse."

Dorrie happily skipped ahead of them then stopped when she came to a sizeable stack of hay bales, which conveniently blocked the pasture from view. She cried excitedly, "Here we are, Joey!"

He laughed. "I see Pop made you a village out of hay bales." Then he stumbled past the bales and froze in astonishment. In the far corner of the pasture nestled in front of a stand of trees sat a small white house with a little front porch. A thin stream of smoke floated out of the tiny chimney.

Joe gazed around at all the happy faces. Then Maggie slipped up and wrapped him in her arms. "Welcome home, Joe."

He stuttered, "What…how? What's goin' on, Pop?"

Maggie pulled him toward the house, explaining as they hurried across the pasture. "It was your folks' idea…and your grandparents'. They did this for us, Joe."

He staggered up the steps and stopped at the front door. Dorrie had her hand on the doorknob, ready to rush in, but Pop caught her up and carried her back down the steps. "You two kids go on in and explore your new home together. We'll see y'all tomorrow."

Dorrie protested, "But I want to show Joey the house, Pop!"

Mom kissed her cheek. "Come on, baby, and help me shell some peas. Then we'll go have a story."

He watched wonderingly as his family trailed off across the pasture. Then he gazed down at Maggie's sparkling eyes and dancing smile. He shook his head in disbelief. "And you knew 'bout this?"

"Mmhmm, I even helped build it," she exclaimed proudly.

"Well, I never!" He grinned down at her and then lifted her into his arms as she reached over and opened the door to the most amazing surprise. He carried her into the house and wandered around the room, shaking his head in wonder.

Maggie kissed him and smiled. "You can put me down,

honey." She gazed blissfully around the little room and exclaimed, "Oh, Joe, look! Your mom and Dorrie put fresh flowers on our little tables, and Rueben and your pop must have finished out the room for us. And they built a fire to welcome us home!" She buried her face on his shoulder. "Your family is so good to us, honey."

"Our family, baby." He gently let her down then strolled over to the tiny bathroom and peeked in. "How'd they manage all this in such a short time?"

"Well, Rueben says when your pop sets his mind on somethin', it's bound to get done, so he did it. He assembled all the folks at the church and asked for their help, and one and all showed up to lend a hand." She strolled up behind him and lovingly embraced him. He twisted into her arms and held her close as she gazed adoringly up at him. "Honey, your pop and Rueben worked so hard to set the water lines and fit in the hardware for the kitchen, and Pop even worked out a deal with a man who will put in a well for us."

He tried to turn on the water, and she quickly finished. "We won't have runnin' water or be able to use the bathroom for a couple weeks, so we'll have to share your folks' till then, but Joe, I was just amazed. Pop was runnin' all over, findin' folks who had skills he could barter with. It surely paid off 'cause later he bartered with a Mr. Wells over in Arlington to come out and put in one of them new pit toilets for us. They're supposed to send out a crew of welfare laborers to install it sometime in the next week or so, and we'll just be charged for the materials only, at a cost of about five dollars."

Her excitement was catching, and he laughed happily as she led him around the room, pointing out all the wonderful aspects of their fine little home. Finally they ended up over by their little kitchen table. "Joe, honey, look at this. Mom even left us dinner and a pitcher of cold water."

He collapsed into one of the kitchen chairs and pulled her down in his lap. "Maggie, you inspire me. You must have inspired my folks as well for them to put out so much time and money on this house. I just don't know how we'll ever pay 'em back."

"They gave it to us as a gift, sweetie, not so much for me, but for their beloved son and grandson. It's a gift from your parents and grandparents, straight from their hearts. And it includes the twenty acres surroundin' our house and the little pond."

He picked at the cloth covering the food and heaved a sigh. "I never expected anything like this." He lovingly caressed her face. "I must be the most blessed man on this earth."

She pulled back the cloth covering the platter and revealed a variety of vegetables, fruits, sweetbreads, and a hunk of farm cheese. She broke off a piece of carrot cake and offered it to him. "You hungry, sweetie?"

He grinned mischievously. "Mmhmm…"

The fire had long died out and darkness descended when reality returned to the room. She floated over to the window and peered out into the darkness, observing the waning moon. She crept back over to the bed and lovingly touched his face. "Ya know, honey, I think it must be well after midnight."

He drew her down beside him and tenderly kissed her shoulder. "And…"

"You're not plannin' on workin' in the mornin', are you, Joe? I don't want you goin' in all worn out."

"Never crossed my mind, baby. I think work can wait till the end of the week, or maybe even till next week. There're much more important matters to take care of right here at home."

She snuggled closer to him and sighed contentedly. "Much more important matters." And soon he sweetly surrendered to her tantalizingly tender touch.

chapter 21

The sound of softly falling footsteps disturbed my dreams, and I struggled hard to wake up and find the source of the noise. But even before I was fully conscious I felt someone gently tugging on my eyelid. I pulled back from the force and rapidly blinked my eyes, finally coming fully awake.

"Mornin', Maggie!" a little voice cried out excitedly.

I drew the blanket up around myself and sat up in surprise. "Mornin', Dorrie. What're you doin' up so early?"

She climbed up on the bed alongside me. "It's not early, silly! I'm meetin' my new friends and walkin' to school. This is my second and a half whole week of school, and I just love, love, love it so much!"

I grinned and hugged her. "That's good, sweetie. You'll have to come by this afternoon and tell me all about your wonderful day."

She gazed thoughtfully at me with her big blue eyes. "I 'membered how you said you missed comin' to school this year, so I just thought to stop by and see if you wanted to come with me today."

I smiled at her innocent charm. "Not this mornin', honey,

but maybe one day I'll come along with you. I have a lot to get done today, so I'm really glad you came by and woke me up."

"You and Joey been sleepin' a lot lately, but I seen Joey head off to work when I was eatin' breakfast."

I grinned at her. "You'd best scoot, or you'll be late to school, little one."

Her laughter rang out as she happily dashed down the steps and flew across the pasture.

I'd promised Mama and Hannah I'd come spend the day with them, so I quickly busied myself cleaning up our beautiful little house then readied myself for the day.

I noticed Mom out working in her wondrous gardens and waved to her as I made my way to the barn. I whistled for Pal, and he plodded over to the fence for his morning rubs and apple slices. After I'd saddled up, I contentedly set Pal to a slow trot. We meandered through the soft September morning down cozy lanes and across golden pastures until we reached the tree-lined road to Hannah's house.

Hannah spotted me coming and promptly hopped up, ready for a new adventure. We'd barely had a chance to talk since the wedding, so I was all fired up to find out how matters were progressing with Rueben.

She scampered down the steps as I dismounted and caught me up in a huge hug. "Maggie, I've missed you!"

I laughed, hugging her tightly. "It hasn't been that long, now has it, Hannah?"

"Seems like it! I miss our girl talks, which we usually have at least once every week, but it's been almost three weeks!"

"Has it really? Seems like just yesterday Joe and I said our vows," I teased her. "My word, Hannah, I've seen you at least three or four times since then."

"I know, Maggie, but Joe and Rueben are always with us, so today it'll be exceptionally nice 'cause it'll be just us girls."

"And Mama," I reminded her.

"Yeah, but that's okay; she likes girl talk too."

I sighed. "Well, we'll just have to make a little time first for just our special girl talk, and then we'll go see Mama."

She laughed happily, called out a good-bye to her mama, and we trotted off back down the tree-lined road.

We were almost to Mama's when I thought about my special path through the woods, so I nudged Pal down the little trail to the banks of Johnson Creek. Hannah slid off and stretched happily. I swung my leg over and jumped down then led Pal to a nice spot near the cool water. I looped the reins around a tree branch and hurried back over to Hannah.

We scooted down the bank to the edge of the creek and happily dangled our feet in the water. I grinned at Hannah, and she blushed. I laughed. "Okay, tell me all the news."

She teased, "You're the one has all the news. Rueben tells me you and Joe barely leave that little house once he gets in from work."

"Well, course not, 'cause we live there; we're not suppose to leave," I teased back.

"Sounds pretty romantic to me," she began.

"Mmm." I lay back in the sand and sighed contentedly. "More than just pretty."

She dropped down beside me and propped her chin in her hand. "Tell me all about it."

This time I blushed. "Some things you'll just have to discover on your own, little girl."

"Maggie!" She sat up and kicked at the water. "I wouldn't mind discoverin' a few things."

"So, how are matters with Rueben?"

She beamed at me. "Pretty good. Last week he showed up at the house."

"Without me? Without Joe? How is that possible?" I kidded her.

She threw a stick at me. "Maggie Bowen ... oops, Gilley! I do have some appealing qualities of my own, ya know."

I hugged her. "I know; I just like to tease you."

"Well, if you'd listen ..."

"I'm ready; tell me what happened." I fixed my eyes on her and smiled mischievously.

"You're in one silly mood today, Maggie. Okay, anyway, Rueben stopped by last week, and Mama was out on the porch enjoyin' the sunset, so when she spotted him ridin' up, she called out to me." She paused for effect.

"And ..."

"And he didn't ask for me! He asked to speak to Papa." She sighed. "My heart started poundin' inside me, and I didn't know if I should go on outside and say hello to him or run back to my room."

"So what'd you decide?"

"I just stood there, and Papa pushed right on by me out to the porch, so I hid by the door and listened."

"No! Hannah the spy!"

"Maggie! Do you wanna know what happened or not?"

"Course I do, sweetie. I'm just playin'."

"You're spendin' way too much time with that Joe Gilley if you ask me. His silliness is rubbin' right off on you." She laughed.

"I'll be serious. What happened?"

"Well, Papa sat down next to Mama, and Rueben parked himself on the steps next to them. After that, he started askin' 'em how they were and how their day had been, and Papa grunted out a few things. Then Rueben commenced twistin' his hat in his hands, so Mama excused herself and wandered inside. Then Papa said somethin' 'bout it bein' a mighty fine evenin', and Rueben just blurted out askin' Papa if he could have his permission to court me."

"What'd your papa say?"

"He hesitated a bit and made Rueben sweat. Then he shook his hand and alleged that he'd be right proud to have Rueben court his daughter." She leaned back and stared off into the sky. "Then they just sat there for another half hour watching the sunset."

"Why didn't you go out with 'em?"

"I don't know; it seemed kind of private."

I about fell over laughing. "Hannah, he's asking to court you, not your papa."

She blushed. "Well anyway, Papa finally excused himself, and I snuck out and sat down alongside Rueben."

"And …"

"Well, I guess some things you'll just have to discover on your own, little girl." She laughed sweetly. "It was right nice, Maggie."

⌖

Pal trailed slowly into Mama's yard. Hannah and I laughed and teased each other as I absentmindedly guided my horse toward the porch. As we alighted, Mama appeared in the doorway, drying her hands on an old dishcloth.

"Well, what a nice treat this is, two of my favorite girls turnin' up on my doorstep."

"Mornin', Mama!" I called happily. "You feelin' okay today?"

She smiled and nodded. "Mmhmm, just a bit drained is all." She embraced me tightly, and I could feel her ribs sticking right out.

I drew away in horror. "Mama, look at you. You're nothin' but skin and bones! Why, you need to eat more!"

She grimaced at me. "You and Will, always on me. I do what I can, baby."

Hannah leaned over and kissed her cheek. "You look right beautiful, Mrs. Bowen."

Mama laughed. "Now here's a girl after my own heart."

"Seriously, Mama, you're worryin' me. I suppose you just went back to work too soon. However, there's plenty of help for you if you'd just take it, and then there'd be no need for you to rush off to work."

She held up her hand to stop me as she sat down on the steps. "Maggie, it's only been two days a week for the past few weeks, and I'm gainin' my strength back more ever' day, but ..."

I hunkered down beside her. "But what?"

She glanced timidly at us both. "Y'all know how bad things are gettin' with the job situation now. It's been a bad spell for a long time, but now with folks from the panhandle of Texas and Oklahoma settlin' here, it's worse than ever."

"Mama, Will has a good, steady job with the railroad, and Joe's stable with his job. We'd all be more than happy to help y'all out so you won't have to go off to work."

She nodded. "Will's a good boy ... man now, I suppose. He gives me just about ever' penny he makes, and I still have my allotment comin' in. But someday Will's goin' to meet up with the right girl and marry, and my allotment's goin' to run out. Then where'll I be? I need to keep this job."

Hannah shook her head. "Well, they should just keep it open for you till you're feelin' good enough to work."

Mama smiled sadly. "That's just not a possibility, Hannah. Too many folks are out of work. Why, there's more than 370 families on the direct relief rolls in Arlington alone, and that's only the families that have asked for help. We just don't know how many more are out there starvin'."

"Mama, Joe and I'd be glad to help y'all any way we can."

"I know you would, honey, but it's not your place to." She sighed heavily and then stared off into the cloudless sky as tears shimmered in her eyes. At last she spoke. "I even set off to the relief offices over at Arlington City Hall last Monday, just seekin' some kind of aid, and it was so crowded. You just wouldn't believe the heartbreaking sights I beheld. Lines and lines of sad-faced people just stood huddled all close together, waitin' on their portion of government rations, ever'one simply hopin' they'd make it to the front of the line before the supplies were all given out."

I held her hands firmly in mine. "Mama, I'm so sorry. I've

just been thinkin' about myself for so long and not even givin' consideration to what you're goin' through."

It was like a dam burst, and her unshed tears spilled over. Her voice was no more than a whisper as she gazed sadly back at me. "Not just me, Maggie. There's so many folks so much worse off than us."

I grasped her hands as she sighed heavily. "Once I made it to the front of the line, I found out that food was only given to folks who don't have able-bodied men in their families to work. And since our Will is a workin' man now, our little family don't qualify."

"But Mama," I faltered. My eyes flamed as anger seared through my soul. I drew in my breath to try to gain control of myself before I spoke. "Mama, there's no reason, no reason at all for you to be sufferin' and hurtin' for money. Look at Papa … paradin' himself around, buildin' that new house, while you and the children go hungry. How can you allow it?"

"Maggie, that's done and buried. I made a bargain with your papa, and it's okay, sweetie. We're makin' it. We still have the home-demonstration agent comin' round once a month, bringin' us some food supplies, and my boss wants me to start back full time beginnin' next Monday, so that'll bring in a bit more money for us."

"Mama, that bargain included Papa providin' for his children." I gazed angrily up at the sky and about bit my tongue off to keep from saying what I truly felt. Instead I knelt down and took her hands in mine as I spoke, "I know for certain it's too soon for you to go back to work full time 'cause you're already so worn down—"

She interrupted me. "It's full time or no job, Maggie. That's the conditions they set down to me yesterday, so I've accepted that I'm goin' to need to work full time." She shook her head sadly. "There's no denying I need my job. I still have six little mouths to feed, ya know."

Hannah frowned and tried to lighten the tension that hung

in the air. "I know everyone's cuttin' back on what they need. My folks have been strugglin' a lot too, but there's only Grace and me now that my brother's married and moved away. Papa's afraid the price of cotton's gonna drop again. Then he said he don't know what we'll do."

I felt like someone had punched me in the stomach as I came down from the cloud I'd been living on for the past few weeks, and the harsh reality of everyday life roughly assaulted my senses.

Mama watched my face fall and smiled tenderly at me. "It's all right to be happy, honey. I want all my children to be care-free and happy, so you just don't fret over me workin'. I'm right blessed to have a job."

"But you do need to eat more and start takin' better care of yourself," I insisted. "The kids are gettin' old enough to help you more, so you should make them." My eyes implored her as I tucked my chin in my hands and heaved a sad sigh.

Hannah plopped down on the bottom step. "What with all the need people have, it was a darn shame about all that milk bein' wasted over in Ft. Worth back at the end of August."

Mama nodded. "Yep, I sure could have made better use of it."

I gazed dumbfounded at them. "Okay, now I'm feelin' really stupid."

Hannah laughed. "Maggie, it come about the day before your weddin', so there's no way you'd have even noticed it, even if it'd took place right in front of your face."

I rolled my eyes at her. "I'm not that lovesick, Hannah." She and Mama both laughed, so I just shook my head. "I give; what happened?"

Mama jumped up. "I believe I still have a copy of the *Arlington Journal* that tells all about it." She dashed into the house and came back out a minute later. "Yep, right here on the front page; they even have a picture to boot."

I prudently held the paper and stared at the glaring photograph depicting irate dairy farmers dumping out huge canisters of fresh milk. The story under the caption read: *"*A milk strike gripped Fort Worth as producers placed a tight blockade around creameries in a fight to increase the price of raw milk. Pickets carried out threats of producers to resort to 'effective' means to thwart inflow of milk by seizing trucks and dumping several hundred gallons of milk. One of these dumpings is shown above, with 15 cans of milk being poured into the gutter."

I opened my mouth to speak, but words just wouldn't form. So I quietly laid the paper aside and buried my head in my lap.

"What a waste," Mama stated frankly. "What a waste."

My spirits didn't improve any on the short ride back to Hannah's, although she tried cheering me up. However, I'd settled into a deep depression worrying over Mama. As we drew near her house, she begged me to stop for a bit. We dropped down under a shady oak, and she doggedly reprimanded me. "Maggie, things have been sad all around us for a long time. You've known it, I've known it, and we're workin' through it. There's no need to hide your happiness just because of the way the world is now."

I heaved a sigh. "It's not just what's goin' on in the world around us, Hannah. It's Mama too. I'm just feelin' so guilty that everything's been so wonderful for me lately, and here she sits hurtin' and needin', and there's not a darn thing I can do about it."

"That's right, not a thing. But you have in the past, and you'll keep doin' it in the future. You've been there for your mama more than anyone I've ever known, and look at you—you're still tryin' to take on her pain." She fixed her eyes on me. "Maggie, I've been singin' in my soul ever since last week when Rueben asked my papa if he could court me, and I don't feel a whiff of guilt bein' happy...and neither should you. You shouldn't have to put your life on hold just because the world's in a muddle."

I brushed away a stray tear and kissed her cheek. "It's right you should feel happy, and I'll be okay. I guess I'm just plum tuckered out." I stood up and reached down to help her up, "Soon as Joe's home, I'll feel a whole lot better."

I picked up Pal's lead, and we walked thoughtfully down the cool, shady road to her house.

I stabled Pal, wandered forlornly down to the little pond, and stared at my wavering reflection in the water. My thoughts tumbled around in my mind like stones in a rushing river as I fell distraught to my knees and prayed hard for my Mama. I prayed for her healing, both of her body and her heart, although I feared her injuries were mending so slowly due to her aching heart as much as any physical damage she'd sustained. Mama had loved Papa so much, and he'd broken her sweet heart. What's more, no matter how much he believed she was strong enough to withstand his leaving, he was wrong, so wrong. I could see it in her spirit today, just as strong as if she'd voiced it. So I prayed and asked God to bless her and ease her suffering heart. Then I sank down onto the soft, damp grass and cried. That's where Dorrie found me as she happily skipped home from school.

I slowly raised my throbbing head as I heard her startled cry. "Maggie!"

I dipped out a little water from the pond and rubbed it vigorously over my face. "Hey, half-pint, you home already?"

She came over and took my tearful face in her little hands. "What's wrong, Maggie. Are you hurt?"

I smiled. "No, sweetie, I'm just a little sad, but I'm not hurt. How was school today?"

She wrapped her chubby little arms around me and kissed my cheek. "The teacher learned us how to write our names. Do you wanna see?"

I smiled in spite of myself. "Mmhmm, I'd love to."

She found a little twig, brought it over to the edge of the pond, and carefully began drawing letters in the mud. She nodded at me as she began, her furrowed brow depicting the depth of her concentration. "This is a D for Dorrie. Then I make a big circle, and that's the O. Next, I have two of the same letter, R. Then my favorite letter comes next. It's an I. I like it 'cause it seems friendly. Then last I have to make a snake letter, a S, 'cause the teacher says that's how to spell my proper name." She stood over her scratchings proudly.

"It's beautiful, Dorrie. Your teacher is probably so proud of you. I know I am." I smiled at her with tender affection.

"I like it best when you smile, Maggie. I just don't like it when people are sad." She plopped down in my lap. "Do you know how to write your name?" She promptly handed me her stick.

"I believe so. I don't think I've forgotten how since last I wrote it," I teased her. Then I copied her sweet way of spelling. "First, I make an M for Maggie, then an A. Next, two of the same letter, G. Then my favorite letter, I, 'cause it seems friendly." She flashed me a wide grin as I finished. "And last I make an E, and that spells Maggie."

She fell down giggling. "You're funny, sister!"

I grinned back at her. "I love you, little sister."

"And I love both of you!"

"Joe! I'm so glad you're home!"

He dropped down beside me and wrapped his arm around me. "Me too."

Dorrie wiggled into his lap. "Me three!"

He traced his finger under my eyes. "Somethin' happen today?"

"Mmhmm, but I'll tell you later."

"You okay?"

I nodded and then turned as Mom called out to us from the garden. Dorrie hopped up and scampered joyfully to her mom. Joe stood up and then reached out his hand to help me up. I stumbled into his arms and fell into his kiss, needing him so much.

His mom called out to us again, so we waved and strolled hand in hand down to the gardens.

He held her lovingly in his arms as she slept, gazing down upon her sweet face as anger at her papa once again surged through him. He knew it was only by default that her papa had hurt her again today, but that didn't change the fact in his mind. He knew she'd hate the thoughts he was having, but he couldn't control what he felt any more than she could.

He dropped a tiny kiss on her forehead as he drew his arm out from under her. Then he turned over to try and sleep, but his restless mind churned and wouldn't settle down. He groaned and sat up on the bed. At that moment he felt her tender touch on his back and sighed softly. "I'm sorry, baby. I didn't mean to wake you."

She pushed herself up behind him and gently massaged his neck and shoulders. "I'm sorry, honey, that I brought all this sadness into our home today. I guess it just struck me all at once, even though I should have known …" Her voice trailed off sadly.

He turned and held her in his arms as he tenderly dropped kisses on her face. She laid her head on his shoulder and lovingly caressed him. He sighed. "I guess we've both been turnin' our backs to what's happenin' around us, but you just bring so much joy and sunshine into my life that it's right hard to notice anything else." He reached over and arranged the pillows behind them then drew her down into his arms.

He brushed her hair back from her face and gazed into the depths of her eyes. "Hearin' what you told me 'bout today just brought back too many images of what I seen up in Oklahoma. I'm sorry I didn't tell you about it, but it was hard enough for me to bear."

He sat up and sighed in frustration. "Seems the more I pondered on the problems of your mama, the more it got tangled up with what I witnessed in Oklahoma, and that just kept boilin' up inside me. After that, all I could picture was the pain on your sweet face this afternoon." He turned back to her. "And that brought me to this point of anger where I concentrated the whole lot back on your papa."

She crawled up beside him and softly brushed his neck with her lips. "That's where my anger centered too, but, Joe, I ... we just can't go back there. We need to let this anger die, or it'll just consume us."

He drew her closer. "I know, baby. We'll just need to spend some extra time helpin' your mama and makin' sure she cares more for herself."

She nodded into the darkness as she snuggled even closer to him, and late into the night with loving tenderness they soothed each other's hurting hearts.

chapter 22

He yanked on his boots and grabbed his hat then sauntered out on the porch. As he opened the door he spotted Maggie, surrounded by his pop's border collies, one and all enjoying her attention. He grinned and shook his head. "Those are work dogs, ya know, baby."

She beamed up at him. "Well, even work dogs need some rubs now and then."

He plopped down behind her and straddled her with his legs. "Just don't let my pop catch you makin''em soft." He swept her hair up and affectionately kissed her neck.

She leaned back against him and sighed contentedly. "Looks like we'll have a beautiful day today."

"Looks like it. You know, next Friday we'll have our one-month anniversary."

She nodded her head as one of the dogs assaulted her face with kisses. She laughed and gently pushed it away. "I enjoyed celebratin' our three-week anniversary last night."

He hugged her against him. "Yeah, but I think a whole month deserves an even bigger celebration."

She scooted around and climbed up on his lap. "It's hard to improve on pure perfection, ya know."

A loud whistle pierced the air, and all four dogs thundered across the pasture toward the barn. He stared up and noticed his pop motioning for him and declared, "I told Pop I'd ride fence with him this mornin', but when I get back we'll head over to your mama's and see what we can do to help her today."

"That'd be good, honey. And, Joe?"

"Mmhmm?"

She leaned over and whispered in his ear, "I love you, Joe Gilley."

He drew in his breath. "It's never easy to leave you, Maggie, even if it's just a couple hours." He kissed her again as he heard his pop whistle loudly for him to come on. He stood up and smiled down at her. "Why don't you go pay a visit to Mom and Dorrie for a bit? Mom has a few things she put together for your mama, and then when I get back we'll take a drive over there."

~

Mama rested on the porch with Lilly comfortably curled up on her lap. I waved happily as we scrambled out of the overloaded car, and she shaded her eyes against the brightness of the afternoon sun then waved as she recognized us.

I hurried over, hopped up the steps, and dropped a kiss on her cheek. She smiled up at me. "Didn't expect to see you quite so soon, sweetie. You and Hannah were just over a few days back."

"Joe and I wanted to come visit and help you some today, and I just needed to make sure you're really okay to start work full time on Monday."

She sighed. "Maggie, I'm goin' to have to be; there's no other way around it."

Joe strolled up on the porch with an armload of supplies. "Get the door for me, Maggie, and I'll take these on in to the kitchen."

I held the door for him as Mama watched in surprise. "What'd y'all bring over?"

"There's more in the car. Joe's mom and pop had a surplus of food from their garden, and they thought it'd be nice to share it with y'all."

"Now, Maggie, I hope you didn't go over there beggin' for me. We're not that bad off."

Joe popped back out on the porch. "No beggin' at all, Mama Jo," he stated as he hugged her and kissed her cheek. "Mom had more harvest than she knew what to do with and hoped you could take it off her hands. She's plum tuckered out cannin' everthing." He jumped off the porch and commenced unloading the rest of the supplies from the car.

Lilly looked up sleepily. "Did y'all bring me a surprise too?"

I laughed. "I'm sure we did, Lilly bell." Then I glanced around the yard. "Where are the rest of the kids?"

Lilly pouted. "They went fishin' down to the creek, but they wouldn't let me come. They said I'm a baby."

Mama hugged her. "You're my baby, Lilly." She cuddled up to Mama and solemnly stuck her thumb in her little mouth.

"Probably they knew Mama needed you to stay with her this mornin'," I offered.

Mama stood up, holding Lilly. "Let's go see what all y'all brought us."

Joe appeared at the door and took Lilly from Mama. "She's gettin' a bit big for you to carry, Mama Jo. Best let her walk from now on."

Mama shook her head and rubbed her face tiredly. "Thank you, Joe."

We gathered in the airless kitchen, and I sat Mama down at the table. "Okay, first off, Mom sent y'all a hot lunch, so you and Lilly just start eatin' while Joe and I put away the rest of the food."

Mama stared hopelessly at me. "Maggie…" She laid her head on the table and sobbed.

I quickly rushed to her and wrapped my arms tenderly around

her. "Mama, don't cry, please don't cry. I'm just so scared for you. I can feel your ribs stickin' out on you, and it simply scares me to death." I irritably swept away my tears and pleaded some more. "I don't want to lose you. Please, Mama, please don't cry, please. We all need you so much."

Mama hid her face in her trembling hands and then tearfully peered up at us. "I'm just so ashamed."

Lilly anxiously watched us, tears welling up in her eyes. Mama stretched out her arms to Lilly as her little lips trembled and her tears began to fall. Mama sobbed softly. "Be careful what you say, Maggie; you're scarin' the baby."

I feebly pleaded, "Oh, Mama, if you keep starvin' yourself, you'll never improve. Then what's goin' to happen to all the kids?"

Joe glanced over at me with concern, and then he nodded and hastily snatched up Lilly. "Come on, kiddo; let's go find Frank and your sisters and tell 'em lunch is all ready." He hauled her up on his shoulders, and she giggled happily as he trotted off out the kitchen door.

Mama's vulnerable eyes followed him. "He's a fine man, Maggie."

I gently grasped her by the shoulders and turned her to face me. "Mama, please listen to me. I wouldn't be sayin' this to you if I didn't love you. You know that." My eyes implored her. "Please tell me, what does the doctor say about your condition? Why aren't you gainin' your strength back?"

"Maggie, there's nothin' wrong with me. I'm just still recoverin' from my accident is all." She shook off my hands and irritably faced away from me.

I paced around the table and stood right in front of her. "Mama, we only have just a few short minutes before Joe comes back with the kids." I took her hands in mine and asked, "I know this is hard to face 'cause it's mighty hard to say, but I have to know. Is it Papa? Are you still pinin' over him, Mama?"

Her ashen face contorted in anger. "Why would you even think that, girl!" She jerked away from me and stormed out of the room.

276

I followed after her, earnestly pleading. "You're still in love with him! I know you are, Mama. I can see it in your eyes. I just don't know how to help you stop—"

She spun around furiously. "Maggie, what you see in my eyes is pure pity." She threw her hands up and practically spit at me. "I pity that man! He's lost you and Will, and he's on the way to losing Frank and Mary. The other girls are too little to see him for what he is. So what you're thinkin' is love is just plain pity. Don't you confuse the two!"

I reached out to her, demanding that she listen. "I'm sorry, Mama, but I just don't believe you. I've witnessed how you act whenever he comes around, and it's not just recently. It's ever since he left us."

Mama's eyes sparked angrily. "Maggie, you're speakin' nonsense, girl!"

"No, Mama, I'm not. Your eyes, your sweet eyes give you away. And I'm just so scared. I just don't want you dying over him 'cause he's not worthy of your love, Mama."

She froze where she stood, and she remained that way for so long I began to worry. Then she turned and stared blankly at me. "Maggie, I just won't tolerate this behavior, and if this is what you call helpin' me, I don't need it. I thank y'all for bringin' the food for the kids, but it'd be real good if you and Joe leave just as soon as he gets back."

My hand flew to my mouth, and I tried to approach her, but she turned her back on me. I sank down on the couch in shock because Mama had never ever sent me away before. And she'd never ever turned her back on me in anger.

I heard footsteps pounding up on the porch and Frank hollering from the kitchen. Mama stubbornly walked off into the kitchen, ignoring me. After a bit Joe poked his head around the door and found me. My lips trembled, and my eyes pleaded with him, so he compassionately helped me to my feet and led me out to the car.

He draped his arms around me and held me close, and I

couldn't even cry. I just stared at the house, willing Mama to come out, willing her to forgive me, but she didn't appear.

Joe kissed my forehead and offered, "Give her time, baby; she'll come around." He started the car and began backing out of the yard, and just at that moment I caught a glimpse of Mama peeking out the door.

"Joe, stop!" I didn't move. I just watched her watching me, both of us stubbornly waiting on the other to emerge first.

"Maggie, what do you want me to do?"

"Let's just wait a bit, Joe. Maybe she'll come outside."

"Maggie, go to your Mama. It'd be the right thing to do." He turned off the engine and moved to open the door.

"Joe, wait."

"Come on, baby. I'll even go with you." He lifted my face to his. "Your mama loves you, honey. She's not goin' to send you away again."

I knew he was right, but a terrifying fear seized me when I remembered the enraged look she'd given me only moments before. My voice trembled as I replied, "I hate this. I've never made Mama so angry before."

He ran his fingers through my hair. "Sometimes facin' the truth is right painful, and it just may be you hit a sore nerve of truth she's been hidin' from herself."

"I don't know, honey, I just don't know."

The door opened a little wider, and Mary slipped out. She silently glided out to the car. "What happened between you two, Maggie? I ain't never seen Mama act like this."

"I just told her how worried I am for her, Mary. She's wastin' away not eatin', and then I said a few other things I probably shouldn't have said. But I never thought she'd get so dang fired up at me."

"Well, she sure did. She sat at the table grumblin' and complainin', never sayin' why, just sputterin' out things about Papa and you. Now she's just standin' at the door starin' out at the car."

Joe shook his head. "I think I'll go take a walk while you girls work this out."

"Joe?"

He looked at me in exasperation. "What?"

"I love you."

He shook his head, rubbed his hand over his face, then chuckled softly. "Go tell that to your mama, baby; then come see me."

"Where you goin'?"

"You'll know where to find me when you need to." He trudged irritably off down the dusty road.

Mary climbed in next to me. "Oh, Maggie, is Joe mad at you too?"

"No, love, he's mad at Papa." She looked at me like I was crazy, so I just shook my head. "It's a long story." I glanced at the door. "Is that Mama comin' out?"

"I'm not sure. No, it's just Frank."

"What should I do, Mary? Mama's never been this mad at me before."

She fixed her eyes on me sadly. "I think you should listen to Joe and go talk to her."

"I know you're both right, but I'm afraid. What if she turns her back on me again and tells me to leave?" I sobbed. "It'd just break my heart."

"Maggie, Mama wouldn't be standin' at the door all this time starin' at you if all she wanted was for you to leave. Come on now; I'll go with you."

I took a deep breath. "Okay, but if she—"

"She won't, Maggie. I promise."

I stared at her. "When'd you get so grown up?"

"Maggie!" She jumped out of the car, tugging me behind her. We solemnly marched up toward the porch, and right before we reached the steps the door flew open and Mama rushed out.

We both cried out at the same time, "Mama, I'm so sorry!"

"Oh, Maggie! I'm sorry!" Then we fell into each other's arms and wept.

⟋⟍

Frank strolled over casually. "Where's Joe?"

Mary rolled her eyes. "Can't you see we're busy, Frank!"

I wiped my eyes and smiled at him. "Down by the woods, sittin' on the rocks." He hauled off in that direction as the three of us wandered back into the house. The girls were all still wrapped around the table enjoying their lunch, unaware of the tension around them.

Mama sat down at the table, and I brought her a cold glass of water. I brushed her hair back and kissed her on the cheek. "I'm really sorry I upset you so badly, Mama."

She nodded. "I think I got so angry 'cause there's a bit of truth in what you said, Maggie, but it's not a truth I want to live with."

Mary wrapped her arms around Mama's neck. "From now on, I'm goin' to make sure you sit down and eat before you go to work, and you're goin' to eat a hearty dinner every night, or I won't let you up from the table."

Mama smiled at her. "Now just who do you think you're orderin' about, little miss? You're startin' to sound an awful lot like your bossy big sister!"

Mary smiled sweetly at both of us. "Let's start right now. Maggie, go get a plate for Mama."

We all made an effort to lighten the mood in the room, and after a while our laughter drew Joe and Frank back home. Joe winked at me then followed Frank back out on the porch. Taking into consideration all that had ensued today, it actually turned out to be an exceptional day.

chapter 23

A bloodcurdling scream shattered the early morning stillness. I sprang up off the bed and stood perfectly still, listening as the horrifying sound grew louder then faded into silence. I fearfully grabbed a blanket, wrapped it around myself, and swiftly flew out the door. The terrifying scream commenced again, and as I peered anxiously across the pasture, I set eyes on Pop trying to get hold of Mom. Yet she couldn't be contained as she ran hysterically from one side of the yard to the other, screaming and screaming. Then I noticed Rueben darting off toward the back of the house, so I hurriedly dashed off across the pasture after him, frantically calling out his name. I finally caught up to him just as he was climbing into his pop's car.

I screamed at him, "Rueben, what the heck is goin' on?"

His face was deathly pale when he answered me. "Dorrie's been hurt; they're takin' her over to the hospital in Ft. Worth now."

Tears shot out of my eyes, and I started trembling. "How? What happened?"

He yelled, "I don't know, Maggie, but I gotta get Mom and Pop there now. They said it's really serious."

"Oh God! Joe, I'll go get Joe, Rueben, and we'll meet you there right away." I don't think he heard because by this time he was already at the house trying to help his pop capture his mom and get her into the car.

I rapidly raced back across the pasture to our tiny little home, threw on some clothes, and raced down to the barn. I hastily saddled Pal and took off at a swift gallop toward the Johnsons' corral.

I spotted Joe on the far side of the corral, talking with a couple other ranch hands. I desperately screamed his name. He spun around, and I saw fear etched on his face. He sprinted across the corral and caught hold of Pal's reins. "Maggie, what's wrong, baby?"

I flung myself off the horse and into his arms. "Oh, Joe, honey, I don't know! All I know is it's bad, and you have to come now, right now!"

He stepped back and stared at me in fear. "Maggie, who's hurt?"

I almost couldn't bear to tell him. "It's Dorrie, Joe. Oh God, I don't know what happened, but they've taken her over to the hospital in Ft. Worth. And Rueben said we'd best hurry because it's serious, honey."

He took charge, called one of the other men over to take Pal, grabbed my hand, and we flew up the road to Mr. Johnson's house. Joe ran in the door and was back out in less than two seconds. "We'll take one of the trucks, honey. It's right over here. Let's hurry."

The truck seemed so slow, and the miles seemed to crawl by. Joe gripped both hands tightly on the steering wheel, and I silently prayed for little Dorrie and all of my new family. Our fear intensified as we drew nearer the hospital, and at long last we pulled up at the emergency room. Joe stopped the truck, left it out in the middle of the driveway, and we fearfully rushed in.

Pop sat bent over in a hard straight-backed chair, his body heaving with sobs. Rueben sat beside him, patting and rubbing his back, uttering words meant to comfort but doing little to ease the pain.

Fear seized me, and I felt as if we'd never reach them. But when we finally did, I fell down on my knees and gathered Pop up into my arms as Joe took hold of Rueben's shoulders.

Rueben stared vacantly at us as if he didn't even see us and then incoherently mumbled, "She's gone, Joe" as he fell back in the chair weeping.

The emergency room doors opened, and Hannah appeared. Her frightened eyes found Rueben, and she rushed to him. I anxiously glanced up at Joe and watched his poor face crumble, so I held out my arms as his knees buckled and rocked him gently in my arms. I heard Pop's heart breaking. Thus as I sat there crying, my arms encircled both Joe and his pop, and I sorely tried to console them with my presence because at the moment I was unable to utter even one word of needed comfort.

After a while Pop heaved a deep sigh and tiredly rubbed his shattered face. "Joe Edward, go to your mom. She won't leave her baby, and they need her to, but she just won't listen to me."

Joe sorrowfully ran his hand through his disheveled hair and nodded. Tears glistened in his eyes as he sadly took my hand and pulled me up with him. We staggered through the double doors of death, down the unending hallway, and paused silently outside the room that sheltered Dorrie's little body.

I felt him stiffen as we took in the horrifying scene before us. Mom lay on the bed in anguish, desperately holding her baby's blood-soaked body, singing softly to her as if she were merely sleeping.

A sob escaped him as I helped him into a chair that was placed near the bed. He scooted the chair closer and reached for his mom's hand. She shushed him. "Sh, Dorrie's sleepin'. She needs rest right now, Joe Edward. She needs her rest to get better."

He begged. "Mom, please, come out with me; let our little girl rest."

Tears streamed down his face as his Mom answered. "I can't, Joey. Dorrie needs me right now."

Her wild eyes pleaded with him and tore at my heart. I sat down on the other side of the bed and tenderly stroked Dorrie's cold little face. I placed my hands over Mom's and whispered firmly, "The doctors need to tend to her, Mom, so you need to come with Joe and me right now." Her eyes flickered across my face, so I continued. "Your boys need you, Mom. Joe needs you so much, and Pop and Rueben are out in the waitin' room needin' you too. Please come with us, Mom, please."

She sadly gazed down on Dorrie's sweet face, and a dreadful sound escaped her lips. She covered her face with her hands, and deep sobs shook her frail frame. Joe's arms encircled her, and he gently guided her out the door and into the hall.

I gently brushed back Dorrie's soft curls from her face and tenderly kissed her cold lips. My tears fell upon her, and I dropped despondently down on my knees in prayer.

Unexpectedly, I felt compassionate arms surrounding me as I prayed. I glanced up at the sympathetic nurse who knelt beside me. I impatiently wiped at my unrelenting tears and then whispered, "Do you know how this happened?"

She nodded sadly. "She was struck by a car on her way to school. I'm so sorry, but I don't know any more than this."

I thanked her then slowly pulled myself up and sorrowfully made my way back down the long, lonely hallway. I pushed aside the door and quickly made my way to Joe. He quickly drew me into his arms and tightly clung to me as if I too might leave him.

The rest of our time at the hospital was all a blur to me. We had a difficult time convincing Mom to leave, and it about broke my heart to see her in such pain. I tried to send word to Mama, asking her to come out to the house and be with us, but I wasn't sure she would get my message. Hannah assured me her mama would be at the house when we arrived, waiting to help in any way she could.

My mind screamed that this could not be real, but in my

heart I knew it to be true. I ached so for Joe and his family. As we drew near the farm, cars spilled over in the roadway, and familiar faces hung in sorrow as we passed by. I noticed Mama standing resolutely on the porch as we pulled in. She bolted down the steps and wrapped her arms lovingly around Mom, gently guiding her into the sad, lonely house. Hannah's mama and several other ladies from the church quietly followed after them.

I sat in the frigid truck, silently holding Joe's hand, shock registering on both of our faces as our tears fell unhindered to the seat below. After a bit he merely drew me close, buried his weary face in my hair, and I held him close as his poor body shook with silent sobs.

At length, Joe wearily sat up and leaned his head back against the coarse seat. He ran his hands through his hair and roughly rubbed his tearstained face. He drew in a deep breath and heaved a long, sad sigh. I caressed his sweet face as his deeply shadowed eyes gazed sadly at me. When he finally spoke, his voice was no more than a faint whisper. "Come on, baby; we need to see to Mom and Pop."

I heard the pastor call out as we crawled out of the truck. He crossed the yard and wrapped his arms around the two of us. His voice broke as he offered, "Joe, Maggie, come; let's pray together for Dorrie, for all of you."

We kneeled together on the cold hard ground and prayed for our beloved little sister. As we prayed, a sweet sense of peace enveloped me, so I prayed even harder that Joe and his dear family would soon experience God's restful peace as well.

We struggled up and headed toward the porch, where Rueben and Hannah sat wrapped in each other's arms. Rueben slowly hauled himself up as we approached, and both brothers fell into each other's arms and cried. I reached out for Hannah and held her tight.

After a while Hannah sniffled and nodded out toward the road. "Rueben, I believe your grandparents are here."

The truth of the day began to sink into my soul, and the weight of the world settled on my shoulders. I gazed sadly as these two dear ones arrived, knowing they would also need our prayers and our love as they struggled to understand and make it through this tragic day.

⁓✳︎⁓

Eventually we discovered all the heartbreaking details about our little Dorrie's tragic accident from one of the older children who had walked to school with our precious little sister early this morning.

The boy's father drove him to Pop's house late in the day. They solemnly climbed out of their old truck, and the horror-struck boy staggered over to us. With a look of sheer terror, he exclaimed, "I'm so sorry…it just happened so fast." Tears welled up in his eyes. "I didn't even know Dorrie had darted out into the road till I heard…" He broke off, crying hard.

Joe put his arm around the distraught child. "Tweren't your fault at all."

The desolate boy stammered, "She'd just wanted to bring flowers to her teacher…that's all she kept sayin'."

Rueben turned away, and Hannah enclosed him in her arms. Joe compassionately patted the young boy on the back. "Come on now; let's sit a spell and talk." Then he wrapped his arm around the boy, took my hand, and drew us over to the steps.

The tension around us was so thick you could have cut it with a knife, and as we listened, Joe gruffly groaned and buried his head in his lap. I rubbed his back gently, desperately struggling to impart my deepest love to him as the boy continued his heartrending tale.

He stuttered, "Well, ya know, Dorrie just kept chatterin' away 'bout the wonderful flowers she'd picked from her own

little garden 'specially for the teacher ... and she was just dancing and laughing all merrily like when up comes a wind gust ..."

He paused for the longest time and then cried softly as he
explained, "That dang wind blew one of her precious flowers out
of her hand, and before we knew it, she'd done gone and rushed
out into the highway after it."

I hadn't realized that Pop was behind us listening till I
heard him cry out in anguish. Joe bolted up and enfolded his
Pop in his arms. Rueben jumped up the steps right behind Joe
and wrapped his arms around both men. They swayed together,
crying.

Dorrie's own sweet teacher, Miss Harrison, arrived at our
house about the same time, distraught and remorseful. She
crept over to the porch, so I quickly stood up and hugged her.
Hannah patted her back as we gazed back at the porch and
watched our men mourn.

I whispered, "Let's walk a bit, Miss Harrison. I fear our
menfolk can't take much more today."

As we glided across the yard, Miss Harrison spoke tearfully.
"When I awoke this mornin' I felt a heaviness in my heart that
I just couldn't explain." She paused for the longest moment and
then spilled out, "Mrs. Morgan's husband was driving her to the
school where she teaches with me ... and they were just talkin'
'bout what their day had in store for them when out of nowhere
little Dorrie appeared right in front of their car."

Hannah squeezed her eyes shut in an effort to restrain her
tears. I simply let my tears flow unhindered as I nodded at Miss
Harrison.

She cleared her throat. "Mr. Morgan slammed his foot to
the brake, but it was too late. He just wasn't able to stop his car
in time." She heaved a sigh and brushed at the tears streaming
down her face. "I'd just arrived at the school myself and was
steppin' out of my car when the most terrifying sound filled the
air. I stared out at the highway, and my heart broke. I simply
couldn't believe what had come to pass."

I shivered violently as vivid, heartrending images swam before my eyes. I quickly turned away and then glanced sadly back at the porch and watched tensely as Joe and Rueben helped their Pop stagger into the house.

An unbidden sob escaped me as I tuned back to Miss Harrison. "I'm sorry, Miss Harrison; please go on with what you were sayin'."

She sniffled. "I rushed out to the road to try and help our little girl, but, honey. I knew in my heart it was too late."

Hannah lost the battle with her tears, sank down on the ground, and wept wildly. I grasped Miss Harrison's hand and drew her away.

Miss Harrison blubbered. "I prayed so hard as Mr. Morgan gathered up our Dorrie and placed her in their car, but I felt in my spirit that it was already too late. Be that as it may, Mr. Morgan rushed Dorrie to Ft. Worth."

I groaned loudly and buried my face in my hands. What my mind couldn't comprehend, my heart knew, and in less than the blink of an eye our little girl had been lost to us, long before she'd ever arrived at the hospital.

Miss Harrison gathered me in her arms and tearfully avowed, "Mrs. Morgan and I have always warned the children to be careful whenever they walked near the highway, but I never in my wildest dreams imagined something this horrendous would come to pass."

Folks slowly drifted off as daylight faded away, and only family remained behind to mourn our little girl. Mama stayed for the night with Mom, and Joe and I sat out on the porch with Pop and Rueben till well after midnight. Pop finally heaved a heartbreaking sigh and trudged mutely into the desolate house. Rueben glanced mournfully at us, his eyes red and his body exhausted. "You two go on home. I'll sit up with Pop tonight." Then he sorrowfully followed Pop into the still, hushed house.

◦✐◦

Summer had come and gone when Dorris Ann Gilley, our little Dorrie, was laid to rest on a beautiful morning in late September just a few short days after we lost her. Almost everyone from our community turned out for the service, offering sweet remembrances to try to ease our heartbroken grief. Dorrie's eagerness to help her parents or anyone around her was kindly spoken of, as well as the joy she took helping her mom with the vegetable gardens and her beloved flower gardens. Moreover, many remembered her as being an extra special joy to both her pop's and her brothers' hearts.

Dorrie loved her flowers and spent many happy hours in her beautiful flower garden with Mom, and everyone cherished this very special memory of our little girl by bringing the most beautiful flowers available to adorn her little grave. However, no amount of sunshine or bouquets of flowers could match the brightness brought to this world by our little Dorrie's smile.

It was pure torture to realize I wouldn't see her innocent smile ever again on this earth or hear her excited chatter or feel her sweet little girl kisses on my cheek or her chubby little arms wrapped lovingly around my neck. My heart was breaking. Yet I could only imagine the sheer anguish her parents and brothers were now suffering.

I held tightly to Joe's hand throughout the short service and tried to convey my deepest love to him through my tender touch. His unrestrained tears saturated his anguished face as he stood beside me, listening to the pastor's droning voice impart intimate details about his precious sister's short life.

I glanced around at all the sad faces and caught a glimpse of Hannah standing tearfully next to Rueben, firmly clutching his hand and anxiously observing him. I sadly took in how Mom and Pop stood apart, each lost in their own grief and unintentionally shattering the bond that once drew them together. I prayed hard that this would not be so, praying that instead they would draw on the love they shared to help each other through this dreadful, heartrending tragedy. My own heart broke as I realized that the precious love they'd shared for so long and had given so freely to each other and their children might not survive this devastating loss.

Tears prevailed as the pastor spoke at length of Dorrie's gentle spirit and loving heart. He completed the sweet service with more than a few memorable scriptures that our grieving family had chosen, ending with, "Well done, my good and faithful little servant. Enter now into the kingdom of God's rest." He closed the service with words meant to comfort and lift our spirits. "May the departure of this little one not shake our faith, but draw us even closer to the God who gave us life."

I prayed fervently that his words would somehow comfort Mom's distraught heart, but I greatly feared we would have many sleepless nights ahead of us.

Chapter 24

Sunset came early on this late October day, and he'd barely made it home before the radiant sun dropped below the horizon. After stabling his horse, he gazed off toward his inviting little home, knowing Maggie would be there waiting to welcome him. Then he sighed heavily as he glanced over at his parents' house. As he rode up, he'd noticed his mom sitting desolately on the porch, sightlessly rocking back and forth, as she'd done every day for the past month.

He trudged reluctantly down the hill to her. His heart was heavy with sorrow as he once again witnessed his mom's profound grief. He knelt down in front of her and kindly took her worn hands in his. "Mom, I'm so worried about you."

"Joe Edward, I want you to get rid of that colt," she grimly stated.

"What? Why, Mom?"

"Every time I see that little colt runnin' up on the hill, I see my little girl there, laughin' and playin', and I just can't stand it, Joey." Her voice broke as she gazed sadly into the distance.

He fixed his eyes firmly on her and tenderly drew her sad eyes to his. "Mom, it's good to remember how happy our little

Dorrie was. It's a good thing. I know how much you're hurtin', and it just tears my heart out too every time I think about what happened, but we have to keep on livin', Mom. Dorrie would have wanted you to—"

"*No!* I shouldn't have let her go off on her own like that. I knew how impulsive my baby was. I shouldn't have done it."

He tried to recapture her attention, but her somber eyes were glazed over with grief, and her mind closed to his pleading. He cupped her face in his hands. "Mom, Maggie and I have been prayin' every day for you, prayin' for God to comfort you and bring you some peace. It hurts us both so bad to see you this way."

She turned her head away from him as fresh tears filled her eyes. "I miss her so, Joe. I just miss her so."

"We all do, Mom, but you still have others here who desperately need you. Look at Pop—he's just about torn to pieces worryin' over you. And Rueben, he don't sleep at night 'cause he's layin' there hearin' your heart break over and over. And me, Mom, I just want you back."

"Every place I look, I see my Dorrie. I can't go out back. Her little garden just reminds me of what I lost. I can't go inside ..." Her voice drifted off, and she turned her face away from him.

He knew he had to keep trying. "Mom, please look at me; don't shut me out."

"She was my baby, Joe."

"And so am I, and so is Rueben; we're your babies too. My God, Mom, you don't know how bad I wish this had never happened, but it did, and all of us just gotta keep livin' and remember the sweetness that was Dorrie. Please, Mom, don't let grief kill you too."

Tears slid down his face, and his body trembled. He turned away from her and slumped over with his head in his hands. All of a sudden he felt Maggie's arms encircle him and her lips caress his brow. She whispered compassionately, "I knew you'd come down here again, honey, and I just didn't want you to have to do this again all alone."

He drew her into his arms and sighed as he laid his head on her shoulder. "Oh God, Maggie, how are we ever goin' to reach her?"

"I don't know, love, but we just have to keep trying."

He heard his mom stir behind him, and then she commanded, "Joe Edward, I want that colt gone in the mornin', you hear me?"

He heaved a sigh. "All right, Mom, I'll take care of it first thing." He stood and helped Maggie up, and they trailed silently across the yard toward home.

An early morning rain had brought a decided chill to the air. I haphazardly finished straightening up the house as a plan I'd been mulling over kept growing in my mind. The only problem was that I didn't know quite how I'd carry it out.

I fell down on my knees beside our bed and asked God to show me the way and if my plan was to be, to please open up the means for me to carry it out. Almost immediately, as if in answer to my prayer, there was a soft knock at my door.

I brushed away the tears shining on my cheeks and hastily opened the door. My mouth dropped open, and I guardedly placed my hand over my quivering heart. After a moment I gathered myself together. "Hello, Papa; do you have your car with you?"

He looked askance at me and nodded. I don't think it was quite the greeting he'd expected, but I'm sure it was better than what he'd anticipated.

I grabbed my jacket and hurried out the door. "Well, come on, Papa; we have a lot to get done."

He followed after me like an obedient puppy eager to please its master. "Where we headed, Maggie?"

"Hurry, Papa! I know it's been a long time comin', but today I really, really need your help."

We drove the few yards to Mom's house, and once again she sat out on the porch in her lonely rocking chair, weeping over her sorrow. I jumped out of the car and flew to the porch as I loudly cried out, "Come on, Mom; let's go."

She stopped and stared at me, her face puzzled, but her grieving thoughts abruptly interrupted. "What, child? What is it you want?"

I grabbed her hands, not giving her a chance to protest, and heaved her up off the chair. "Hurry, Mom! We have to go now!" I'd caught her off guard, and that made it much easier to manipulate her. She docilely complied with my request and simply followed me to Papa's waiting car. At that juncture, I gently helped her slide into the backseat, and I hurriedly slipped in close beside her.

Papa glanced anxiously over his shoulder at me. "Where to, Maggie?"

I commanded, "Drive us to the road just past Mama's house. I'll tell you when to stop."

He set the old car in motion, asking no more questions, just curiously peeking back at us from time to time. Mom sat silently lost in her tortured thoughts, and I truly felt my ruse to get her into the car had been a worthy one.

We'd driven past Mama's house and rounded the bend in the road when I suddenly cried out, "Stop here, Papa."

He complied, and I hastily hauled Mom out of the car. I held on tightly to her lifeless hand, half-afraid she might turn and run. Then I sternly directed Papa, "Stay here, and no matter what you hear, don't follow us, and don't let anybody or anything follow us either."

He stared at me as if I'd gone plum crazy, but he wordlessly nodded in agreement.

I quickly towed Mom along my well-worn path through the woods and right down to the edge of the creek. She gaped blankly at me, her tortured mind fractured and fearful. Nevertheless, she serenely submitted to me when I gently pressed her tired shoulders, grasped her cold hands, and helped her carefully sit down on the cold, hard ground.

I clasped her hands in mine and fixed my eyes on her. "Mom, I brought you here today because this place, these woods, this creek have always been a place of peace and healin' to me."

She gazed fearfully at me. "I need to get on back home, Maggie. I have so much needs tendin' to."

"Mom, darlin', that's why I brought you here, because there is so much of life left for you to tend to, so many joys and sorrows you're never goin' to experience if you keep mournin' our little Dorrie the way you are now."

Her eyes filled with tears. "I don't deserve to go on. I shouldn't have let my baby go off that way."

"Mom, Dorrie loved school, and she'd walked that same road with her friends every day for near on a month. You can't blame yourself for her death."

She wailed. "No, my baby can't be gone."

I sat silently beside her, fervently praying for the right words that would help her most. I listened sorrowfully to her deep weeping, silently waiting and praying for God's sweet inspiration. At length, I tenderly caressed her sunken face and softly whispered, "It's really okay to be angry. It's even okay to be angry at God, but you just need to let all your anger out, Mom. You just gotta let it out and let it cleanse you so you can be open to God's healin' of your heart."

She glanced gloomily down at the dark, swirling water. "I just wanna let that water take me and never have to feel again."

I shivered. "That's a good way to express how you're feelin' right now, but think of the heartache you'd cause to those you'd leave behind. Think about Joe, Rueben, and Pop, and think about all the little grandchildren you might never know if you're not here."

She buried her face in her hands and sobbed. "What am I to do? I just don't know what I'm supposed to do."

Compassion overflowed within me as I held her tightly. I laid my tearful face close to hers and softly pleaded, "Mom, I'm goin' to go sit over yonder under that tree, and I want you to cry, yell, and scream as much and as loudly as you need to. I want you to release all this anger you're shoulderin' so you can start to heal." I kissed her cheek and then wandered forlornly over to one of the towering old oaks and bleakly plopped down on the hard ground. I felt monstrously afraid to just leave her completely because I didn't want her actually jumping into the creek.

I wordlessly waited, ardently hoping and praying something good would come of this when all at once Mom let loose. She violently kicked at the ground and then passionately threw fist-sized stones and any type of brush she could haul into the creek. She screamed piercingly into the silent woods and harshly ranted and raged for well over an hour. At one point I heard Jack barking like crazy, but then he was silent, so I knew Papa had kept his word and kept Jack away.

After she'd finally exhausted herself, she dropped dejectedly down on the cold ground, weeping wildly. Tension hung in the air as I crept over near her, drew her close, and gently stroked her wild, tangled hair. We lingered there for the longest time, but at length, she cautiously reached for my hand and pulled herself up. After that she hiccupped loudly, unthinkingly grabbed up a handful of her skirt, and wiped her red, tearstained face. Then she surprised me when she even used her shabby skirt to loudly blow her nose.

She laughed softly. "I'm not in the habit of doin' that, but at this moment, I just don't care."

I downright hugged her tight. "You're doin' fine, Mom, and I pray you're not too angry at me for kidnappin' and bringin' you out here. But I really prayed about it, and this is where God led me."

She heaved a tired sigh. "It did help, Maggie. You're a real sweet girl to want to help me after all I've put you and Joe Edward through."

I rubbed my face tiredly and then offered her a smile. "Do you need a few more minutes here, or are you ready to head on home?"

"I think, no…I know I need to go to her grave, Maggie. I need to speak to my little girl. I never even said a proper good-bye, and I just need to, honey. Then I'll be ready to go on home."

We strolled leisurely out of the woods and found Papa waiting patiently beside his car. He peered questioningly at me as we climbed into the backseat, but I ignored his look and quietly instructed him to take us to the little cemetery over near Sublett.

Once there, Mom asked to be alone, so Papa and I stood attentively next to the car, respecting her wishes. After a bit Mom quietly ambled over to us, her reddened eyes wet with fresh tears, but a new air of peace surrounding her.

Back at the house, she scurried past the old rocking chair she'd been married to for the past month and hurriedly headed for her kitchen. We heard the familiar sounds of pots and pans rattling around, and I smiled sweetly as I glanced favorably over at Papa. "Thank you for your help today, Papa. I'd prayed for a way to open so I could help Mom. As a consequence, God sent me you, and I'm certainly pleased you turned up when you did."

He sighed. "I'm glad I was here when you needed me, girl. I'd just had a notion to come over here and try to make peace with you and your new husband, but I'm right pleased I's able to help y'all." He stretched out his hand to me, and I quickly reached over and lovingly hugged his neck. I gently whispered, "Good night, Papa."

I watched wordlessly as his car drove slowly away then turned as I heard Pop and Rueben trudging down from the barn. As they approached me, they searched the shadows for Mom. I shrugged my shoulders. "Something just snapped today, and Mom's feelin' a little better."

Their eyes about popped out of their heads when Mom came out on the porch and called, "Maggie, when Joe gets home, you tell him y'all are havin' supper with us tonight. I feel a need to have all of my family around me." She whirled around and marched back in the house.

Rueben quickly caught hold of Pop's shoulders as he collapsed down on his knees and whispered, "I just don't believe it. I thought I'd lost her too." Then he rushed into the house after her.

I glanced over at Rueben's stunned face and smiled. "I think your pop is feelin' better as well." He still looked taken aback, so I waved my hand in front of his motionless face. "You all right, Rueben?"

He mumbled, "Mmhmm, I am now." Then he hurriedly followed his pop into the house.

I thankfully sank down on the porch steps to wait for Joe to ride in and soberly gave thanks for the healing that had begun today.

Laughter didn't prevail, and the meal was anything but normal as we all sat on pins and needles trying not to upset Mom. She'd laid out a heaping platter of crispy fried chicken, creamy mashed potatoes, hot gravy, and fresh string beans, which we all made a pretense of eating.

Everyone tried to make casual conversation, but it came out stilted. I think Mom noticed, but she tried really hard to keep herself together. Every once in a while she'd glance over at Dorrie's empty chair and her eyes would tear up. Then she'd look around the table with a semblance of a smile touching her trembling lips.

Pop cleared his throat and turned to Joe. "How was your day, Son?"

"Pretty much usual. I've been workin' with them two-year-olds we brought back with us from Oklahoma. Johnson wants 'em trained as cuttin' horses for a rancher down near Waco. I believe they'll be mighty pleased with 'em once I put 'em through their ropes."

Mom piped up, "Joe?"

"Yeah, Mom?"

"What'd you do with that colt?"

His knuckles turned white under the table, and a trickle of sweat appeared on his brow. "I turned him out in that pasture down by Gramps'."

She smiled sadly. "That's good, Son; that's real good."

We struggled through another half hour of exhausting conversation before Joe and I decided to leave. We hugged and kissed everybody. Then I drifted quietly back over to Mom. "Are you sure I can't stay and help you with the dishes, Mom?"

"No, no, Maggie, it'll give me somethin' to occupy myself with." She looked shyly at me. "Thank you for today, Maggie. It's still tearin' me up inside, but I think you're right; gettin' rid of some of my anger helped me."

I held her and spoke softly so only she could hear. "Anytime you need to go back, our secret place will be waitin', and I'll always be right here by your side if ever you need me."

She sadly brushed away a tear and nodded. Pop crept over quietly and tentatively placed his arm around her waist. "It's good to have you back in the kitchen, Laura. I've missed you somethin' awful."

She moved shyly into his arms and rested her weary head on his welcoming shoulder, so we all slipped silently away, leaving them alone to heal together.

Rueben restlessly wandered after us and followed us part

way back home. Then he broke off suddenly and headed up toward the barn, calling over his shoulder, "Think I'll ride over and see Hannah for a bit."

Joe stopped under the oak tree next to our little pond. The hazy moonlight shimmered on the water, and the wintry wind chilled me. I shivered, and he wrapped me tightly in his arms. Then he whispered tenderly, "Thank you, baby. I don't know what you said to her, but thank you."

I gazed up into his remarkably beautiful eyes. "It wasn't me, honey. I've just been prayin' so hard for God to open a window or a door and let me know what to say or do to help her." I dropped my gaze, not wanting him to see the tears trailing down my face.

He tilted my chin and kissed me sweetly. "I know how much you care, honey, and your strong emotions are one of the reasons I fell so hard in love with you."

I nodded and sniffled a bit. "Papa came by this mornin'."

"And …"

"I'd had this idea turnin' round in my mind all mornin' long, but I didn't know how I could accomplish it, so I just prayed and prayed. Seemed like just a minute later that I heard someone at the door."

"Your papa?"

I shivered again. "Mmhmm."

He drew me close. "Let's go make a fire and warm you up, sweetie. Then you can finish your story."

We rushed the rest of the way to our little house, and Joe quickly stoked up the fire. We huddled together in front of the fireplace, and he vigorously rubbed my cold hands to warm them.

Only the flickering flames of the fire cast light on my face as I quietly described the tumultuous events of the day. He sat wordlessly listening, his eyes mirroring his dismay as I described his Mom's outpouring of raw emotion deep in the woods by the banks of Johnson Creek.

At length, he ran his hands through his hair then buried his face in them. "I know it seems to have helped her, but I just don't understand how, Maggie."

I stretched out on the floor and heaved a lingering sigh. "You remember what a mess I was when Uncle William died and Papa—"

He lay down beside me and lovingly stroked my face. "You could never be a mess, baby."

"An emotional mess. I had so much anger pent up inside me that it just about consumed me. As a result, I had a breakdown just about like your mom's. Afterward, I found more peace with myself and God than I'd had in more than a year. I still had, have even now, a touch of sorrow and anger that haunts me at times, but gettin' rid of all that anger and hate that was just so bottled up inside me helped me start healin'."

"And that's what helped Mom today." His eyes darkened. "You are so beautiful, Maggie, and such a blessin' to me and my family."

"Joe, honey, it's not gonna go away overnight. Your mom still has a long row to hoe, but it's a start. She's ready now to start healin', but it's goin' to take all of us supportin' her to help her make it through each day."

"I recognize that, and I also know that without you here with us, none of my family would be healin' right now." His fingers delicately stroked my face. "It's your tender heart, baby, that keeps me breathin'."

I rolled over next to him and propped my chin in my hand as I gazed starry-eyed into his intense, passionate eyes. "And it's you, Joe, that keeps me—" His fiery kiss captured my eager lips, and our passion ignited as heated as the fire blazing beside us.

chapter 25

Cold, crisp air greeted me as I drifted lazily toward the pond. October had quietly faded away into a bleak November, and the weary trees shivered under the white winter sky. A touch of melancholy settled heavily upon me as I solemnly gazed out over the barren pasture.

It was already nearing noon, and I hadn't yet even mustered the energy to go saddle Pal for our morning ride. I stretched sleepily and decided I really should run back inside for my coat, but I'd barely started up the steps when I heard the rattling racket of an old truck approaching. I watched with pleasure as Hannah jumped out, waved good-bye to her papa, and happily hurried over to me.

"Hannah! I wasn't expectin' to see you this mornin'. What a wonderful surprise!"

She beamed. "I just couldn't wait to come over, Maggie, and have a private chat with you. I know we planned to meet later in the week, but this was just too important to keep!"

I hugged her tightly, my mood vastly improved by her presence. "Come inside. We'll make some tea, and you can tell me all your secrets."

She frowned. "It has to be kept private for a bit, Maggie, but I couldn't contain myself from sharin' it with you."

I sat the teapot on the stove then added another log to the fire. "It's positively wintery out there today. That must be why I feel so weary this mornin'."

"Maggie?"

"Mmhmm?"

"Stop ramblin' and come sit down." She patted the seat next to her and smiled.

I set two cups on the table and dropped down in the chair. "So tell me."

"You know, it hasn't been too long since Rueben and I started courting."

"I do know, about two or two and a half months, I'd say."

"Close enough." She fiddled with her empty teacup and then conceded, "We've shouldered a lot together during these months, and I think it's drawn us closer together than might otherwise have happened."

I sighed sadly. "It's been a really hard time for the whole of us, Hannah, and I do know you've been a true blessin' to Rueben."

She nodded as she wiped away a solitary tear trailing down her face. "We'd really started carin' for each other quite a spell before we were rightfully courtin'."

I reached over and held her hands in mine. "I could see that, honey. You and Rueben were smitten with each other practically from the time we went to the races way back last May."

Her face puckered up. "It seems almost a lifetime ago what with all that's come to pass."

The teapot whistled loudly, and I quickly jumped up to tend to it. I felt a bit light in the head as I approached the table, so I quickly dropped the hot teapot onto the table and shakily grabbed the back of my chair to steady myself.

Hannah anxiously sprang up and took hold of my shoulders. "Maggie, are you sure you're feelin' okay?"

"Mmhmm, I must have caught a bug or somethin'. On the other hand, I was feelin' fine last night, so I simply haven't a clue."

Hannah's eyes took on a dreamy look as she implored, "Maggie..."

"No, no it's not, Hannah."

"How do you know?"

I squeezed her hand lightly. "I'm okay, sweetie; however, I do know you can't wait to confess, so..."

She smiled shyly and bit her bottom lip. "Rueben stopped by last evenin', and I invited him in like most times, but he asked if I'd walk with him a bit instead."

"And?"

"We had some special time together as we strolled along, although that wind was really blowin' cold. Consequently, Rueben tried to find a shelter for us. Then we stumbled upon this little abandoned shed." She paused, lost in thought.

I clasped her hands in mine. "Hannah?"

"I'm sorry, Maggie, it was just so tender and sweet." She laid her head on the table and peeked up at me, her bright blue eyes glistening as she whispered, "Anyway, he wanted to know what I'd think about us gettin' married."

"You said yes?"

"I did. I told him I'd be right proud to be his wife." She pursed her lips and sighed reflectively.

I squeezed her hands. "I'm so happy for both of you! Rueben is mighty lucky to have captured your heart, Hannah."

She blinked back tears. "I'm very blessed." She sighed heavily and scooted her chair closer to mine. "What with all the sorrow in the family these past months, we decided to wait till early spring. However, if Rueben's mom is doin' better, we'll make our plans known on Christmas Day."

Footsteps pounded up the steps, and we both jumped at the sudden interruption. I fluttered to the door and flung it open as Joe practically fell into my arms.

I stared at him in surprise. "Honey, what are you doin' home in the middle of the day? Is everything okay?"

He kissed me sweetly. "Mmhmm, I just took a bit of time off work—"

He noticed Hannah. "Hey, Hannah, how ya doin'?"

I stuttered. "I'm mighty glad you're home, honey. I just wasn't expectin' you, so it gave me a fright."

He led me out on the porch then declared, "I was hopin' to find you home 'cause I kinda had a little surprise planned for you, baby."

I raised my eyebrows at him with a smile, and he grinned broadly. "Not that kinda surprise, Maggie!"

I laughed and hugged him. He grinned as he held out his hand. "What say we all walk over to Pop's for a bit."

I called out to Hannah, and we headed straight away across the chilly pasture. Hannah kept watch on me, which made me feel jumpy, but fortunately, Joe didn't appear to take the hint.

As we neared the house we caught sight of Rueben and Pop ambling slowly down the hill from the barn. Hannah enthusiastically called out to Rueben, and they rushed hurriedly to meet each other.

Smoke rose cozily from the stone fireplace, beckoning us into the warm house. I wished once again that our little girl would be waiting inside, but I knew I had to put such thoughts aside.

We crowded into the snug little kitchen and found Mom stooped down over near the stove. She looked up at us with a cheery smile. "Why, isn't this a nice surprise, my whole family home for lunch." She remained where she was, which somewhat surprised me, but then Joe wrapped his arm around my waist and drew me over to the stove.

Mom sheltered a little basket, tied prettily with a bright red bow. As she moved her hand aside I heard a tiny whimper, so I crouched down next to Mom and peeked into the basket.

I let out a little whimper of my own. "Oh, honey!" I reached into the basket and scooped up a wee little black and white puppy and held him gently in my hands. "Joe, is it for me?"

He grinned from ear to ear. "Yep, baby, just for you. I know how much you miss Jack, and Pop here keeps gettin' on me 'bout his cow dogs, so when I saw this little fellow, I knew I had to get hold of him for you."

I sank down into his lap, holding the little puppy. "Thank you, sweetie! It's just precious." I kissed his cheek and then eagerly found his lips. At that moment the little puppy gave a tiny yip, so I quickly turned my attention back to it.

Rueben chuckled softly. "Watch out there, Joe. I think you just bought yourself some competition."

chapter 26

An unseasonably warm November day greeted us as we stepped out on our tiny front porch this morning. I paused to admire the radiant golden sun shining softly through the rusty brown leaves, which still clung hopefully to the now dormant trees.

Mama had sent word by Frank last evening that Jessie had come down with a cold, so she wondered if I'd come over and stay with her since everyone else would be at work or school. Hence, I'd rolled out of bed early this morning when Joe arose, and we'd headed over to Mama's. I'd elected to ride with him instead of taking Pal out and consequently enjoyed sharing this beautiful morning ride cuddling close to my beloved husband.

Mama had long been at work, and Mary scrambled around trying to rouse the little ones as I strolled in the door. Mary took one look at me and screamed impatiently, "How'd you ever deal with these babies, Maggie? Not a one of 'em will even listen to me!"

I hugged her and laughed. "Seems to me you used to be just as hard to stir in the mornin'."

"Nope, that must be another sister you're thinkin' of."

I marched back to the bedroom and peeked in the door. Jessie was curled up in the far corner of the bed, sniffling, Kate and Janie had their heads buried deep under the pillows, and Lily had climbed down over to the corner and was happily playing with her doll.

I smiled and used my sternest motherly voice. "What'd I tell you girls? You best be up and ready for school this very minute!"

Their eyes flew to me as they screamed in unison, "Maggie!" Suddenly, four little girls excitedly clutched onto me, dragging me down to the floor.

I hugged them close and kissed them till they yelled at me to stop. Then I plopped Jessie back in bed, rounded up the rest, and hauled them down the hall to the kitchen. Frank sat at the kitchen door whittling on a piece of wood, Mary stood at the sink chewing on a piece of toast, and to my delight, my long, lost brother, Will, sat sideways in a chair at the table, long legs sticking out, bolting down a bowl of oatmeal.

I grinned at him. "Well, I see you're just about as much help as always."

He scratched his head and brushed back his still shaggy hair then grinned back at me. "Dang right, if I weren't here none of this gang would likely roll out of bed 'fore noon."

I hurried over and embraced him. "It's so good to see you, Will. Seems like forever since I've caught even a glimpse of you."

"You've had other concerns lately, Maggie. I usually make it home one or two days a week, just never know which days. I rolled up here last night, but I'm off again in a bit, headin' down to Sulphur Springs for a few weeks."

"Mama misses you somethin' awful, ya know, and all these little rascals as well."

"Yep, they're the reason I keep going."

Janie stared at him. "Hey! That's a mean thing to say!"

We both laughed. Then he pulled her up in his lap and hugged her. "Naw, I like y'all just fine. I just meant I wanna help

Mama earn some money so she can buy all you kids shoes and other such wants."

She nodded. "I guess that's okay."

Mary impatiently tapped her foot and looked needles at us. "All these kids need to be dressed and ready to leave in five minutes. Is anybody even goin' to help me get 'em movin'?"

Will shook his head. "Nope."

I eyed him and then glanced over at Frank. "The men in this family need a little lesson on helpin' out around the house."

Frank whooped. "I got better things to do."

I picked up a broom and started sweeping toward the door and accidentally on purpose swept dust all over him.

He coughed. "Hey, Maggie, what's wrong with you!"

"Move, son. Go help your sister get the kids to school. You should take a lesson from Joe, the both of you. He sure don't have any problem helpin' me around the house."

Frank grumbled, but a new look of respect appeared in his eyes because he just about worshiped Joe.

Will pushed back from the table and walked to the window. "Mama seem all right to you, Maggie?"

"Some better. Why?"

"She just looked as if she was plum worn out last night. I don't want her doin' too much too soon, and now that she's gone back to work full time, she just appears tuckered out all the time. Think maybe you can talk to her again about slowin' down?"

"Course I can. I guess I've been pretty tied up what with all the distress we've had out at our place. I've been tryin' to take care of Joe and his mom and pop. Rueben has Hannah, but everyone's been devastated by Dorrie's death."

"I know, Maggie, but talk to Mama this evenin' before y'all leave. I tried last night, but in spite of everything she's determined to work even if she's still feelin' bad." He sighed heavily and walked over to me. "I'll be gone 'bout three weeks, so I'd 'preciate you and Joe lookin' in on Mama and the kids."

I hugged him tightly. "Do you think you'll be back home by Thanksgiving?"

"Mmhmm. Should be back a day or two before." He frowned. "Tell Mama I'm earnin' enough that she don't need to worry 'bout workin' what with the money she's gettin' from her settlement."

"I'll try, Will, but you know how stubborn Mama can be."

A frantic rush of small bodies roared by us, amid cries of "See ya later," "Hurry up," and "Dang it, I forgot my lunch!" My heart fluttered with remembrances that only a short while ago Will and I had been a part of this mad dash.

Will strode off a few minutes later, and I wandered down the hall to check on Jessie. She'd fallen back to sleep, curled up cozily around her pillow. I felt her little head to see if she had a temperature, and she felt just a little warm. I occupied myself tidying up the house and doing the laundry while Jessie slept most of the morning.

Around noon I heard her stir, so I checked on her and found her sitting up on the bed. She held out her little arms to me, and I cuddled her close. "Feelin' better, baby?" I kissed her forehead, and she felt cool to my touch.

"Mmhmm, but I'm real hungry." She snuggled up closer to me. "I sure miss you, Maggie. I wish you could still be home with us."

"I know, Jessie. I miss all of y'all so much too, but I'm married now, and I'm supposed to live with Joe."

"He could live here too. He can sleep in Will and Frank's room." She rubbed her sleepy eyes and stretched lazily.

I sighed heavily and picked her up, and she wrapped her little arms and legs tightly around me. I waddled down the hall to the living room the best I could what with Jessie all snuggled up around me. I tenderly kissed her soft curls and plopped her down in Mama's rocking chair. At that point I suggested, "How 'bout I make you a sandwich, sweetie, and you can just eat it in here since you've been sick."

She nodded happily as I tucked a warm blanket over her pale little legs. A bit later I sat with her as she cheerfully gobbled down her sandwich with a cold glass of milk. I'm not sure how she ate so quickly because it seemed as though she chattered constantly as she ate. Afterward, I brought her a doll and her favorite book, carefully tucked the blanket back around her, and then wistfully wandered back into the kitchen.

I rested my weary head on the hard table. I seemed to be overly tired from rising so early and from all the work I'd done around the house this morning. As I dozed off, I heard a soft knock at the kitchen door. I glanced up and spotted Mom posed at the door. As a result, I jumped up frantically and in my haste, clumsily knocked over the chair.

Her face mirrored my agitation, but she held out her hand to me and asserted, "Everything's okay, Maggie. I just felt a need to visit the creek today."

I wrapped my arms around her. "Oh, Mom, you frightened me so." I stepped back and looked askance at her. "Do you need me to walk you over?"

She smiled sadly. "No, no, I've done been. I knew you was here, so I just stopped by to rest a bit 'fore I walk on back to the house." I led her over to the table, picked up the chair I'd knocked over, and helped her sit down.

She sighed and nodded. "I've been back several times since that day you took me. It helps me release some of what's hurtin' inside of me. Then I can go on back home and tend to Pop and Rueben."

I took her hands in mine. "I'm so glad." I paused as I heard Jessie singing in the front room. Mom's eyes took on a glazed look as she too absorbed the healing words Jessie sang in her clear, sweet voice. *"Tis so sweet to trust in Jesus, just to take him at his word, just to rest upon his promise, just to know, thus saith the Lord! Jesus, Jesus, how I trust him! How I've proved him o'er and o'er. Jesus, Jesus, precious Jesus! O for grace to trust him more!"*

Jessie's melodious voice softened, and a sweet sense of peace filled the house as she sang the last verse. *"I'm so glad I learned to trust thee, precious Jesus, Savior, friend; and I know that thou art with me, wilt be with me to the end."*

I glanced over at Mom. Tears streamed down her fretful face. I leaped up and anxiously moved to her side, and then I drew her lovingly into my arms and cried with her.

After a long while she leaned back in the chair and dabbed at her weepy eyes. "You know, honey, trustin' Jesus, that's somethin' I haven't done in a long while."

I caressed her agonized face. "Sometimes it's right hard to have faith when it looks as if our world's crumblin' 'round us, but we always tend to find our way back, Mom."

She patted my cheek then hesitantly headed off into the front room. After a bit I quietly peeked into the living room and watched as Mom gently scooped Jessie up, sat down in the rocking chair, and tearfully held our sweet girl lovingly in her arms.

Sunlit shadows slanted lazily across the room as Mom, Jessie, and I contentedly cut out paper dolls from old newspapers. Jessie appeared to be feeling much better, and she was thoroughly enjoying all the attention shed on her this afternoon.

I looked up as I heard the soft patter of Mama's shoes crossing the porch. The front door opened, and she smiled sweetly as she took in the scene before her. As she quietly closed the door, she declared, "That sure looks like fun, girls. As a matter of fact, I'd like to play too."

Mom jumped up. "Why time has certainly flown this day! I didn't mean to linger so long."

Mama kissed her cheek. "I'm right glad you're here, Laura."

Mom nodded. "And it's so good to see you, Jo. I haven't been out too much lately, not even to church, but I believe that's goin' to change soon."

I laid down the newspaper and scissors, pulled myself up, and wrapped an arm around each one. "Why don't you two sit down and talk. I'll go bring y'all a cool glass of water. Then I think I'll run over and see Joe for a bit."

Mom started to protest. "Oh, Maggie, I've stayed too long as it is. I'd best get on home and see to supper."

Mama drew her to the couch. "Sit a spell, Laura. It's been a long time since I've just relaxed and enjoyed the company of a good friend."

"That's truth, Jo, and I guess it won't hurt if supper's a bit late tonight."

I grinned. "That's without doubt. You both deserve a little time off of work." I strolled cheerfully to the kitchen and rapidly put together a little plate of crackers and cheese, three glasses, and a pitcher of cool water. I called Jessie to come help me, and we carried my masterpiece into the front room.

"We thought you two might like a bite to eat," I offered. Jessie presented each a napkin and then sat down on the floor at their feet. Mama unconsciously stroked Jessie's hair as she contentedly leaned her head against Mama's legs. I gazed happily at the three, and my smile widened as I noticed how Jessie's ecstatic eyes shone with joy because she had Mama practically all to herself, even if it was only for a few short minutes.

I quickly gathered myself together and started for the door. "I'll be back shortly. I just fancy a few minutes of my husband's valuable time."

I skipped down the steps and into the warm November sunshine. Jack barked joyously and bounded across the yard to join me in my walk. We happily raced down the road for a bit. Then

I had to slow down. Jack darted ahead of me, stopped in the middle of the road, and commenced barking at full volume for me to hurry and catch up.

I laughed. "I'm comin', Jack." We wandered the last half mile at a more sedate pace, enjoying the unseasonably warm afternoon. As I took in the splendor of God's creation, my heart spilled over with a sweet sense of satisfaction. I stretched out my arms, spun around, and then gazed up into the clear blue sky.

The sun shimmered softly in the sky as we arrived at Johnson's corral. I climbed up on the fence and dotingly watched Joe expertly riding one of the quarter horses around a series of obstacles.

Jack stood up on his hind legs and barked his approval as well, which instantly caught Joe's attention. He reined in the horse, slipped off, and sprinted over to the fence. Jack fell into his ecstatic, quivering state that he seemed to get into every time Joe was around. I felt pretty much the same way. I just didn't demonstrate it quite so well.

Joe hopped up on the fence and kissed me. "Hey, baby, everthing okay?"

"Is now." I climbed over the fence and wrapped him in my arms. "I simply needed to feel your arms around me, and I just didn't think I could wait another two hours."

He grinned. "I was feelin' the exact same thing, so I'm mighty glad you turned up." Jack wiggled his way under the fence and jumped up on us, begging for attention. Joe rubbed him down good, and then Jack bounded happily away to visit the horses.

I took his hand, and we walked over toward the gate. "I wanted to let you know your mom came by Mama's today." He frowned as I continued. "No, honey, she's fine. She visited the creek again today and then stopped by the house to rest 'fore headin' home. Only thing is, she cuddled up to Jessie for a long while, and I really think it helped her some, but I don't want her walkin' home this late. I thought maybe you could ride on home after work and then bring the car back for us."

"I believe I can handle that." He held me close for another minute or two then kissed me sweetly. "I best get back to work, baby, but I'll be over to your Mama's in a couple hours. What say we just stay for supper? I could fetch Pop and Rueben over with me."

"'Less Rueben's headin' off to Hannah's," I interjected.

"Yep, that's a good possibility. I'll bring some of that ham you cooked up yesterday if you and Mary can pull together the rest."

I stretched up and hugged him, dropping little kisses along his neck till I captured his willing lips with mine. Then I cuddled him close and whispered, "I'm pretty good at takin' care of all kinds of things, ya know."

He nuzzled my neck and groaned. "I set great store by how well you handle every single thing you do, baby."

I sighed longingly as I broke away from him and then half-heartedly called out to Jack. Joe ran his hand roughly through his hair, watching me wistfully as I declared, "See you in a bit, sweetie."

"Now you're just gonna walk away and leave me to go on back to those horses, I suppose?" he teased.

"You'll see me later," I promised with a grin.

Epilogue

I reckon my life has come full circle, or at least that's how I deem it. So many heartaches came to pass in such a short length of time, yet despite my sorrows, I'm blessed in so many wondrous ways. First and foremost, by the love I've found with my sweet Joe.

As I laid beside him and reflected back on the day, I felt amazed at how deeply and completely I loved this man. My hopeful heart yearned to always be near him, and it soared with joy as I gazed upon his sleeping beauty.

We shared a joyous day with our families, a most heartening Thanksgiving surrounded by those we love. Everyone gathered at Pop's for a magnificent Thanksgiving feast, and each family had pitched in and provided his or her favorite dishes to share.

Even Hannah and her family arrived early and helped us ready the house and prepare all of Mom's traditional recipes. She practically glowed with joy all day, and I just couldn't believe she and Rueben would be able to contain their delight in each other much longer. I'd prayed hard that they would decide on a Christmas wedding, even if Christmas is only a month away.

Speaking of weddings, we all about fell over earlier in the

week when my dearest little brother Will came home from Sulphur Springs. Joe and I had spent Sunday afternoon visiting with Mama and the kids, and we'd about decided to head home when Will popped his shaggy head in the door. His sappy, broad grin conveyed to us that something astonishing had happened, but it was like a bolt from the blue when he strolled in the door with a pretty petite young woman attached to his arm. Then he laughed merrily at our bewilderment and proudly introduced us to his new wife.

Will turned seventeen just a few short weeks ago, but as Joe avowed, he's lived the life of a man for quite a while now. We determined that Rose was the daughter of one of the men Will had worked alongside of for the last half year. She'd traveled everywhere with them, seeing as her papa was the only family she had left in this world. She and Will struck up a friendship right away, and over time it blossomed into so much more.

Will announced that the two of them would move in with Mama and lend a hand so she wouldn't have to work anymore, or at least not until she was fully recovered and had gained all her strength back. Will proudly explained that he'd received a promotion at work, along with a fine raise, so he felt comfortable supporting both a wife and his family. Nevertheless, life would be a hardship for them, but his determination to provide for our family just warmed my heart so.

He and Rose appeared to fit right in with our entire family. Rose eagerly helped all of us in the kitchen this morning and delighted us with tales of Will's exploits over the past several months. Her papa even elected to join us for Thanksgiving dinner. Thus it seemed our welcoming family had not merely expanded but simply spilled over with tenderness and love.

Our laughter filled Pop's house today, a hopeful, joyous laughter that hadn't been present in all the weeks since we lost our little girl. Mom placed Dorrie's little chair close to the fireplace, and one and all of us took time to remember our dear, delightful girl. Her sweet little presence could be felt even today, living on in the love of her family. Mom tried so hard not to sit down and weep, but late in the day I did come across her standing silently in Dorrie's little bedroom with unshed tears shining in her sad eyes. I wrapped my arms lovingly around her and held her for a bit. Then she smiled sadly and whispered that she was just remembering last Thanksgiving and Dorrie's special sweetness and smile.

We wandered back into the kitchen, and I stood quietly at the door, reflecting back on the past two years and on how all our joys and sorrows had drawn us all so much closer together. My eyes fell on Lilly, snuggled up on Mama's lap, and our little Jessie all cuddled up in Mom's lap, excitedly explaining how she and Lilly had helped Mama make her famous molasses cake.

As I stood watching, I felt Joe's arms encircle me, so I leaned back contentedly into his sweet embrace. His lips gently brushed my cheek, and I sighed happily. My joy exploded as I sank against him, and my grateful heart acknowledged that on this, our very first Thanksgiving together, we had so very many blessings to give praise for and a most wondrous future to look forward to together.

I covered his strong hands with mine and recalled the chat I'd shared with Hannah a few weeks back, feeling tender and a little sad that it really had been a trifling illness bringing about my dizzy spell. Nevertheless, I knew whatever disappointments might befall us, Joe and I would bear them together.

Later, we strolled off outside and found Mary, Frank, Janie, and Kate chasing around after my little Muffin, which is what I'd fixed on naming my adorable little puppy. Their laughter blended joyfully with Muffin's tiny yips as they darted merrily around the yard, heedless of the cold, frosty air. After a bit, we struck off toward our snug little home, built up a nice warm fire in our cozy fireplace, and snuggled up comfortably together.

My eyes teared up as I thought back over this precious day, and it set off shivers of joy all through me as I remembered all our beloved family surrounding us with their presence and their love. I unconsciously let out a contented sigh and sank sleepily into the downy softness of my pillow. Blissfully, I felt Joe's arm snake comfortably around me, so I snuggled up closer into his warm embrace as he tenderly kissed my neck. "What's wrong, baby? Havin' a hard time sleepin'?"

I lovingly kissed his sweet lips and gazed adoringly into his deep, dark eyes. "Just thinkin' 'bout the day and everything and sayin' a prayer of thankfulness for you, honey, and for all of our family."

His fingers caressed my face. "It was a good day, now wasn't it? I'm mighty glad Mom tolerated the holiday so well. I feared she might just break down again, it bein' the first holiday after our loss."

"Your mom's still sufferin', but all told, she's a strong woman, sweetie, and she's bearin' up even though her heart's still breakin'. But I know for certain your pop's the glue that's holdin' her together, so I'm right glad they've bonded back together in love to help each other keep goin' through each day."

He heaved a sigh. "Maybe it'll help 'em when Rueben and Hannah are married. Ya know, Rueben talked to me today and admitted he'd told Pop about their engagement, and Pop offered to let 'em live at the house after they're married. We all concluded it'd be mighty good for Mom to have 'em living at home 'cause she don't need to lose all her children at once, so to speak."

I fell sadly back on the pillow. "Oh. Joe, honey, it's a hard thing one way or another, but I guess I never rightly thought of her losin' you when we married."

He laid back beside me and asserted, "None of us looked at it from that angle, baby, but what with everything now … anyhow, it's somethin' Hannah and Rueben discussed 'fore he ever brought it up with us."

I rolled back into his strong arms. "I understand, honey, I do, and it'd be right nice to have Hannah so nearby. In view of that, I really hope they decide to marry sooner than springtime. They just need each other so much." I snuggled closer, confessing from the bottom of my heart, "Almost as much as I need you, my love." I closed my eyes and rested my weary head on his sturdy shoulder as he unconsciously caressed that wonderful spot just behind my ear.

After a bit his breath fluttered in my hair as he whispered sweetly, "Have I told you yet today how much I love you, baby?"

I entwined myself around him. "Mmhmm, maybe once or twice, but not anywhere near enough."

He gathered me closer in his arms, his lips caressing me. "Well now, what say I try and convince you just how much I love you, adore you, desire you ..." His voice trailed off, and once again I feverishly melted under his magical spell.

Bibliography

Arlington Journal circa 1934 (no author cited) * information acessed by author Sept. 2008. <*http://arlingtonlibrary.org/research/localpapers.aspx*>.

Kahn, G. and Schwandt W. (1931). "Dream a Little Dream of Me."(Anderson, N). SAI. Essex Music, Inc. (1958).

Simons, S and Marks, G. (1931). "All of Me" (Palma, JoAnn). SAI. Bourne Co. (1931).

Stead, L. and Kirkpatrick, W. (1890) "Tis So Sweet to Trust in Jesus."